"Richard Cooper thought he w[
The death of his father brings a shocking past into his present
life. The events force him to struggle with a personal history
that is too terrible to comprehend. Alan Clegg's "Where birds
don't sing" brings to life what happened during the last months
of the Holocaust and delivers it powerfully into today's
consciousness."

"A novel that deals with the other side of death camp
Auschwitz. What did the perpetrators of the killing believe they
were doing? How did a Jewish refugee lawyer-come-soldier deal
with the terrible truth about his family? Alan Clegg provides
the answers in the most graphic and compelling detail."

Alan Clegg writes "faction" - a heady mixture of fact and fiction.

The Other Planet
AUSCHWITZ

Times were different than on this planet.
Life changed by the minute.
We did not have names.
We did not have parents.
We did not have children.
We did not wear clothes like other people.
We were not born.
We did not give birth to life.
We were breathing the air filled with the smoke from the crematoria.
We did not live life according to the rule of law.
We talked to each other in silence.
Our number was our name.
Our families continually left us.
They became separated from us.
I can see them, and they are looking for me.
Auschwitz - the largest cemetery in history,
where most of us lost our parents and families,
must always remain a warning against indifference
to all forms of violence and racial, religious and national hatred.
Auschwitz - the other planet.
We must never forget.

by

Mendel Beale - a survivor of Auschwitz

To Emi

Where birds don't sing

the second story in the Dutch Holocaust trilogy

alan clegg

HORSESHOE PUBLICATIONS . WARRINGTON . CHESHIRE

ISBN 1.899310.14.2

British Library Cataloguing in Publication Data
A Catalogue record for this book is available from the
British Library

Printed and bound in Great Britain by
REDWOOD BOOKS LTD
Trowbridge, Wilts

for the Publishers

HORSESHOE PUBLICATIONS
Box 37, Kingsley, Warrington,
Cheshire WA6 8DR

Cover designed and illustrated by David Nolan

With thanks to Mendel Beale, a survivor, for allowing me to use his poem, 'The Other Planet -AUSCHWITZ'.

Thank you to Simon Wiesenthal for checking part of the manuscript and allowing me to use him as a character.

In memory of Ilse Meyer-Hecht (Lottie Cohen), a survivor aged ninety years who sadly died just before this novel was published.

With thanks to Eve for her story.

"I swear by God by this sacred oath I shall render unconditional obedience to Adolf Hitler, the Führer of the German Reich, supreme commander of the armed forces, and that I shall at all times be prepared, as a brave soldier, to give my life for this oath."

The Führer Oath taken by all members of the armed forces.

"I swear by Apollo Physician, Asclepius, by Health, by Panacea, and by all the gods and goddesses, making them my witness, that I will carry out, according to my ability and judgement, this oath and this indenture. .... I will use treatment to help the sick according to my ability and judgement but never with a view to injury and wrongdoing. I will keep pure and holy both my life and my art. In whatsoever houses I enter, I will enter to help the sick, and I will abstain from all intentional wrongdoings and harm .... now if I carry out this oath, and break it not, may I gain forever reputation among all men for my life and for my art; but if I transgress it and forswear myself, may the opposite befall me."

The Oath of Hypocrites.

SELECTED BIBLIOGRAPHY

The Diary of Anne Frank, The Critical Edition, Viking. 1989.

Clay, Catrine & Leapman Michael,*MASTER RACE. The Lebensborn experiment in Nazi Germany,* Coronet. 1995.

Clegg, Alan, *WINDMILLS,* Horseshoe Publications. 1997.

De Jong, L. *De Bezetting,* Querido's Uitgeverij N.V. 1966.

Gilbert, Martin. *Atlas of the Holocaust,* revised edition, Routledge. 1993.

Gilbert, Martin, *Second World War,* FONTANA / Collins. 1989.

Goldhagen, Daniel Jonah, *Hitler's Willing Executioners,* Little, Brown & Co. 1996

Edited by Gutman, Yisrael & Berenbaum, Michael, *Anatomy of the Auschwitz Death Camp,* Indiana University Press. 1944

Lifton, Robert Jay, *The Nazi Doctors - Medical Killing and the Psychology of.*

Naumann, Bernd, *AUSCHWITZ - A Report on the Proceedings Against Robert Karl Ludwig Milka and Others Before the Court at Frankfurt,* Pall Mall Press. 1966.

Dr. Nyisli, Miklos, *Auschwitz.* Mayflower. 1979.

Pick, Hella, *Simon Wiesenthal - A Life in Search of Justice,* Wiedenfeld & Nicolson. 1996.

Read, Anthony & Fisher, David, *The Fall of Berlin,* Pimlico. 1993.

Ryan, Cornelius, *Berlin 1945 - The Last Battle.* New English Library. 1985.

Sayer, Ian & Botting, Douglas, *Nazi Gold,* Granada. 1984.

Speer, Albert, *Inside the Third Reich,* Sphere Books. 1971

Taylor, Telford, *The Anatomy of the Nuremberg Trials,* Bloomsbury. 1993.

Genocide, Harper Collins. 1986.

Trevor-Roper, H.R., *The Last Days of Hitler,* Pan Books. 1968.

Whiting, Charles, *The Hunt for Martin Bormann - The Truth,* Whiting Charles, Leo Cooper. 1996.

ONE

The distant clanking of a train came through the thick curtains and the sound forced him to sit upright. Rubbing sleep from his eyes, he swung long legs off the bed and onto the wooden floor.

A tall man, over six feet, with a shock of short blonde hair and wide-open eyes.

A white bath-robe hung neatly from its hanger. Quickly slipping it over his body, he gently opened the door and stepped out into the freezing corridor. The man walked the short distance to the showers and found an empty cubicle. With a quick glance at the shower-head, he threw off his robe and let the hot water run over him.

The blonde hair covered a heavily muscled body. A handsome face. Long, angular with a patrician nose. In a totally masculine way, the lips were full. It was the eyes that caught the attention, blue flecked with black. They saw everything and moved constantly, taking in every detail. Long, strong fingers topped by perfectly manicured nails. The right forefinger touched the day's growth of beard.

His other hand wiped the mirror dry and the brush whipped the shaving foam into a heavy froth. The first swipe of the open razor was from the ear to the chin. The free hand stretched the skin taught and the blade cleaned away every spike of blonde stubble. A quick, efficient strop on the leather, two more sweeps below the nose and he was finished.

TWO

Richard Cooper parked the Saab in his usual spot near the front of the school. Stretching his six foot body, he opened the door and stepped out. Nodding at some children, he strode up the steps. He always strode everywhere. It was part of the image he wanted to project. An energetic headmaster, head up, shoulders back and a firm stride.

Glancing at the clock, Richard pushed open his office door. A largish room, a reflection from the generous sixties when the school was built. In his eight years as head, he had made it his own. Lots of potted plants and framed childrens' paintings on the walls. A huge desk littered with papers: Richard was not a tidy man. Large french windows threw light across the room. Opening the door to his private wash-room, he hung his coat on its coat-hanger behind the door. Richard stared into the mirror, pulled a comb through his brown hair and straightened his tie. With a final smoothing of his grey, double-breasted suit jacket, he left the small room and crossed to his desk. A few letters, some opened and others closed. Nothing unusual for a Tuesday morning.

Assembly was dead on time and Richard made the short journey from his office to the hall. Squaring his shoulders, he straightened his silk tie and pushed open the doors. As Richard entered, six hundred children, as one, rose to their feet. Some turned to smile, most stared stonily ahead. He paused for a moment at the door and waited for the signal from the deputy-head near the stage. He caught the brief nod and walked alone down the narrow aisle.

With a measured stride, he ascended the eight steps onto the stage. Turning, he looked down at the sea of faces in front of him. There was not a sound and they waited for him to begin. The wind stirred the black curtains to his left and he watched the second hand of the clock on the wall at the rear of the hall. Their eyes looked into his and he glanced back full into theirs. Most he knew by name, all he knew by sight. Taking a deep breath, he began.

'Good morning, everybody. Please sit down.' His voice was deliberately quiet. As the children sat down, there came an almost audible sigh. He began slowly. 'For me, today is a special day. It is a day, that for my family, is very important.' He continued, quietly flexing his voice to the acoustics of the hall. 'Exactly fifty years ago to the day, on September 4, 1944 during the Second World War, my relatives were taken from their homes by the Nazis and moved to a transit camp. My father's family were called the Cohens of Leeuwarden. That's a small town in the province of Friesland in the north of the Netherlands.' Bending forward slightly, he let his voice rise. 'The Germans gave orders that all Jews had to leave their homes and be taken to help in the resettlement lands to the east of Germany that had once belonged to other people. Whole families were rounded up and taken to the railway station. They were allowed to take only one suitcase and the clothes they stood up in. They travelled in carriages pulled by steam locomotives to a transit camp called Westerbork, located on a piece of wild heathland, miles from anywhere. My father's family arrived on a Monday morning.' Richard leant against the oak lectern and his heart began to pound as he relived the familiar story told so often to him by his father. 'By that evening, the family had been assigned to a train that took six hundred other Jewish people away from home and friends. That is exactly,' and he waved his hand over the assembly, 'the number of people who sit here in the hall this morning. Grandmothers,' and he tapped on the lectern to emphasise his words, 'grandfathers,' another tap, 'brothers, sisters, nephews, nieces and mothers and fathers. Children the same age as you and some younger and some older. Babes in arms; old people in wheelchairs; men in dark coats and long white beards; pregnant women and brash teenage boys; business men in neat ties and shiny shoes; women in high fashion with beautiful hair and manicured fingers. Yes, everybody, all humanity was on that train. They were jammed into cattle wagons that normally were supposed to hold, "6 horses or 20 men". But then, each one held 80 people with one bucket of water and another bucket as a toilet. They travelled across Holland, Germany and Poland to arrive at a camp of death called Auschwitz. By the time they arrived there on the morning of Friday September 13, 1944, a hundred people had died on the train. Within an hour of arriving at Auschwitz, everybody was dead. Murdered in a horrible way by the guards.' There was a silence in the hall and he wondered whether he had gone too far. Richard stepped round from behind the lectern and folded his arms. A look of sadness crossed his face. 'You may be wondering why this terrible thing happened? And you may be wondering that if my family died in that awful place, then why am I here today? I cannot explain, nor can I understand, why one group of human beings can do that to another group of human beings. People for fifty years have tried to explain why the same race that created the genius of Mozart and the philosophy of Goethe, also created the death camps called Auschwitz, Belsen, Sobibor and many more. Long ago, I gave up trying to understand. I do think about it a great deal, because my mother is German and my father is Jewish.' Richard walked down the top step and stopped. 'Just before the war, my father chose to leave Holland to travel to Manchester to study law. By the time he had finished, Holland had been invaded and the persecution of the Jews had begun. My father was told by his father to remain in Manchester. There were over forty members of my family in Holland. They were all gassed to death. At the end of the war, there were only two left. My father in Manchester and an aunt called Lottie Cohen. She was saved by the brave members of the Dutch resistance and she is still alive and living in Holland.' A quick smile flickered across his face, 'But, that's a story for another assembly.'

Richard walked back up the single step and again turned to face the children. 'I'm sorry to begin your day with such a depressing story. I really believed it was my story about my family and then I thought that it was something that I must share with all of you. Because, what happened in a war so long ago, must never happen again.' He took a deep breath. 'And so today, if you have a second of your busy time, may I ask you to remember the lives of those people on that train.' Richard looked at the bright faces in front of him and caught the curious glances of their teachers. This was the first time he had ever told anybody about his family. 'Let us bow our heads for a moment, and remember them in silence.' The heads in front of him drooped. He waited for no longer than half a minute. 'Amen,' he said, 'and thank you for listening to me.'

Richard walked down the steps as, with a scraping of chairs and a scuffing of shoes, the children rose to their feet. He nodded and quickly strode down the aisle to the open doors at the rear of the hall. His story had drained him and he had to be alone.

THREE

The blast of cold wind shook the wooden building to its shallow foundations. Rolf Müller walked quickly back from the showers to his room. As he opened the door, the welcoming warmth hit him. With his hair still wet, he pulled on his long-legged underpants. The heavy, light green, serge trousers hung neatly over the back of the chair. Yanking them down, he laid them neatly on his bed. Taking a deep breath, Rolf reached into the wardrobe and found the white starched shirt. It crackled as he unfolded it from its paper wrapping. Throwing the cold material around his shoulders, he smoothed its whiteness over his still damp chest.

Tying the knot of the tie precisely, he pulled it exactly into position in the V of his shirt collar. Black against white, perfect. The single knock on the door made him jump.

'What is it?' he called out sharply.

The voice was hushed with respect.

'The train is arriving early, sir.'

'All right, damn you, ... I heard you.' Heavy boots clattered away down the wooden corridor.

Rolf snapped the leather braces over his shoulders and fastened up the brass fly buttons. With a grunt of effort, he pulled on his gleaming black boots and pushed his arms into the sleeves of his jacket. Grabbing his peaked cap and overcoat, he pulled open the door of his room and stepped into the corridor.

FOUR

There was fresh coffee waiting in Richard's office. Closing the door behind him, he grabbed the cup. As he swallowed the first welcome mouthful, he began to doubt whether he should have given the assembly at all. All his life, he had lived with the memories of what his father had passed on to him. Although a Jew, Simon Cohen had become Simon Cooper and, after the war, he had forsaken his birthright and turned away from his religion.

There came a single knock at the door.

Betty Corrigan came with the job and she saw her boss sitting with his head in his hands. 'Good morning, Mr Cooper,' she said softly. 'I'm so sorry to interrupt.'

He lifted his head. 'No,' he said quietly, '.... It's all right.'

She remained in the door way and nodded and her grey lacquered hair nodded with her.

He knew that look. 'Yes?' he asked, raising an eyebrow questioningly.

'In the office, we heard about your assembly this morning.' She paused. 'Well, we all wanted to say how sorry we are to hear about your family. It's fifty years ago today and you must be thinking about what happened.'

Richard pulled his ear-lobe, a personal habit that irritated him. 'Thank you. I appreciate you saying that. Today is an important day and it's very special for my family.' As she gently closed the door the phone rang.

He reached across his desk.

'Hello, Richard. I just phoned to remind you about tonight. How did the assembly go?'

He was taken aback. 'Jane, ... how the hell did you know about my assembly?'

She chuckled. 'Wives always know about their husbands. I know you by now and, anyway, I saw the notes on your desk in your study. .... Was everything all right?'

'I think so. I'll know for sure, when I get home tonight. Our critical children will, no doubt, inform me.'

'All right, darling, I'll see you later. Please don't be late.' The phone clicked into silence.

FIVE

Dawn streaked the sky and there was the usual harsh, chill wind from the north. Rolf Müller shook himself as he quickly walked down the wooden steps. A man appeared at his side.

'Good morning, sir.' He received a grunted reply.

They walked together, although the newcomer walked a respectful one pace behind his superior. Rolf stared fixedly ahead and there was no further conversation.

The piercing whistle of the train made them both jump. A whistle that searched the soul and echoed and re-echoed across the flat, bleak countryside. Rolf drew his overcoat collar tighter round his neck and squinted into the wind.

Along the footpath, the lights on the concrete lamp-posts cast puddles of pale yellow, broken only by the passage of the two men. The men did not see or even want to see the grey faces that watched their every move. A gate swung open and they passed through. It snapped closed behind them.

Standing silhouetted against the billowing morning mist, a high brick archway, topped by a four-sided, sloping roofed building, Sometimes the arch was complete, other times it disappeared in the mist. The arc lights on its roof cast hellish halos of yellow and white eddies through the swirling mist.

The round steel front of the locomotive's boiler burst through the arched opening and its single light stabbed into the darkness. The piercing shriek of the train whistle penetrated the fog, and the thick, black smoke from the locomotive mingled with the dense, white mist.

Rolf watched it travel slowly towards him and his eyes were drawn to the circular light as it cast its pale beam over the shining steel rails at his feet.

'It's a full load, sir!' shouted the man in his ear. Rolf nodded.

The hugeness of the engine dwarfed the two men at its side. Its great driving wheels turned slower and slower and still the greasy pistons pulled the train forwards. Behind, the wagons stretched back through the archway and the locomotive ground onwards towards the waiting men.

Rolf Müller stepped backwards and raised a gloved hand in half salute. The locomotive stopped and the driver peered down from his cab. With a hissing of steam, there was one final shattering whistle.

Rolf Müller clapped his hands and followed the other men that had appeared at his side. This was his duty, this was his job. This was the first train of the day and this was the Ramp at Auschwitz-Birkenau on Friday, September 13, 1944.

SIX

Richard took great pleasure in driving his car. The Saab responded to his driving and he felt absolutely in control. Flicking the CD player control, he waited for Shostakovich's Seventeenth Symphony to fill his head. The slow, rolling Third Movement settled his thoughts and he hummed the tune to himself. Richard arrived home, as usual, late. The gravel on the drive crunched satisfyingly and he pulled to a halt in front of his house.

A solid traditional building. 1930's red brick with a touch of the Tudor. Detached and surrounded by a large garden with mature trees and sloping lawns. Not an average house, more of a small vicarage. Between them they had a good income. Richard's school was large and he was well rewarded. Jane's work as a solicitor was satisfyingly sufficient.

As he opened the front door, Jane walked down the hall and gave him a great hug. 'Richard, I'm so glad you're home.'

She was dressed in what he called her Laura Ashley kit. A long blue skirt with a small floral print and a matching blue sweater. Black ankle boots of the softest suede encasing small feet. Richard's nose caught a swirl of her perfume, Estée Lauder, his favourite. Returning her hug, he kissed her full on the lips. She recoiled slightly and he saw her grimace.

'Richard, you reek of school. Before your parents arrive please have a shower.'

Richard knew exactly what she meant. Jane described it as a mixture of chalk dust and adolescence.

In the bedroom, he undressed and stepped into the shower. Jane sat at the antique dressing table and stared into the mirror. An attractive face with a strong forehead accentuated by a good bone structure and wide open eyes. With careful, deliberate strokes, she brushed her long, brown hair down and then back, each time flicking the strands into shiny bands over her head.

In a swirl of steam, Richard strode naked back into the bedroom. She turned and they both stared at each other. Jane caught his glance. 'No way,' she said, waving her finger. 'No way at all.' And she continued brushing her hair, piling it up on her head and pinning it closely at the back. Hearing Richard laugh, she smiled at her own reflection.

They dressed. Richard in casual trousers and a polo shirt. Jane in a green silken dress that clung around her slim figure.

In the kitchen, their son waited. A teenager, as tall as his father and with his mother's eyes. Dressed in a standard uniform of sweatshirt, jeans and trainers. 'Hi,' he said, 'when's dinner?' A grin split his face.

Almost on cue, the kitchen door opened and in walked a carbon copy of Jane. A face composed and expectant. She flicked her head and the brushed hair dropped neatly into place.

David was seventeen, in the upper sixth and, surprisingly, working quite hard. Rebecca was a totally different person. Sixteen years old with a maturity that hardly matched her youth. Richard looked at them both, marvelling at how children can be so totally similar to their parents. His thoughts were interrupted.

'Richard,' said Jane, staring through the hall window. 'Your parents are here.'

Hearing the familiar crunch of gravel on the drive, he opened the front door. His father's black Jaguar had arrived and Richard walked across to meet him. For a moment they paused and their eyes met.

'Richard, good to see you,' he said, in a deep voice. 'How are you?' They shook hands.

'I'm fine thanks, Dad.'

Simon Cooper stood in that special way that older people adopt when it is painful to stretch the back. But his head was up and the lined face fully alert. 'Home from work already?' With a laugh, he nodded and his brown eyes sparkled. 'You teachers, …. you don't know what long hours mean.' It was a banter that had gone on for years. Richard pulled at his ear-lobe and took his father's arm.

Behind them, the other car door opened and a smallish woman stepped out. For her age, Sabina Cooper was remarkably youthful. The blonde hair had retained most of its colour and she had tied it back in a neat coil on the nape of her neck. Her relatively unlined face bore a permanent slightly questioning look. Her eyes were the deepest, clearest blue. She leant against the car door and the simple dress that she wore was in the very best of taste. 'Hello everybody.' Her voice was soft with a trace of an accent.

Jane waited in the hall and welcomed them into the house. 'Good to see you both. Do come in.' She hugged them and Richard took their coats.

In deep, leather arm-chairs, father and son sat opposite each other. The living-room was warmed by a log fire burning steadily in an open grate. Half the room was oak panelled and the remainder brick. The wooden parquet floor gleamed and Persian scatter rugs gave a splash of rich colour. Newspapers and magazines lay over the coffee table. It was a lived-in family room.

'Richard,' Simon's lips formed a thin line. 'You look a little tired.'

Richard ran his fingers through his hair. 'Really, I'm fine. No problem.'

Simon nodded and a flicker of concern passed across his face. 'All right. But just be careful, son.'

Richard rose from his chair and walked towards the panelled wall. He pulled the cornice of one of the panels and it swung open, revealing a small cupboard. 'A drink before dinner?' he asked. There were nods and he filled six glasses. Placing them on a silver tray, he passed them out to his family. Without a word or a sign, Simon rose from his chair. He paused, as he looked at the faces in front of him. They waited, each holding their glass, ready for what he had to say.

He paused for a moment and looked at each of them. 'Sabina, my wonderful wife. Richard, the best son I could ever have. .... Jane,' and he smiled, 'my special daughter-in- law.' The smile widened. 'Rebecca and David, my two fantastic grandchildren. .... I give you a toast.' His lined face became serious and he took a deep breath. 'Fifty years ago on this day and almost to the minute. All my relatives, apart from Lottie Cohen, perished in the Holocaust. .... I still find it hard to believe.' Simon gripped his glass. 'Let us drink, and, for a minute and remember them.'

Richard felt Jane's hand in his and he glanced at her, she was crying.

The minute elongated and the room around them was silent. The heavy smoke from the log fire curled up the chimney and nobody wanted to talk.

SEVEN

The greyness of dawn spread across the Ramp. Everything was grey; the hard ground, the sky and the people who disgorged themselves from the train.

Black and brown Alsatian dogs, and their viciousness was seen and heard. They howled and barked and snapped, ready for their prey. Children began to wail and mothers cried with them. Ten wagons with six hundred people crammed into every centimetre space. One by one, the heavy wooden doors slid back and the people poured out. Over all lay the stench of humanity. Six days in unventilated cattle wagons and the smell of fear showed on the faces of the people who scrambled down onto the compacted earth. Voices shouted and bellowed and screamed at them.

From inside the barbed wire of the camp, more men and some women arrived at the Ramp. Some wore the green uniforms of the SS. Others wore the striped blue and grey of the camp inmates, the *Rampe Sonderkommando*. The uniforms made no difference, each was committed to the routine of the first train of the day. For the new arrivals there was a chaos that numbed the mind. To the people who had journeyed for six days, there was terror, horror and the unknown. Either screamed at by the guards, bitten by the dogs or struck by the inmates, they tried to retain their friendships and keep hold of what little was left of normality. The one metre drop from the darkness of the wagon to the floodlit grey earth was a drop into hell. Some made it, others fell, most were dragged.

It took fifteen minutes to empty the train. Wheeled wooden carts arrived, pushed by inmates. They scrambled into the wagons and removed the dead. Thrown onto the carts, the bodies were trundled away and disappeared into the mist. Soon there were queues of people, all in five's, each holding the regulation suitcase and each staring about them in shock. The organised cacophony of orders and screams quickly died away. The smoke from the engine cleared at the same time as the mist and the Ramp was clearly seen by everybody.

A bare corridor of ground, a hundred metres wide and a kilometre and a half long. On both sides, lines of concrete fence posts strung with electrified barbed wire. Beyond the wire, row after row of squat wooden huts. On the left, the women's section. On the right, the men's. In the near distance, chimneys poked into the air from low brick buildings. The twin tracks of the railway lines gleamed dully in the early morning sun.

The train was at rest, its awful job done. The locomotive waited quietly, the odd wisp of steam escaping from its driving pistons and black smoke rising lazily from its squat stack. Small groups of men ran down the ramp in front of the wagons, they carried cleaning tools. It took five minutes for each wagon to be serviced. The dead removed. Bucketsful of water and a quick scrub. The excreta and urine carefully washed away and the heavy sliding doors left open to allow the free passage of fresh air. If there was any left in this foul place.

EIGHT

The Cooper family sat down for dinner. A long, antique table fitted the proportions of the room and each place was carefully laid with its correct complement of silver cutlery and cut glass. Eight candles set in two gilt candelabras cast a warm, flickering glow over the faces.

Whilst they ate, they chatted about family matters and enjoyed being together. After a short time, David, his voice edged with curiosity, said, 'Grandpa, can you tell us a little more about the end of the war and what happened to our family?'

Taking a deep breath, Simon frowned across the table at his grandson. 'David, I think you're old enough to hear the answers.' He nodded, picked up the carving-knife and cut the first wafer-thin slice of beef. 'Rebecca,' he glanced at her, 'you carry a family name. If your family namesake had lived, then she would've been a woman of seventy or so. I remember her as a beautiful little girl, full of life and very intelligent. She always wanted to be a teacher. Perhaps that's why your father took up the profession.'

'I never knew that,' said Richard, curiously.

'Ah, ah, there's lots of things you don't know about your past,' replied Simon, lifting his eyebrows. He sat down.

'Grandpa,' asked Rebecca. 'Where did my Rebecca live?'

Simon re-adjusted his gold-rimmed spectacles and tucked his napkin into the collar of his shirt. 'I'll start from Rebecca's question.' His voice was steady and he stopped only once to carefully chew a piece of food. 'Rebecca was a relative. We all lived in Leeuwarden, the capital of Friesland, a province in the north of the Netherlands. Before the war, we'd lived in Breslau in Germany. After Adolf Hitler came to power, my father realised what was going to happen because he'd read 'Mein Kampf' and Hitler had said very clearly what he would do to the Jews. Most of our friends thought we were crazy when we moved, lock, stock and barrel, to Holland in 1934. Our business prospered and we had an office in Amsterdam but we lived in Leeuwarden.' He took a deep breath. Rebecca chose the moment to interrupt.

'Grandpa, last year, for our exams, we had to read "The Diary of Anne Frank." Have you ever read it?'

'Rebecca,' he said, nodding, 'If you've read that famous book, then you've some idea of what happened in Holland.'

'I've read it as well,' said David brushing his hand across his face. 'It's a fantastic story.'

Simon's eyes filled. Turning to his plate, he cut a piece of beef and forked it into his mouth. It gave him time to think. 'Yes,' he said slowly. 'I've read it. ... Reading Anne Frank's Diary made the past come back to me. .... It always makes me cry. David, I'm so glad it's had the same effect on you.'

As the table was cleared, the aroma of fresh coffee wafted across the room as Richard brought in the pot and filled the cups. Simon continued. 'In the late Thirties, life for the Cohens was good. We had a big house, a car and we were totally accepted into the local community. My father was quite successful. He desperately wanted me to practise law and he pushed me hard.

'Sounds familiar,' muttered Richard.

Simon ignored the comment. 'His idea was to send me to Manchester in England. In the city there was a very good university and a large Jewish Community.' He turned to his grandson. 'Anyway, David, in those days, sons did as they were told. Within two months, I was living in Manchester and there I began my law studies. I came home whenever I could and then in September 1939, Britain declared war on Germany and I was unable to go home again. The last time I spoke to my father on the phone, he told me to stay put. I really had no other choice. In May 1940, the Germans invaded Holland and I was completely cut off from my family. The odd message came back though all sorts of unofficial channels and that was it.' He slowly stirred his coffee and sighed. 'You know, apart from Lottie Cohen, I've no other relatives.'

'How did Lottie survive?' said Rebecca quietly.

He held his granddaughter's hand. 'The Dutch were wonderful towards their Jewish friends. They hid a quarter of the total Jewish population of 98,000. A man called Frank van de Meer and his wife Marieke saved Lottie's life.* They actually took her out of a hospital and hid her for the remainder of the war.' His eyes glazed. 'In all, forty-two members of our family were murdered in the gas chambers.' He stopped talking and his eyes closed. For several minutes, there was silence.

Richard rose from his chair and walked round to stand at his father's side. 'Come on now, Dad.' He put his hand on his father's shoulder. 'Let's go and sit in the living-room.'

---

*(See Alan Clegg's **'WINDMILLS'**, published by Horseshoe Publications, for the story of the van de Meer family)

The old man hesitated for a moment. His shoulders straightened and the head lifted. 'Thanks, son. A good idea. Today is a day when I want to tell you all exactly what happened.' His gnarled hands pushed at the table and he levered himself into a standing position. He turned to his wife at his side. 'Now, my darling, take my arm and I'll lead the way to the living-room. Rebecca, take the other one.' A log crackled in the grate, sending a shower of sparks up the chimney.

NINE

The conditioning of the arrival process had taken effect and the rows of humanity were strangely still.

From nearby, there came the sound of a bicycle bell. It rang several times and the quiet rows turned curiously to see where it was coming from. The man on the bike stopped, swung his leg over the saddle and passed it to one of the waiting inmates.

In his early thirties, slender and impeccably dressed in a purest white SS uniform and glossy, black boots, Josef Mengele seemed strangely out of place on the Ramp. But this was his second home and he acted as if he owned it. Straightening his shoulders and, with a black leather-gloved forefinger, he dusted imaginary specks of dust from his trousers. All eyes focused on the white uniformed figure as he controlled the stage in front of him, something he had done so many times before. A face glowing with health and good living. Cold brown eyes surveyed the waiting queues. They lined-up, five in a row, mixed by sex and age.

Rolf walked to the man's side, smiled a welcome and raised his hand to the peak of his cap. 'Good Morning, *Herr Doktor* Mengele, and how are you on this lovely day?'

'Very well, *Herr Doktor* Müller .... I think today, I will make the selection.'

Rolf Müller clicked his heels. 'As you wish, *Herr Hauptsturmführer*.'

Josef Mengele walked casually towards the front of the queue. He nodded at a guard and the grinning man propelled a Jewish girl towards the *Herr Doktor*.

She was beautiful. In her late teens and she held her head high and looked Mengele full in the face. The grey dress was torn but it fitted her lithe figure perfectly. With pale hands clasped in front of her, she stood casually at ease, almost daring the German to do something; and he did.

Mengele spoke quietly in a clear, well modulated voice and his eyes looked into hers. 'What is your name, my dear?'

She cocked her head to one side, unsure what to say.

'Well ....,' he said, with the slightest edge of impatience, 'what's your name?'

She stared him in the eye. 'My name is Rebecca Cohen.'

'And how far have you come?'

Her voice gained in strength. 'From a town called Leeuwarden in the Netherlands.' The waiting hundreds stood silently behind her.

He smiled and nodded. 'Ah yes. I know it well. I've often sailed on your Frisian lakes.'

For a moment they looked at each other.

Mengele unfolded his arms, raised his gloved hand and placed it on her shoulders. She flinched and froze. Slowly and gently, he turned her to the left. His eyes never moved from hers.

He pointed with his other hand. 'Just go that way, Rebecca Cohen. Down that path. The guard will show you the way.' Stepping away from her, his eyes settled on the next person.

All the promises of resettlement in the east and work for all, vanished in twenty minutes. Each person was quickly examined and each, with a casual wave of the hand, was sent on their way. Columns of five marched past Mengele. Occasionally he stopped the flow.

'Who is your favourite artist?'

The mouth gaped with astonishment.

Mengele shook his head. 'Not quick enough, my dear. Go to the left. Hurry now.'

He separated men from women; husbands from wives; children from parents; babes in arms from their mothers. Many jumped to the wrong conclusions.

'Please, sir,' said the mother. 'Let me go with my son, …. please?' Her eyes yearned for acceptance. There was a pause and the guards began to scream obscenities.

'Wait a minute,' said Mengele, with a polite smile and they quietened. 'Of course you can go together. Both of you, off to the left.'

On that particular morning, the short journey to the right meant hellish life. To the left, meant murderous death.

TEN

The fire in the living-room settled into a dull red glow and the curtains were closed against the chill September night. A single light from a tall, shaded standard lamp lit the room.

'Cognac, Simon?' said Jane, holding the bottle in one hand and a crystal glass in the other.

Simon dropped into the old Chesterfield near the fire. 'Thanks,' he replied and looked across the room as the others followed him in. He patted the sofa. 'Rebecca, sit next to me on this side and David on the other.'

The chatter was of everyday things and the trivialities of life. Glasses were filled and refilled. After a short time, there was a break in the conversation. Simon leant forward and placed his half-finished drink on the coffee table. Prising himself up from the Chesterfield, he walked slowly across the room.

With a slight stretching motion, he leant back against the top of the fireplace. 'Where was I? …. Ah, yes, …. in Manchester. Money stopped coming from my parents. But, my father had been a wise man. Before Britain declared war, he was able to transfer some of his money to London and that money helped me to survive.' He ran his hand through his thick, grey hair. 'At that time, British Intelligence in Holland was in chaos. The Germans had broken the British codes causing the deaths of hundreds of British and Dutch agents. I asked at my Embassy if I could return to Holland but nobody would let me.'

David politely interrupted. There was a look of awe on his face. 'Grandpa, do you mean that you wanted to be a …. a spy?'

Simon picked up his glass from the table and drank the last drop. 'No David, not quite. …. I helped out with things and translated a lot of radio messages and I wrote reports.' He nodded at Richard, as he refilled the glass. 'With my studies and the war, the years flew by. I only heard bad news from Holland. I knew Jews were being sent to the east for what was called "resettlement" and at that time nobody knew what it meant. In 1942 some news came out that Jews were being systematically murdered. But nobody believed that such awful stories could be true. I'd also heard about a place in Holland called Westerbork. The Dutch Government had built it before the war to help to resettle Jewish refugees from Germany. Many of my parents' friends came through the camp. The Germans were using it to reverse the flow of Jews back to Germany.' Simon shook his head. 'Oh dear, it's such a long story.' Glass in hand, he took another deep breath and sat down.

'Are you all right?' said Sabina, with a worried frown.

He looked across the table at his wife and smiled, a smile without humour. 'I'm fine, thanks .... I just want to talk. I think this is the right time to tell these things. I know you've heard them before but I want my grandchildren to know.' Reaching into his trouser pocket, he took out a bright red handkerchief, clapped it to his nose and blew loudly into it. 'Sorry,' he muttered. 'Bit of a cold coming on. .... One day, I was told by my exiled Dutch Government that I was to be commissioned into the British Army. It came as quite a shock. They wanted lawyers and I soon found out why. I was told to report to an office in Baker Street. It was only later that I found out it was the headquarters of the Special Operations Executive. I was interviewed for an hour or so and then they made me a lieutenant working for the Army legal department. That same day, I bought my uniform and, two days later, I moved into Woolwich Barracks outside London. A brigadier explained to me that when Europe was liberated, there would be a need for multi-lingual lawyers because the Allies were considering doing something about the Nazis. At that time there was no mention of war crimes. In the following months, I learnt a great deal about international law and, I must admit, I enjoyed it. Army life wasn't bad. The mess I lived in, was occupied by a crowd of loony gunners and I had the time of my life.' He chuckled, as the memories came back. 'D Day arrived in 1944 and then things happened so quickly that I thought I'd be back in Holland by Christmas. But, as we all know, it didn't happen like that. Parts of southern Holland were liberated and then I asked again if I could go and help. I was surprised when my CO agreed. The whole thing was very exciting. Then I began to hear more rumours about the plight of the Dutch Jews. The rumours backed up what I'd heard in London. It's something that I don't want to go into tonight.' He paused for a moment to empty his glass. 'I was attached to the Princess Irene Brigade as a legal advisor. It was a brigade entirely staffed by Dutch citizens. The CO was Prince Bernhard, the husband of Queen Wilhelmina's daughter, Princess Juliana.' Simon's head lifted and he smiled grimly. 'I was in Nijmegen a month after the airborne landings at Arnhem. What a bloody mess that was. Hardly a building left standing and bodies everywhere. In Nijmegen, I had the job of interrogating German soldiers and that's when I first came into contact with the SS. After coming through Holland, I thought I'd seen it all, but these swines were different. Arrogant, self-seeking and completely without any morality whatsoever. Some spoke, most of them refused to say anything. By this time, the Allies knew exactly what was happening in the concentration camps. It was my job to see if I could extract any information from these men and it was damned hard work. I learnt little, apart from their hatred of the Jews. I remember mentioning the word Jew to an SS major and he laughed. Then he said, "The Jews? What Jews? By now, they've all gone up the chimney." It was the first time in my life I'd ever hit somebody. I just punched him in the face and then I went to hit him again. My sergeant managed to stop me. I informed my section commander and he told me not to worry about it. I did, because after I'd hit the man, he just smiled and told me it was too late to do anything about the "*Juden Untermenschen.*"' Simon looked at a frowning Rebecca. 'Quite literally, when translated, it means "subhuman" or just, "nothing". .... After that incident, I learnt quite a lot.' Simon's voice faded away and his head sagged onto his chest.

Richard rose to his feet and said quietly, 'He looks a bit pale.'

'Don't worry,' said Sabina. 'He often falls asleep like that. Just let him be alone for a few minutes.'

'Come on, let's go into the kitchen,' said Richard concernedly. They rose to their feet and tip-toed out of the room. The flickering flames of the fire cast long shadows across Simon's still body.

ELEVEN

A feeling of absolute dread filled Rebecca Cohen's heart. Josef Mengele moved away to her right and, to her left, the SS guards began pushing and heaving the mass of crying humanity forward. Many sick people fell to the ground and the *Sonderkommando* rushed to drag them to their feet. Lorries parked in a single row were steadily filled to brimming with the sick and the elderly. Around Rebecca was the panic of her people and she tried to stand upright as bodies fell, and stumbled, and grabbed, and kicked and screamed; each in their individual torment. A young soldier grabbed her arm. Rebecca paused for a moment in her panic and looked into his face. He was no older than she was and she saw him stare into her eyes. For a split second, the man faltered and his eyes froze into surprise; then it was gone to be replaced by hate and his deep-throated spittle caught her full in the face. She ducked to her knees and crawled away through the churned, grey mud.

The crowd shuffled from the Ramp and slowly, painfully, they were driven like cattle towards their final goal. It took only twenty minutes and they were there. In front of them stood a two-storied, brick building. They stopped and the SS shouted their instructions.

These damned Germans wanted her to take a shower. In front of her, appeared concrete steps leading down into darkness. Rebecca placed her foot on the first step and glanced upwards. The sun had broken out from behind heavy, black clouds. A single slanting beam of pure white light caught the top of the squat, tapering, red brick chimney. It made her shiver and she edged downwards, seemingly into the depths of the earth. The azure blue of the sky and the bright sunshine vanished.

The crowd quietened as the large, bare room filled up. Signs in Dutch hung on the brick walls, "**Disinfection**", "**This way to the Baths**". They gave some solace to the waiting hundreds. Rows of wooden benches lined the walls. Numbered brass hooks above each place. Inmates handed out bars of fresh soap. Their blue and grey striped clothes stood out incongruously against the clothing of the new arrivals. Four days ago, most had dressed in their best and everywhere there were splashes of colour. The SS shouted and signalled that all were to undress. There were roars of indignation and downright refusal.

Rebecca sat on the hard bench and looked at the faces in front of her, hoping to see some of her family. She had not seen any of them since Westerbork. Around her, the screaming began all over again. Some took off their clothes and stood, hands covering their nakedness. Two SS men explained in so patient voices that people had to undress to take the disinfecting shower. Towels appeared for people who wanted them. A huge German loomed over Rebecca and stared hard at her face. Leering at her, he shouted something. She rose from her seat and tried to listen. In one sweeping movement, he ripped off her coat and threw her to the floor. Rebecca refused to panic and she scrambled to her feet, gently pushing an old woman out of the way. Turning her back to the German, she yanked her pullover over her head and slipped off her skirt. Carefully, she folded both garments and laid them on the bench. Glancing sideways, she saw that the man was still watching her. She again faced the wall and, staring hard at a crack in the brick-work, she removed all her underclothes and completed the neat heap. Something in her heart calmed her. She turned, the man was gone.

In the bare undressing room most of the people were naked and they huddled into groups to protect themselves. The dogs arrived down the steps and their handlers let them roam at will. Anybody not naked was screamed at and the dogs barked and barked and barked. An air of acceptance came over the faces of the people and their panic began to subside. A tall SS officer, speaking Dutch, announced in a clear voice that the disinfection room was ready. The faces looked up and watched his face. He smiled at them and some smiled back. A row of SS guards moved to one side and the doors at the end of the undressing room were open. The crowd noisily pushed forward.

The disinfection chamber had bright lights and whitewashed walls reflected the light harshly. From overhead came the hum of ventilation fans. The floor, apart from square drain holes, was bare and clean. Four tall, ventilation columns reached to the ceiling. There was no sign of showers.

The inner calm that flowed through Rebecca made her at peace. She smiled at the faces around her and several times she touched somebody. There was no response; their faces were expressionless. The crowd began to edge forward and she found herself carried along with them. Rebecca felt no pain, she loved her people and drew strength from them. The clear German voice spoke again and told everybody to go in for the disinfecting shower. There was plenty of space and groups of twenty or so people, young and old, men and women, babies and children, walked steadily forward. It was then that Rebecca saw her mother and their eyes met. She tried to reach her but the group hemmed her in. Her mother shouted something, Rebecca heard nothing. At her side appeared the young soldier. She glanced across the room at her mother and back to the man. With her eyes, she pleaded. His eyes saw nothing, only her young body and his fat red face split into a huge grin. Slowly he shook his head and motioned her towards the disinfection room.

Suddenly Rebecca knew she was going to die. It was a feeling that swept through her body and she gritted her teeth with the agonising terror of the knowledge of death. Looking around her, the same feeling overtook the faces that looked at hers. The voices began to rise and a child screamed. Surprisingly, some of her people raised their voices in song. Glancing back from where she had come, she watched the great wooden door slam tightly shut.

Now Rebecca knew she was going to die; in the disinfection room there were no SS.

TWELVE

'He's been asleep a long time, Sabina,' said Richard, with concern in his voice.

'Don't worry,' she replied, stepping off the high stool. 'I'll go and see him.' The conversation stilled for a moment.

Sabina's shout was loud and penetrated the thick walls of the house. 'Come here, ... QUICKLY!'

Richard jumped out of his chair, ran across the kitchen and down the hall. He was the first one to drop to his father's side.

Trying to be calm, he said, 'Sabina, what's the matter with him?'

Simon lay exactly as they had left him. Chin on his chest, legs wide open and arms at his side. His face a florid red.

'I don't know. .... I don't know,' she said frantically, smoothing his cheek with her hand. 'I can't waken him.' She turned to face Richard. ' ..... Oh, for God's sake, what's happened?'

Richard knelt at his father's side and, with the tip of his two fingers, touched the neck. It took him a few seconds to find what he was looking for. 'There's a pulse and he's alive. But it's faint.' He snapped into action. 'Jane, phone for an ambulance. .... Sabina, help me to lay him down and loosen his clothing. .... David, give me a hand.' Together, they gently pulled Simon sideways across the Chesterfield and placed cushions under his head.

Richard put his face close to his father's and raised his voice. 'Simon, wake up! .... Come on now, wake up!' There was no response. His mother began to cry and he slipped his arm around her. 'Don't worry,' he said, trying to speak calmly. '.... Don't worry.'

The sound of a wailing siren came through the windows. Richard rose and said, brusquely, 'David, go and let them in.'

They came along the hall carrying the paraphernalia of high-tech medicine. A man and a woman, their green overalls standing out sharply against the soft hues of the living-room. The woman spoke first.

'We'll just give him a quick check over. Please stand back.' She slipped an oxygen mask over Simon's mouth and clamped the stethoscope on her ears. Opening his shirt, she listened to his chest. The room was quiet as everybody worriedly watched them go about their work. She rose to her feet, nodding.

Richard looked at her. 'I'm Richard Cooper. How's my father?'

'Yes, hello. I think your father's had a heart attack. I don't know how bad it is until we get him back to the hospital.' She glanced around the room. 'We ought to move him as soon as possible.'

Sabina stepped forward. 'You and I, Richard. .... Come on, let's go.'

The paramedic left and returned with a wheeled chair. David helped him to manhandle it into position. 'Dad, look ....,' he cried. 'I saw Grandpa move. His eyes flickered. .... Look, ... they moved again.' The family stared and gathered round the couch.

Sabina dropped to her husband's side and stroked his forehead. 'Come on, my darling, Simon. Talk to me, ... please.' It had some effect. Suddenly he let out a low moan and his eyes opened and then quickly closed. Sabina held his hand tightly. She looked up, her eyes shining. 'He squeezed my hand,' she said, with joy. 'He's all right.'

'Excuse me,' said the paramedic, quietly. 'We have to get him to the hospital.' They cleared the way and wheeled Simon out to the waiting ambulance.

As they sped away, Richard heard the siren rising and falling. At the hospital, the ambulance doors flew open and before Richard and Sabina could move, Simon had been lifted out, placed on a trolley and rushed away.

She was small, neat and smart. 'Hello, I'm the Cardiac Care Sister. Would you please follow me?' She led the way past the hubbub of casualty, down a long corridor and into a room. Patterned walls, a low table with magazines and four chairs. 'Please sit down and I'll explain what happens next.' They followed her request. 'Mrs Cooper ', she said softly, 'there's no need to worry. Your husband is in the best of hands. The Doctor has just given him a good check over. Mr Cooper has had a heart attack and it's not too serious.'

'Thank God,' whispered Richard.

The sister stopped talking and waited for the questions that always came.

Sabina was first, with her hands to her face. 'Sister, will he be all right? .... I mean, you know, ... all right?'

'Oh, don't worry. .... No, ... all things being equal, he should make a reasonable recovery.'

'Is he conscious?' asked Richard, anxiously.

'Yes, he is. In fact, when I left him, he was asking for both of you.'

'Can we see him?' said Sabina.

'Of course you can.'

Simon lay connected to everything imaginable. Plastic tubing hung out of his arms and he was surrounded by clicking and whirring machinery.

Green and white were the predominant colours.

They made their way across the gleaming floor to Simon's bed. Richard stood on one side and Sabina on the other.

The nurse leant over him. 'Wake up, Mr Cooper. Your wife and son are here.'

Sabina held Simon's hand and, for a moment, nothing happened. One eyelid opened and then another. The eyes focused and then slowly his face split into a faint grin.

'Hello, Dad,' whispered Richard.

'Darling, how are you feeling?'

Simon took a deep breath. 'I feel as though I could sleep for a week.' His voice was clear, although he spoke slowly. Screwing up his eyes, he recognised them. 'Richard, old man. It's that bloody brandy of yours. You know I can't stand Hennessy, give me Remy Martin any day.'

Richard smiled and held his father's hand. 'Nonsense, you old cheat. You don't know one from the other.'

Simon's eyes snapped closed and he drifted off into medicated sleep.

After a few minutes, Richard took his mother's arm. 'Come on,' he whispered. 'There's nothing we can do now. Let's leave him and come back later.'

Together they walked slowly back down the long corridors. As Richard looked for a phone for a taxi, he saw the rest of his family come through the doors of the main entrance.

'We had to come.... How is he?' said Jane, gently putting her arm around Sabina's shoulders.

She tried to be confident. 'They said it was only a small heart attack and he could be well quite soon.'

Before they could say another word, the Sister came towards them almost running. Her face was expressionless.

'Please,' she said, sharply, 'come with me. I'm sorry to say that Mr Cooper's just had another heart attack.'

'Oh, God, ... no!' shouted Sabina.

They followed the sister back down the corridors, none of them speaking a word. People moved out of their way and they quickly arrived at the ward. A grim faced doctor waited for them.

'Please come through.'

'.... Is he? .... Is he?' Sabina could not complete the sentence.

'I'm sorry, everybody,' the doctor said, respectfully. 'I have to inform you that Mr Cooper has just passed away.'

Jane sobbed and held onto Richard, her eyes filled with tears.

'I can't believe it,' said Richard and a great sob wracked his body.

Richard and Sabina walked through the curtains to the side of the bed. He looked at the scene before him. 'Sabina,' he said, reaching for her, 'he died peacefully and he's had a good life.'

'I know, ... I know. .... And .... .' And she choked back the tears.

Carefully, Richard moved away from her side and walked over to the window. Outside, the world carried on as if nothing had happened. Leaves fell gently to the ground and clouds scudded across a leaden sky. He took a deep sigh and turned to his family.

'Dad, can I see him, ... please?' Rebecca fought back her tears.

'Of course you can,' Richard replied and led her through the curtains to the bed.

'He looks so beautiful,' she said, with wide-open eyes. 'Can I touch him?' Richard nodded and tears sprang back to his eyes.

David waited quietly at his grandmother's side. 'I'm sorry, ... I'm sorry. I really am. I can't see him. I just want to remember Grandpa as he really was.' His eyes searched Sabina's face.

She held his hand tightly. 'Don't worry, she whispered. 'It's quite all right. We all understand how you feel.'

THIRTEEN

'Hurry them up, damn you!' shouted Müller. 'We're twenty minutes behind schedule.'

Steam rose from the mass of people on the Ramp. The morning mist had gone and the sun shone weakly from a cloudless sky. The youngest and the fittest were quickly forced marched away and the straggling line of the very young and the elderly made their way to the waiting trucks.

'Use the dogs! Come on!' snapped Rolf, impatiently. 'There's another transport due in two hours and this lot has to be cleared before then.' Rolf was angry, he liked perfection. He stood, arms folded, near the barbed-wire fence of the women's compound at the side of the Ramp. Quickly darting to one side, he dragged an old woman to her feet. 'That way, madam. Follow the crowd to the trucks.' With a gloved hand, he pointed the way. The woman was in her eighties and, for a moment, stared at this handsome man.

She frowned and thanked him. '*Dank U wel, mijnheer.*' And she joined the crowd.

The shouting and screaming ebbed and flowed as people followed their orders. Rolf resumed his place near the fence. He knew exactly what he was looking for. After five minutes, as the Ramp emptied, he spotted his prey.

'*Rottenführer*, over there! .... Behind the old man! Get them! Bring them here!' The corporal rushed forward.

Twins, both girls, about eight years old. They wore the same clothes, pretty dresses with long skirts and flowered tops. Short black hair cut to a fringe over their foreheads. Their white shoes were muddied but the black stockings were unmarked. They waited-arm-in-arm, with big staring eyes. Their young mother stood close. The soldier grabbed them by their shoulders and they began wailing with fear. The mother's cry of utter despair cut through the air.

'No, ... idiot! .... Bring the mother as well,' shouted Rolf, striding across to the family group. They waited, frozen to the spot. Rolf touched the peak of his cap and gave his most charming smile.

'*Mevrouw*, no need to worry.' His smile disarmed the mother completely and she stopped screaming. 'Bring your children and follow the *Rottenführer*. Take your time.' Reaching her side, he fondled the children's hair.

'Sir, my husband!' she shouted back over her shoulder. 'My husband! I must find my husband.'

Rolf laughed. 'Don't worry. Don't worry, we'll find him later. He'll have a shower and then catch you up.' The corporal held a child's hand and they followed him as meekly as lambs.

The Ramp had cleared. The *Sonderkommando* gathered up lost suitcases and filled the waiting trolleys. With a shrieking whistle, the locomotive came to life and slowly its driving wheels began to turn. With a squealing and a clanking, the wagons moved backwards and, giving out a final belch of steam and smoke, the locomotive crept down the track and the train disappeared through the arched entrance.

The guard gave a swift salute. '*Herr Hauptsturmführer*, they're ready in the undressing rooms.' Rolf followed him, walked down the long track and turned left towards a low, brick building. On each side of him, the rows of dismal huts stretched away into the distance.

The chill wind of an early winter blew across the flat plains of Upper Silesia and it cut to the bone. The Auschwitz-Birkenau concentration camp provided no break from the wind; it was always cold. There were four places in the camp where heat could be found and *Hauptsturmführer Doktor* Müller was walking steadily towards one of them. Rolf neither looked left nor right. It didn't matter, because any of the inmates in his line of sight were forbidden to look at him on pain of death. It took three minutes to walk briskly from the Ramp to Crematorium II. Passing through barbed-wire gates, he returned the salutes of the SS guards. As he approached the concrete steps, he noticed something by his foot, glinting in the sunshine. Bending over and, with his gloved forefinger, he moved the object in the mud. Picking up the gold wedding ring, he straightened. With a smile, he wiped off the dirt and slipped it into his trouser pocket.

A squat building, red brick with a low, sloping roof. Like the coldest iceberg, most of it lay beneath the surface. Broad concrete steps led downwards and quickly the daylight faded away.

The stench of human sweat hit Rolf full in the face and, even though he was well used to it, it still made him flinch.

'My God, why do these Jews stink so much?' he muttered.

The sergeant near him smiled. 'You get used to it, *Herr Hauptsturmführer*.'

The scene in front of them heaved and boiled. Some of the people were naked, others were dressed. Faces stared and faces cried. Bodies cringed and some lay on the floor. The noise was deafening. Screaming, crying, wailing, sobbing and the barking of the dogs.

Rolf saw nobody individually, he was immune to these people. The disorganised panic upset him. Standing in the fetid air near the entrance to the undressing room, he shouted, 'Everybody, please listen to me.' It was probably because he spoke in Dutch that everybody turned to listen. He was well versed in five languages for the standard phrases used in Auschwitz. Immaculately dressed, smartly polished black boots and standing, legs apart, hands on hips; the classic SS pose. He waited for another full minute, watching his audience. Slowly they stilled and stared. Smiling, he lowered his voice. 'Before you work here in the camp, you must be clean and free from any infection. Therefore, you must undress and then make your way through the door at the end of the room.' He pointed behind them. 'Leave everything here, spectacles, jewellery. It'll all be safe. Everything will be returned when you've finished in the shower room. When you get in there, we'll organise you into smaller groups. We don't want any epidemics in the camp. Then you'll go to your barracks and receive some hot soup and then you'll be assigned jobs according to your profession.' The smile broadened and he clapped his hands. 'There's no need to worry. Everything will be taken care of. There's soap available for when you go into the showers. The *Rottenführers* will give towels to those who need them.' He nodded. 'I'm very sorry you've been inconvenienced like this. But, it's the only way we can handle such large numbers.' He stepped down and waited in the corner. His eyes saw everything.

The guards and the inmates made sure everyone was undressed. Some had to be persuaded; the dogs did their work well '*Rottenführer*, is all ready in the disinfection room?' Rolf said quietly to the corporal at his side.

'*Jawohl, Herr Hauptsturmführer*. All is ready.'

'Send them through. .... Quickly now.'

The mass of naked people moved forward leaving behind their belongings. Small cases and bags piled high in disorderly heaps. Clothing, either folded or thrown to the floor. The undressing room was a mess but already the *Sonderkommando* were hard at work.

Rolf followed the corporal across the room and along the narrow passage to the ante-room. It was empty and, as he walked, he nearly slipped on the steaming piles of human excreta. Shaking his head, he stepped sideways and nodded at one of the *Sonderkommando*. The cowed man bent over and, with his bare hands, cleaned the stinking brown mess off Rolf's boots. Without as much as a second glance, Rolf strode to the door at the far end of the ante-room.

It was an interesting door, two metres high and a metre and a half wide, made of layers of planks sandwiching a solid sheet of wood. The edges of the door and its frame were padded with felt. At head height was a circular peep-hole, filled with glass and sealed by rubber gaskets.

'*Hauptsturmführer*, all is secured.' The corporal waited patiently.

The door was held firm by massive bolts and hand driven screws. But no door could deaden the sound of the screaming from within. Rolf put his eye to the glass. Inside was a hell no words could describe. Some people were running backwards and forwards. Others crouched on the floor. Many stood with arms around each other. Their faces expressed the horror of what they knew was going to happen. It was a scene that always fascinated Rolf. Because it was a scene he controlled. For a few moments, he watched. A new sound came through the thick insulation. The condemned Jews were singing. Their voices increased in volume and the screaming was stilled. They all rose to their feet and turned to stare fixedly at the door. Rolf saw nothing of their nakedness and their despair.

'*Hauptsturmführer*, what's that noise?' said the corporal, eyes wide open.

Rolf knew exactly what it was. It was the '*Hatikvah*', the Jewish anthem of hope. He whirled round and his eyes blazed. Pushing his peaked cap firmly onto his head, he took a deep breath and gave the order.

'Release the crystals. Quickly! .... Do it now!'

The corporal stood stiffly to attention. 'But *Hauptsturmführer*, the temperature inside the chamber is not yet high enough. The crystals will not make gas.'

'Obey my orders, immediately!' Rolf snarled.

'*Jawohl*.' The salute was brisk and the corporal stared fixedly ahead. A guard ran out of the room. With the '*Hatikvah*' ringing in his ears, Rolf waited.

The guard shouted to the SS medicinal disinfectors on the roof at ground level outside and they began their deadly task. Four men broke open the small, round drums, each one clearly labelled '*Zyklon B*'. The men wore breathing masks to avoid inhaling the dangerous fumes. Dragging off the steel shrouds that covered the tops of the four induction columns, they tipped in the contents of the drums. The mauve crystals fell softly down the columns into the disinfection room below. In the body heat of the room, the '*Zyklon B*' vaporised into cyanide gas and began its awful work. The men swiftly replaced the shrouds, removed their masks and left.

Rolf always watched the effects of the gas take place. As one of the camp doctors, it was his job to do so. The ringing sounds of the singing still penetrated the door and he swiftly fastened his eyes to the peep-hole. For a few minutes nothing happened and then people's faces swung towards the columns. The singing stopped. It took another long five minutes. The effects of the gas caused people to frantically scramble away from the invisible gas. Very quickly, a deadly, helpless terror gripped the victims inside the chamber. They ran hither and thither and Rolf gave an involuntary jerk as faces passed before his peep-hole. A single eye stared back at him and, through the door, they faced each other. One, a person about to die a horrible, painful, lingering death and the other eye, the cause of that death.

As he stepped away from the door, it was all over very quickly. The one period in the whole process that Rolf disliked was the opening of the gas chamber door. He checked the time on his gold wristwatch, waited for an expectant five minutes and nodded to the waiting guard. The ventilation system switched into top gear and the deadly residual fumes were noisily sucked from the gas chamber. The door was unlatched, unscrewed and swung open. There was no need to hold the door, because the pressure of dead bodies against it, caused it to swing open by itself. Rolf took five steps backwards and coolly watched. The dead slithered out like wet fish from a net.

Already the *Sonderkommando* were dragging the bodies across the ante-room ready for disposal. He watched them going about their job. Any remaining jewellery was removed and thrown into specially numbered boxes. Hair of all colours was quickly shorn from the dead. It fell softly to the floor, was scooped up and stuffed into sacks. Apart from the sound of the hair-clippers, nobody spoke. Three men grabbed a corpse between them and threw it onto the small elevator. A tug at a rope and the electric motor sent it up to the ground floor.

Rolf quickly glanced around to check that all was in order and walked out of the room into the fresh air. Above him, the chimneys of the crematorium began to roar, sending up enormous tongues of yellow flame and clouds of dense, black, greasy smoke.

FOURTEEN

They left the hospital and Richard sat in the taxi, his mind a complete blank. Upon arriving home, they sat in the living-room, each one lost in their thoughts.

Sabina spoke first. She rose to her feet and everybody watched her. She began speaking slowly, almost in a whisper. 'I can't believe what's happened and I want to talk. I just have to get things out of my system.' She took a deep breath, her face creased with concern. 'I really don't think I could face organising a funeral. As you all know, I'm German and my parents died during a bombing raid on Berlin. There was no funeral because they were never found. Perhaps, ... Jane, and, if you wouldn't mind, please, could you and Richard sort out the arrangements for me?' She raised her hands, helplessly.

Jane gently placed her arms around her. 'Of course we will and you mustn't worry. Richard and I will look after everything.'

'Grandma,' said David, after a few moments, 'May I ask how you met Grandpa.'

Sabina sat back in the deep winged chair and, in a voice edged with sadness, began. 'I was an orphan at eighteen and I'd leant how to survive. I saw Simon for the first time on a spring day in May, 1945. During the war, I'd been a very good secretary for a firm of lawyers in Berlin and my English was quite good. In those final days before surrender, life was as awful as it could be. There was virtually no food and the only water came out of filthy rivers. I can remember it tasting pretty foul but there was nothing else. In May, the Russians conquered the city, or, at least, what was left of it. We were terrified of what the Russians would do to us. I suppose I can't blame them, we did much the same to them. Anyway I hid in the sewers with hundreds of other people. The Russians knew we were there and they sent down teams of men with flame-throwers and dogs. I was lucky, I escaped; many didn't.' She lifted her head and took a sip of brandy from the glass that Richard placed in her hand. She nodded and ran her fingers down the creases on her pleated skirt. 'I stayed in those sewers for over a month. I was totally alone and I stank and I felt dreadful. At times, I would've sold my soul, and anything else I could sell, just for a single crumb of bread. I remember coming out from the darkness towards the end of May. There was a smell that I'll never forget. About a hundred metres from where I stood, there was a smouldering heap of what I thought were old rags. The rags were human beings. I ran away and hid in a building. I thought I was going to die.' She stared about the room and looked at the faces of her family. Sabina wondered whether she was saying the right things at such a difficult time but she knew she had to open her heart.

She sighed. 'I wandered about for days with no food and almost no water. For some time, I hid in a ruined church. Eventually, I walked out of the place. It was then that I saw my first British soldier. I looked at him and he looked at me. We stared at each other for ages and then he smiled. What I looked like, I can't imagine. I hadn't washed or changed my clothes for six weeks. I was laughing and I must have looked like a mad woman. He held out his hand and I took it and then he offered me a cigarette.' Sabina's voice dropped to a whisper. 'One whole cigarette. Can you imagine it? I'd known people who'd killed or prostituted themselves for a cigarette-end, never mind a whole cigarette. And do you know what I did? .... I said, in my best English, "No thank you." Then another man appeared. I could tell he was an officer because the soldier saluted him.' She turned to look at her grandchildren. 'The officer,' she said to David and Rebecca, 'was your grandfather.' Sabina stopped talking and began to cry. David rushed to comfort her and she kissed him on the cheek.

'Sabina,' interrupted Jane, gently, 'would you like to stay the night?'

Another deep sigh. 'Yes, please. I might as well. There's nobody to go back to.'

The day had nearly passed and dusk was falling. They talked and subjects came and went. Suddenly Sabina's head dropped and her eyes filled up.

'What's the matter?' Richard said, anxiously.

'It's just hit me..... My darling Simon died today. Oh my God, what am I going to do?'

She pushed herself up from the table. Kissing each of them on the forehead, she turned to Richard. 'I'm so tired, I really just want to go to bed.' Jane helped her to the door. 'After the funeral, Richard,' Sabina said slowly, 'you must help me to sort out your father's papers. There are boxes of them and he always said that you must have them if anything ever happened to him.'

'Good night, Sabina,' said Richard, quietly. 'Don't worry about the papers. It'll give me great pleasure to sort them out.'

FIFTEEN

As he left the underground rooms of Crematorium II, Rolf Müller gazed around, noted the steps were clear of rubbish and nodded at the efficiency of his men. Pulling his gloves on tighter, he approached the ground floor entrance of the crematorium itself and pushed open the door. The blast of heat hit him full in the face and he winced.

'*Herr Hauptsturmführer*, all is going well,' said the duty corporal, with a beaming smile.

The dead, naked body of a young Jewish girl was laid out on a marble slab ready for Rolf's inspection. She was in her late teens with long, black hair and a beautiful face. Apart from a slight blueing of the skin on her feet, her slim body was unmarked by the gassing process and it seemed as if she was asleep. Her eyes remained wide open, giving her face an expression of surprise, although blood oozed from her nose. Rolf stared at her for a moment and then carefully removed his black glove. Pressing his two fingers against her soft neck, he felt for the jugular vein. For a moment his eyes caught hers and quickly he looked away. Wiping his fingers on his sleeve, he pulled the glove back on his hand. 'She's dead,' he said, with a bored expression. Another part of his job was complete. By declaring this girl to be dead, he had declared all the people in the gassing to be dead.

Rolf watched the carefully organised processing of the 1,400 human beings that had been the Dutch transport. The "pieces", as the dead were known in Auschwitz, arrived quickly on the elevator from the ante-room below. They were dragged off the steel transport trays by the *Sonderkommando* and thrown onto small railed trolleys. Another inmate forced open the mouths and, with pliers, quickly removed any metal or gold fillings and threw them into labelled boxes. Overall was the deathly roar of the coke fuelled incinerators.

Fifteen furnace retorts in banks of three dominated Crematorium II. Quite crude in their construction, roughly laid bricks and coarsely made cast iron-frames. Although they were carefully polished and well maintained. Located directly below each retort were three other doors where the ashes were shovelled out. All were connected to central flues leading to a single chimney above the building. The suppliers, J.A.Topf and Sons of Erfurt, had done a good job for a cheap price. The retorts they had developed and built could process 2,500 corpses a day. With this particular transport, the job would be finished in four hours.

Rolf rubbed a gloved finger across his forehead. It was always hot in the crematorium and he wanted to leave because there was other work to do. Walking outside, he paused for a moment to cool down. Still the stench of burning flesh and singeing hair hit his senses.

He strolled back along the ramp and whistled to himself as he approached the low building that was the entrance to Birkenau. A single floored, brick structure spread out on each side of the two storied tower. Under the tower was the tall, rounded arch that permitted the trains to enter. The windows on the first floor looked blankly down on the single railway line that stretched and split into three tracks on the Ramp. The arch was blackened by the smoke of the hundreds of locomotives that had passed beneath it over the last two years. Every stride Rolf took was watched by the guards in the wooden watch-towers lining the electrified barbed-wire perimeter fence. With a nod, he passed through the railway arch and turned left onto the road.

Taking care not to trip over the sunken railway lines, he stopped for a moment as a black Mercedes pulled up at his side. Bending over, he peered through the side window to look at the occupant. The man inside beckoned him closer. Rolf stiffened to attention and threw up a *Führer* salute. The door opened.

'Would you like a lift, *Hauptsturmführer*? I'm on my way to the Mess.'

'Yes please, *Sturmbannführer* Bär,' Rolf replied. He stepped into the car and sat on the deep leather seat. It was not everyday that he was given a lift by the Camp Commandant.

SS-Sturmbannführer Richard Bär had recently taken over command of the camp from Rudolf Höss. Bär was a career officer, who had seen earlier service at the first concentration camp at Dachau in 1933. Not one for being too friendly, it surprised Rolf when he began to talk to him in earnest tones.

'I'm glad we've met, Müller. I've already told *Doktor* Wirths that I must meet the medical section as soon as possible.'

'Is there a problem, *Herr Kommandant*?'

Bär turned and looked at Rolf. The man had a shinily smooth face and slicked down brown hair. Bloodshot eyes peered out from the under the peak of his cap. There was an unusual edge to his voice. 'There could be. .... This morning, I heard that the Russians have taken most of Rumania and are within two days of Budapest. It seems the swines'll outflank us to the south. This means, my dear Müller, that here, in Poland, we are in the middle of a pincer movement that may encircle us.'

Rolf was surprised at such openness. 'Yes, *Sturmbannführer*,' he said respectfully. 'I understand what you're saying. But surely our army is powerful enough to push back the Russians? The *Führer* said only last week that we would drive them back all the way to the Urals. It was just a matter of time .... .' He stopped as the car drew to a halt and the *Kommandant* touched his arm.

'From where we are now,' said Bär, biting his bottom lip, 'the Russians are the other side of Krakow, only a hundred kilometres away. .... Think about it, Müller.'

Lunch-time in the Mess was a time of hurried conversations and quick meals. Carefully, Rolf unfastened his belt and holster, hung it on a hook with his cap and sat down in his usual spot near the window. He nodded at one or two friends and the steward took his order. The triple *schnapps* arrived and he downed it one gulp.

'Hello, Rolf,' said a friendly voice. 'How are things? .... Mind if I join you?' Rolf placed his glass on the table and looked up. *Obersturmführer* Hossler and Rolf had been together through the SS training centre at Bad Tolz. They had remained firm friends.

'I see you had a lift from our *Kommandant*,' said Willi with a grin, sitting down opposite Rolf. 'Going up in the world aren't you?'

Rolf folded his arms. The tone of his voice expressed his worries. 'Willi, the *Kommandant* told me the Russians are only a hundred kilometres from here. Is that true?'

Willi shrugged his shoulders. 'There are rumours. Although, I've heard Model's Army Group Centre is in full control.'

'I don't like it. I've never heard Bär talk like that before.'

The steward arrived with their lunches. Two *bratwurst* lay in their pools of fat. Rolf cut them neatly into slices, stirred the potatoes and mashed it all together. He filled his fork and pushed the heavy mess into his mouth.

Willi played with his pork pie. Leaning forward, he whispered, 'I'll tell you one thing though, my friend. There's a strong rumour that Berlin are going to move five thousand women out of the camp.'

Rolf stopped eating. His face split into a grin and then he laughed. 'Willi, Willi, ..., where do you get such ideas from. Nobody leaves this camp through the gates. They only leave from the bakery over there.' He waved his fork at the distant column of thick black smoke pouring from the chimney of Crematorium II.

'Rolf, I'm only telling you what I've heard.'

They ate in silence whilst the mess chattered and buzzed around them.

'*Doktor,*' said a familiar voice, 'I'm sorry to interrupt your meal. Perhaps you could spare me a moment?' Rolf looked up from his plate. He rose from his seat, as did Willi.

'No, no, gentlemen. Please sit down,' With a slight smile on his face, Josef Mengele stood at their side '*Doktor* Müller,' he said, 'I just wanted to thank you for the samples you sent to me this morning.' The fish-like eyes glittered. 'They're beautiful.'

Rolf was used to Mengele's phraseology. 'I only spotted them at the last minute. I thought you'd be pleased.'

With an airy wave of his hand, Mengele went on. 'Those twins, ... ah, magnificent.' Without another word, he left their side as quickly as he had arrived.

Willi pushed his chair back. 'Sorry, Rolf. .... I'll have to go now. Another transport arrives in two hours. I'll see you later.'

Rolf sat quite still, oblivious to the activity around him. For the first time since he had joined the SS, a pang of worry flickered across his soul. All the time, the conversations with Bär and Willi re-echoed through his brain.

Fortunately, there was a Red Cross truck parked near the Mess and Rolf was soon on his way back to Birkenau. The truck pulled up outside the medical block. Stepping out, Rolf walked briskly into the building that was almost his second home. He strode through the entrance hall towards an open door. Twenty inmates lined the wooden walls of the corridor and they stared ahead, not daring to even glance at the tall *Herr Doktor*. Each wore a dirty, striped shirt, standard wooden clogs and clutched ragged blankets around their skin and bone bodies; men, women and children.

To be called "prisoner" was, in itself, a privilege. They were selected on the Ramp and made to work in every medical section of the three Auschwitz camps, and automatically made *Sonderkommando*. A privileged group who rarely survived for very long. Prisoner Doctor Benjamin Blum worked in the medical block of Birkenau and every day cursed to God that he was still alive. For a year and a half, he had swallowed the daily bile of the breaking of his Hippocratic Oath. On this particular day, he had been detailed to assist with killing by phenol injection.

Humming to himself, Rolf closed the door quietly behind him. He glanced at the equipment carefully laid out on a wooden table. Two small thermos flasks contained the concentrated phenol. Two hypodermic syringes lay in a white enamel tray. They were unusually large and the long needles protruded over the lip of the tray. In front of the table stood a strong wooden stool.

The room was small and neat and the floor spotlessly clean. The light from three windows was carefully shaded out by thick coatings of whitewash. A single electric bulb cast a brownish light over the room. There was a smell of carbolic soap. A black rubber apron hung on a peg behind the door.

'Is everything ready?' said Rolf, breaking the silence.

'Yes, *Herr Hauptsturmführer*,' replied Benjamin, keeping his downcast eyes focused on a single knot on the wooden floor.

Flexing his shoulders, Rolf yawned. The schnapps usually made him sleepy. 'Fill the syringe,' he said, loudly.

Benjamin stepped to the table, unscrewed the lid on the flask and poured out some if its contents into a metal bowl. The innocuous yellowish-pink liquid was ready and its pungent smell filled the room. Lifting the syringe from the tray, he lowered the needle into the fluid. Carefully, withdrawing ten cc's, he held the syringe up to the light to check the measure.

'Call the first patient,' said Rolf, as casually as if he was in a village surgery.

Benjamin smiled grimly to himself. To be called a patient in this hell was indeed a misnomer. With a heart that hammered away threatening to burst out of his chest, he gave a quick nod and shouted, 'FIRST ONE.'

Two inmates, led in an old woman. She had snowy white hair and, through her sunken eyes, shone a light of defiance. Not a word was spoken as they sat her on the stool. Her eyes never left Benjamin's face, for she knew what was going to happen. The men went through their well-practised routine. One of them pulled the old woman's right arm cross her face. Very quickly, the other man lifted her arm up into a horizontal position. With his hand, he snatched at her blouse and pulled it open. Her breasts, like old rags, lay empty with starvation. Rolf leaned against the wall and yawned again. Still her eyes watched Benjamin, who stood immobile with the syringe hidden behind his back. Praying to his God, he revealed the syringe, stepped forward and with his free hand, felt for the fifth rib and immediately plunged the long needle into the cardiac cavity.

'May your God forgive you,' were the old woman's final words. Within ten seconds, she rolled off the stool, giving Benjamin just enough time to withdraw the syringe. Her life slipped away before him and he watched her die. The atmosphere in the room was filled with a stultifying horror. The inmates quickly carried the dead woman through the door and returned later with a young man. He began to shout and squirm. They clubbed him senseless and held him in the correct position on the stool. Chest out and a hand held across the mouth and eyes. Benjamin had just enough time to fill the syringe and inject in another ten cc's of phenol.

It was worse when the children came into the killing room. They never knew what was going to happen and they were always silent, watching his actions with big soulful eyes. The final exhalation of their breath was something that Benjamin could hardly bare and yet he could not cry. Crying was a luxury in Auschwitz, crying meant nothing; crying was only for people who had a future.

As he left the building, Rolf saw, with some satisfaction, that the corridor was clear. The twenty inmates had suspected typhus and hepatitis and their bodies would be checked before being taken to the crematorium. He remembered only too well the stories about the Auschwitz typhus epidemics of '41 and '42.

As he walked away from the medical block, it began to rain. Heavy black clouds rolled across the sky and the lights on the perimeter fence glowed dully over the mud and the huts. He just reached the next group of buildings before the clouds opened up. And the rain drove hard against the roof above his head.

Rolf stood in the entrance to 'Canada II' so called because the treasures that it contained the inmates likened to the riches of Canada. Canada II consisted of thirty barracks which served as the main sorting and storage areas for plundered loot and the personal effects from the victims. Rolf entered a long room and his eyes swept the scene before him. A space steamy with body heat. Rows of women sat at long benches. Powerful lights shining down from the low, wooden roof. There was a heavy smell of old sweat and stale clothes. Two rows of tables had clothing laid out in neat heaps. Pairs of hands removed sewn on Jewish stars. Other felt the seams of trousers and the padding of coats. The search for hidden money and gems never stopped as shifts of inmates worked day and night. This job was regarded as a privilege because it gave them better chances to obtain goods illegally for food. For that reason alone, the guards were extra vigilant. To take something meant a short trip to the gas chamber or instant death on the floor of the sorting room.

Rolf liked the hustle and bustle of the place and he was always on the look out for precious things to touch and hold. Walking down the space between the sorting rows, he arrived at the secure holding area.

'Can't keep away, can you, my friend?' whispered a voice.

Rolf jumped and turned. *SS-Hauptsturmführer* Emanuel Glumbik stood at ease, leaning against a heavy steel box. A thin man, his green uniform hanging on his cadaverous body.

'Good afternoon.' Rolf smiled. 'How are things today?'

Glumbik nodded. 'You keep sending them through the bakery and I keep sorting out their shit.' He spoke in the broad vowels of Berlin. Glumbik gave an enormous wink and motioned Rolf to follow him behind the stack of boxes. There was not as much light here, just enough to see by. Glumbik removed his peaked cap, felt in the lining and the smile on his thin face widened into a grin. He held up in front of Rolf's staring eyes, a necklace of glittering diamonds. They sparkled and sent shafts of radiance across Rolf's uniform. Glumbik's eyes narrowed. 'Aren't they beautiful?'

Rolf was hypnotised by diamonds. The gems had always fascinated him and touching them gave him an almost sexual pleasure. 'Where did you find it, Glumbik?'

'You'll never guess, my friend. Not in these stinking clothes and not up a Jewish cunt. I found the necklace hidden in the cracks of the timbers in one of the cattle wagons and what's more, it's from the transport you selected this morning. One of the *Rampe Sonderkommando* brought it to me. Fortunately, he died and I disposed of him not an hour ago.' He winked again and ran the diamonds through his fingers. 'Look at the settings, silver and platinum. They must be worth a fortune.' He glanced slyly at Rolf's face and saw the flash of envy. 'Here, you hold it.'

Removing his gloves, Rolf wiped his hands down his trousers, licked his lips and took the necklace into both hands. He felt its icy coolness and the weight of the gems. He touched each stone with his finger almost in the same way he touched necks.

'Wonderful, they're wonderful,' he breathed. For a moment, he hesitated. 'Has the necklace been fumigated?'

'Yep, ... I did it myself. You could eat those diamonds.'

Rolf reverently raised the necklace to his lips and kissed the biggest stone. The stink of the sorting barracks was gone as the glitter of gems flashed before his half-closed eyes.

Glumbik spoke quietly in a greedy monotone. 'Would you like to keep the necklace, my friend? It's yours. That is, ... if you want it?'

Through Rolf's brain rushed delicious thoughts of owning such a treasure. In the past, he had acquired small articles of gold. He had been brought up in a strict Catholic family and taught never to steal. He was tempted and eyed Glumbik with concern.

'Look here, Rolf,' muttered Glumbik in his oily voice. 'Let's forget about our beloved Himmler's orders to abide by the "principle of the holiness of property". We're going to lose the war and, after it's finished, I want to live in comfort and so do you.'

It was the first time Rolf had heard such treason from an *SS* officer and it only took him a moment for him to understand that Glumbik was correct in his assumptions.

'Give me some more of your morphine and we'll call it straight,' whispered Glumbik. Over the last six months, Rolf had supplied him with an addict's needs. The gems became heavier by the second. This time, it was different and he did not hesitate. If he gave him the morphine, then there was no way Glumbik was going to tell anybody.

'Right,' said Rolf, slipping the necklace into his pocket. 'See me outside the Mess before dinner.'

Glumbik's eyes shone with the anticipation of a night's pleasure. 'That, my friend, will be perfect,' he said. 'Tonight I've got a date with somebody very special in the entertainment block.'

Rolf did not want to hear. His thoughts were already with his wife back in Berlin. On his next leave, the necklace would grace her beautiful neck. Glumbik darted back into the bustle of the sorting benches. Rolf patted his prize into the folds of his trouser pocket and strode back to the entrance.

His work was not yet finished and he returned to the medical experiments block. On his way, he saw nothing of the misery and horror surrounding him. Wretched inmates scrambled out of his path or froze into servile mobility. Somebody opened the door for him and he entered, still thinking about the necklace. Turning sharp right into the first laboratory, he removed his cap, hung it on a peg and donned a white coat.

Another room with walls of wood and spotlessly clean; always spotlessly clean. In a flick of a glance, Rolf recognised Prisoner Doctor Blum. Three other inmates waited quietly in the corner. Again whitewashed windows, although they were wide open. Two powerful studio spotlights focused onto a small wooden platform. Overall was the familiar pungent smell of carbolic disinfectant.

'Good afternoon, *Doctor* Müller.' Josef Mengele stood quietly in the long shadows cast by the spotlights. His voice was, as usual, obsequiously polite. 'Thank you for coming to help me and thank you again for these magnificent specimens.' He was relaxed and smiling. All eyes converged on the platform.

The identical twins from the morning selection sat primly naked on low stools, staring eyes with legs closed and toes pressing onto the floor. There was an air of terrible fear about their demeanour and they held each other's hands tightly. The room was chillingly cold and occasionally they shivered making tiny goose pimples rise on their small, white bodies.

Mengele stepped forward, hands lightly clasped in front of his stomach. The voice purred. 'Girls born within three minutes of each other. Ruth on the left is the older and Eliza is the younger.' He chuckled. 'Why, they must have been born at the same time. ..... Some mother, .. eh? .... Blum has already photographed them and now we must measure them. And remember, Rolf,' he added quietly, 'always with the greatest precision we can possibly achieve.' Producing two notebooks and rulers from his pocket and walked to Ruth's side. 'Eyes first and then the head,' he said, firmly.

Rolf smiled, he had no idea why Mengele had such an interest in eyes. It was time to satisfy his curiosity.

'*Doktor* Mengele,' the tone of his voice made his colleague stop and turn. 'For many months, I've wondered why you have such an interest in eyes?'

Mengele smiled. With a finger, he delicately opened Ruth's left eye. He explained, almost revelling in the professional intimacy of the question. 'Whilst I was at the University of Frankfurt, I specialised in anthropology and genetics.' He saw Rolf's interest. 'Genetics is a relatively new area of medical research. I studied under the famous Otmar Von Veschur who was in charge of the University Institute of Hereditary Biology and Racial Hygiene. It was from him I learnt that precise measurement is the essence of racial studies.' He paused for a moment to jot something on his notepad. 'Perfect,' he muttered quietly and looked up. 'I had three dissertations published. They are well respected and one of them was quoted in the medical journals only last month.' He stroked the girl's soft hair. 'Don't worry, little Ruth, everything is all right. In a short time you can go with your sister and have a good meal and a rest.'

Frowning, she looked at Mengele, 'Where's my Mummy?' Her faint voice cut through the room.

Mengele threw a broad wink at Rolf and smiled at her. 'Don't worry, little one. Your Mummy's gone to work. You'll see her in a couple of days.'

Apart from the twins, everybody in the room knew that mummy was already gassed, cremated and gone.

'Hazel eyes are the best,' said Mengele, holding a magnifying glass. 'They show the deepest hues and you can actually see the refractive area of the cornea much easier than with other colours.' Rolf did not give a damn what colour the eyes were but he was still fascinated by the man and his work. Mengele was totally absorbed.

'Keep still, Eliza,' he said softly. 'I just want one of your eyelashes.' She jumped, as he pulled one free with his tweezers. 'Now, that didn't hurt, did it?' He pulled something out of his pocket. 'Here's a piece of chocolate for you and your sister.' The label on the chocolate bar surprised Rolf. It was written in English and he wondered where Mengele had obtained such a thing. Josef Mengele rubbed his hands. 'I love children, especially twins.'

Rolf helped him for over an hour. He filled eight pages of the notebook with measurements. Eliza began to cry and Mengele frowned at the disturbance. 'We can't possibly continue our work with all that wailing.' With a peremptory wave of his hand, he stopped the measuring. In an instant, his mood changed from that of a serious physician, to a friendly colleague and he laughed. 'Rolf, my dear friend. You're obviously interested in my research. Come with me.' The two men left the room.

Benjamin Blum gathered up the girls' clothes and began to tenderly dress them. He held their bodies close to his. Benjamin stared into the distance, his heart beating like a sledgehammer. They would survive for another day. Many that cried, did not.

Mengele took a brass key from his pocket, undid the lock on another door and swung it open. There was an overpowering smell of phenol preservative. He rubbed his hands dryly together and a new look of concentration came over his smoothly-shaven face. 'This,' he said, carefully closing the door behind him, 'is my personal collection.' He waved his hand towards a large glass case on the wall and turned to watch Rolf's reaction.

Eyes, more eyes. In pairs and singles. Each of a different hue from brown to purple to blue. All carefully mounted on a white board like pinned and labelled butterflies. Even Rolf was shocked, they seemed to follow his gaze as he looked from one specimen to another.

Mengele pointed to two sets. 'Look, four eyes from a pair of twins. Precisely the same.' His voice rose with excitement. 'How is it possible for nature to reproduce such perfection?' His own brown eyes stared at Rolf. He continued explaining. 'The simple answer to my question can be found in the new world of genetics. From my work here at Auschwitz, *Reichsführer* Himmler chose me to take part in the research into the creation of an Aryan master race. All my work, and most of yours, must lead to this final goal. Scientists have always been able to study twins after they have been born together. But only in the *Third Reich* can Science examine twins who have died together. We can learn much from our work here.' Rolf had never seen the man so physically excited. 'The Jewish scum is being eradicated. *Obersturmbannführer* Eichmann is making sure of that fact.' He paused for breath. 'The Jews are inferior and our race is superior to theirs and that gives us the right to eradicate them as if they were a disease.' Suddenly Mengele stopped talking.

Rolf took a deep breath. 'Very interesting, *Doktor*. It's all very interesting.'

Smiling, Mengele folded his arms. 'I'm just a small part of the *Führer's* plan for the future of the *Reich*.'

Rolf was unsure what to do next and he again stared at the glass case. Mengele watched him. 'In this room I keep some of my records,' he said, pointing to heavy steel chests lining one wall. 'Everything is in date order and each racial stereotype is carefully described. Ah yes, ... these records are of inestimable value for all of us.' A far away look cast itself across Mengele's face and, with a forefinger, he tapped one of the chests and his eyes stared penetratingly across the room. 'I'm talking to you like this, Rolf, because I trust you. You and I can give Germany its future. You're an excellent officer. Loyal, and I've never heard you once complain about your duties here at Auschwitz. The other rabble, you know, ... steal.' Rolf felt the necklace and the gold ring against his thigh, 'and do things to Jewish women that are totally forbidden.' For the first time in the two years that Rolf had known Josef Mengele, he saw sweat sheening his brow.

Rolf suddenly wanted to get away from this man. Glancing at his wrist-watch, he tried to excuse himself.

'*Doktor* Müller,' Mengele's voice took on a new edge of hardness, 'before you go, remember one thing. When we have to leave Auschwitz, remind yourself that we have always obeyed our orders and we were loyal to the *Führer.*'

'Of course,' replied Rolf, with his most charming smile and a half salute. Mengele gave Rolf the shivers and he was never quite sure how to behave in his company. The prisoners, Jew and Gentile alike, hated him. But again, for the third time in a day, the possible end for Auschwitz was mentioned.

One more place to call at and Rolf could prepare for dinner. SS Headquarters was located just outside the perimeter fence and not far from the main entrance to Birkenau. As he entered, a corporal rose from his seat at the reception desk..

'*Herr Haupsturmführer*, the *Kommandant* wishes to see you.' Rolf nodded and walked through to the small waiting room near the *Kommandant's* office.

Sturmbannführer Richard Bär remained seated. Rolf stood stiffly to attention. 'My dear Müller,' Bär said softly. 'These are busy days.' He waved towards a chair. Rolf removed his peaked cap and sat down. Swiftly, he glanced around the office. The staring eyes of an Adolf Hitler portrait watched him. It could have been the office of any successful business man, which, in reality, it was. The SS ran Auschwitz-Birkenau strictly as a business.

Bär's bloodshot eyes flickered across Rolf's uniform and then to his face. 'You're looking tired, Rolf.' The informality surprised him. '*Doktor* Wirth tells me you've been working very hard.' He nodded to accentuate his words. 'You've done a good job on the Dutch transports and I want to reward that work.' Rolf's heart leapt, he sensed promotion or even a medal.

The voice was silky smooth. 'Berlin has ordered me to select an officer of superior breeding to have the honour of taking part in the *Lebensborn* Project. .... As an *SS* doctor, you must know about the Project?' Rolf nodded, his brain searching for the information. Bär continued. '*Lebensborn* was originated by the *Reichsführer* himself. It is a project for the purpose of transforming the German nation into a super race through positive eugenics and selective breeding. We in the *SS* have always been regarded as racially superior and I'm sure it comes as no surprise to you that you've been selected?'

Rolf was trying to take it all in. '.... A great honour, thank you, *Sturmbannführer*.'

'The honour is yours,' replied Bär, scratching the tip of his nose. 'You know, the girls in the Project are superb. I hear that they're the pick of the bunch. Blonde-haired, blue-eyed maidens all beyond reproach. You're a lucky man. I know you're married but the *Reich* tells us that children born out of wedlock through *Lebensborn* are perfectly acceptable. It is the duty of the German woman to bear children and it is your duty as an *SS* officer to father such children. I have your orders here.' He waved the fat grey envelope. 'In four days time, you'll leave Auschwitz for Berlin and report directly to the *Lebensborn* offices on *Voss Strasse*.' Bär smiled. 'You'll represent the whole of the Auschwitz *SS* and we're proud of you.' His right hand pivoted upwards into the *Führer* salute. '*HEIL* HITLER!' Rolf jumped from his seat.

'*HEIL* HITLER!' he shouted back.

Rolf walked slowly back to his quarters. A distance of no more that five hundred metres but it gave him time to think. He had not seen his wife for two months. He wondered whether or not to inform her and then shook his head. Bär's comments about blonde hair and blue eyes made his heart thrill and suddenly he yearned for a woman. The wind changed and he glanced back towards the camp. The dark sky of dusk mingled with the black clouds and the roaring flames from the chimney of Crematorium II and, for a moment, his thoughts about beautiful women faded.

Willi Hossler walked past the entrance to the officers' accommodation. 'Hello, Rolf.' He frowned. 'You're looking a bit pale. Are you feeling all right?'

'No, I'm not. I think I've got a temperature,' replied Rolf, brushing past his friend and walking quickly down the corridor. In his room, he undressed and threw everything into a corner. Grabbing his white bath robe, he strode out of the room to the showers. The hot water coursed down his body and he realised that it was exactly twelve hours since he had stood in the same shower and much had happened. The water did not cool him down.

SIXTEEN

The funeral was a quiet affair, private and with only the family present. Afterwards they had a light meal in a local hotel. It was late afternoon and through the tall windows of the restaurant the pale sun was rapidly setting. There was a silence as the normally busy hotel quietened before the evening rush for dinner.

'Grandma,' asked David, curiously. 'Why did Grandpa stop being Jewish?'

'Ah, ah,' replied Sabina. 'David, you never stop being Jewish. It's a bit like being born with black skin. It was just one day when Simon said he no longer considered himself to be behaving like a Jew and therefore he was not a Jew.' Sabina took a deep breath and leant across the table. 'In Berlin, when I first met him, I knew I would marry him. It was one of those strange things. I've never believed in love at first sight. I just, ... well, I knew.'

'Oh that's great,' said Rebecca, 'You sound ever so romantic.'

Sabina smiled. 'It was romantic. At that time, I thought I was going to die, never mind meeting a handsome officer.'

'Did you know he was Jewish?' asked David.

'I guessed it, because of his name.' Folding her arms, she sat back in the chair. 'On the day that we met, he took me back to the British barracks. It was all very strange. The Allies were the only people with food or money.' She laughed in a brittle way. 'In those days, any Allied soldier could have gone with any woman he wanted, just by nodding his head. For another week, I lived in a hole somewhere. Eventually, when I became hungry, I went to his barracks but they wouldn't let me in. Then I saw Simon again. Or at least, he saw me. We started going out with each other. A difficult thing to do at that time.' Sabina stared into the distance and everybody listened. 'It was a time when my city lay in utter ruin. The *Kurfürstendamm*, Berlin's Regent Street, was battered into mere shells of buildings. And yet, you could still buy a newspaper and, in some parts, there were still policemen on duty. There were shortages of everything. Everything depended on money. So many things happened.' She abruptly stopped talking and shook her head. There were tears in her eyes and, with a quick dab of her fingers, she brushed them away.

Sabina stared into the distance and then she abruptly stopped talking and shook her head. There were tears in her eyes and, with a quick dab of her fingers, she brushed them away.

'What is it, Sabina?' said Richard, gently.

She shook her head. 'I really can't talk any more and tonight I'd rather go back to my home. That is, if you and Jane don't mind?'

Jane reached over and kissed her gently on the cheek. 'Of course we don't mind. Perhaps you'd like Richard to stay with you?'

He drove the car through the darkness to his mother's house. It took a good hour and gave him time to think. After ten minutes, he glanced sideways and saw she was fast asleep. Slowly, he let the day pass before him.

At the house, he drew the car gently to a halt. Sabina awoke and looked up. 'Oh, it's good to be home,' she sighed. 'Now, I feel like a cup of tea. How about you?' He nodded and they walked into the house together. They went into Simon's study and, for the first time in his life, he sat in his father's leather chair.

'You look good in it,' she said, attempting a smile.

Sipping at his mug of tea, Richard glanced around. It was a room he had always liked. Panelled in warm oak, with a thick carpet of the same light brown colour. The desk was a Victorian roll-top, salvaged from Simon's first law practice in Ormskirk. It was incredibly neat and tidy, everything was in its place and carefully labelled. Richard smiled, because he was the most untidy person in the world. The paintings represented the best his father could buy. Pride of place was an original Chagall. Richard never asked where his father had obtained it.

Sabina interrupted his thoughts. 'It was always his room. I rarely came in here.'

'I remember it very well,' said Richard gripping the worn arms of the chair. 'He used to talk to me about all kinds of things.' He chuckled. 'Most of it, went in one ear and out of the other. But he always did the right thing for me.'

'You were very close to him and he loved you dearly.' A sad look crossed over her face and then it was gone.

'I loved my father too but I was never really close to him. There was ... ,' he paused in mid-sentence, 'something missing between us.'

Sabina frowned with understanding. 'He was a father of his generation. You always went to the best schools and Simon always said you would get into Oxford, and you did.'

Richard tossed his head back and laughed. 'My God, I felt as if I had to.

Well,' he added, stretching, 'that's all in the past. We now have to get on with our futures.' The chair creaked, as he swivelled to face his mother.

Before he could continue, she rose from her chair and crossed the study to the desk. Pushing open the roll-top, she stared at the cubby-holes and the piles of paper. Removing a stack of paper-clipped bills, she found what she was looking for and triumphantly produced a scrap of paper. Turning to the Chagall, she removed it from the wall, quickly blowing dust off the top edge of the frame. With her thumb and forefinger, she eased the revealed panel open. A small Chubb safe nestled in the plaster behind the panelling.

'I don't believe this,' said Richard, with wide eyes.

'Your father never told me what the combination was and I only found out when I opened his will this morning.'

'His will?'

'Yes, it was in the bottom drawer of his desk. He left specific instructions that I was to open the safe and give you its contents.' There was twist of impatience in her voice. '.... Now let me see,' she said, holding up the piece of paper to the light. The tumblers clicked into place and there was a clunk as she turned the stubby handle. Sabina stepped back and faced him. 'Richard, it's all yours.'

He stepped up to the safe and peered into its dark recess. There was a heavy manila file, two envelopes and a single sheet of paper. Carefully, he took everything out and laid them on the desk. He felt his mother's hand on his shoulder.

'I'll leave you to it,' she whispered. 'Just call if you want anything.' Closing the door quietly, she left the room

SEVENTEEN

Climbing into the back seat of the Mercedes staff car made Rolf realise he was taking a break from Auschwitz. With his case safely stowed in the boot, he began to relax for the first time in months. There were five transports and selections due in and he heard the first one arrive just as the car pulled away from the barracks.

It was only ten minutes to Auschwitz town station and, by the time he had thought about the journey, the driver was opening the door. As Rolf stepped out of the car, his nose caught the stench of the chimneys, even though Birkenau was four kilometres away. The driver carried his case through the station entrance and Rolf produced his rail pass and leave warrant to the clerk in the booking office. The booking hall was as nondescript as the clerk behind the window. The man nodded sourly, loudly hammered the pass with two rubber stamps and handed over the ticket. The train waited on platform two. The driver found the correct compartment, threw the suitcase onto the rack, saluted his officer and left the train. Rolf slumped into the worn brocade of the seat and removed his hat.

Glancing around the carriage made him realise just how much the standards on the *Reichsbahn* had fallen, even in the last six months. Old cigarette burns on the seats, greasy head rests and the lingering smell of unwashed humanity: and this compartment was first class.

'Good morning, *Hauptsturmführer*. I have a reservation for this compartment. Do you mind if I join you?' He was in his sixties, fat as a pig and with a pale, gleaming bald head. His face had beads of perspiration dripping onto a shiny blue suit. Rolf took an instant dislike to him. A year ago an SS officer would have had such a compartment to himself.

'Now this is what I call a really nice compartment,' the man said, wiping a grubby handkerchief across the sweat on his forehead. The guttural Hamburg accent grated on Rolf's nerves. 'My last train was just filthy and full of foreign workers.' He wriggled down into his seat and slipped his collar loose. Rolf felt the eyes flickering over him and he tried to look through the window. 'It's not very often I get the pleasure of travelling with an SS officer.' Rubbing his hands sweatily together, he extended his right hand. 'My name is Karl Boese and I work for the Hamburg shipyards.'

Rolf stared hard at the man's eyes, forcing him to drop his hand back onto his lap. 'Ah, yes, *Hauptsturmführer*, I understand. You don't mix with working men like me.' A fat grin spread across his face. 'Quite right too. The SS are the elite of our fighting forces.' The locomotive let out a piercing whistle and the man jumped. As the train moved slowly away, Rolf saw another train pass along the parallel platform. He recognised the wagons and smiled. It was one transport he would not have to deal with.

'Another load of Jewish meat,' said the man, with a wolfish smile. 'All kosher, I believe.' Rolf ignored him.

The train gathered pace and the drab, flat land of Lower Silesia slipped past the windows. The monotonous clickety-clack of the rails lulled Rolf into a half-slumber. Jumbled pictures flashed through his mind. He saw his wife, the lovely Angela, lying naked on a bed. Every time he moved close to her, her eyes opened and she vanished. The train changed track and the sound altered. Just as they entered a tunnel, the whistle shrieked. Rolf was curious about his dreams. One particular thing always made him curious and that was why he never dreamt about his work at Auschwitz. With a blinding flash of light, the train roared out of the tunnel and Rolf sat up, eyes wide-open. Somebody was tapping on the door of the compartment.

'Ah, it's the refreshments, *Hauptsturmführer*,' said the man from Hamburg, wetly licking his lips. 'Just what the doctor ordered.' Rolf swivelled on his seat.

'Good morning, gentlemen,' said the steward. He held a small trolley with one hand and the door open with the other. Rolf reached into his pocket.

'No, no, *Hauptsturmführer*.' said the man opposite him. 'This one's on me.' He looked at Rolf questioningly.

'Coffee, please,' he begrudgingly replied.

'Coffee for the *Hauptsturmführer* and a double of your best schnapps.' He peered at the trolley. 'On second thoughts, leave the half-bottle and the two glasses. The *Hauptsturmführer* might like to share a glass with me later. Keep the change.' The steward passed the cup of coffee across to Rolf, who placed it on the small table under the window.

The coffee was ersatz, probably ground acorns. 'At least,' Rolf thought, 'we have real coffee at Auschwitz.'

'Travelling far, *Hauptsturmführer*?' The man emptied a full glass of schnapps down his throat in a single gulp and his eyes rolled with pleasure.

'Berlin,' replied Rolf, eyes fixed on the fields that rolled past. He was beginning to regret this journey.

'That's good. Me as well. It'll be nice to have some good company on a long journey. Do you know, *Hauptsturmführer*, I've never met an *SS* officer before. I mean, well, ... you know, eh, ... never actually talked to one.' He refilled his glass and watched for Rolf's reaction. 'I couldn't help seeing the address on your case and that you work in that place near Auschwitz. I've heard that's where the Jews work for I.G. Farben. Damned good, I say. Those swine's have robbed us blind for long enough. Make 'em work harder, I say.' He chortled to himself as Rolf stared stonily through the dirty glass. 'Mind you, I stayed for a night in Auschwitz and that smell. Jesus Christ, that smell! What the hell are those Jews making out there?' There was a silence. '*Hauptsturmführer*, did you hear me? What the hell are they making there?'

Rolf turned his head and said quietly, 'Materials for the war effort.'

The man edged forward in his seat and dropped his voice. His eyes glanced to the compartment door and then back to Rolf. 'Somebody in the hotel told me that we're gassing the Jews at Auschwitz and then burning them and that's what the awful smell is.' He sat back and raised his glass. 'I say, "cheers" to that. Let the bastards burn.'

Rolf made no comment and took a deep breath. The man fell asleep with the empty glass clutched in his fat fingers.

The train stopped at Wroclaw. Rolf put on his hat and edged past the half-asleep man. The air was fresh and clear and the autumn chill made him shiver. The station was full of troops. Some saluted, most ignored him. Again he realised times were changing. These men looked tired and their uniforms were muddy and dishevelled. From behind a pile of ammunition boxes appeared an officer. He wore the shoulder insignia of a captain in the *Wehrmacht*.

They exchanged quick smiles. 'Morning, I wonder if you could spare a cigarette? I'm clean out,' said the captain.

'Sorry, I don't smoke,' replied Rolf with a ready smile.

The man shrugged his shoulders. 'Going far?'

'Berlin, ... and you?'

'Fuck knows. Anywhere except where we've just come from.' He whistled silently through clenched teeth. The captain looked Rolf up and down and noticed the lack of medals. 'From where we're standing now,' he said, 'the Bolsheviks are only eighty kilometres away and Jesus, can they fight.' He sniffed loudly and spat a string of phlegm near Rolf's feet. 'If I was you, *Hauptsturmführer*, I'd stay in Berlin. ..... Although, that'll go within the next six months, believe me.'

There was a blast of sound to Rolf's left and another train arrived on another platform. He recognised the wagons. The captain wiped his nose with his sleeve. 'Look at that,' he waved across towards his train. 'The cream of the German Army moving by cattle wagon. My God, what next? I've travelled in them before and the fucking stink is awful. What kind of cattle travelled in there, I'll never know.' He threw up a casual salute. '*Auf Wiedersehen*, have one for me in the *Adlon* Bar.' He turned on his heel as his men began to shuffle towards the wagons.

During the rest of the journey through Germany, Rolf hardly slept. The train stopped frequently before it pulled into Berlin *Görlitzer* Station. His travelling companion snored away and Rolf left him. The station was not as he remembered it. Huge holes in the curving glass roof let in the pouring rain and the platforms were slippery with sodden rubbish. Surly people scuttled quickly about avoiding eye contact with anybody near them. Pulling his greatcoat round his shoulders, he looked for a porter and there was none to be seen. An official in uniform approached him and gave a sloppy *Führer* salute. Six months ago, Rolf would have had him arrested for insulting the *Reich*.

Outside the station, the view that greeted Rolf was even worse than inside and, for a full minute, he just stared. Around him lay piles of rubble and smashed vehicles. Broken statuary lay jumbled with uprooted trees. Most of the roads in front of him were blocked, others were being slowly cleared by old men with long-handled shovels. A man approached, dressed in the uniform of the Home Guard. His salute was crisp and he stood to attention.

'Good evening,' he said politely. 'Am I addressing *Hauptsturmführer* Müller? ' Rolf nodded. 'I'm your driver. Where do you wish to go to?'

Rolf saw the battered *Kübelwagen* car. 'Thank you, *Rottenführer*. ... 22 *Voss Strasse*.' The man collected his case and opened the car door. The engine started on the second pull of the starter and the car drew away from the kerb. The beautiful *Unter Den Linden* was unrecognisable and the car ground onwards. Suddenly, above the whine of the engine, sirens started wailing.

He heard the driver shout over his shoulder, 'Oh, Christ, another air raid!' And, slamming on the brakes, he pulled up sharply. '*Hauptsturmführer*, quickly now, down into the *U-Bahn*. ..... It's the only safe place.' And he was gone, like a rabbit down a hole.

The sirens continued their howling and soon, apart from some horses jerking restlessly at their carts, Rolf was alone. A stillness settled over Berlin and nothing moved. 'Damn it,' he said aloud. 'I'm not running from some bomber I can't even see.' Almost before the words were out of his mouth, a low drone sounded to the west of the city. Stepping out of the car, he watched and waited. The rain lashed down over him and he pulled his greatcoat collar higher.

He saw the flash before the sound and then it hit him. It was like nothing he had ever felt in his life. Waves of noise and earthquake shocks rippled past exactly where he was standing. The blast knocked him off his feet, throwing him like a rag doll against the side of the car. It seemed to go on forever and then it was over. Clouds of fine dust and soot mixed with rain water sluiced over his immaculate uniform. He lay numbed and utterly desolated. Screaming reached his ears and he tried to pull himself upright. The sound came from two horses. One had lost its legs and the other had blood pumping like a red fountain from its neck. He watched them die.

The corporal emerged from nowhere and began to pull rubble away from Rolf's side. 'Are you all right, *Hauptsturmführer*?'

Somehow he managed to stand, and tried unsuccessfully to brush the mud off his boots. He found his cap and jammed it back on his head. 'Thank you,' he replied. 'I'm all right.'

'It's always best to go down into the *U-Bahn* when those bastards come across.'

'Who was it this time?' said Rolf, looking anxiously into the leaden sky.

The corporal glanced at his wrist-watch. 'The British. They normally start at this time.' The wail of the sirens began again. Rolf moved quickly towards the dark entrance to the *U-Bahn*. The old man smiled. 'Don't worry, *Hauptsturmführer*, it's the "All Clear".'

The journey from the *Brandenburg* Gate to *Voss Strasse* normally took ten minutes but on this miserable evening it took twice as long. Eventually the car pulled up at number 22. It had no roof but there was still an *SS* guard at the bottom of the steps. When his eyes saw Rolf's uniform, he snapped up a salute. The soldier opened a door at street level and Rolf stepped down into half-light. Another larger door opened and bright lights made him blink.

'This way, *Hauptsturmführer*,' said a thin *SS* captain, sitting behind an ornate desk. The large room buzzed with activity, phones jangled and clerks hurried from one door to another. 'Your orders, please.' Rolf handed them across, conscious of his muddy uniform. 'I see you braved the bombs,' smiled the man. 'It's difficult to keep smart nowadays.' He scanned the orders, humming to himself. 'Ah, *Lebensborn*, eh? Lucky devil.' He stood and beckoned Rolf towards a door near his desk. 'Follow me, please.' He opened his drawer, removing a bulky file.

The room was basic but comfortable. 'Please take a seat.' The man smiled again and Rolf dropped into the chair. 'Right, sir. .... Let's have a look at the file.' He thumbed over the pages and then glanced upwards. 'Did your commanding officer explain anything about *Lebensborn*?' His question was answered by a shaking head. 'It means,' and the man took a deep breath, 'that you're ordered to mate with a pure German girl to produce a child of such purity that it can be our hope for the future.' He glanced into his file again. 'You've been selected by the *Reichsführer* himself for this important task.'

Rolf kept control. 'What exactly do I do now?'

'A car'll collect you tomorrow morning at 0800 and take you to Kallinchen. It's not far from Berlin. The castle in the village is one of the special buildings used by the Project.' He scanned the file again and looked up. Yes, I think that's all. May I ask where you'll be staying tonight? .... I can arrange for transport.'

In a flash of guilt, Rolf decided to stay with his wife. He had not seen her for six months.

'I'm staying at my home tonight and I'll take that transport,' said Rolf, rising from his seat'

'Ah, yes,' again glancing at the file, 'that'll be Apartment 4a on *Friedrich Strasse*.' The captain snapped the file closed and there was a smile on his face that Rolf did not like.

The corporal waiting in the *Kübelwagen* jumped out when he saw Rolf approaching.

'4a *Friedrich Strasse*.' The old man nodded.

Total darkness everywhere. The car ground along in first gear until it reached its destination. Rolf sighed with relief when he saw number 4a was still standing. The front door was open and he stepped through into the dark interior of the hallway. Quickly, he walked up the stairs. Finding his keys, he took a deep breath and opened the door. Dropping his case on the floor, he gently closed the door behind him. Glancing around he saw their familiar things and the smells and sights of home.

'Angela,' he called quietly. 'It's me, Rolf.'

For a minute there was no reply. Then a door creaked open and she stood framed in the soft light of the bedroom. A silk night-dress clung over the curved outlines of her slim figure and he felt a rush of desire.

'Rolf, is that really you?' she said incredulously and began to move down the hall towards him.

'It's me,' he said, throwing his cap onto an antique table.

She rushed into his arms. He smelt her perfume and felt her body close to him. 'Darling, why didn't you tell me you were coming home? Your last letter only arrived this morning.' Her face shone up at him. 'Oh, Rolf, Rolf,

... it's so good to see you.' Winding her arm around his neck, she pulled his head close and kissed him hard on the lips. He felt her tongue sinuously slipping into his mouth and the fresh sweetness of her saliva joined his.

'Angela, darling,' he whispered. 'I'm happy to be home.' Somehow, he had to regain control of his emotions. Rolf was not a man to lose control.

She was pulling him along the hall towards the bedroom. 'Rolf, ... oh my dearest Rolf. It's been so long, come to be bed with me, ... NOW!' The bed covers were thrown back and his closeness in the room only served to arouse her further. Within a minute, he was on the bed and she was pulling at his tunic. 'Now, please darling, ... now.'

To Rolf, this was a new woman. In the past, it was always he who had made love to her. The positions were reversed. He let go and managed to pull off his boots. The door bell rang. They ignored it and soon they were both naked. The bell rang again.

'Damn,' said Rolf loudly, reaching for a robe.

'Leave it, darling,' she whispered frustratingly. 'For God's sake, leave it. It's only the blackout warden.'

In an instant, his passion dropped and he forced himself off her prostrate body. As Rolf lunged for the bedroom door, he glanced back at her. She lay quite still, brown hair flowing over the pillow, her legs wide open revealing her Venus mound ripe ready for the taking.

Yanking the door open, he was about to shout something at anybody who was there.

'*Hauptsturmführer* Müller?' He was in full dress *SS* officer's uniform. Black shiny boots, silver piping on his tunic and the gleaming *SS* dagger swinging at his side. The steel helmet was burnished to a deep glow and the twin silver runes on each side stood out sharply. The face was cast in stone and stared rigidly ahead. 'May I please come in?'

Rolf groaned, 'Yes, if you must.' He stepped to one side.

'I am *Obersturmführer* Otto Tauber. One of *SS-Reichsführer* Himmler's personal aides.' He paused for effect.

'Who is it, darling?' called Angela. Rolf ignored her.

The officer delved into a slim, brief-case. '*Herr Hauptsturmführer*, here are the final orders and briefing details for the *Lebensborn* Project. The *Reichsführer* orders you to read everything before your meeting tomorrow morning with *SS-Obersturmbannführer* Eichmann.' The man clicked his heels and threw up a dazzling salute and thrust the envelope into Rolf's hand. Rotating to the left, he stepped smartly out of the door and closed it quietly behind him.

With a sigh, Rolf walked back down the hall. Angela stood at the side of the bed, a pale blue silk peignoir draped tightly round her body. Her face was expressionless.

'What is it, darling?' he asked, eyebrows raised.

Her voice was as cold as her demeanour. 'I heard that officer say the word, *"Lebensborn"*.' Her eyes narrowed. 'I know what it means.'

Rolf, for a moment, was unsure what to say. One second at the height of desire and the next in the depths of panic. He tried to make excuses. 'Of course, darling, don't worry. It's something to do with my research at Auschwitz.'

'Well?' she said, hands firmly on hips, eyes ablaze. 'You'd better tell me exactly what the hell's going on.'

He decided to bluff it out. 'Angela, please listen,' slipping his arm round her waist. '*Lebensborn* is a project that needs doctors and I'm a doctor.'

Pushing herself away and grabbing a packet of cigarettes, she pulled one out and jammed it between her lips. 'Get my lighter,' she ground out from round the cigarette, glaring straight into his eyes.

Rolf searched the chest of drawers and found a box of matches. The light flared and he held it to her cigarette. She inhaled deeply and turned away. There was a silence in the apartment. Angela stopped at the bedroom door and turned to face him.

'I don't believe you and now I'll tell you what I know about the fucking *Lebensborn* Project.' With dragon-like clouds of smoke coming from her mouth and nostrils, she spat out the words. 'It's a brothel where "pure", and that's a joke, SS men can screw blonde-haired, blue-eyed whores. All in the name of making a new German super race. …. Jesus Christ,' she shouted, tossing her head back, 'and we dutiful wives are supposed to accept it all. Well, I'll tell you right now, *Herr Doktor Hauptsturmführer* fucking Rolf Ernst Müller, not me. I'll not let Himmler dictate my morals and decide who my husband can screw.' She threw the half-smoked cigarette onto the wooden floor and left it smouldering. 'So what's it going to be my loving husband? Himmler and his whores or me and our marriage?'

Her questioning devastated him. As long as he had known her, she had never used foul language. And her denying of the *Reichsführer* was inexcusable. He smiled and leant against the drawers. 'Darling, I'm not taking part in the mating routines. I'm assisting as a doctor and it's only for two days.'

Her posture changed slightly and her eyes dropped. 'Rolf, I don't know what to believe any more,' she said, with a tremor in her voice. She put her hand on his arm and spoke in almost a whisper. 'You do realise that we've lost the war, don't you?' Rolf tried to interrupt but she squeezed harder.

'That bloody madman Hitler, will be the death of us all.' She stopped and looked up at him.

For Rolf, she had gone too far. He squared his shoulders and spoke firmly. 'You must not speak like that about the *Führer*. I know these are difficult times. But, I've been told on the highest authority that it's only a matter of weeks before we'll push back the Russians and the Allies and then .... ' The interruption was clinical.

'Rubbish, absolute rubbish.' Angela shook her head in frustration. 'The Bolsheviks will be in Berlin within six months. Only three days ago, the British and the Americans landed thousands of paratroopers in Holland and, if your geography is any good, and it never was, is only ten minutes from the Fatherland.'

'I didn't know about that,' Rolf said, quietly.

'Since you were posted to that damned place in Poland you seem to have lost touch with reality.' Angela made her way back towards the bedroom and shouted back at him, 'There's a lot you don't know about.' Sitting on the stool in front of her dressing-table, she began brushing her hair. Rolf watched her and waited expectantly. She remained silent and the silver brush went up and down her long brown hair.

'I'm going to take a shower,' said Rolf.

'You'll be lucky, the water's off.'

'Off, ... off? What do you mean off?'

'It's the war, darling or haven't you noticed?' she muttered, sarcastically. Lowering the hair brush to the table, she rose from her seat. 'There's a bowl of water in the kitchen, you could use that. Don't try heating it, the gas is off.' She watched his face and her eyes glittered. 'I'm sure you'll want to read the report from your beloved *Reichsführer*. You can read it in the living-room and sleep on the sofa. Now, my loving husband, pour me a glass of brandy and I'll say good night to you.' Her chest was heaving with suppressed anger and Rolf, with a twist of pure lust, watched her breasts tautly move.

Pulling the belt on his robe tighter, he walked into the living-room and opened the drinks cabinet. Something had changed his wife. He was used to instant obedience and Angela's new attitude excited him. He reached into the bottom cupboard, apart from a small bottle of schnapps, the cupboard was bare. And then he realised where her strength and temper had come from. Filling the two glasses half-full, he closed the door and returned to the hall. Placing the glasses carefully on the chest of drawers, he unstrapped the buckles of his case. Slipping the necklace into his robe pocket, he collected the glasses and strode down the hall.

She lay in bed and, sitting down next to her, he gave her the glass. As she reached forward from the pillow, he again watched her breasts tremble under the sheer silk of the night-dress.

'Thank you,' she whispered. Her eyes watched his and she knew what he was looking at. Drinking deeply, she nearly emptied the glass.

Taking a good mouthful of the schnapps, he rolled it round his mouth and swallowed, relishing its fiery power as it coursed into his stomach. With his other hand, he withdrew the necklace from his pocket. It flashed and sparkled in the soft light of the bedroom and he toyed with it like a rosary. Angela watched, with eyes becoming greedier every second. She rolled off her pillow and tried to touch the biggest diamond. Rolf moved away. She moved closer.

'It's for you,' he said, simply.

'It's fantastic,' she said softly and he dropped it into her hand. With eyes wide-open, she ran the stones through her fingers and touched every facet, making noises in her throat. Gently, he took the necklace out of her hand. Frowning with curiosity, she watched him unclip the catch and hold it out to her. With a smile of anticipation, she reached round her neck and, with that most feminine of movements, lifted up her hair. Rolf lowered the necklace around the curve in the nape of her neck and the diamond swung into position between the pale whiteness of her breasts. The very act of placing the necklace around Angela's neck aroused Rolf almost beyond his iron self-control.

She found some words and they came out huskily. 'Is it, ... is it for me?'

'Yes.' And he emptied the glass and dropped it gently to the floor. In one smooth motion he slipped his hand around her waist and pulled her towards him.

A low moan came from within her and her eyes closed. Her hands reached out and gripped his face. All she said was, 'Yes,' and pulled his head to the necklace nestling between her breasts.

Angela was the first to climax and she ground out the ecstasy in grunts of delight. Rolf fell to one side and, with his mind crystal clear, he reached for her again. She came to him but there was nothing there. He strove to enter her and she opened wider and wider. She stiffened when he could not and she faced him across the pillow.

'What's the matter?' she said, with a trace of annoyance.

'Nothing,' he whispered, pulling her soft, creamy thighs closer. Mounting her again he tried with all his might to enter her and then flopped to one side.

Sitting-up, Angela slipped the night-dress over her head and reached between his legs. 'Come.. on .. you .. bastard, I'm not finished yet,' she said, stroking and squeezing. After five minutes, she gave-up and fell back onto the bed. Turning over, away from him, she took off the necklace and threw it to the floor.

'I'm sorry, Angela,' he said, frustration making him sweat. 'It's because I'm so tired.'

'Go to hell,' came the muttered reply.

Rolf slept in fits and bursts and, for the first time in his life, he had nightmares. Great white blobs of faces came and went. Trains with clouds of black smoke intermingled with Angela's body thrusting upwards, always thrusting upwards and then always disappearing into a gaping hole. At one point, he jerked upright with a cry on his lips. Desperately, he searched out Angela in the half-light. She remained curled in the foetal position and stiffly out of reach.

Rolf jumped out of the bed, found his robe and left the bedroom. Gritting his teeth with frustration, he walked into the bathroom and stared hard in the mirror. A proud body, well proportioned and in peak condition. He felt his flat stomach and flexed the muscles. Using his medical knowledge, and his fingers, he examined his testicles and the flaccid penis. There was nothing wrong that he could find and he left the bathroom feeling angry and disgusted.

Switching on the light in the living-room, he sat down and stared at the familiar things around him. A turn of the century apartment, high ceilings and plaster cornices. A marble fireplace with the remnants of a log fire sitting in its grate. The pictures they had collected on the trips round Europe before the war had started.

Rolf picked up the briefing papers from the chair. Most details he already knew and then the directions caught his eye.

"*At 0730hrs, SS-Hauptsturmführer Müller will be collected and taken to the old Reich Chancellery and there he will report to SS-Obersturmbannführer Eichmann.*"

He had met Eichmann before when he had visited Birkenau. He was a man who had impressed Rolf from the start of their short meeting.

Dropping the papers back onto the chair, he slumped back on the sofa and tried to sleep. Almost before his eyes had closed, the sound of the sirens cut through the stillness of the night. With a sigh, he raised himself and made his way to the door. Angela pushed past him and, without a glance in his direction, grabbed a heavy fur coat to cover her half-naked body and disappeared through the front door. The sound of the door slamming and the ever rising wail of the air raid sirens made him shrug and return to the living-room. Walking over to the tall window, he snatched back the curtains.

Apart from the ghosts of shadows, there was nothing to be seen and he waited patiently for the bombers to arrive. They came in great roaring waves of sound and he heard the bombs screaming to their targets. Searchlights stabbed the sky and the staccato burst of anti-aircraft fire echoed across the city. It was over in ten minutes and in that time Rolf remained motionless. Before the all clear sounded, he turned, opened his wardrobe, removed a clean uniform and quickly dressed. Rolf collected his suitcase and walked down to the hall to the front door. The stench of burning debris and clouds of dust wafted in and he wrinkled his nose and waited. He smiled to himself when the black Mercedes drew up outside the door. Rolf handed his case over to the SS driver.

The inside of the huge car enveloped Rolf in its leather and chrome luxury. He saw nothing of the city and, clutching the brief-case to his chest, he stared at the shaved neck of the driver. A slowly rising sun spread a grey light over the mess that was *Wilhelmstrasse*, Rolf saw none of it. The car drew to a halt and the driver swung out of his seat and opened the door. Rolf stepped onto the cracked slabs of the pavement and the entrance steps of the *Reichskanzlei* loomed up in front of him. For a moment, he hesitated and then, with a snap of decision, he straightened his shoulders and walked forward.

Two guards saluted him and the heavy wooden doors of the *Reichskanzlei* creaked open. Inside, all was calm and the lights on the walls occasionally flickered sending ghostly shadows around the cavernous interior. Marble and stone formed a structure that was massive and daunting. The geometric patterns on the floor of the hall led forward towards a wide flight of stairs illuminated by huge, cut-glass chandeliers. Standing stock-still, Rolf felt surprisingly alone.

'*Hauptsturmführer*,' the words made him jump and he turned round. 'Follow me, please.' The corporal walked back from where he had silently emerged and Rolf meekly followed, his footsteps echoing back from the marble walls. There was not a soul in sight. After two echoing corridors, the corporal opened a tall door. Rolf was curious.

'Where are we going to, *Rottenführer*?'

The man stopped and turned to face Rolf, 'To the *Führerbunker*, *Herr Hauptsturmführer*.' To Rolf it meant nothing.

Together they walked into the gardens of the *Reichskanzlei*. There was bright sunshine with heavy, scudding clouds rushing across a blue sky.

The once beautiful gardens and the ornate water fountains were gone. The rear of the main building was severely damaged. Most of the windows were boarded up with sheets of painted steel. The whole area was like a battlefield, with massive water-filled bomb craters, uprooted trees and smashed stonework. The smell that assuaged his nostrils was strangely familiar. Rolf picked his way through the rubble, his mind taking note of everything around him. In the far corner they approached an oblong blockhouse guarded by two sentries. They saluted and asked for papers and identity documents. A close scrutiny took several minutes, as they double checked from a list clipped to a board. Nodding, they pulled open a reinforced steel door.

Rolf placed his papers back into the brief-case and waited as the door closed behind him. He walked into an underworld he would remember clearly for the rest of his life. Grey concrete walls and spiralling concrete steps led downwards and the light became fainter. As Rolf turned a corner, he entered a brilliantly lit hallway. People dressed in a bewildering array of uniforms walked purposefully past him. The hallway opened up into a larger room. Domed lights let into the ceiling gave out a warm glow. Comfortable chairs stood against light beige walls and on the floor lay a richly-coloured Oriental carpet. It had obviously been moved from a bigger room, because the ends were neatly turned under. Although comfortable, the chairs did not match and the oil paintings on the wall seemed out of place.

'Excuse me, *Hauptsturmführer*.' The voice brought Rolf out of his wandering curiosity. Two young SS officers in full dress-uniform stood at attention in front of him. 'Sir, I have to search you,' one of them said. 'It'll only take a moment and we apologise for any inconvenience.' Before he had time to think, the men patted his white gloved hands all over Rolf's body and then he remembered the July bomb plot. The other officer searched the brief-case carefully feeling the folds and stitching of the black leather. It was all over in a minute and one of the men threw up a crisp salute.

'HEIL Hitler!'

'*HEIL* Hitler!' replied Rolf, a swell of pride beginning to replace his earlier worries.

For several minutes, he waited at the side of a small mahogany table. He recognised some of the people who walked past but nobody recognised him.

A voice at his side made him jump. 'Good morning. *Hauptsturmführer* Müller, I believe?' The accent was pure high German. *SS-Hauptsturmführer* Günther Schwaegermann was a tall, elegant man and he smiled at Rolf.

'*Obersturmbannführer* Eichmann will be ready in a few minutes. Would you like the guided tour?'

'Sorry, ... the guided tour?'

He smiled, 'Oh yes, indeed. Not many officers have the chance to visit the *Führerbunker*.' Before Rolf could reply, he began to rattle on. 'We are under three metres of bomb-proof reinforced concrete. On top of that, is another five metres of compacted earth. Down here nobody can touch us. The *Führerbunker* is divided into two sections. The *Führer's* personal quarters are over there,' and he pointed to his left. He smiled when he saw Rolf's interested glance. 'I'm sorry, the *Führer* is not in residence today. He's at the Wolf's Lair at Rastenburg.' He walked out of the room, back into the corridor and Rolf followed. 'In that room is the control centre.' His hands pointed hither and thither. 'That one houses the wine cellar and the pantry. That one is the armoury.' And then he stopped. Down the corridor trotted an Alsatian dog. Rolf froze, because he knew exactly who the dog belonged to. 'Ah, hello, Blondi,' said the officer. 'Come on girl. ... Come on now. ..... There's a good dog.' Rolf felt a warm muzzle in his hand and looked down. Two brown eyes looked at him and he patted her on the head. A pink tongue licked his fingers and then, with a wag of a brush-like tail, she padded away down the corridor. 'She's the most famous dog in the whole of Germany,' said Schwaegermann. 'The *Führer* thinks the world of her and so do we. She's a sort of good luck symbol.' He glanced at his watch. 'She'll be off for her walk. *Hauptscharführer* Mansfield is waiting by the main door.' Rolf took a deep breath and waited for the next piece of history.

'Here we are. Just knock and go in. Good bye, Müller.' He walked away down the corridor. Rolf waited exactly ten seconds and he suddenly felt terribly alone. The door swung open and the bright lights made Rolf squint. A baroque desk and a huge chair, above which hung a portrait of Adolf Hitler. He felt his eyes drawn to the face.

'Good morning, *Hauptsturmführer* Müller. And how are you?' The man in the chair rose and walked round from behind the desk. *Obersturmbannführer* Adolf Karl Eichmann gave a gentle smile. Small and slim in stature, a long, thin nose being the dominant feature on his face. Angular eyebrows raised alternately as he spoke. Eichmann was not a brilliant man but he had blundered and bluffed his way to the top of the *Reich* Central Security Office in Berlin, the department that looked after all Jewish affairs. The handshake Rolf accepted was firm, although the palms were slightly damp. 'Do sit down,' Eichmann said politely.' He waved him to a straight-backed chair.

Returning to his desk, he sat down and watched Rolf composing himself.

He spoke very quietly. 'There are one or two things I wish to discuss.' Rolf nodded and waited. 'Firstly, I wish to congratulate you on the excellent work you're carrying out at Auschwitz. You may think nobody has noticed what you've achieved.' His forefinger tapped the blotter pad. The sound was the only noise in the room. 'I have received excellent reports from *Kommandant* Bär and *Doktor* Mengele about your loyalty to the *Reich* and your uncomplaining approach to this vital work.'

'I do my duty, *Sturmbannführer*.'

'Yes, yes, Müller. But some do it better than others.' His eyes narrowed and he stared hard at the desk top. 'The work you do is not easy. I know that, because many years ago, I myself did similar work.' He saw Rolf's eyes widen. 'Yet, I never gave up. Oh yes, Müller, I kept on and I succeeded. I was noticed by my superiors and they promoted me. Believe me, I know what it's like to have to follow orders.' He paused and a smile crept across his face. 'This time, it is I who have noticed you.' Eichmann took a deep breath. He knew exactly how impressed his junior officer was with his reputation. He paused for a moment whilst thinking. 'I know, that your brother, Edvard Müller, is doing a wonderful job for the SS in Holland.'

Rolf had frequent contact with his brother and he was delighted to hear Eichmann's words. 'Thank you, *Herr Obersturmbannführer*. May I tell him of your praise when we next meet?'

'Of course,' Eichmann replied. 'But we can do a little more than that for one of our most loyal SS officers. When you leave my office, you'll find your brother waiting for you.' He saw the astonished look on Rolf's face and added, 'The *Reich* thanks you for your hard work.'

In the distance, Rolf heard the rumble of bomb explosions and across Eichmann's face flickered a worried smile. Rolf was surprised when he felt a trickle of sweat run down his back.

'On January 20, 1941,' droned Eichmann, 'I was present at a highly secret conference held at Wannsee, not ten kilometres from where we sit. The meeting lasted less than an hour and a half and, in that time, the fate of the Jews was sealed. We called it the "Final Solution".' He rubbed his hands together, a gesture that Rolf found strangely Jewish. 'So far, my dear Müller, we have dealt with over five million of them. You personally,' he glanced at a file on his desk, 'have dealt with nearly a quarter of a million.'

The damp trickle became a drenching cold sweat. In the harsh light of the marble room, his head swam and, for the first time since he had worked at Auschwitz, Rolf began to think about what he had been doing. "Pieces", "units" and "filth" suddenly became almost real people and his heart pounded.

Eichmann saw the change in the face of the man seated in front of him. Rising from his seat, he came round from his desk and gently placed a hand on Rolf's shoulder. 'I can see, *Hauptsturmführer*, that my words concern you'

The shock of the personal contact made Rolf stiffen and he lifted his head to look at the brooding portrait of Adolf Hitler. 'Not at all, *Obersturmbannführer*,' he said quietly. 'I was doing my duty for the *Reich*.' The standard words gave a him a breathing space.

Eichmann nodded and removed his hand. 'I know what you're feeling. We do our work for the benefit of the *Führer* and the German people. It's not easy work but the rewards are many. Being an *SS* officer and carrying out our orders are reward enough.' He paused, straightened and his thin lips compressed into a narrow line.

'Did you say over five million, *Herr Obersturmbannführer*?' Being asked a question, surprised Eichmann.

'Yes, ... I said over five million. Why do you ask?' Folding his arms, he stared hard at Rolf's face.

'It's a lot of people.'

Eichmann threw his head back and laughed. 'It is a lot of people. But I don't regard the Jews as people. And, ... I suppose, *Hauptsturmführer*, you may be worried about the Allies?' Rolf shrugged and tried to smile. 'Listen, Müller,' said Eichmann, mockingly. 'A hundred dead people is a catastrophe. Five million is a statistic. Stop worrying.' Eichmann looked at the ormolu clock on his desk, pulled open a drawer and took out a slim, leather-covered box. He opened the case. 'I have a little surprise for you. *SS-Hauptsturmführer Doktor* Rolf Ernst Müller, with the *Führer's* fullest authority, I hereby invest you with the Iron Cross First Class.' With a flourish, he took out the black and grey ribbon and pinned the medal onto Rolf's tunic. Feeling the damp hand slip into his, Rolf shook it. The cold eyes bored into him. 'Congratulations and well done.' Unable to speak, Rolf felt himself swaying. 'And now,' Eichmann said, 'the *Lebensborn* Project. When you leave here, you'll be taken by car to Kallinchen Castle.' Using his phenomenal memory, Eichmann filled in the details. 'You're being mated with a woman called Ulrika Hannsen. She is racially pure and has an excellent German background. You'll have two days to carry out your orders and then you must return to your duties at Auschwitz. There, you still have much to do.' The eyes searched Rolf's face. 'That's all. Enjoy your leave.' Rolf stumbled to his feet.

'Thank you, *Herr Obersturmbannführer*, thank you very much.'

'*HEIL* Hitler!'

'Of course,' stuttered Rolf. '...... *HEIL* Hitler!'

Eichmann pressed a brass button on the corner of the desk. 'Good bye. I have urgent business in Budapest. There is still much work to be done there. Good luck and keep up the good work.' His eyes shone. 'And enjoy *Lebensborn.*'

Rolf left the office and carefully closed the door behind him. He made his own way back out of the bunker and into the long corridors of the *Reichskanzlei.* Close to another massive steel door, he stopped.

'Hello there, Rolf. You're looking a little pale. How are you? .....Ah congratulations on the medal.'

He knew the voice and turned. They shook hands and embraced. *SS-Hauptsturmführer* Edvard Müller was young and very good looking. A deep tan and a handsome face. The uniform fitted his physique perfectly. The eyes were a penetrating blue, exactly the same as his brother's, and as cold as ice. They stepped back and calmly surveyed each other.

'You're looking well,' said Rolf, grinning.

'Yes, indeed,' Edvard replied. 'I live very comfortably. The Dutch enjoy life's little luxuries.'

'Plenty of cheese?'

He shrugged and smiled. '*Reichskommisar* Seyss-Inquart promised me an easy time in Holland but the Dutch are not easy to control. There's resistance everywhere.'

Edvard Müller smiled at his brother. 'At least I keep sending plenty of Jews down the line for you to,' he laughed, '.....to dispose of.' They chatted earnestly for another five minutes.

'It's been good to see you,' said Rolf. 'And this is some place to be in.' He waved his hand around the corridor.

'Yes indeed,' replied Edvard. 'Who would've thought that we'd ever be so close to the *Führer* himself.'

Rolf smiled and nodded. 'Edvard, I really have to go now. I've got urgent business.'

'I quite understand, Rolf. Keep in touch.' They shook hands and parted.

As Rolf left the Reich Chancellery, he walked through the dust clouds, just as the sirens sounded the all clear. He passed through another steel door and along a damp corridor. It led into a basement garage where, with its engine running, a black car waited. The driver saluted and opened the rear door. With a sigh of relief, Rolf slumped into the back seat. 'Your bag is in the boot, sir,' he said, as he closed the door. Revving the engine, the car slipped across the oily concrete floor and made its way up the ramp towards the opening steel shutters. Rolf stared out of the window at his ruined city. Near the Berlin Zoo the car passed the tall G Tower. Forty metres high, it dominated the western part of the city. Massive concrete walls three metres thick. The driver slowed.

'Ah, ... sir, the G Flak Tower. It'll last forever. Do you know, it has a complete hospital with two fully-equipped operating theatres. I was in there last week and it's fantastic.' Rolf listened with interest. 'They say the cellars are full of treasures from the museums.' He slowed, almost to a stop. Rolf had seen enough.

'Drive on,' he said. The man nodded and pulled away into the rapidly thinning traffic. As they left the centre of Berlin, the damage to the buildings lessened. The *autobahn* to the south was almost empty and they made good time. The drumming of the tyres on the concrete road lulled Rolf off to sleep. Faces, people, smoke and bombs. It seemed as though the dream would go on forever. A jolt awoke him. Through the mists of his dream, Rolf struggled to sit up. Shaking his head helped and, as the car lurched round steep bends, he managed to clear his brain.

'We're here, sir,' said the driver.

It was indeed a castle. Thick stone walls and a bridge over a water-filled moat. The fading sun cast long shadows and Rolf shivered. The car rattled over the bridge and through the high arched gate. The courtyard surprised him. It was a garden, full of late summer flowers and trickling fountains. The door opened and Rolf stepped out. His head cleared instantly and he looked all around him. Gone was the dust of Berlin and the stench of Auschwitz. It was the first fresh air that Rolf had breathed for over three months.

'This way please, sir.' The hotel porter beckoned Rolf forward.

The interior of the castle impressed him. Gleaming floors, deep sofas and long drapes at the windows. For a moment, he was totally confused and stood stock-still in the lobby.

'Good evening, sir.' Another man, dressed in hotelier's uniform, a dark jacket and pin-stripe trousers. Rolf was dumfounded.

'Am I in the right place? This is the Castle Kallinchen, isn't it?'

'Yes, sir, you're in the right place. This is the Castle.'

'For the *Lebensborn* Project?' he asked quietly.

The man smiled, crossing his hands over a generous stomach. 'Here we run the castle as a hotel and as a leave centre for special guests. There's no mention of the Project.' Glancing at Rolf's uniform, he added, 'Sir, here only civilian clothes are worn.'

'Where are the other, ... "guests"?' he asked.

'Ah yes, sir.' He gave a professional smile. 'I see what you mean. It does appear to be rather quiet. Actually we're only half-full. That's about thirty guests. Most of them are changing for dinner.' Rolf nodded. 'Anyway, sir, ... if you could please sign the register.' Leaning over the desk, he opened the leather-bound book.

Rolf picked up the pen and signed his name. He smiled, it was the first time since the start of the war that he had used the title, "*Herr*".

'Porter,' the receptionist called. 'Take *Herr* Müller's bags to room 4.' Rolf followed the old man to the lift. 'Oh and by the way, sir,' the manager called. 'Dinner is at eight.' Rolf stepped into the lift.

The thick carpet on the long corridor deadened his steps as he followed the porter. The man opened the door and led the way.

Rolf was surprised. It was more of a suite than a room. A big lounge with three doors. The French decor was superb. Hung from the centre of the ceiling, a single, glittering, cut-glass chandelier. At the end of the room, the long windows were wide open and the porter rushed to close them.

'Don't close them,' said Rolf. The man stopped in mid-stride.

He nodded and placed the suitcase on the floor. 'Sir, this door leads to the bedroom.' He walked over and opened the heavy door. Inside was sheer luxury. A huge bed covered by a green silken canopy. The paintings on the panelled walls were all of cherubs and nymphs. 'And this door, is the way to your bathroom. .... In here is your wardrobe.' And he opened a door. The wardrobe was neatly full of clothes. The old man watched Rolf's face. 'They're all your size, sir. The manager does a good job.' He turned and walked across the room. 'Do you wish me to unpack your bag?'

'No, thanks.'

The porter gave a curt nod. 'The champagne is ready on the table,' and then closed the door behind him.

EIGHTEEN

Richard stared hard at the contents of the safe laying on the desk. Picking up the single sheet of paper, Richard recognised his father's neat italic script. There was no date.

'My dearest son,
By the time you read this letter, I will be gone. Please don't grieve too much for me, life must go on and I've had a good innings.'

Richard felt tears beginning to well up inside him.

'Everything is prepared for. If Sabina has followed my instructions, then she will have read my will and know she has no financial worries. I have also made good arrangements for you and your family.

I know I have not been a particularly good father. But, I suppose every father at some time in his life says the same thing. When I was younger, I always remember the happy times in Holland. The war changed all that and, when I came to England, life there made me harder.

You now have much to learn and, for a change, I'm going to be your teacher. The file near your right hand is to be read and then you will learn much about your family that you never knew. Your mother will tell you other things. Don't be too upset when you discover information that may hurt you. Some of what you read about, will effect you and your family for generations to come.

The envelopes are to be opened when you've read the file.
Good luck in life and, one day, God willing, we'll meet again.

Your loving father,

Simon.'

Richard read and re-read the letter a dozen times. Rising from the deep chair, he walked across the study. Finding a bottle of brandy, he poured himself a full measure. Drinking deeply, he felt the liquid seep warmly into his stomach and he sat down again at the desk. The house was asleep and there was not a sound to be heard.

The manila file was slightly faded and over it lay a sheen of fine dust. Taking a deep breath, he lifted the cover. The file opened with a faint crackling sound and the papers inside had a yellowish look.

His father's script filled the pages and there were occasional alterations and margin notes. Each page was numbered and the odd rusty paper-clip fastened some of the pages. The first page said, quite simply, '**NOTES MADE BY SIMON AARON COHEN.**' Placing it to one, side he began to read.

'Holland was at peace, although the rumblings from Germany were beginning to echo across Europe. The last time I saw my parents was in September 1939. In that last summer before war, I had the time of my life. Sailing on the Frisian lakes in the day and drinking in the cafes of Leeuwarden at night. I saw most of my relatives and visited friends all over Holland. I clearly remember one night in August 1939 when my father told me to return to my studies in Manchester. He must have known something was going to happen. By pure luck, I had a ticket on the ferry for the 31st. Without that ticket, I would not have survived the war. It was the old 'Amsterdam', the last ferry to sail from Holland to England and the ship was packed with people. Whilst I was eating breakfast, an announcement came over the loudspeakers. It was September 1st and Germany had invaded Poland. At the time, it really didn't worry me because Holland was neutral and had been since the turn of the century. Britain and France declared war on the 3rd and I expected it all to be over by Christmas. I spoke to my parents on the phone, then all communications with Holland ceased. When the Germans invaded my country on May 10th, I couldn't believe it. It was as though a light had gone out. I'd never felt so completely alone in all my life and there was no way I could contact my family. After months of misery, I went back to studying and all the time with no news from home.

A year later, I received a letter asking me to go to an office somewhere on Baker Street in London. When I arrived, it all seemed very mysterious. Eventually, I met an Englishman and, although he was in a sports jacket and flannels, he was so obviously military. He told me that a message had come out of Friesland to the effect that my family were all safe and sent their love. I asked the man how he had received such information and he said that the British were in contact with resistance groups in Holland. At that time, I really didn't believe him. Three years later, when I met the man again, I realised that the visit had been to the offices of Churchill's newly formed Special Operations Executive.'

Richard placed the sheets of paper back on the desk and sighed. Emptying the brandy glass, he stared fixedly at the file. His thoughts kept returning to his father's letter and slowly his eyes closed.

The tapping at the door made him jump. His mother walked in and glanced at the file. 'Is it interesting?' she said softly.

Rubbing his eyes with finger and thumb, Richard relaxed back into the chair. 'Very interesting, and it's going to take some time to read it. I'll give it another go and then I'll go to bed.'

She touched him on the shoulder. 'I think we've both had a busy day so I think it's bed time for you as well. I've already switched on the electric blanket in the guest room.'

'Just like the old times.' He grinned.

'Nonsense,' she retorted, 'we never had an electric blanket. You had to make do with a hot water bottle.'

'Those were the days,' he said, rising and putting his arm affectionately round her shoulders.

Together they climbed the stairs and he kissed her gently on the cheek. 'Sleep well.'

'And you,' she replied quietly, brushing away a single tear.

Without showering, he collapsed into bed only just remembering to switch off the electric blanket. In an instant, he drifted into a dreamless sleep.

'Richard, wake up. ....'

He thought he was dreaming and, with a moan, turned over.

Slowly realising where he was, he opened his eyes.

'Good morning. How are you today?' A fully-dressed Sabina sat on the side of his bed and looked down at him. 'Breakfast is in the kitchen in precisely twenty minutes.' She kissed him on the cheek and left the bedroom.

Richard's brain slowly began to function and he slipped out of bed. Sabina had thought of everything, the razor and soap were laid out in a neat row. Another five minutes and he was finished. Over the chair lay his black tie, at its side were four others. All had belonged to his father. He picked one up and slipped it on.

As he walked down the stairs, the aroma of fresh coffee came from the kitchen. Taking a deep breath, Richard opened the door. Over the sound of John Humphrys' BBC voice, he heard his mother call out to him.

'About time, your eggs are nearly hard.' He smiled.

Lifting the toast from the toaster, she placed it on a plate and walked across to the table. 'My God, I miss him. I hardly slept a wink and when I got up this morning and realised you were here. Well, ... it just made all the old memories come flooding back.'

His heart went out to his mother. 'I'm so sorry, Sabina. I really am. It's going to take some time for us all to get over this.'

She cracked her egg. 'I know, I know, ... but believe me, it's very difficult.' She stared hard at his face. 'Richard, I've got to say this, ... when you read your father's notes, please try to understand me.' Richard had no idea why she was saying such a thing.

They ate their eggs in silence and Richard re-filled the coffee cups.

'Oh hell, I can't eat any more,' she said, banging her knife on the wooden table. 'Look here Richard, before you leave, I want to explain about Simon's will.' He folded his napkin neatly and waited.

Reaching across the table, she took down a long envelope off the shelf. Extracting the sheets of paper, she laid them flat on the table. 'I won't go into all the detail. It's really quite simple.' She squeezed her eyes closed and then opened them again. 'Right, ... I'm left the house and everything in it. I also have a very generous allowance. Our grand-children receive fifty thousand pounds each, placed in a trust-fund.' Richard's eyebrows raised. 'As the only child, you receive five hundred thousand pounds.' She scrutinised the document. 'This will be provided when various shares and insurance policies are sorted out.'

'Wow,' he exclaimed.

'There are other bits and pieces. Twenty thousand for Lottie Cohen in Holland and for the van de Meer family, five thousand pounds. All Simon's books, papers and other documents are left to you.'

Richard shook his head, 'Sabina, I can't believe it. I mean, I knew he was a successful lawyer but, ... all this money. Had you any idea of .... well, you know?' Shrugging his shoulders, he bit his lip.

The tears came again. 'I feel like you. We've never had to worry about money.' Another glance at the will. 'Assets and capital total over a million pounds.'

There was silence in the kitchen.

'Sabina,' said Richard, still thinking about what she had just said, 'do you mind if I take the contents of the safe away with me.'

'Of course not. Take anything you want to take.' For the first time that morning, she smiled. 'I'm just going to potter about and sort out one or two things.'

'Can I do anything for you?'

She thought for a moment. 'No, not really.'

Richard rose from his chair and began to clear away the breakfast.

'No, please leave everything,' she said, with a frown. 'I'll tidy away.' It took him a few minutes to collect the papers together and he stood quietly in the hall. As he paused Sabina appeared from the kitchen. 'Have a safe journey, Richard.' He nodded. 'Phone me tonight.'

For some reason, after a couple of miles, Richard stopped the car. Driving through an open gate into a field, he switched off the engine. A fine day, the odd cloud and a chill wind heralding winter. Stepping out of the car, he took a deep breath and glanced around at the view. The flat, Lancashire countryside always pleased him. There was the smell of damp earth and the not so distant sea. Nobody in sight and a quietness broken only by the odd cry of a lonely crow. The fields stretched away in front of him, some ploughed, others with their fading stubble. Richard was a man who could be at ease with himself and being alone was one of his great pleasures. How long he stood there for, he had no idea. It was the sound of a tractor that brought him back to reality. Jumping back in the car, he picked up the file and flipped open the cover. Without thinking of the time, he began to read.

The Jewish community in Manchester made me very welcome. As the war ground on, news from Europe became worse. I had no time to get depressed because my tutors worked me hard. Rumours began to circulate about the German treatment of Jews. One day, a man, actually a Polish Jew, told me that the Nazis were systematically killing Jews by the thousands. I remember actually laughing at him and walking away.

In March 1944, I received a letter. The brown envelope was headed, "On His Majesty's Service" and I remembered that it looked the same as the one I'd received years ago. It just asked me to go to London and meet somebody.

London had changed. Uniforms everywhere and a new sense of urgency. The office in Baker Street was crammed full of military and civilians. I met the same man as last time and he remembered my background. At his side was a woman with a notepad. Easy to remember her, because she had superb legs! The man and I chatted for over an hour and she took down every word. At the end of the discussion, he asked me if I would like to work for the Allies as a legal advisor. I jumped at the chance. I explained that my studies would take another year and would it be possible for me to finish them when the war was over? For the first time, he smiled and said not to worry about my studies. There was nothing to sign and he shook hands with me before I left. For a month, I waited for the post to arrive and it never did. I gave up, thinking that the man had enough to worry about.

The professor of the law faculty was a god whom I'd only met once. I was surprised when I received a summons to go to his study. A nice enough man. We talked about all sorts of things and then he dropped the bombshell. He told me that I'd be allowed to graduate a year early. I asked him why and he replied that my services and background were required for the war effort. Within two weeks, I'd been awarded my degree. I couldn't believe it, Simon Aaron Cohen, Bachelor of Law! Then I was gazetted lieutenant in the British Army. They billeted me in the Royal Artillery Barracks at Woolwich. They were pretty good to me there and tolerated a Jewish Dutchman with no experience of war. Then I was summoned to a law practice in the City. I was told not to wear my shiny new uniform. Upon my arrival, I was asked to sign the Official Secrets Act and then, I found out why. I was ushered into a large room, all wood panelling and leather chairs. Six men and one woman. All very important. Somebody asked me to take notes and to answer any comments when asked. The following is a re-drafted version of those notes:-

'The purpose of the meeting is to assist in the framing of a policy for the summary execution without trial of German war leaders who have taken part in war crimes. Mr Templeton-Jones of the Army Legal Branch put forward the list that had been so far suggested. This list contained the names of the top Nazis. There then followed a discussion with many names being added to the list. The German Commissioner for the Netherlands, Arthur Seyss-Inquart, was mentioned by Mr James Johnstone, MP for Wigan

This time, I asked some questions. "Gentlemen, may I ask why Seyss-Inquart's name needs to be on the list?"

"Ah, yes, Lieutenant Cohen,' said Mr Johnstone in rounded Lancashire vowels. '"Of course you're Dutch and, I presume, ... Jewish. We know from information received that the transportation of the Dutch Jews for forced labour in Germany and Poland has been going on for the last three years."

"All the Jews in Holland?"

"Well, yes, ... our reports say they send them out on trains through a transit camp called Westerbork in the north of the Netherlands."

"I've heard about Westerbork."

"Look here," he continued. "I'm afraid the news is not good. We hear nobody ever returns from the forced labour."

"What exactly do you mean, 'they never return?'"

"We now have strong evidence that Jews throughout Europe are being murdered by the Germans." His comment hit me hard.

I found out they wanted my linguistic skills and I was able to translate some German documents for the group. Not once did I read anything about the Jews of Holland. I left the meeting feeling very depressed and, in my mind, I almost knew that something awful had happened to my family. After that day, I became totally immersed in the legal intricacies of tribunals and the laws of war.'

NINETEEN

The evening suit fitted him perfectly and the starched wing collar was exactly his size. Rolf marvelled at SS organisation. As he firmed back his hair with perfumed pomade, he heard the chimes of the dinner gong. A quick glance in the full length mirror and he was ready.

Waiting at the stairs stood the manager. An imposing man with a clear, rather high-pitched voice. '*Herr* Müller.' He have a half bow. 'Please follow me.' As the double doors swung open, Rolf hesitated. He need not have worried, an air of gaiety engulfed him.

A long room, at the far end, large windows thrown open to the cool night air. In the corner, a musical trio played soft music. Candles everywhere casting a soft, flickering glow. And then he saw his fellow guests, all ages, all types, every one of them was smiling. Rolf stepped forward.

'Champagne, sir.' The waiter hovered and Rolf removed a glass from the silver tray.

The guests greeted each other like lost friends and Rolf sipped at his champagne. The chatter was composed and calm. Each person in the room tried carefully to measure the others around them. Rolf watched the ladies and they watched him. There were equal numbers and then he realised why. Not a woman was over thirty and all of them were blonde. He smiled and wondered which one was for him. A voice came over his shoulder.

'Lovely, aren't they?' A man about the same age as Rolf. A little fatter but with an open smile that prompted contact.

'They certainly are,' replied Rolf.

'I keep wondering which one is mine.'

'How do we find out?'

Grabbing a glass of champagne from a passing waiter, the man sniffed loudly. 'Well, I know her name but I don't know what she looks like.' Chuckling, he added, 'Although, looking at this lot, I wouldn't mind any of them.' He turned to examine Rolf more closely and lowered his voice. 'I won't ask your rank but I'm curious about what you do?'

'I'm a doctor.'

'Really, I'm just a simple *Wehrmacht* administrator. My name's Bruno Lippert.'

'I'm Rolf Müller.'

They paused, sizing each other up whilst glancing around the room.

'Rolf,' said Lippert, 'does this *Lebensborn* thing really work? I mean, can we actually say what will be produced from our, ... ' He shifted on his feet and took a good mouthful of champagne. 'What's the word they use? Our ..... "mating"?' The smile broadened into a grin. 'Because, to be quite honest, I don't feel like a superman.'

Rolf warmed to his subject. 'We've all been selected because of the blood of our families and our loyalty to the *Reich*.'

'And the ladies?'

'For the same reasons and ....' He was politely interrupted.

'And how do we know that our "mating" will produce the next generation of heroes?'

The cynicism surprised Rolf and he frowned. 'Today the women will be at the fourteenth day of their menstrual cycle; the most fertile time for mating.'

Bruno shrugged and waved his hand over the assembled group. 'How the hell is that possible? You know, ... all these ladies at your "fourteenth day"?'

'There are certain treatments now available to delay or speed up the cycle.'

Bruno cocked his head to one side and the grin faded. 'Just what sort of doctor are you? Are you actually involved in this project?'

'Yes, I'm involved in medical research into certain aspects of genetical science.'

'Oh, really, and where do you work?'

'In a research centre at a place called Auschwitz in southern Poland.' As gentle music rolled over them, the *Wehrmacht* officer flinched.

'I've heard of that place,' replied Bruno, quietly and the smile vanished, 'It's where we kill Jews.'

The music changed tempo and conversation between the two men was broken. Rolf, shrugging his shoulders, walked towards the larger group.

Champagne lubricated their conversations and eyes sparkled in the flickering candlelight. The warm air was filled with the very best French perfumes. Subtle fragrances of sweet flowers mingled with the zest of fresh green grass. All the men wore dinner-suits but it was the ladies who set the scene. Ball-gowns in every colour and style imaginable. Dark blues, flashing reds and purest whites. Sheer silk and glowing velvet, cut to fit bodies that were perfection. Nipped at the waist, the gowns flowed and rippled in folds to the polished floor. Although they were all dressed differently, each had one facet in common. Every women wore a gown cut low over her breasts. Every man's eyes were drawn to those breasts like a baby to its nipple.

Rolf found himself watching how his fellow guests were beginning to interact. He was as curious as they were. Everybody smiled, everybody bowed low and they all had the look of hunters.

The gong stopped the talking and the manager announced, 'Ladies and gentlemen, please take your seats for dinner.'

At the far end of the room, long, heavy curtains were pulled aside by unseen hands. Rolf found himself walking slowly forwards. Nobody spoke and the ensemble played gentle Mozart.

The long table was a work of art. Glittering silver on fresh white damask. Crystal glasses sparkled in the lights from the gilded candelabra. There was a moment's hesitation and then the manager spoke again.

'Ladies and gentlemen. There are place-names set ready for you all.' And then Rolf understood. Without appearing to show any interest, he glanced at the small silver-framed name boards set neatly at each table placing. The group slowly sorted itself out. Waiters appeared and drew chairs away from the table. Rolf's heart began to pound and he could feel sweat on his forehead. Most of the guests were already seated and then, forcing himself to walk slowly, and avoiding any eye contact, Rolf moved steadily around the table. Then he noticed that men and women were seated alternately.

As soon as he took his seat, he saw her. Slightly turned way from him, he glimpsed her profile. A gentle curve of forehead and sweet red lips. As he sat down, she turned to look at him. Bright blue eyes that settled on his, then demurely turned away. Throwing a glance at the silver stand, his heart flipped. *'Ulrika Hannsen'*. The feeling brought back days from his youth. Days he thought he had forgotten.

'Good evening, my name is Rolf Müller.'

'So I can see.' She replied with a gentle smile and a slight tilting of her head.

Rolf felt like an awkward schoolboy He caught the faintest trace of her perfume, then he took the initiative. 'Tonight is a very unusual night,' he said softly. 'It's as though we meet as friends but we've never been introduced. I must say that it gives me great pleasure to be here with you tonight.' He watched her face. She was not a beauty but the overall impression was one of attractiveness. She bent forward slightly to reply and Rolf saw the cleavage shadow of her breasts.

'I feel just the same way as you do and it's a great honour to be here.' A melodic voice with a trace of a well-covered Berlin accent. 'Where in Germany do you live?' The question was genuine and then she put a gloved hand to her face. 'Oh dear, we're not supposed to mention things like that, are we?'

Rolf smiled, 'I don't know what we're not supposed to talk about. Anyway, the matter of where we live can't be that important. .... I live in Berlin.'

'The same as me,' she replied, clapping gloved hands.

He was beginning to warm to her. 'Most of the time I live in Poland.'

She looked interested. 'Poland, I've never been there. What's it like?'

The champagne glass at his elbow was refilled and he took a sip. 'A miserable place. Cold in the winter and hot in the summer. Lots of coal mines and stinking chimneys.' For a moment, he realised he was talking about the chimneys at Auschwitz. And then he shivered; she noticed.

'What's the matter, Rolf? Are you unwell?' Her hand hovered near his.

'Not at all. I've been rather busy recently.'

Rolf snapped the starched napkin over his knees and broke his bread neatly onto the side plate. The quiet chatter resumed and he smiled at Ulrika. The pale-blue silk dress fitted her perfectly, showing off her snowy white shoulders and slim figure. The elbow-length blue gloves moulded her delicate arms. He watched her placing small spoonfuls of soup into her mouth and smiled. 'This is some place,' he said between mouthfuls. 'Do you know anything about it?'

She nodded. 'Yes, actually I do know a little. The castle used to belong to a very rich Jewish family. They were sent to work in the east and never returned.' Rolf's brain flickered with interest. 'It was taken over by the *Reich* and used as a rest home for officers. Don't you think they've made a wonderful job of restoring it?'

'How do you know all this?' asked Rolf, curiously, ignoring her question.

'I work in the office of a government department which occasionally deals with such appropriations.' Rolf nodded as the main course arrived. She continued, lowering her voice, 'Rolf, I hear the Jews go to the east to work for us. I don't hear of many coming back. At least not in Berlin.'

He took a deep breath and changed the subject 'This food is excellent. I do believe we're eating roast boar. I've not had it for years.'

'I used to eat a lot of it when I was girl.' The comment surprised him, from the moment he had met her, he thought of her as just a girl.

It was like a dinner party at any good country house. The guests were talking earnestly and the wine flowed. The ensemble played light Strauss to wild Wagner, music that suited the occasion. Bodies became closer and faces more earnest. The waiters scurried about in organised efficiency.

To Rolf , Auschwitz seemed a million miles away. No worries about his work and he realised that not once had he thought about his wife. Time flew by and he was drawn ever closer to her. Her décolletage made his heart race and he felt her silken thigh slide against his.

An evening that was cool with the gentlest hint of autumn. A marble paved terrace with an edging of stone balustrades. Beyond, in the darkness, stood the silhouettes of tall trees. Rolf's arm slipped easily around Ulrika's slender waist. He felt her warmth and that same fragrance he had noticed when he had first met her. The waltz came clearly through the high, open windows. Some of the couples made their way across the terrace and back into the main room. Others remained entwined, each lost in their duty for the Fatherland.

Rolf suddenly felt a stirring of excitement. His head began to spin and an unreal sense of exhilaration flowed through him. For a moment he stopped dancing and Ulrika looked up at him.

'Rolf, are you feeling all right?'

'Yes, I'm fine. Just a slight dizzy spell.' He held her closer and moved slowly. She seemed to accept his excuse and burrowed her head against his chest. As a doctor, he knew exactly what was happening to him. Somebody, somewhere, had given him a dose of stimulant. Smiling, he heard the beat of the music and let the drug take effect.

'Rolf,' and he noticed that her voice was husky, 'I really am a little tired. Perhaps we could sit for a while?'

He looked into her shining blue eyes and saw the dilated pupils. The drug lifted him again, because he realised she was also in its hold. They found a low sofa and sat down.

'Ulrika, let's leave here,' he whispered. She looked beautiful and his eyes kept glancing down between her breasts. Resting his hand gently on her thigh, he could feel her blood heat. Together they rose from the sofa and he led her gently back through the open windows and into the lobby. With the music fading away, they ascended the grand staircase. Walking quickly down the long carpeted corridor, they arrived at the door to his suite. They stopped and he turned to face her. It was unnecessary for them to speak. Rolf tightened his arm around her slim waist.

Rolf opened the door and was surprised; the room was softly lit by candles.

'Somebody's been busy,' said Ulrika, with sparkling eyes.

'Yes, indeed,' replied Rolf, watching her flow onto a low chaise-longue. He sat next to her, reaching for the bottle resting in the silver champagne bucket. With a pop, the cork flew across the room and he deftly caught the seminal gush in the fluted glasses.

Ulrika took a deep breath and he watched her breasts rise and fall. 'Rolf, I give you a toast.' Raising her glass, she announced, 'May the war soon be over!'

'May the war soon be over!' replied Rolf, smiling when he realised it was the first time for years he had given a toast without a *Führer* salute.

Her blue eyes looked at his face. 'When did you know we were going to meet here?'

'Only a week ago.'

'Yes, it was the same for me.' She sipped at the champagne and her blue eyes watched him. 'What do you think of this *Lebensborn* thing?'

It was a question that had been going through his mind and he dismissed it with a quick answer. 'When I see somebody as beautiful as you, I completely agree with it.' She laughed in an open-mouthed way and he saw a row of perfect white teeth.

'You know,' and she spoke in a husky whisper which he found so exciting, 'I've never done this sort of thing before. But, ... I think I'm enjoying it.' For a moment they laughed. 'It's strange,' she continued, 'I feel as though I've known you for such a long time.'

Rolf took it as a hint. 'I agree with you and I must say that whoever organises these things has got it absolutely right.' Again he felt the same surge and glanced at the empty bottle, knowing he had taken a second dose.

Without warning, he felt her lips on his. Soft, luscious, with a yearning that surprised him. Her tongue slid into his mouth and he tasted her warm sweetness. A mixture of champagne and something so femininely aphrodisiac. Rolf threw his arms around her shoulders and pulled her to him. There was a groan from deep within her and her body pressed against his. He felt it all. Her soft neck cradled in his hands; warm thighs alongside his; firm breasts pushing into his very heart and a heat that aroused them both.

Rolf had never felt such lust, it was deep and consuming. Whilst their mouths locked, he lowered his hand into the dark canyon that his eyes had watched all night. Silky smooth and hot to touch. His fingers found her nipple, as tender as a ripe grape. Their lips unlocked and they stared at each other, open-eyed and open-mouthed. As though in a panic, she tugged his clothes away from his body. Yanking the gown from her shoulders, he exposed a white-skinned heaven.

'Rolf,' she said huskily, 'please don't hurt me. I'm scared.'

What she said surprised and aroused him even more. He was the first to be naked. Kneeling at her side he stared down at her body. She was clad in a black silk basque. It contrasted sharply with her pure white skin. Long suspender straps led to slim legs encased in the sheerest black stockings. Her legs were locked together but they moved slightly and he heard the sexual rasp of silk against silk.

There was no time to think and he stood and straddled her, both legs reaching over the chaise-longue. His feet felt good on the cool pile of the carpet. She looked up at him and her legs opened wide like a flower. A flash picture of his wife's body flew across his eyes. With a smile of superb pleasure, he knew his manhood had risen to match the coursing desire that powered through him. Remembering Ulrika's words of caution, he slipped his hand between her thighs and so gently parted her, ready for penetration. She shouted, urging him on and in.

Rolf rode her like a hunter on a horse. So mad with passion, he thought it would be over quickly. She orgasmed twice before opening her blue eyes and staring at him. Panting hard, he wanted to fill her with his seed. Slippery with sweat, he withdrew and sat back on his haunches. Still he had not reached his climax.

'What is it, Rolf? …. What's the matter?' Sitting up, she pushed her hair back out of her eyes and lowered her slim legs off the chaise-longue.

Forcing himself to concentrate, Rolf watched her body uncoil itself towards him. 'I'm saving myself for later,' he said quietly, managing a smile.

She stood up and, staring down into his eyes, stretched out her arms and held him close. He felt himself being drawn off the chaise-longue and led across the floor.

The sheets were thrown back. She sat on the bed, unhooked the suspenders and slowly slipped off her stockings.

She rose and said, huskily, 'You do the rest.' There was a greedy smile on her face and she watched him like a cat with a mouse.

Rolf carefully unhooked the basque, the unfastening of each hook making his lust rise in ever-increasing intensity. The boning of the corset slipped loose and he caught tantalising glimpses of tiny blonde hairs on sleek skin. And then she was free. Shiny, fine hair flowing down over creamy shoulders. Turning to face him, he saw her breasts full with desire, each nipple standing proud. Her body sloping and curving downwards to the blonde triangle at the top of her white thighs. Ulrika's face shone with a sexual intensity. She spoke again, urgently, 'Do it now! Quickly, …… please quickly.' She pulled him over and they fell, already locked together, onto the sheets.

Rolf saw her writhing beneath him. He thrust deep within her and rutted like a stag. Then she mounted him and he watched her head thrown back in ecstasy as she used his body as if it was a sexual machine. He never reached his climax. Eventually, she was exhausted and flopped back onto the pillow. Feeling his utter frustration, she turned to face him and, in the glow of the bedside light, she used her hands to try and satisfy him; she did not succeed.

'Don't worry, my darling,' Ulrika said. 'We'll try again tomorrow.' And she fell into a deep, exhausted sleep.

Rolf tossed and turned, soaked in sweat and a rising anger. He slept in short bursts and was always half awoken by the same nightmare. Smoking chimneys and the pale faces of children and young women. He heard screams and smelt the acrid smoke of death. Since he had left Auschwitz the dreams had intensified.

'Wake up! Please, ... wake up!' In the inky darkness, he felt her presence at his side and jerked upright. 'Rolf, what's the matter with you?'

'Don't worry,' he mumbled, as his mind cleared. 'It was just a bad dream.' The night was cool and she had put the sheets back over his body.

'You were shouting something I couldn't understand.'

'What did I say?' Rolf asked urgently.

She moved at his side and he felt her warmth. 'You kept shouting, "Send in the crystals!" And, "They're dead now! Burn them!"' The bedside light clicked on and he was momentarily blinded. In a frightened way, she held the sheet to her throat. 'Rolf, what were you dreaming about?' There was a demanding note in her voice. Between them rose an awful silence.

Blonde tousled hair and the whiteness of her skin. On her face there was a look of real concern. There was something in her eyes that he trusted.

'Don't worry, Ulrika. It's only a dream.'

'No, it isn't,' she said. 'I know there's something terribly wrong.'

Maybe it was the final effects of the drug, or the look in her eyes. A curtain in his brain parted and then he told her everything. Everything that he had done at Auschwitz. The transports, selection, torture, the gassing, the killing, the experiments and the job he had done as a doctor, all for the *Führer*. It all came tumbling out in jerky, staccato sentences, making his brain buzz with unusual clarity. Things he had only told himself. Memories that chilled the soul.

It took an hour and she quietly listened to every word. Eventually, he stopped talking and closed his eyes. It was as though a huge shadow had partly lifted from his heart. He seemed to lie for an age and was nearly asleep. Her whisper made his eyes open.

'It can't be true. It's unbelievable.' He turned to glance at her face. She was staring at the ornate ceiling, her face pale with anger.

'It is. …. Every word.'

'I know we're at war but nobody could carry out such a …….. a ……. ,' she sought out words that did not exist and then her lips closed. She wiped a hand across her forehead. 'How do you do it? …… Why in God's name do you do such things?'

Rolf turned on his side and her body pulled away from him. He used his words carefully. 'I was following orders. I had no other choice. If I'd disobeyed, then I would've been gassed as well.'

She spoke in a voice stiff with anger. 'That would have been the best thing to happen.'

'You don't understand.'

'I don't want to understand!'

Rolf felt a frustration rising within him. 'It's all right you being angry but Germany has been doing this to people for ten years.'

'That's not an answer!'

'It is, because thousands of people have known about it and done nothing.'

'That's not possible!'

'Who do you think supplied the *Zyklon B*? Who made the gas ovens? Who took over the Jewish properties? Who drove the trains?' Rolf took a deep breath. 'You could smell the stench of Auschwitz from twenty kilometres away. Nobody ever complained. Nobody ever tried to stop it. You deal with the appropriation of Jewish property. That means you're part of it.'

Ulrika sat up in bed. The sheet fell to her waist. Eyes flashing, with a finger pointing into Rolf's face, she said angrily, 'If I'd known what sort of monster you were, then I would never have taken part in this stupid project.'

'I'm not to blame. I was a serving officer in the SS and there are thousands of others.'

'Yes, you're an officer and you've taken you're oath of allegiance to the *Führer*.' Drawing herself upright, she gazed down at him. 'But, ……. but you, Rolf Müller, you're a doctor.' She struggled for strength. 'God in heaven, …….. you're supposed to save people, not take part in their murder.'

Her simple logic hit him hard. She voiced the terrifying worries that had bothered him for so long. The SS conditioning still made him waver and he made another attempt to rationalise his confession. 'Yes I'm a doctor but the Jews and the other undesirable elements of the *Reich* must be eliminated. My Oath does not apply to the Jews. We need to cleanse ourselves of such people and be free to create our master race.'

The interruption was swift and deadly. 'Create!' Ulrika shouted, 'Create! How could you create anything? You can't even fuck a woman properly.' Rolf had no answer and a great blackness returned.

Packing his bag in the early light of dawn, he left the castle as soon as he could. Somehow, he felt better wearing his uniform. As he finally clicked closed the locks of his suitcase, he saw her stockings lying on the floor. Staring hard for a moment at the wisps of black silk, he leant over and picked them up. They slipped through his fingers with a single thread catching on a finger nail. He lifted a stocking to his nose and inhaled deeply. It was her smell, the fragrance of fading perfume and something special; the musky aroma of sex.

'Damn!' he cried aloud and pushed them into his pocket.

He picked up his bag and left the suite. The carpeted stairs cushioned his steps. In the lobby there was a half-asleep porter. He jumped to his feet and waited expectantly.

'A car, ... quickly!'

'Yes, sir.'

Rolf was angry with himself. The utter frustration of the night and the questioning of his way of life had struck deep into his soul.

A grinning Bruno Lippert faced him. Dressed in casual trousers and a shirt, a huge cigar dangled from his fingers. He was the last person Rolf wanted to meet. 'Morning, Rolf,' he said. 'Have a good time?' The grin widened. 'Yours looked good, mine was bloody fantastic. If this is working for the *Führer*, then he can give me as much work as he likes.' He waited for a response from Rolf; there was none. 'What's the matter, Doctor, couldn't you get a hard on?' Laughter bubbled out of him. He prodded Rolf in the chest. 'What the hell's that stuff they put in the champagne? Jesus, if they sold it, they'd make a fortune.'

The porter said quietly, 'Sir, your car is waiting,.' Rolf nodded, turned and walked to the car.

TWENTY

Richard reached for the thick file. The slightest whiff of old documents and dust reached his nostrils, it was a smell he would always associate with his father's past.

'My work was more and more connected with the impending trials for Nazi war criminals. The invasion of Europe seemed to happen very quickly. There was nothing to do and so I read reports and translated yet more documents. I used to sit in my small office with a typewriter and a stack of dictionaries and I wondered just how I was helping the war effort.

Some of the reports I read painted an awful picture of what was happening to the Jews. One special document really brought home to me the plight of my people. It was a long report sent from Switzerland. Apparently, two men had escaped from a concentration camp called Auschwitz in southern Poland. Rudolph Vrba's and Alfred Wetzler's thirty-three page report, "The Extermination Camps of Auschwitz and Birkenau in Upper Silesia", was hard to take in. It was all there, the transports; the Ramp at Birkenau; the gassings and the killings. The estimates of the dead were unbelievable. I must have read and re-read the document a dozen times. At times, I cried with disbelief. There were accounts of the gassing of the Dutch Jews and, it was then I knew what had happened to my family. I wrote an analysis on the Vrba-Wetzler Report and sent it to the Director of SOE. Two days later, with the words and the photographs still playing through my brain, I was summoned to the office downstairs, something that didn't happen very often. What the Director said surprised me even more. The Prime Minister had read my analysis and I was to meet him at number 10. It all happened very quickly.

When special things happen in your life you always remember them; this was special. Apart from a policeman at the famous black door, there was nobody else in Downing Street. Number 10 was just as I imagined it would be. A black and white tiled hall with doors leading off into secret places and it made me shiver with excitement. A man in a dark suit took our hats and my swagger stick. He informed us that the Prime Minister would meet me alone in the cabinet room. I felt the Director's hand on my shoulder and he just smiled and nodded.

Another room smaller than I imagined. Dominated by a table that was neither oval nor round. But my glimpse of the table was soon overtaken by another presence. Smaller than me, dressed in a morning suit with a gold chain looped across an ample stomach. He was standing with his back to an ornate marble fireplace. The hunch of his shoulders gave out a great sense of purpose. The watery blue eyes held mine and then I saw the cigar clenched between his lips. We looked at each other for a full thirty seconds. Then a podgy hand removed the cigar and the tip of a pink tongue licked the lips.

"Good morning, Lieutenant," said Winston Churchill, in that familiar growl.

"Good morning, sir," I heard myself saying and unsure what to do next. The cigar waved in the air, throwing out eddies of blue smoke. "Do sit down." I saw him smile and I was filled with confidence. He lowered himself into a broad leather chair. "Lieutenant, I know you're Dutch, so I'll give you a little history lesson." He sucked at the cigar and I remembered his fascination with history. "This room has been used by the British cabinet for over two hundred years. The table at which we sit is a peculiar shape." The rise and fall of those vowels thrilled me. "No matter where you sit, nobody has precedence." Another puff and he nodded that round head. "But I always sit here." And he tapped the table with his finger, sending flakes of ash spiralling down onto the polished surface. There was a pause as the Prime Minister gathered his thoughts. He saw the effect his words were having on me and the lopsided smile spread over his face. "I remember when I was a young lieutenant. Indeed, I was a war correspondent working for the 'London Times' in South Africa." Winston Churchill's eyes became dreamy for a moment and then, giving himself a mental shake, he reached onto the chair at his side. Lifting a file onto the table he began flicking through it. The gimlet eyes stared right into me. "Lieutenant Cohen, let us move on. I've read what you have written about the Vrba-Wetzler Report. I was most impressed with your clarity of thought. Now, ... I must ask you what you really believe?"

I hesitated, feeling the man's enormous presence. "Sir," I replied quietly, clearing my throat, "I believe the report to be entirely genuine. Awful though it is, I can draw no other conclusion." I paused for a moment, shifting in my chair.

"What about the gassing? Do you think it's practically possible for the Nazis to achieve such a thing?" The shoulders hunched again.

"Yes, sir, I've thought about it a great deal and, understanding the Nazis technical expertise, I think they can carry out what appears to be happening

at this place called Auschwitz. All the reports I've read, show that the Nazis, and particularly the SS, are more than capable of carrying out such horrifying and unbelievable acts of murder."

Churchill nodded and smoke came from his mouth like a dragon. "I brought you here this morning because there's a question that has been going through my mind for some time." I nodded, waiting for the question. "You're a young, Jewish man. A Dutch citizen and with German blood. I hear you're an excellent and highly efficient officer. But, tell me, if you believe these reports to be true, then why do thousands of your people climb into cattle wagons, travel for days in the most awful conditions and then walk into gas chambers and quietly die?" The cabinet room was totally silent and neither of us moved a muscle.

It was something I'd been thinking about since I'd read all of the reports. I phrased my answer carefully. "Sir, I think I can give you an answer in three parts. Firstly, there was a belief, or a need to believe, that Jews would really return home when they'd finished their labours in the east. Secondly, in the earlier years of the war, any thought that such an enormous crime could be committed, was out of the question. Thirdly, by sticking together, we've always believed somehow that we'd be able to save each other. It's happened in the past and, I think it's happening again today."

Churchill chewed on the stub of his cigar and looked at my face. He nodded slowly. "Good answers. I've asked the same question of Jewish leaders in London. They give similar reasons."

I didn't want to miss the opportunity of talking to this great man. "Sir, may I ask, " a frown crossed his face, "what you think the reasons are?"

He sat back in his chair and ground the cigar into a silver ashtray. "Well," he growled, "if what the report says is true, then the Nazis are committing the greatest crime the world has ever seen. But then, I believe the Hun is capable of anything. I think, in similar circumstances, anybody would probably do exactly as your people have done."

After the last word had rolled from his tongue, I knew, instinctively, the meeting was over and I rose to my feet. Winston Churchill's arms rested on the table and I noticed, with some slight amusement, that the cuffs of his black jacket were frayed at the edges. I don't think he saw my quick smile.

"Lieutenant Cohen," he said, softly, "thank you for your thoughts and comments on this matter. I want you to continue with your valuable work. Now the invasion of Europe is proceeding well you may find yourself leaving your office." He smiled and I was surprised at his knowledge of my personal life.

When I walked back into the spring sunshine, my head was whirling with the thought of the meeting. Glancing at my watch, I was surprised when I realised the meeting had lasted only fifteen minutes.

It took twenty-four hours for Winston Churchill's parting words to come true. I was quickly attached to the Dutch Government in exile with orders to continue to work as a legal liaison officer for Nazi war crimes.

I returned to Europe during the first week of September and I was able to set foot on Dutch soil for the first time for five years. I'd never faced war at first hand and now I saw it. It was the utter desolation that shocked me. I saw dead animals, dead people and refugees. In the end, you somehow became used to it.

It was arranged for me to meet a member of the Dutch Resistance and question him about the activities of the SS in his area. Hulst had been liberated some weeks previously and I was made very welcome. The Resistance man I was to meet came to the house where I was billeted. The meeting lasted two hours and I just listened. Taking careful notes, does not give the opportunity for discussion. What I heard, only backed-up what I'd read. What I saw was a different matter. The man led me out of the village for about two kilometres. A long country road leading to the Schelde estuary. After twenty minutes, during which we hardly spoke, he stopped at the side of the road. Deep parallel ditches and flat fields as far as the eye could see. On the ground lay a small bunch of dead flowers. The man bowed his head and prayed, I waited quietly. When he was ready, he told me the story of what had happened. Five weeks previously, somebody had blown up an ammunition dump located at the back of the school. The Germans had taken the first six people who'd watched the ensuing fire, marched them out of the village and then shot them in the back of the head, throwing their bodies into the bottom of the ditch. The youngest had been a girl of fourteen and the oldest a man of eighty-five. I cried with the man and then we walked back to the village. I never saw him again.

After Hulst, I had to report to the CO of the Princess Irene Brigade. This was a properly formed, brigade-strength army, composed almost completely of exiled Dutchmen. Meeting the CO was another exciting moment in my life. Prince Bernhard had married Princess Juliana before the war and, even though he was German, he was a great Dutch patriot. My orders were to remain with the Brigade and to question any prisoners about illegal activities. At the end of our brief meeting, the Prince handed me a letter. It was from the Director in London reminding me that I was to continue collecting information for future Nazi prosecutions. My biggest surprise came at the end of the letter. I'd been promoted to captain.'

The journey home was without incident and, after braking to a stop, he grabbed his brief-case and crunched his way up the drive. The children were home and he called out to them as he dropped his case and strode up the stairs. Taking a deep breath, Richard went to the bedroom and removed his clothes, ready for a shower. It was his routine to always change after work. The act of changing clothes seemed to relax him. Dressing in a grey polo shirt and matching cotton trousers, he slipped into comfortable shoes and walked back down the stairs.

David dashed back to the hall from the kitchen. 'Dad!' he shouted. 'There's a letter for you and it has Dutch stamps on it.' He placed the envelope into Richard's hand and watched his face.

Richard stared at the stamps for a moment and then made up his mind. With his finger, he ripped open the envelope.

'Read it out, ... please,' said David, frowning.

Another envelope fell out after the letter. Richard held it in his other hand as he read out the words.

'Phone/Fax 00 31 481 659238

Dear Mr Cooper,
I have heard that your father, Major Simon Cohen (or should I now say Cooper) has recently passed away. Please accept my sincerest condolences. Now that your Father has died, I have some very important information that concerns you and your family. It is about your father's past and mine. The documents and artefacts that you need to see must not leave my house. I have therefore made arrangements for you to visit me in one week's time. This will be convenient because it is half-term at your school. Your local office of Thomas Cook in Southport, Lancashire, will assist in making your travel arrangements. Naturally, I will pay all costs.
I shall be at my home all that particular week and perhaps you will be kind enough to let me know just when you will be arriving. I will then send to you my address and directions. You are very welcome to stay at my house or at the local hotel.

Yours sincerely,

Jan Bildt.'

'That's really weird,' said David. Rebecca heard them and came down from her bedroom.

'It certainly is,' said Richard softly, wandering what the hell it could all be about.

Friday night was always fish and chips night and he knew Jane would be home any minute. Putting the letter and the envelope on the kitchen table, he opened a bottle of Chardonnay.

Jane's car pulled up and they heard her opening the front door. The rich aroma of fish and chips came into the kitchen. 'Hello, everybody,' she shouted, walking down the hall. 'Put them in the oven. Quickly now, or else they'll be cold.' She stopped in the kitchen doorway and then sensed the atmosphere. 'What's the matter?'

'Dad's had a strange letter from Holland,' said David, excitedly.

Jane frowned with curiosity and picked up the letter. Turning the sheet of paper in her hands, she said, 'It's not word processed. Somebody's typed it. ....You can see the indentations on the back of the paper.'

The family watched Richard. Tapping the envelope and pursing his lips, he said quietly, 'I find this letter very interesting. Nobody has called my father Major since the end of the war. And how does this man know that my father died? How did he know my address?'

Jane glanced again at the letter. 'What does he mean by "important documents and information"?' She shook her head. 'I don't like this one little bit.'

'Dad, don't you think all this is a bit strange?' David put his hand on his father's shoulder. Richard nodded.

'Dad,' asked Rebecca, 'what's in the other envelope?'

He slit it open and pulled out a single sheet of paper. What he saw completely surprised him. 'I don't believe this,' he said. 'It's an old copy of my birth certificate.'

'What's a complete stranger in Holland doing with your birth certificate?' said Jane, shaking her head. 'How did he get hold of such a thing?'

'Questions, questions and I haven't got the faintest idea but I intend to find out,' replied Richard, placing the papers back into the envelope. Tapping it, he said firmly, 'Tomorrow, I'll go to Thomas Cooks and find out what's been arranged.' Jane remained silent, knowing that when her husband had made up his mind to do something, then there was no stopping him.

The meal ended quickly and the talk was of work and the weekend. Richard waited until they had stopped talking, then he picked up the envelope and left the kitchen. When he left, Jane quietly asked Rebecca and David to leave her alone. She wanted time to be with her husband. When Richard returned, several minutes later, Jane was tidying things away.

Raising her head as he came through the door, she frowned. 'Well?'

Richard shrugged his shoulders. 'David's right. It is strange. The phone number's an answering machine with a woman's voice in English telling me to try again later. Directory enquiries said the dialling code was a small village in the south east of Holland, called Kekerdom. It must be small, because my road maps don't show it.' Grabbing plates, he placed them into the dishwasher.

'Don't you think this is a stupid thing to do?' Jane said, sorting out cutlery. 'It's somebody you've never even hard of and yet, you're thinking of going off on what, at least, could be a wild goose chase and ....' She walked across the kitchen and held his arm. 'At the worst, it could be damned dangerous. The war's left many scars.'

Richard spoke in a voice edged with frustration. 'This man Bildt has mentioned my Father and my family. The two things that are closest to me. Do you think for one minute that if I don't go, then he'll leave me alone? .... Jane, if it was to do with your family, would you do the same as me?' Without realising it, he saw his fingers drumming on the table.

Jane knew all the signs. 'Of course I would,' she said indignantly. 'But first, I would want to talk to the man or at least send a fax back asking what the details are.'

Richard nodded. 'All right, ... I will. I'll ask him.' Grabbing the fax, he turned and strode out of the kitchen.

Jane smiled to herself, she knew her husband. Ten minutes later, Richard returned holding a piece of paper. Without a word, he thrust it into Jane's hand.

'Read it,' he said tersely.

She read out the words.

'Dear Mr Cooper,

Thank you for your fax. I am so glad that you are showing so much interest in my proposal. I must repeat that the information that I have in my possession cannot be sent in the post, neither can we discuss it on the phone. I must meet you personally, although I can add that your mother may be able to throw some light on what I know.

Yours sincerely,

Jan Bildt'

'Now, Jane,' he said softly with a slight smile. 'Do you now see why I have to go to meet this man?'

She did not answer.

TWENTY-ONE

At Auschwitz the waiting car was driven by a smiling Willi Hossler. Rolf expected the humorous comment and it came. 'Good morning, *Hauptsturmführer*, I bet you had a great time, you lucky bastard.' And then he saw Rolf's new decoration. 'I see they gave you the Iron Cross for devoted duty to the Fatherland.' Willi threw his case onto the back seat. 'All that lovely screwing, by order of the *Reichsführer*.' As he slipped the car into gear, he thumped Rolf on the shoulder. 'Come on, tell me all about it.'

Rolf hunched into the seat, his mouth gritty with tiredness 'It was good enough.' He managed a half-smile. 'And lots of excellent champagne.'

'But what was she like?' Willi's eyes shone. 'This perfect example of German womanhood? Was she blue-eyed and blonde-haired?'

'Yes to both questions and really I'm far too tired to talk about it. Maybe later.' He stared stonily ahead.

'I understand,' answered Willi and his face became more serious. 'Whilst you've been away things have been happening at Auschwitz. There're very strong rumours that we may have to evacuate.'

The comment brought Rolf out of his thoughts. 'Evacuate.' he grunted. 'Has it come to that?'

'Most certainly,' said Willi. 'On quiet days, when the wind is blowing from the east you can hear the Russian artillery.' Rolf shook his head.

The car bumped over the single rail track stretching under the towered entrance to Birkenau and continued towards the SS blocks. As they stepped out of the car, the familiar stench of the chimneys hit them..

Willi saw Rolf wrinkle his nose and said, 'Good to be back is it?'

Rolf made no comment. The Mess was in turmoil. Men rushing around trying to look unconcerned. Willi and Rolf took up their usual spot near the window.

'Well, Rolf,' said Willi, emptying his glass. 'In an hour, the *Kommandant* wants to speak to us. Bär hasn't done that before. So there's time for another drink.'

The last hour had made Rolf think. His secure world was beginning to crumble and he knew it. Berlin was in ruins and now his important work was seemingly at an end. In the back of his mind, he was worried about what the Allies would find when they arrived at Auschwitz.

'Willi,' he said, calming himself, 'is there anything else I need to know?' Willi scratched his chin. 'The rumours are getting stronger every day. A friend of mine in communications told me some of the concentration camps in the east have already closed down.'

Rolf, hungrily ate the sandwiches that arrived with the drinks. The mess began to fill up as the word spread of the Commandant's meeting.

'*Hauptsturmführer* Müller.' Rolf whirled round. '..... Do you mind if I sit with you?' Josef Mengele paused and settled himself into the chair. Mengele smiled. The brown, half-dead eyes gazed at Rolf and then at Willi. Willi nudged his friend. 'Here comes the *Kommandant*.' The mess hushed and there was a scraping of chairs as men rose to their feet.

Sturmbannführer Bär stepped onto a small platform that acted as a stage for mess functions. Heavily-built, he stood at ease, hands clasped behind his back. Bär had learnt his trade in all the right places. 1943 had seen him gain valuable experience at Auschwitz. After a spell in the concentration camp inspectorate, he returned to Auschwitz in May 1944, as *Kommandant* and Garrison Commander. Bär waited for the last noise to cease. Without moving his body, he spoke quietly, forcing his men to lean forward in their seats. A hand emerged from behind his back and he waved a finger like an admonishing schoolmaster.

'Gentlemen, I'm taking this opportunity to inform you about the future of Auschwitz.' There was a squeaking of chairs, as men turned to look at each other. 'It's quite simple, ... the camp will be evacuated. All prisoners will be marched to other camps within the *Reich*. The disposal of prisoners will continue for as long as possible. All staff will be evacuated in due course. Wait for your orders and do nothing until then.' Folding his arms, Bär nodded and his voice rose. 'Gentlemen, I'm proud of you. Since Auschwitz was opened in 1940, all of you, past and present, have done a wonderful job. Sometimes it's been difficult but we have won through and followed the orders of the *Führer* to the letter. Germany will never forget what you have done.' Jerking to attention, he threw up the salute. 'HEIL HITLER!' The returning shout echoed round the hall. Stepping down from the stage, he walked briskly out of the mess to his waiting car.

The moment the doors closed behind him, the mess erupted into chatter. The stewards again began serving drinks. 'That,' said Mengele, laying his hand on Rolf's shoulder, 'is the end of our medical research here at Auschwitz. I suggest you start to gather up all your notes and specimens and arrange for their transport back to Berlin.'

'I wouldn't bother,' replied Rolf, with an unusual show of indiscipline. 'There's nothing left of Berlin.' Mengele stiffened and rose from his chair.

'*Doktor* Müller,' he said, ignoring Rolf's comment. 'I must speak with you. Alone, if you please.' Rolf nodded and Mengele led him to a corner. He thought his flippancy had gone too far but Mengele was utterly charming. 'My dear Rolf, I'm worried about you.'

'Why?' replied Rolf, half knowing the reason.

Mengele reached out and touched his forefingers to Rolf's neck, making him jump. 'Ah yes as I thought. You may have a touch of jaundice.'

'Jaundice!' retorted Rolf. 'What are you talking about?'

'I've suspected it for several days,' said Mengele. 'You've looked a little yellow around the eyes. .... Have you been running a slight temperature?' His fingers probed the neck glands. Rolf flinched and nodded. 'I thought so. It's probably jaundice. Prescribe yourself something and rest. It'll soon go.' The smile of worry was genuine. 'I can't have my best doctor falling ill, can I?' He touched Rolf on the arm, smiled and walked away.

Rolf returned to the medical block with little heart. Menage's diagnosis had confirmed his own worries over the last few days. A glance in his small mirror on the wall showed the yellowing around his eyes and neck. Throwing his cap on the hook on the back of the door, he slipped his white coat over his tunic. There was a pile of reports on his desk awaiting his signature. Exact counts of gassings and totals of transports for the week, all had been left for him during his absence. Plucking his pen out of his breast pocket, he began to sign them, placing each document neatly in the out-tray. Rolf knew it was now a waste of time but the conditioning of routine was too strong.

'Prisoner!' he shouted.

Benjamin Blum had been waiting in his allotted place in the passage. Knocking gently, he opened the door and walked slowly towards Rolf's desk..

'Hurry up, damn you.'

'Yes, *Herr Hauptsturmführer.*'

'Take these reports to administration and be quick about it.' He saw Blum hesitate.

'What's the matter with you?' he said, testily.

Benjamin had never asked Müller a question before but, throwing his normal caution to the winds, he asked, politely, head down, '*Herr Hauptsturmführer*, is it true the camp is going to be evacuated?' He knew death could be quick.

Rolf paused and thought for a moment. Blum, even for a Jew, was a good worker. 'It's true,' he said, without looking up. Blum nodded and left the office.

The events of the last few days made Rolf stop and think. Looking around the room, he saw the cabinets full of notes and record cards. Mengele's words echoed through his head. Stepping away from the desk, he opened the first filing cabinet and glanced at the tightly packed files. Rolf shook his head, the cabinets represented two years of hard work. Behind him, the office door opened and Rolf whirled round, thinking Blum had entered without permission. Josef Mengele closed the door quietly behind him and, smoothing his hair back, waited for Rolf's reaction.

'Good afternoon again, *Doktor* Mengele.'

'Good afternoon. I hope you're remembering my advice.' He smiled. 'Another matter. I wanted to congratulate you on your Iron Cross. It was well deserved. Your research here has been very useful for the advancement of genetical science.' He touched his own row of medal ribbons. 'In August, I received my War Cross of Merit Second Class with Swords. I'm very proud that my work has been recognised by the *Reich* as I am sure you must be.'

Rolf nodded. As much as he disliked the man, he was still the chief physician of the whole Auschwitz-Birkenau complex.

Walking over to Rolf's desk, Mengele lowered himself into the chair. Nodding, he pushed some of the papers on the desk to one side. 'Over the past few weeks, I've been making arrangements for my safe passage away from this place. Whilst you were in Berlin,' Mengele allowed himself a smile. 'I completed the packing of my most important records. I strongly advise you to do the same.' Steepling his fingers, he stared at Rolf .

'I agree,' replied Rolf, realising that what Mengele was saying made good sense. 'In fact, just as you were coming into my room, I was thinking exactly the same thing.'

'Good, good, excellent. You know, I have come to respect your work. The job at the gas chambers is not an easy one. A weaker man would have given up a long time ago.' Rolf enjoyed the words of praise. 'Therefore, I've decided to help you to leave here. When you've selected what you wish to save, then let me know and I will have it put with my records.'

Rolf leant against the window-frame looking at the man behind his desk and he understood that if Mengele was leaving, then there was real trouble ahead. 'Thank you, *Doktor*. That's very kind of you. May I ask where the documents will be going to?'

'In two weeks, there'll be a train leaving here.' A smile flickered across the smooth face. 'The train will consist of thirty cattle wagons.' The smile changed, and for the first time, Rolf heard Mengele laugh. 'Now that's what I call a real coincidence. .... On board will be the remainder of the gold and precious metals from the crematoria. A thousand kilos in total. All jewels and art objects are ready to be transported to the *Reichsbank* in Berlin. There're two wagons specially detailed for my records and there's plenty of room for yours.'

'Thank you very much, *Doktor*. I'll see to my things tomorrow.'

Mengele rose from his chair and said, quietly, 'Tomorrow, Müller, may be too late.' Brushing past the desk, he left the office.

There was another knock at the door. 'Rolf that man never leaves you alone,' said Willi, walking into the office. 'What did he want this time?' Rolf explained. Willi stuck his hands deep in his trouser pockets and pursed his lips. 'Well, ... I don't know about that kind offer. I wouldn't trust that bastard as far as I could throw him. He could, of course, steal your reports and hard work and claim them for himself.'

Rolf nodded. 'Yes, ... I've thought of that. But it could be one way of getting out of here.'

'Don't worry about getting out of here,' retorted Willi. 'A group of us have been planning that eventuality for the last couple of months.' He saw his friend frown. 'Yes, Rolf, I know you're surprised. The writing's been on the wall for some time now and I think the war'll be over in the next six months, if not sooner.'

'I can't believe that,' said Rolf, frowning. 'The *Führer* will ....'

'The *Führer*, ... the *Führer*!' replied Willi, his voice rising, 'The *Führer* will do nothing. There're rumours he's gone mad.'

Rolf glared at his friend, eyes flashing. 'Now you're talking treason!'

Willi calmed. 'No, ... I'm talking survival.' He changed the subject. 'Another thing, Rolf. You don't look well. .... Come on, ... what's the matter?'

'It's a touch of jaundice,' replied Rolf, quietly. 'Probably some infection I've picked up from the medical block. Jaundice soon goes away. Some rest and good food will do it.'

'Neither rest nor good food are available in this cursed place,' said Willi, his voice showing genuine concern. 'I'm no doctor but jaundice can lead to hepatitis and that's a killer.'

'Thank you *Doktor* Hossler,' said Rolf, with some professional irritation. 'I can assure you that my diagnosis is correct.' The two men looked hard at each other. A knock at the door broke their mood.

'Who is it?' shouted Rolf.

Benjamin Blum quietly opened the door and waited, head down.

'What's the matter?' said Rolf, casting his anger with Willi onto the man in front of him.

'*Herr Hauptsturmführer*, I've been asked to bring you a message.' Benjamin stared at a fixed spot on the floor. He removed an envelope from the pocket of his blue and grey striped inmates suit and laid it on the table. Backing away, he flicked a glance at the two SS officers, and left the room.

Rolf remained motionless for a moment, staring at the envelope. With a quick motion, he snatched up the envelope and opened it.

'Well, Rolf? asked Willi.

'It's a message from Mengele saying he wants to see me in his experiments barrack.'

'Jesus, the man never lets go, does he?' Willi passed Rolf his peaked cap and together they left the room.

The rain lashed down, forming muddy rivers under Rolf's boots. It was early evening and already blackness had descended. He half-ran across the road to the first wooden block, dashed up the steps and into the building. Shaking water off his tunic, he slowed and knocked politely on the open door of the first room.

Mengele, stood legs apart with hands on hips. His white medical coat was spotless. 'Ah, Rolf. There's something I wanted you to see.' In the corner waited Benjamin Blum.

Three medical operating tables lay parallel to the wall, two higher than the third. Over the whole scene shone a single bright light. There were no windows. Mengele's voice took on a professional tone. 'This is an experiment I've been preparing for some time.' Rolf, not knowing what to expect, stood at ease and listened. The man always surprised him.

Picking up a small, steel baton from the table, Mengele carefully explained. 'It's all a matter of blood.' The baton pointed. 'On this table is Isaac. He's fifteen years old. On the other table is his twin brother, Simon. Over the last six months, they've had the best of food and the finest medical treatment in Auschwitz.' The boys stared in terror at each other and their pale feet stuck out like twigs from under the white smocks covering their small bodies. Thick leather straps held them down. From Isaac's thin left arm, a rubber tube hung over the side of the table and joined in a Y-shape to the other tube leading from Simon's right arm. Both boys had a tourniquet locked into position above their veins. Rolf's eyes followed the snake-like tube as it passed down along the floor to the third table. 'They have an intravenous connection from here,' the baton jabbed into Isaac's arm, 'and here.' The baton moved to Simon. 'The tube is then connected to this man.' Mengele paused, 'Prisoner Doctor, what's his number?'

'A42869, *Herr Hauptsturmführer*.'

'Yes, A42869.' Mengele glanced at the chart hanging from the bottom of the table. 'He's a Hungarian Jew I kept back from the last selection. A good specimen, strong fit and very virile. I've heard he fucks anything in sight.' The man's face was set, with broken teeth biting his bottom lip. Sunken eyes flickered from Mengele to the twins and then helplessly to Benjamin. The end of the tube went straight into his right arm leaving a bloody clot where the needle entered the vein. The straps held his body to the table like a fly caught in a web. The baton tapped on the man's forehead. 'A42869 has the same blood group as the twins.' The cold brown eyes fixed onto Rolf. 'I believe that by giving the twins' blood to A42869, it will make him capable of reproducing twins. When this transfusion is complete, he will be rested for twenty-four hours and then mated with Jewish women. I'm sure that in nine months, the women will give birth to twins.' Taking breath, his eyes rested again on Rolf. 'Your comments please, Doctor.'

What amazed Rolf was the idea that the experiment was going to take at least another nine months. After his earlier conversation with Mengele, he doubted it would last nine weeks and the Russians were only days away. At the same time, there was the strange fascination the man held over him. 'It's very interesting, Doktor Mengele' he replied respectfully. 'Very interesting. On what proof do you rest such an experiment?'

The room was totally silent and the scene was frozen as in a snapshot. One of the twins whimpered and Mengele was all concern. He strode to the side of the table and stroked Simon's forehead, nodding and smiling down at him. He turned to face Rolf and spoke quietly and with great deliberation. 'Many of the greatest scientific discoveries have been made by chance rather than by method. I've studied twins very closely and I'm the Reich's most important expert on every aspect of their lives. There are many theories about why women have twins. I've discounted all of them. The only logical explanation is in their blood. By transferring the blood from one to another, twins will be produced.'

'Yes but why not just mate the twin directly with the partner?'

'A good point, Müller. A good point. I've already tried that dozens of times. It doesn't work. No, …. this is the only logical way it can happen.' Mengele turned and nodded to Blum. 'Release the tourniquets. …. Careful, you idiot! It must be done simultaneously.' Blum with his back to Mengele, smiled grimly at the boys and, using both his hands, slipped the tourniquets. The veins pulsed with life as the blood flowed.

'Why do you want women to give birth to twins, Doktor?' said Rolf.

Dropping the baton to the table, Mengele clapped his hands. 'Now that's the question I hoped you would ask. It is all quite simple. In producing the genetical master race, I can get two for the price of one. Think of it man. For every one mating using *Lebensborn*, we can produce two children. If we transfuse male twins' blood into you, then you can mate and produce twin boys. .... It's perfectly feasible.' Five minutes passed and still the blood pulsed along the tubes. 'This could be the greatest discovery for the future of the *Reich*.'

Rolf was unsure what to say and the thought of being strapped to a table whilst Mengele pumped alien blood into him made him break into a cold sweat. And still the blood coursed.

'Why, Müller, just think what a service Isaac and Simon are doing for mankind.' Already the twins were semi-conscious and deathly pale. 'Blum, check A42869.'

Benjamin Blum knew what to do. He stood at the man's side and, away from Mengele's sight, he slipped a hypodermic syringe from out of his sleeve. Pretending to examine the arm, he quickly plunged the needle into the vein. There was no fluid in the syringe, only air. The effect was instantaneous. The inmate stiffened and, with a cry, pushed himself up against the heavy restraining straps. Blum stepped quickly away.

'An embolism, *Herr Doktor*,' he shouted. 'The connection was bad. The man is dead.' Without waiting for instructions, he strode towards the twins and, in a quick motion, pulled out the intravenous tubes and folded their arms; thus closing the veins.

Rolf knew exactly what Blum had just done and he surprised himself by saying nothing.

Mengele's voice rose to a scream, an unusual occurrence. 'Jesus Christ.' The words seemed strange coming from this man. 'You fucking idiot! You set up the transfusion. You've made the mistake!' Blum crouched, knowing he was a dead man. Mengele had shot people for less.

Rolf strode to A42869's side. Opening the eyelids and examining the intravenous tube, he turned to Mengele. '*Doktor* Mengele. This rubber tube is perished.' He pulled the needle out of the vein and passed it across the table. His fingers pushed the thin tube apart. 'Here, have a look for yourself.' Mengele grabbed it and scrutinised the tiny slit.

He was a transformed man and his temper subsided as rapidly as it has risen. 'Ah yes, Müller. I see what you mean.' The frozen smile slipped back onto his face. 'It was a simple error that could have happened in any experiment. The problem is that I'm given such poor equipment for work of such importance.' He walked towards the twins. It was then that Rolf saw Benjamin Blum staring at him. Their eyes locked and Rolf saw the slightest of nods and then Blum's eyes cast down to the floor. Rolf then knew why he had saved Prisoner Doctor Benjamin Blum, it was for his own survival.

'What a waste of good material,' muttered Mengele and he stooped, rubbing his forefinger into a pool of the twins' blood. Quickly, he made a red cross on their foreheads; the cross of death.

Rolf had had enough. '*Doktor*, thank you for letting me watch your experiment. I'm really tired and it's been a very long day.'

Mengele was already making meticulous notes in a small book and he waved him away. 'Yes, yes, of course, Rolf. Good night.'

Benjamin Blum opened the door for Rolf and again they glanced at each other.

TWENTY-TWO

'Richard,' said Jane, as they sat together before an open fire, 'this thing is becoming very involved and it worries me.' The flickering flames from the logs cast sharp shadows on the walls.

Richard, his arm draped over her shoulder, replied, 'I don't find it worrying. In fact, I find it very exciting.'

Jane searched for his hand. 'How the hell does somebody know so much about you? Is it connected with what your father says in his papers?'

Richard shrugged his shoulders. 'As far as I know there's only one copy of his notes.'

'How are they written?' asked Jane, stretching her long legs.

'It's a bit like a diary. Comments, notes and all manner of thoughts.'

Her eyes looked into his. 'Since Simon died, you've not really been with us.' Jane was worried about him. 'Is it really important for you to read every word?'

He took a deep breath and ran his hand through his hair. 'Yes, I'm afraid it is. I always knew I had a strange background, half Jewish and half German.' Richard chuckled, and he pulled her closer.

'I've been thinking,' said Jane. 'With your father's inheritance and our savings you could easily retire and do all the things you've wanted to do.'

'Such as?'

'You enjoy writing, and that publisher said he was interested in your work.'

'Would you retire from your job?' His voice altered slightly.

'Probably not. …. I mean, it's not as though you'd be home all day. In fact, you could be away from us more often than you are now.'

Richard touched her hair. 'Yes, I'd never thought of it like that. But I suspect that there's more on your mind than me just retiring.'

She stirred at his side and snuggled into his shoulder. 'Two of your headmaster friends have had heart attacks and I don't want you to be the next.'

'Jane, I'm as strong as a horse. Don't worry.'

They relaxed in each other's arms. The fire began to die down and Jane looked up at him. 'Will you really go and meet this man?'

'I've thought about it a lot over the past few days and I think I will.'

She hesitated. 'Would you like me to come with you?'
Richard thought for a moment. He knew Jane would ask, it was just like her. 'Thank you,' he said. 'For now, this is something I have to do alone.'
'OK, I thought you'd say that.' She rubbed her eyes. 'I'm really tired, I think I'll go to bed.'
Richard kissed her softly on the mouth feeling her warmth. 'Darling, I'll be up later.'
Standing near the couch, she shook her head and smiled. 'I bet you won't. You can't wait to get back to Simon's papers.'
Richard laughed, rose to his feet and, for a moment, held her close.
'See what you're missing?' she said quietly, her eyes bright in the flickering embers of the fire. With a lilt of the hips, she left the room and he heard her climbing the stairs.
'Shit,' Richard muttered, with a grin. He walked back to his study and reached for the file. Within a minute, he was totally immersed.

'I'd heard about the big push towards the Rhine bridges in Holland. It was on Sunday morning September 17, 1944, when I saw the air armada fly towards the Rhine. It was a sight I'll never forget. The whole sky was thick with aircraft, hundreds of them, mainly C-47 Dakotas. I jumped into my jeep with a driver and drove as hard as we could out of Eindhoven. Within five minutes, our way was blocked by a mass of tanks and troop carriers. They were part of "Operation Market-Garden", the Allied attack on the important bridges.

I was the tail-ender at the back of 30 Corps, a huge column of British troops following up towards the airborne landings near the bridges. I managed to thread my way past the armour and then I had to stop. The advance was along a road no wider than an English country lane and the Germans fought along every inch of the way. Everything happened very quickly and, within a week, I was on the outskirts of Nijmegen. It had once been a beautiful medieval town, now it was in ruins, the Americans and the British had bombed the heart out of it.'

Richard glanced at a newspaper cutting paper-clipped to the page. It was the announcement in The London Gazette of his father's promotion.

'I was heavily involved in checking prisoners of war. A fairly routine job. I was on the look out for Waffen-SS, particularly those involved with the bad treatment of civilians and Jews. The name Auschwitz kept being mentioned and I remembered the Vrba-Wetzler Report. I was sitting in my small office

*where I carried out interrogations and a knock came at the door. A civilian
waited, tallish, about my age. A drawn face with an English cigarette dangling
from his mouth. He didn't give his name, unusual because the Dutch are
very formal about names.*

"Excuse me," he said in Dutch, "are you kapitein *Cohen?" I nodded. He
walked past me and, uninvited, sat down in my chair which made me a little
angry.*

*"Are you Jewish?" I nodded again. "I've heard you've been making
enquiries about what's happened to the Jews and about what's happened to
your parents?" I just listened as he talked. "Most of the Dutch Jews are dead.
The Germans rounded them up and transported them to special camps in
the east. None have ever returned." The man smiled. A thin smile without
humour. He inhaled deeply on the cigarette. "They go to German death
camps." He saw the look on my face. "You just have to wait,* kapitein. *Only
when Friesland is liberated, will you find out what's really happened." Another
cigarette was stubbed out on the floor. "I have to tell you this. The Germans
are still transporting Jews out of Westerbork. If the Allies don't hurry up,
there'll be no Dutch Jews left."'*

Richard read more of his father's notes and soon the neat handwriting
began to blur. Yawning, he put the papers back into the file and laid it to
one side. Shivering with the midnight chill, he rose from his chair and
tapped his finger on the desk. 'Richard Cooper, what are you getting
yourself into?' He spoke in a whisper but the sound seemed to echo loudly
around his study. 'Bed for you, before you fall asleep on your feet.' Walking
across the carpeted floor and made his way to bed. Jane was asleep and
she murmured as he crept into the shower. Later sleep came quickly and
he had no dreams.

Southport was only twenty minutes away and the journey gave him
time to think. He turned into Lord Street, a grand but rather faded Victorian
road full of shops. A normal Thomas Cook travel agents. Bright travel
brochures everywhere. Pictures of brown girls and yellow beaches.

The girl in a red uniform gave the official smile. 'Good morning sir.
How can I help you?' Richard dropped into the chair and explained.

She turned to her screen and tapping the glass with a pen, said, 'Ye .. es,
I can see your name here. Yes, that's right. A thousand pounds has been
sent by bank transfer for your travel arrangements. It says, "To facilitate
travel for Mr Richard Cooper to the Netherlands."' She turned to look at
him.

'Thanks,' he said. 'I'll book later.'

'Of course, sir. Wait a minute.' She selected a small stack of brochures and handed them to him. 'These are all the ferries and there's also a list of flight times.' Richard left the shop and walked back towards his car. With a snap of his fingers, he remembered to call into Waterstones bookshop for maps.

The children were home and, he could hear music from their bedrooms. Walking through the house, he hung up his coat and flopped into the chair in his study. He was used to ferry journeys, the family often travelled abroad. The maps he carefully unfolded and sought out Kekerdom. He smiled when he found it, a small dot near the River Waal.

'Dad,' shouted Rebecca down the stairs. 'Mum's car's just coming up the drive.'

Glancing out of the window, he saw Jane closing the car door. Leaving the heap of brochures, on the table he went to meet her.

'Hello, Richard,' she said. Jane knew that look on his face. 'Come on, darling. Let's talk about it.'

The family gathered in the kitchen. Richard waited until they were settled. There was an expectant hush as he explained what had happened during the day.

'So you're going?' she said, with the same worry in her voice.

He nodded. 'I've been thinking about it all day and here's what I want to do. I'll leave on a Sunday and travel by car overnight on the ferry from Hull to Rotterdam.'

'That's nice, Dad,' said David, enviously.

Richard nodded. 'If this man wants to pay a thousand pounds for me to travel, then I'll travel the best way I can.'

David grinned. 'I suppose it's the state room and the free booze?'

'Yep. ..... The journey will give me time to read more of Simon's notes and get my brain together.' David opened his mouth.

Jane quietly interrupted, 'Let Dad explain. I want to know what's happening.'

Richard nodded. 'I'll go to Friesland and stay with Lottie Cohen. I'm sure she won't mind. It's been a long time since we met. Then I'll go south and meet this Jan Bildt.'

'And then?' said Jane, eyebrows raised.

Richard shrugged. 'I'll listen to what he has to say, decide what I'm going to do and then come home. I should be back in a couple of days.'

There was a silence. Rebecca's brown eyes opened wide. 'Dad, do you think you'll be all right? It still sounds dangerous.'

He paused and looked at Jane.

'Richard,' she said. 'I don't really want you to go on this trip.' Her face took on the straight look that he recognised as her most serious. 'But, I know it's important for you. I quite understand that you've got to find out what the connection is between this man and your father's life.'

'I agree,' said Rebecca.

'Me too,' added David.

'Thank you for the vote of confidence,' grinned Richard. 'It's important for me. The more I read Simon's notes, the more I want to find out what really happened. I'm sorry to worry you all but I have to go'

'Have you thought about telling your mother about your journey?' said Jane.

'Yes, I have,' he replied. 'When she comes round here on Friday night, I want to explain everything to her and see what she thinks. I have the feeling it may upset her. The last three weeks have been difficult and I have to be very careful what I say.'

'Dad,' said Rebecca, quietly, 'I think Grandma will want you to go.'

'I hope you're right,' said Richard, pulling at his ear lobe. For some inexplicable reason, Richard doubted his daughter's comment and he smiled to cover up his thoughts.

Jane felt the change of Richard's mood, and rose to her feet. 'Well, everything seems to be decided and that's that.' She still did not really want him to go.

Richard saw the concern on her face, hooked his arm around her slim waist and pulled her close. Her head nestled on his chest. Richard shivered and it was not just the chill of the onset of winter. The enormity of his journey made him think about his father and he turned to her. 'Darling, I need a few minutes to myself.'

She kissed him on the lips. 'I know. It's Simon's notes again.'

Switching on the light, he selected the large scale Michelin map of the Netherlands, and unfolded it flat onto the table. Scrutinising the bright colours, he moved his fingers backwards and forwards along the reference lines until he found the tiny dot. 'It's a small place.'

'What's a small place?' Jane's voice made him jump. She stood in the doorway with two half-full, balloon glasses of brandy. She had changed and was wearing a green silk dressing-gown that moulded itself to her figure. Brown hair tied back in a neat bun. 'I thought you might like me to join you and I bring your favourite tipple.'

He patted the chair at his side and said, quietly, 'You and the brandy are very welcome.' She joined him and stared at the map.

'The number of the phone is at this little place called Kekerdom,' he said quietly. 'It's about ten kilometres from Nijmegen. The village is right on the Waal, that's a tributary of the Rhine. It branches just near a small town called Millingen aan de Rijn very close on the border.' They both sipped their brandy and stared hard at the map.

She swirled the brandy glass in her hand. 'Have you any idea who this man Bildt might be?'

'Not really,' Richard replied. 'He could be anybody. Simon had an interesting and multi-faceted life.' He stopped and stared, pausing before continuing, 'Now there's a strange coincidence.'

'What's that, darling?'

Scratching his head, he again looked at the map, quickly circling a small area near Nijmegen. 'When I was last reading Simon's notes, he was explaining about meeting a man in Nijmegen near the German border.' And Richard went on to explain.

Jane sighed. 'In this story, there are far too many coincidences.'

Richard sat back in the chair and folded his arms. The glasses were empty and Jane put her hands into his. She spoke softly, wanting to be closer to him. There was a feeling within her that wanted to share his emotions and feelings. 'Richard, please read Simon's notes to me.'

He was surprised but reached for the file. Holding Jane's warm hand, he began to read, the mellow taste of brandy still in his mouth.

'The closer I got to the fatherland, the harder and more arrogant the Germans became, particularly the SS. I interrogated all day and half the night. Most of the men I talked to were junior ranks with little real information.

What really angered me was the utter desolation in my country. During the last year of the war, it had been stripped bare. There was starvation, desperation and, above all, a feeling of horror followed by deep anger. It took another six months for Holland to be liberated. During that time, I was called back to London twice and, on each occasion, I had to provide the Director with a summary of my reports.

I became more and more involved with the preparation for the impending trial of war criminals. The big push for war crimes came from the United States. The British wanted execution without trial. I was one of the officers told to look out for such people in Holland. My biggest problem was finding the evidence that would stand up in a court of law, or at least, a court of law I understood. Over and over again, I came up against 'orders are orders'. It's military law that a German soldier obeys orders from his superior.

Particularly if it is a 'Führerbehefehl', *an order from the Führer. I've never believed that to be legally correct. I believe a soldier only obeys an order that is lawful. All of this area called 'superior orders' became of great interest to me. I learnt by heart a quote and it went,* 'No international law of warfare is in existence which provides that a soldier who has committed a mean crime can escape punishment by pleading as his defence that he followed the commands of his superiors. This holds particularly true if those commands are contrary to all human ethics and opposed to the well-established international usage of warfare.' *Reichsminister* Goebbels *wrote those words in a German newspaper in May 1944. I still have the cutting and I quoted it frequently when I was interrogating SS prisoners.*

I was determined to find out what had happened to my family. Most of the Germans had surrendered and I managed to get four days leave complete with my jeep. I left on a bright sunny day, determined to make it to Friesland by the evening. The main roads were fairly clear and I was sure of a safe journey, or so I thought. The peaceful farming land I remembered so well was still there. Some villages I'd passed through showed no signs of the war. Others were shattered beyond belief. On the sight of my battered jeep and my Princess Irene Brigade uniform, I was made very welcome and sometimes it was difficult to get away from the hospitality. I never really thought of myself as a liberator but being in uniform and wearing the Dutch orange shoulder badges, meant that I had to act like one. I usually smiled, nodded and saluted. It was a real ego booster.

I had been advised to travel up the middle of Holland and not to go near Amsterdam. There were still pockets of German troops in the west. I kept to the east of the IJsselmeer lake and the main roads.

The road was completely deserted and I managed a reasonable speed. The jeep is a good little vehicle, it drives well, although mine had an annoying whine from the gearbox and a squeak in the steering. At times it seemed as though there was no war. Cows were grazing on spring green grass and the fresh shoots of corn sprouted in serried ranks from the fields. It was this feeling of rural tranquillity that lulled me into a false security. I shouted aloud when the first shots whistled and whined over my head.

I stamped on the brakes, ducked my head and wrenched the steering-wheel. I was out of the jeep in a flash and landed belly down in a ditch. With a thumping heart, I pushed myself upright and slowly raised my head above the road. A large black and white cow loomed over me and then friskily disappeared as another round ricocheted off the cobbled road. I waited a full minute and then tried again. This time there were no shots. I could hear the sound of an engine revving hard and then I saw it. A big, dirty brown German

BMW motor-bike. One man sat astride the pillion and the other crouched in the sidecar. A tripod-mounted machine-gun poked out from on top of the cowling.

I knew I had no more than a minute and I surprised myself by reacting very quickly. Running low across the road, I stopped near the jeep, grabbed the Sten and the clip of ammo, and dashed back to the ditch. Finding the safety-catch, I slipped it off, pulled back the cocking lever and waited. The ever-louder sound of the motor-bike slowed. I heard something shouted in German and that was it. With a terrific surge of adrenaline, I jumped up, saw the BMW, the two men, roughly pointed the Sten and let fly.

I'm not quite sure what happened because it all happened so quickly. I saw blood and I saw open-mouthed astonishment. There was the heavy chatter of their weapon. I was shouting some obscenity, I don't know what it was and I can't remember. Without thinking, I managed to remove the clip and jam in the spare and then I let loose with that one. Again the shattering cacophony of noise. I ended up shooting at the clouds as the recoil forced the snout of the weapon ever higher. And then it was over as quickly as it started.

They were both obviously dead. The driver lay slumped over the handle-bars with blood streaming from gaping chest wounds. The other man made me feel ill. The head was almost completely severed from its body by a series of bullet perforations across the neck. There was a complete and utter silence. Then I dropped the Sten and it fell with a clatter on to the cobbles; it was red hot. They say you can empty a Sten clip of thirty-six rounds of 9mm ammunition in eight seconds and reload in another ten, which meant that my little escapade was over in half a minute.

As I stared at them, I didn't know what to do. Suddenly a great surge of emotion welled up inside me. Tears streamed down my face and I tasted their saltiness. I broke the silence. "God in heaven," I cried. "What have I done?" These were the first men I'd ever killed. I wanted to know more about them. I started on the driver first. He wore the standard field-grey uniform of the Wehrmacht. *The heavy steel helmet had fallen off and then I realised that this so called man was really only a boy. A blonde-haired teenager with a fuzz of hair on his cheeks. Pale blue eyes stared up at mine. Wiping my tears with one hand, I used the other to gently close the boy's eyes. Trying unsuccessfully to avoid the blood, I slipped my hand into the pocket of his tunic. I found the wallet and flipped it open. There was a bright photograph of a middle-aged couple; obviously the parents. The man, upright in a neat wing collar. Light coloured hair and, with a quick downwards glance, his son had the same features. The woman smiling, well-dressed, legs primly crossed. It hit me again; I'd just killed their son.*

The other German was a bit older and I didn't have the stomach to examine him. He was too much of a bloody mess. Flopping to the ground, I attempted to get a grip on myself. I tried to wipe the blood off my gloves and eventually gave up and threw them into the sidecar. The shaking started in my legs and then spread all the way up my body. I suppose it was a sort of secondary shock.

I don't know how long I sat on the road and it was the sound of approaching vehicles that brought me round. The Sten was empty and, apart from my big Webley revolver, I had no other weapons. I tried to yank the mounted machine-gun round on its mounting but the field of fire was all wrong. With a grunt, I jumped back into my friendly ditch.

I was really worried because the sound increased in volume and it was the sound of tanks. One pistol against tanks! .... It was laughable. I need not have worried. A couple of minutes later, they appeared round a bend and I cheered with relief. It was a long column of Shermans. They stopped a hundred yards away and the long barrel of the lead tank suddenly erupted a spout of flame. I ducked and dropped into the deepest cranny of the ditch. The crack lashed at my ear drums and I almost saw the shell as it roared past me. It crashed into the cobbles further up the road sending shattered stones into the air. The tank ground on and pulled up near the jeep and I carefully rose up from my hiding place.

"Good morning, Capn'," drawled a deep, loud voice, "and what the hell are you doin' down there on this bright and sunny day?" Not a young man. Clipped moustache and bright green eyes.

He seemed a long way away. I was in my ditch and he was up there leaning out of the turret, grinning down at me. The steel sides of the tank seemed enormous. Blue smoke belched out of its rear and the whole bulk of the thing trembled and shook like a living beast.

I stepped out and, still holding my revolver, smiled back at up him.

"Did you do that, Capn'?" and a gloved hand waved at the motor-bike and the dead Germans. I nodded and stuffed the Webley back into its webbed holster. "Not bad, not bad at all," he said as he climbed out of the turret and stepped onto the steel carcass of his tank. On his arm, I saw the red maple leaf on a white background. "That was a helluva good job you did there." I blushed with pride. His hand reached out. "I'm Lieutenant-Colonel John Landell, Royal Canadian Dragoons."

I shook his hand and saluted him. "Captain Simon Cohen, Princess Irene Brigade. Thanks for coming along."

"No problem, Capn' Cohen. No problem." He straightened. "Now what do you want to do? Take a lift with us, or jump back into that jeep?"

'I'll take the jeep." And I thought of my name on the loan chit back in Nijmegen.

He began to climb back into the turret. Calling back over his shoulder, he said, "OK, that's fine. Just drive on and then pull over and let us pass." With a final heave, he dropped into the turret and clipped the headphones over his peaked cap. He gunned the tank engine and I leapt towards my jeep.

The jeep engine started first turn and, as I drove away, I glanced back. The Sherman drove straight over the BMW. The blonde head turned towards me and, as the heavy linked tread crushed the sidecar, the young German's hands seemed to rise in farewell, before he disappeared under the black underbelly of the tank.'

Richard stopped and yawned. Jane's eyes were closed. He closed the file and, without thinking, it dropped to the floor. Most of it remained together glued by age. A single sheet of heavy vellum separated and fell onto the carpet. Richard muttered something and reached down to pick it up.

'Jesus Christ,' he said, softly.

Jane sat up. 'What's the matter?'

'It's this document,' said Richard, staring. 'I can't believe it.'

'But, what is it? What's it all about?' There was a trace of tired frustration in her voice.

Richard said quietly, 'It's a certificate awarding my father the German Knights Cross with Oak Leaves. And it's signed by Adolf Hitler.' With his finger, Richard touched the embossed golden eagle holding the swastika in its claws.

Snatching it out of his trembling hands, Jane peered at the black Gothic lettering and Hitler's scrawling signature. 'Don't be silly,' she retorted. 'It can't be real.'

'It is, …. it must be. It says quite clearly, *"Major Simon Cohen"* and the date's *April 28, 1945*. That's the day before Hitler died. What the bloody hell was my father doing in Germany the day before Hitler committed suicide and why the hell did Hitler give him one of the highest decorations you could get?' They both stared at the certificate and then Richard carefully folded it, and placed it back in the file.

Turning to Jane, he said quietly, 'Let's go to bed.' She nodded and, without a word, they left the study.

Richard, as he undressed, said, 'When I visit Lottie Cohen, I want to hear her side of the story.'

'Do you think that's wise?'

'How else can I have some idea of what happened in Holland during the war? She may be the only person who can help me.'

Richard had never met Lottie. There had always been a distance between her and his father and Richard had never understood why. Whilst Jane showered, he carefully brushed his hair and waited for her to finish.

She emerged from the shower, drying herself with a fluffy towel. Richard watched her as he undressed and she saw his obvious interest and smiled.

'I think a cold shower may cool you down,' she said, mischievously.

'That I doubt,' replied Richard, pulling her close.

'Shower first, fun and games later.' Jane laughed and pushed him away.

He was out of the shower in five minutes flat. Jane lay in bed wearing a black, silk night-dress. Through her half closed green eyes, she watched him. As he slipped into bed at her side, he felt her warmth and need. Her personal fragrance intermingled with her perfume and it instantly aroused him.

She wanted him. Her worries increased her need for him. She wound her long legs around his and pulled him close. The silk night-dress slid up over her thighs as her mouth sought his. The feel and the sound of the rustling silk on her body made Richard gasp. She dominated him and pushed her body over his. It was pure sex and, as their mouths met, he devoured her tongue whilst his hand pushed her legs apart. Straddling his body, she reached down and pushed him into her, uttering a low moan as he thrust hard, over and over again.

'Bloody fantastic,' groaned Richard.

'Shut .... up,' she replied, grinding out the words as she moved over him.

It was Jane who awoke first and, as the early morning sunshine streamed through a crack in the curtains, she slipped out of bed and entered the shower. The sound of the running water made Richard stir and, with one eye open and without saying a word, he watched her begin the feminine process of dressing. Jane tossed a grin towards him and quietly left the bedroom closing the door behind her. He lay for five more minutes thinking and then the aroma of fresh coffee filtered up the stairs. It made him climb out of bed and, before he had finished his shower, there was a full cup waiting for him on his bedside table.

Downstairs, they started breakfast. He opened his mouth to speak and she leant forward and put her finger over his lips. Before they could say anything, David and Rebecca joined them.

'Morning all,' muttered David.

'Hi, Mum, Dad,' said Rebecca, kissing Richard on the cheek.

'Dad,' continued David, 'if you see that new Bon Jovi CD cheaper in Holland, can you buy it for me? I'll pay when you come back.'

'You haven't paid for the last CD I bought for you,' replied Richard, smiling and David shrugged.

'How long will you be away?' asked Rebecca.

Breakfast was not rushed and Richard took his time. 'I'll cross over on P & O North Sea Ferries next Sunday. Then on to Lottie's and then to see this man, Jan Bildt. I'll probably stay in Millingen and come home the following day.'

'Dad,' enquired Rebecca, very quietly, 'we're all very worried about you going on this trip.'

Richard recognised their concern. 'Listen all of you. There's no need to worry.'

TWENTY-THREE

Rolf slept for fourteen hours and his orderly had to wake him. Drawing the curtains open, he saw the clouds of oily black smoke belching from the chimneys. After quickly showering, he slipped on his tunic and left the block. It was a still, cold morning and he walked away from the barracks, across the road, past the *Kommandant's* house and under the gateway into Birkenau. His office in the medical block was quiet. Busying himself with paper work, he began to sort some of the records. When he was finished, he flopped into his chair and pulled open a drawer in the desk. A glass was unnecessary and he up-ended the brandy bottle to his mouth. Like drinking water, he gulped it down, wanting its effects to take over as quickly as possible. The work of the last few days and the brandy made him sleep. A gentle knocking at the door quickly woke him up. A blinding headache caused flashes across his eyes and his stomach heaved. Vomiting into the waste bin, he tried to regain his self-control, wiping sticky mucus off his tunic.

The door opened and Benjamin Blum stood quietly, head down. Rolf glanced up. 'Get out!' he hissed and his stomach gave one more heave. Blum remained in the doorway.

'*Doktor,*' said Benjamin softly. 'Thank you for saving my life. I know why you did it.' The door closed behind him.

Rolf flopped back onto his chair and, with a spinning head, he tried once again to reassert his self-control. Blum's comment finally sunk in. Slowly, he stood and began to walk up and down the small office. Gradually, his stomach settled and the room stopped moving. Another sharp knock at the door and, just as Rolf was about to shout something, it opened.

Willi's usual smile was missing. 'Christ, Rolf you look like shit.' He glanced at the half-empty bottle. 'Do you mind if I have one?'

'Help yourself,' Rolf muttered.

Willi tapped his finger on the desk. 'I see you're packing your records.'

Rolf looked up. 'I am and I'm worried because they're evidence that could be used against us.' He toyed with a silver paper-knife. 'Yes indeed, a week ago, for saying such things, I would've been reported to the *Kommandant* for treason against the *Reich.*'

'What *Reich*?' asked Willi, angrily, leaning over the desk. His face an unnatural red. 'Not this *Reich* we see here. I want the *Reich* that made us proud to be Germans. The Germany that after the depression gave us jobs and a sense of belonging.'

Rolf thought for a moment, using the paper-knife to carefully scrape pieces of dried vomit off his green tunic. 'I'm an SS officer,' he said. 'I've sworn my oath to the *Führer*. I've followed my orders to the letter and I'm proud that I have done so.'

Willi shook his head, 'You're proud to have followed your orders in,' he waved his arms towards the window, 'this shit hole? This abomination of mankind?'

'I follow orders. I do not make them.'

'Like hell you do. Every time you stood on the Ramp to make a selection, you give the order to kill.'

'I was passing on a more supreme order from the *Kommandant*, who in turn received that order from *Reichsführer* Himmler and down from the *Führer* himself.'

Willi laughed, smoothing a crease from his trousers. 'Semantics, my friend. Just semantics. When you stand in front of the Russians, I would be very careful what you say about orders from the *Führer*.' Rolf had no answer. 'And there's another point you need to think about. You've also taken the Hippocratic oath as well as the *Führer* oath. Only your conscience can sort out the conflict between those two. I'm not a doctor, so I've only one oath to worry about.' Willi watched his friend's eyes drop and they both stopped talking.

Through Rolf's mind went thoughts of his future and he knew, that eventually, somewhere, sometime, Benjamin Blum would be involved. The shrill whistle of a train echoed across the camp disturbing his thoughts. Rolf slowly rose and walked to the window. 'What's going on?' he said, turning to Willi. 'I thought the number of transports were down.'

Willi joined him at the window and replied, 'Our work today is not yet finished. Three more transports are due in.' Outside, the wind changed direction slightly and the smoke rolled across the camp and into the hospital. His nose wrinkled. 'It's the Jews from the family camp at Theresienstadt. We're processing them faster than ever. Orders say we must exterminate them as quickly as possible.' There came a gentle knock at the door.

'Come,' shouted Rolf, half-expecting Blum to be waiting. The door opened and a guard respectfully saluted.

'*Herr Hauptsturmführer*.' Rolf waited. '*Herr Doktor* Mengele sends his compliments and asks you to report to the Ramp.' Rolf nodded.

The long drawn-out screech of the train re-echoed across the camp. The locomotive slowly passed under the arch and Rolf waited in his usual place. Wearing a huge smile, Mengele saw him and strode along the Ramp.

'Good morning, Rolf. There's still plenty of work to do.' He rubbed his gloved hands together. 'This transport carries 1,789 from Theresienstadt. Families and plenty of twins.'

The train ground to a stop and the familiar routine of emptying, sorting and selection began. The trucks waited and the *Sonderkommando* rushed hither and thither pushing and dragging men, women and children into rows of five. At Auschwitz, it was always in fives. The white smoke of the locomotive intermingled with the black clouds of the crematorium. Waves of sound from the roaring of the crematoria chimneys hit the ears of the assembled crowds. The flames spurted into the sky, blotting out the early morning sun. The contents of the last transport burned with such a ferocious intensity that the sides of the furnace chimney cracked and the bronze lightning conductors bent to right angles with the heat. The purpose of Birkenau was known to everybody on the transport and there was an air of terrified acceptance. Mengele warmed to his task. With his thin conductor's baton, he elegantly waved his patients to the left and to the right.

The transport was a big one and it took over an hour to clear. Rolf watched Mengele select four sets of twins and three dwarfs for his experiments. For the first time, Rolf felt himself looking into the eyes of the Jews that passed before him. They stared back, some with horror, some with anger but all of them with heads held high. He knew he should have been at the crematoria carrying out his duties of death but, for some reason, on this particular day, he turned away. Josef Mengele followed him.

'*Hauptsturmführer* Müller,' he said loudly. 'There's a job I must ask you to help me with. Follow me, please.' Together they walked off the Ramp towards the medical block. It took them ten minutes and during that time Mengele's eyes were everywhere. Occasionally, he stopped and stared at some inmates. They moved heads down out of his way. Whistling a merry tune and immune to the living hell all around him, he beckoned Rolf to his side. 'Such a pity that we'll have to leave all this behind.' An inmate opened the door to the block and the roaring flames of the crematoria were dulled. Mengele glanced at his watch. 'You know, Rolf, that last transport has now gone up in smoke.' He folded his arms. 'We've made extermination so efficient that from selection to hot dust takes exactly eighteen minutes.' There was a sense of achievement in his voice. 'Now, that's what I call technological progress. It takes great brains and skill to create such perfection.' Rolf was unsure what to say. Mengele walked towards a door at the end of the small hallway. Producing a key on a long steel chain, he inserted the key in the door and turned the lock. The door was surprisingly heavy and, pushing it open, Mengele clicked the securing latch into place.

No windows, just strong lights lining the walls. Rows of grey metal filing cabinets stretching away into the distance. There was not a speck of dust in sight. Mengele paused for a moment, hands on hips, legs apart. He took a deep breath. 'These are the records of the prisoners over the last two years. Personal files, charge sheets and death certificates. Remember, my dear Rolf, not all that are selected, are recorded. Perhaps only sixty per cent.' Turning his brown eyes on to Rolf's face, he said quietly, 'Now, our job is to destroy them all.'

'I quite understand why *Doktor*,' said Rolf, without hesitation.

Mengele gave a wolfish smile. 'Yes, my dear Müller, my signature and yours and our colleagues are on all the death certificates. The Allies are already preparing a list of officials in the Nazi party who can be held responsible for places like Auschwitz. They're fools, because we've almost rid Europe of its greatest evil; the Jews. Another six months and our solution to the Jewish problem will be achieved.' He wagged a finger in Rolf's face. 'But we must protect ourselves. As I've already explained to you, my research records, even now, are being moved.' Wrapping a knuckle on the nearest cabinet, he gave his orders. 'Select a group of the most trusted guards and empty all the files into cardboard boxes. I've ordered two vehicles and a prison van to be here in five hours. When the transports are full, take them to Crematoria V and burn them. I want no inefficiency. Keep filling the vehicles and burning files until the filing cabinets are empty.'

'How long do you think it will take?' asked an astonished Rolf.

Mengele scratched his smooth chin. 'There are over a million records on this site and probably about the same at Auschwitz 1. I would say several days. But,' he emphasised, 'but, the records do not take priority over the exterminations.' Then he smiled again. 'The *Kommandant* wants every record to be destroyed. I will leave it to your judgement. Do what you think is right.' Walking out of the room, Mengele waited in the hallway and handed over the key to Rolf. Standing so close that Rolf could smell his heavy cologne, Mengele said in a whisper, 'In three days time there are also valuable goods leaving Auschwitz.' He tapped the side of his nose. 'Be ready to move as quickly as possible.' Rolf shivered as Mengele touched him on the shoulder. 'Remember my friend, under your armpit is tattooed your SS number. The only thing that you share with these Jewish swine is that tattoo. Thank God, there's no tattoo under my arm.'

There was an air of panic over the Auschwitz complex but still transports arrived daily. Rolf's routine had changed forever. As the camp emptied, his medical skills were no longer needed. He became used to being given different orders every day. He remembered one day in particular.

Again all officers were summoned to a briefing by the *Kommandant* in the officers' club. Bär stood at ease, waiting for his men to quieten. The large room was not full, many had already departed from Auschwitz, some officially and most, unofficially. Rolf waited near to Willi. Bär spoke quietly and the men craned forward to hear. 'Good morning, gentlemen,' he said briskly. 'Today is a sad say for all of us. The *Reichsführer* has ordered all crematoria to be dismantled or destroyed.' He paused, whilst a ripple of whispers passed round the room. 'Already the *Sonderkommando* have begun the task and it's expected to take at least a month. Preparations are being made to evacuate all personnel after Christmas.'

Willi whispered in Rolf's ear. 'Like hell, I'll be away long before then. The Russians are only weeks away.'

'There is much to do,' continued Bär. 'Guard escorts are needed for all inmates being evacuated. All records must be destroyed and the contents of the Canada warehouses will be transferred to the *Reich* within the next three weeks. *Hauptsturmführer* Mengele is in charge of all records and I ask you to co-operate fully with him.' Licking his lips with the tip of his pink tongue, he surveyed the men in front of him. 'Are there any questions?'

An older officer raised his hand and Bär nodded. '*Herr Sturmbannführer*, what happens to the Jews still arriving on the transports?'

'A good question. Yesterday was the last day for the operation of the crematoria. The *Reichsbahn* have been informed but, because of the advance of the Allied armies, there may be a delay in the information being received in the right places.' Bär waited for a moment and there were no further questions. There were no good byes and he quickly left the stage and walked out of the club.

'That's it,' said Willi softly. 'It's over.'

Rolf nodded his head. 'This time, I think you're right.' The club was beginning to clear and men glanced self-consciously at each other.

Willi clapped his hand on his friend's shoulder. 'Soon, it'll be every man for himself and I intend to make absolutely sure that this man is safe and sound. So I'll be off home as soon as I can volunteer for one of those escort duties.'

Rolf sighed. 'And where's home?'

'Emmerich on the beautiful Rhine. .... You know, north-west of Essen. Or what's left of it. What about you? Is it home to the loving wife in Berlin? Or off to that bit of stuff you met on *Lebensborn*?'

Willi's questions upset Rolf and he answered sharply, 'I'm not sure yet. .... I'll be here long after you've gone.'

'A bit upset aren't you?' said Willi. 'I'm bloody glad this thing is all over. I've always obeyed orders but I never really enjoyed this work and my wife'll make me more than welcome.'

Rolf grabbed Willi's arm and squeezed, making his friend wince. 'Willi, you're a damned fool. Don't you realise that when the war is over, and Germany has lost, that the Allies will be looking for people like us. We may not have been front-line troops but what we've done here in this place will not get their approval. They'll hunt us down like dogs. There'll be nowhere to hide and nobody to turn to for help.' Willi had never seen Rolf like this before. 'Willi, we've all got to try and help each other. You make jokes about my relationship with Mengele but he's the only person at Auschwitz who's offered me any help.' Rolf paused for moment and watched his brother officers leave the mess. 'Now, ... we must go back to work and organise the closure of our departments.'

The *Kommandant's* orders were obeyed to the letter. Within days, streams of inmates left the gates with *SS* escorts and *Kapos* shouting instructions. There were long dejected columns of people, many without footwear, most of them walking and struggling to move in the flimsiest of prison clothing. Even before they had stepped through the outer perimeter fence, some had died and their thin bodies were left to rot at the side of the path.

TWENTY-FOUR

They stood together in the hall and Jane watched his face. 'Listen, darling,' said Richard firmly, 'this is something I have to do and I have to do it alone. I know what I'm doing.' He gave her a reassuring grin. Jane's face was paler than usual and she smiled, running her fingers back through her long, brown hair. Richard held her very close and kissed her full on the mouth.

Pulling away from him, she whispered, 'Richard, do be careful.'

Gently, he placed his hand over her mouth. 'Stop worrying, you silly woman.' Then a final hug and she returned his kiss. Richard watched her leaving the house. The front door closed and she was gone.

He was alone. He checked and double checked his tickets and placed the note from Bildt into his pocket. Richard packed a set of casual clothes into a hard Samsonite case that had served him well for many a journey. His small shoulder bag held tickets and travel papers. Last of all, he slipped Simon's file into the bag.

It was time to inform the mysterious Jan Bildt about his travel arrangements. Richard found the note with the fax and stared at it again. Using his PC, he sent out the details of his journey and waited. The reply only took five minutes, almost as though Bildt was waiting for him. The message was simple.

'Dear Mr Cooper,
So nice to hear from you again. My address is "Grosse Bauernhof", Bimmen. After travelling through Kekerdom and Millingen aan de Rijn look out for a small church on the left. My house is directly opposite. The guest room is ready, although you may wish to use the local hotel in Millingen.
I very much look forward to meeting you.
Yours sincerely,

Jan Bildt.'

Richard read it twice, folded the fax and placed it in his case. Backing the green MGB out of the garage, he gave the long curving bonnet a quick polish and went back into the house. The MG GT was something that he had bought in a moment of nostalgia. He only used it for special occasions and this was one of those occasions.

Leaving home at 2 o'clock meant the journey to Hull was fairly quiet. Richard relaxed as the MG purred gently along in the fast lane and he revelled in its power. The M62 climbed away from Manchester up into the high Pennines. Switching on the CD player, Richard warmed to Ella Fitzgerald and found himself humming along to the haunting "*I'm beginning to see the light*". Through his mind flashed thoughts of his father and he kept glancing at the brown file sticking out of the bag on the passenger seat. Richard enjoyed the isolation of driving and pushed the car up to 100 miles an hour and watched a Range Rover trying to catch up with him. The mist vanished and a pale sun dried the road. The M1 crossing from north to south came and went and he steadily cruised towards his destination. The last fifty miles flew by and soon Richard was under the north tower of the Humber suspension bridge and slowing for the short distance into Hull and then quickly through to the docks in the east. He threaded the car across the early rush hour traffic and drove straight to the reception area at the King George V Dock.

The two massive P&O Ferries lay quietly berthed, their rear loading doors gaping open ready for the cargo of cars. Richard loved ferries and these were his favourites. Few cars waited and he was quickly through ticket formalities and edging the MG towards the loading ramp of the Rotterdam ship. Always worried about the low exhaust, he edged carefully over the lip of the ramp, ignoring the loading supervisor who became visibly angrier at this fussy Englishman. Richard laughed, cleared the ramp and parked behind a lorry. As he gathered his bag and stepped out of the car, a voice boomed down at him.

'Nice car, mate.' The driver climbed down from the cab of a lorry and jumped onto the steel deck. 'I used to have one of those.' He was dressed in blue overalls and big boots.

'Oh, really,' said Richard, politely.

The man touched the wing. 'The MGB is a smashing car. People say it's not a real sports car but I don't believe them.' A big man with a driver's physique, all fat and muscled forearms; probably in his early thirties.

Gathering together his bag and coat, Richard locked the car door. 'I agree with you but this MGB is a bit special.'

'Why is that?' The man leant forward with interest.

'A bigger engine than normal. Stage two tuning and up-rated suspension.'

The man whistled and then turned as the deck crew began to loop heavy securing chains around his trailer. 'Sorry, have to go.' And he dived under the trailer to help with the fastening down of the load.

Richard threw his small travel bag over his shoulder and dodged between the vehicles to the nearest lift. He had taken the best accommodation on board. A de-luxe, two berth cabin with a free drinks cabinet and plenty of room. Richard was not a cabin dweller, he preferred the interesting activity of the public areas. Just as he checked his hair in the mirror, there was a knock at the door.

The steward was polite. 'Good evening, sir. There's a message for you at the information desk.' Richard nodded and followed him down the corridor. He was surprised, when the door to the cabin next to his opened. It was the lorry driver, now dressed in smart casual clothes and wearing a beaming grin.

'We meet again.' He saw Richard's surprised glance and laughed as he locked the door. 'I always go first class. I own four lorries and, with the amount of travelling I do, I like to sleep in comfort.' Giving a huge wink, he added, 'Anyway, I claim it all back on tax.'

'It's all right for some,' replied Richard, beginning to warm to this larger than life character. Together, they walked along the corridor and the chatter was of engines, cars and lorries. At the information desk, they parted.

The young woman at the desk smiled as she handed over the envelope. Richard smiled back at her and strolled to a nearby chair. Opening the envelope, he pulled out the P & O North Sea Ferries headed note-paper and his heart skipped a beat. The message was in clear writing saying, "Have a safe journey." Apart from his family, the lorry driver was the only other person who knew he was on board and, even so, they had not exchanged names.

People came and went but Richard's thoughts were only on the message. Instinctively, he glanced at every person before him, desperately seeking a face that might be the writer of those words. The excitement of the journey had gone and there was the realisation that something strange was happening. Striding back to the desk, he waited patiently. Passengers booked cabins and collected keys.

'Excuse me,' he said.

She gave the official smile. 'Yes sir, can I help you?'

Showing her the slip of paper, Richard asked, 'Please, have you any idea who left this message for me?' Scrutinising the envelope and the slip, she shrugged and replied, 'It certainly came through this office. Please, wait a minute.' She disappeared into a back room returning after a few minutes, nodding. 'I've checked with the Purser. The message was left on the desk by a man. I'm sorry, we have no name or description.'

'Was it on this crossing?'

'Oh, yes. We've just changed crews so it must have been within the last hour.'

'Thank you,' said Richard, turning away from the desk. Tucking the envelope back into his pocket, he thought for a moment and decided he needed a strong drink.

The Moonlight Bar beckoned and, although nearly empty, the pianist was already playing. Richard slumped into a comfortable chair and signalled to the waiter. The brandy arrived double quick and he downed it in one gulp. Placing the glass back on the table, he tried to rationalise his position. Everything passed through his mind and the brandy took its effect.

'Ah, it's the MG man. Can I buy you a drink?' The lorry driver was all smiles.

Richard turned and inwardly groaned and then realised he probably needed some company, even if it was a stranger. Smiling politely, he replied, 'Yes, eh ...... thanks. I'd like another brandy.'

The man stuck out his hand and smiled. ' My pleasure, mate, and the name's Tom, Tom Ogden.'

Richard grinned, 'Mine's Richard, Richard Cooper.' And shook the hand. It was a firm grip, dry but warm and somehow reassuring. The waiter came across and Tom ordered.

'Ah, ah,' Tom commented, seeing Richard's empty glass, 'another brandy man. Is Remy Martin OK.'

Richard grinned. 'Great, Remy Martin is fine.'

The drinks arrived and Tom raised his glass. 'Cheers, have a safe journey.' He saw Richard stiffen. Frowning, he said, 'Are you all right? I mean, ... you look kind of worried.'

Richard shook himself, realising that Tom had boarded the ship at the same time as him and it made him think the worst. 'No, ... thanks, I'm fine, just something I've forgotten.'

Tom beamed. 'Funny you should say that. I always forget something.' Taking a good slug of the brandy, he wanted to talk. 'Tell me about the MG and that great engine.' They continued until the glasses were empty and Richard called the waiter over. 'No, no,' insisted Tom, 'this one's on me. Come on, the tax man'll pay.' Richard sighed and nodded.

Three brandies and his head was beginning to feel comfortably sleepy. There were two calls for dinner and it was Tom who rose from his seat.

Richard surprised himself. 'Shall we have dinner?' he said.

Tom hesitated and then a big friendly smile lit up his face. 'That's kind of you. Sure I will. Normally I sit with the other drivers but all they talk about is screwing and the price of diesel oil.' Leaving the bar, they walked down two decks to the restaurant.

The ship had left the dock and was edging its way towards the massive lock into which it precisely fitted. Within ten minutes, it cleared the gates and turned east towards the North Sea. A gentle swell caused Richard and his guest to pull their chairs a little closer to the table.

Tom looked hard at the man sitting opposite him. 'Tell me, Richard. Why are you making this journey?' The question was asked in a way that all travellers ask.

Richard forked a spoonful of beef into his mouth, chewed and swallowed it. 'I'm going to Holland to find out about my father.'

Tom leant forward and a frown crossed his face. 'Now that sounds really interesting. Would you like to tell me about it?'

For some inexplicable reason, Richard told him most of the story, only leaving out the part concerning Jan Bildt and the contact in England. Tom listened as he ate. The restaurant was nearly empty and the staff were clearing the tables. Pushing away the empty cheese plate, Tom took a deep breath. 'That's a helluva story. Jesus, I can understand why you're going to Holland.' Falling quiet for a moment, he rubbed his hand over a stubbly chin. 'Do you think you'll find out anything more about your father?'

'I sincerely hope so.'

'And what about this Jewish lady? What's her name, Lottie Cohen? Can she tell you any more than you already know?' What about .... ?'

Richard held up his hand. 'Hang on, hang on. One question at a time.'

'I'm sorry, really sorry, it's just so fascinating.'

'Lottie is eighty-six years old and, from what I remember, has all her faculties. I've not seen her for some years.'

'Where does she live?'

Before Richard could answer, a waiter hovered at the table and informed them that the restaurant was closing. 'Tom,' said Richard, 'let's go back to the bar and continue this discussion,' He pushed his chair back. 'That is, of course, if you're still interested?'

'Jesus, am I. Lead the way.'

The Moonlight Bar was almost empty. Most of the passengers were in the popular Europa Bar one deck down. They sat in the corner with the sound of the piano playing gently in the background.

'Just a coffee for me please, Richard. I'm driving in the morning.' The aroma of the hot coffee wafted over them and Richard tried to answer the questions.

'Lottie Cohen now lives in a small village called Oudemirdum. It's in Friesland in the north of the Netherlands.'

'I know Friesland,' said Tom with interest. 'I quite often drive through there when I collect a load of cheese.'

'That's Friesland. .... After the war, Lottie was the only surviving member of her family. All the other forty-two had been gassed in Auschwitz.'

'The bastards.'

'She's my father's niece. I hardly know her. She's still as bright as a button, although her eyesight is poor. I want to find out what happened at the end of the war and exactly what my father did.'

'So you're half-Dutch, half-German and Jewish?' Richard nodded. 'That's a difficult mixture.'

'You're right. But I'm a British citizen and a non-practising Jew.'

Tom shook his head and smiled. 'You're a very interesting man. I've travelled all over Europe but I've never met anybody like you.'

'Come on now, Tom. Europe's a big place.' He paused for a moment, wanting to change the subject. 'Let's hear about your life.'

He blushed. 'Not much really. I left school at 16. I hated school.'

'I'll let you into a secret,' smiled Richard. 'So did I.'

'I always loved driving. I drove anything on wheels. Then I started driving long distance and I ended up driving into Russia. I delivered televisions to Siberia and carpets to Moscow. I got fed up with all that, it was bloody dangerous. I then won a good amount on the Football Pools and I bought myself four new trucks and here I am.'

'And a family?' inquired Richard, quietly.

He shook his head. 'Nope, that didn't work out. The wife left me after I won the money and I've not seen her since. We didn't have children.'

The pianist closed the lid of the grand and nodded to his few remaining guests.

'I think that's a sign for sleep,' said Richard, yawning.

'That's fine by me,' added Tom and they rose from their seats.

In his cabin, Richard felt the gentle swell of the North Sea. Even though it was dark, through the window, he could see the white tops of the waves and the rise and fall of the bow. It was after midnight and, strangely, he was not tired. Richard knew what he had to do. The file lay on the other bed in his cabin and he yearned for Jane to be with him. Piling up the pillows, he switched on the bedside light and reached across for the file.

'Before I'd left my last night's camp, one of the Canadians had told me to head directly to Leeuwarden. And, hopefully, there I would discover precisely what had happened to my family.

I felt the warmth of the spring sunshine and somehow it made me more confident. The closer I got to Leeuwarden, the more Dutch flags I saw and I wondered how people had managed to keep them hidden for so long. There were cheering crowds. Twice I was stopped by men wearing blue boiler suits and with a red, white and blue arm band tied around their arms. They were well-armed with British Sten guns and captured Luger pistols. The first group stopped me.

"Kapitein, may we ask where you're going?" I was tempted to ask them just who the hell they were but then curiosity got the better of me.

"I'm kapitein Cohen of the Princess Irene Brigade. Who are you and why are you stopping members of the Allied forces?"

They looked at each other rather nervously and lowered their weapons. The taller one spoke first, "Sorry, kapitein but we have our orders to stop everybody in uniform." They saw the question on my face. "We're the new Dutch Interior Forces and we're just following orders.' He hesitated. "I'm sorry to ask this but did you say your name was Cohen?"

My heart beat a little faster. "Yes, why do you ask?" I could see their curiosity.

"Well, you see, ... it's a Jewish name. Are you Jewish?"

"Yes."

"We haven't seen many Jews for the last couple of years. Most of them have been transported to the east by the Nazis."

"And the others?"

Shrugging his shoulders, the man looked at me and answered carefully. "In hiding, you know, sort of hidden."

"Hidden?"

"Kapitein, for the last four years, people in Friesland and Holland have been hiding Jews and other people. We call them 'divers.'"

Now at last I had some idea as to what had been happening and I could hardly contain my excitement. "Where can I find out about these, 'divers'?" The men looked at each other.

"We never had a lot to do with the divers. We were always KP. You know, involved in active resistance. The divers were looked after by the LO. That was another organisation specially formed by the Church to help divers."

My heart was pounding away. "Come on, come on, where can I contact these people from the LO?"

"It's difficult to know, kapitein. Most of us have been hunted by the Nazis." His eyes narrowed and he stared into mine. "Can I ask you why you particularly want to contact the KP?"

I found it difficult to speak. The thought of possibly being close to discovering the fate of my parents and my family unnerved me. The sun shone even more brightly and I could feel the warmth through my uniform and I suddenly remembered I'd not had a bath for four days. Why I thought of such a thing at this particular moment, I'll never know and then I saw the two men staring at me and I answered their question. "It could be that my family are hidden somewhere in Friesland and I have to find them."

The smaller man nodded. "I understand, kapitein. Try looking in Hotel de Kroon. The LO and the KP use it as a meeting place. You can't miss it, it's just round the corner from the station." He raised the Sten gun in salute. 'Good luck. I hope you find your family." I returned their salutes and climbed back into my jeep.

Passing tanks and armoured columns, I made good time into Leeuwarden. The town was going mad and I managed to squeeze my way down streets packed with cheering people. National flags and streamers of orange, the colour of the Dutch royal house, fluttered everywhere. I found the station and I watched the scene before me. Three massive Shermans, engines running, were parked outside the main entrance. There was a straggling queue of people waiting near the ticket office and they all carried a single suitcase.

On the nearest platform, stood a row of cattle wagons, about twenty in all. A mixture of types, some with 'Deutsche Reichsbahn' stencilled on them. Made from heavy brown almost black wood. Chalk marks scratched over the sides and some with barbed wire over the tiny ventilation windows. A greasy locomotive waited, water dripping from corroded pistons and rust staining its steel sides. Some men in tattered German uniforms, women in torn clothes and crowds of people watching them. The heavy doors of the wagons slammed shut and the locomotive began to belch smoke and steam. Slowly the train moved away and the cheers became louder. A fat old woman at my side shouted an obscenity and it shocked me.

"What's going on here?" I said loudly.

Her lined face showed surprise. "It's the Nazis, they're leaving. And do you know?" I shook my head. "We're sending them to Westerbork. And they're paying for their tickets. First class prices for first class bastards." Her body shook with laughter and she wobbled away down the street.

A man stood watching me, there was something about him. An air of quiet authority and a great presence. The woman at his side stared in my *direction and a smile crossed her face. Older than me, very attractive, slim with a yellow skirt and a matching jumper that fitted her perfectly. Just behind them stood a girl, quite obviously their daughter. The man frowned curiously. For a moment, I thought he was going to speak to me and then they all turned and walked away.*

Away from the station, there were fewer people. I found Hotel de Kroon *very easily and I parked the jeep outside the front entrance. Walking into the lobby, I glanced around. A standard Dutch interior, dark brown wood, bright Persian rugs on the tables and faded paintings on the walls. Crowds of men and women sat in groups and the chatter was earnest and real. Blue cigar and cigarette smoke wreathed heads and faces. I stood near the reception desk and suddenly everybody stopped talking. All heads turned towards me and there was a shuffling of chairs on the wooden parquet floor. For a moment, I was unsure what to do. Towards me, walked a short man dressed in the hoteliers' uniform of dark jacket and striped trousers. Neat brown hair parted in the middle over a round head.*

He spoke with a Frisian accent. "Good morning, kapitein, *welcome to* Hotel de Kroon. *My name is Dirk Haan and I'm the owner of this wonderful establishment." A good handshake and the smile was genuine. He was a man I instinctively trusted.*

"Good morning mijnheer Haan," *I said. "Perhaps you could explain to me exactly what's happening round here?" Speaking my native Dutch was easy*

"It's wonderful," he replied, with a broad grin. "We've just been liberated and we intend to celebrate. These people," and he waved at the groups before him, "are the brave members of our Resistance groups." Cocking his head to one side, he asked, "And now, kapitein, *exactly what are you doing here? We don't very often see members of the illustrious Princess Irene Brigade in* Hotel de Kroon. …. *Do sit down." His grin was infectious and I dropped into a worn brocade chair.*

*"*Mijnheer Haan. *My name is Simon Cohen." At the mention of my name, I saw the grin vanish from his face and he leant forward over the table.*

"Did you say your name was Cohen?"

"Yes, why do you ask?"

Shrugging, he nodded and his eyes widened.

*I told him my story and slowly conversations stopped and people turned to listen. I kept my most despairing question until the end. "*Mijnheer Haan, *I must ask you this. Can you tell me what's happened to my family?"*

He shifted in his chair and his eyes saddened. "I can only tell you that the news is bad. I can't tell you just how bad. The Jews have had a terrible time." He glanced up at the slow ticking wall-clock. "In five minutes, a man'll be coming in here. He'll be able to tell you what's happened to your family." He rose and walked away.

My mind was whirling. I was conscious of glances and interested nods from the people in the hotel. For me, it was the end of a long journey. Several people came up and shook my hand. Most of them had lined, grey faces. I felt the suffering they must have gone through. Occasionally the door opened and people came and went. The roar of military vehicles passing the entrance echoed through the hotel.

I recognised them as soon as they walked through the doors and they saw me straight away. The woman smiled and I instinctively rose from my chair. Dirk Haan intercepted them and said something I couldn't hear. I saw a flicker of surprise pass over her face. They all crossed the lobby and Dirk spoke first.

"I would like to introduce Frank van de Meer and his wife Marieke. Also their daughter, Aukje." My judgement had been correct.

Frank van de Meer was tall with thick, brown, wavy hair and streaks of grey. The blue eyes looked gently into mine and his face crinkled into a smile. "Kapitein Cohen, I think our paths have already crossed." The handshake was cool and lingered slightly.

"Yes indeed," I replied. "Events at the station were not pleasant."

"We've met before the station," said Marieke van de Meer, quietly. "We last met you when you were, ... let me think now." Her blue eyes stared at the floor and then lifted. "Yes, ... when you were about eight years old. It was at the skutje sailing races in Sneek. You were there on holiday from Germany visiting with your family and we were with our friends, the de Bruin's. It was a beautiful summer and very special for us because our second child, Aukje was born."

Frank van de Meer snapped his fingers and laughed. "Now I remember. You fell in the lake and cried."

Searching my memory, the scene came as a flashback. "I can remember falling in the lake. But I'm sorry, I can't remember any faces." As I spoke, the double realisation came to me that these two people knew my family. They must have seen it on my face because Marieke van de Meer gently took my arm.

"Simon, let's go into Dirk's office." Her hand clasped mine and we went together.

A youngish man walked through the hotel door. He was in his early twenties and a mirror image of Frank. All I could do was stand and watch.

Marieke stared at the heavy bandaging around his shoulder and it stopped her dead. "What's the matter? What's happened?" She gently eased him into a low chair.

"Your son is a hero," laughed Dirk. "Please, all of you, have a seat," and he waved to a long couch. Then he introduced me. I walked across the office and reached down to shake hands. A bright young face but with heavy shadows under the eyes. "Hello, kapitein," he said. "I'm Harmen van de Meer." I smiled and sat down next to Aukje van de Meer.

"Two days ago," continued Dirk, "we took over the town. The SS tried to disguise themselves as soldiers of the Wehrmacht. Harmen here and three others got to SS headquarters just as Müller was about to leave on a bike." He laughed again, "Can you believe it, Haupsturmfuhrer Edvard Müller on a bike? Anyway, your son here rammed him with his bike and jumped on the bastard. Oh, sorry, Marieke." She smiled. "It was a good fight until Harmen swiped him across the face and laid him out cold. Harmen arrested him and took him to the prison in town."

Dirk glanced at me. "The Allies want Müller but we've refused to hand him over. We want our people to deal with him when the rest of the country is liberated. Meanwhile, he can rot in hell."

Harmen spoke quietly. "I went to see him last night. People want to shoot him but I don't."

I watched a family and its friends try to deal with problems that the Allied lawyers had argued about for three years.

"Why, son?" said Frank van de Meer, gently, with his eyes on Harmen's face. "Why don't you want to shoot him?"

"It's what you said sometime ago. 'Let's deal with them by the due process of law.' Our people need to see him dealt with properly and with justice."

I watched Frank smile and I knew that his son had learnt something from the war.

All the noises from the hotel had gone and it was time for me to ask the question. My throat was dry and I moistened it with a mouthful of the beer; it didn't help. "I have to ask you something that's very important to me." The van de Meers listened. "Do you know what's happened to my family?" My hand gripped the glass until it threatened to shatter.

Marieke leant over and gently held my hand. She glanced at her husband and he nodded. Her blue eyes stared hard into mine. "Simon, it grieves me to say this but, apart from Lottie Cohen, all your family have gone." Tears came to her eyes.

"Gone?" In a way, I'd half-expected her answer.

"Yes, gone. They were transported by the Nazis to the east and, as far we know, all people transported are killed."

"*Everybody?*"

She nodded and squeezed my hand even harder. For some time, I'd feared the worst but hearing it from the mouth of another human being made it true. My first feeling was of a tremendous anger and I drank the contents of the glass in one massive gulp. The next was of sadness and tears poured down my cheeks and I felt their hotness and tasted the salt. I managed to say, "When did it happen?"

"1944," answered Frank, "the whole family were transported to Westerbork and then on to the death camps."

"Then why is Lottie Cohen still alive?"

Dirk explained. "Frank and Marieke saved her life. She became a diver." I looked at him and he could see that I wanted to know the whole story. "Your family went to get on the transport from the railway station to Westerbork. Lottie was deliberately delayed by Marieke. As they walked with her to the station, Frank made sure that the road bridge over the canal was raised and Lottie missed the train. Lottie swore she would go on the next transport." He smiled grimly. "In those days, transports left every two weeks. Lottie fell ill and was taken into hospital. These two brave people," and he nodded towards Frank and Marieke, "went into the ward where Lottie was lying and smuggled her out from under the noses of the SS guards. They found a hiding place for her and she remained hidden until today. I'm sorry, Simon but there's no possibility that your family have survived."

I rose from my chair and walked to the window. Outside, people paraded up and down the streets and I watched them celebrate their liberation. Leeuwarden was not my town and it was somewhere that as a child, I'd only visited a few times but today it felt as though I'd found my past and discovered my future.

"Would you like to meet Lottie?" It was Frank who spoke and I felt his hand on my shoulder. I turned to face him. "She'll probably be coming into town later," he said, "and I know she'd like to see you."

I sat down heavily and thought for a moment. I heard myself saying, "Yes, I'd to meet her." She was a distant relative I'd met in my youth and only the faintest recollection came to my mind's eye. I shook my head. Out of a family of forty-two, she was my only living relative. Then my thoughts turned completely around and I said, "Thank you for saving Lottie."

"It was our pleasure," said Marieke, with her smile. "Your family will be in heaven now and resting with God." It was a simple statement and I'd never been a very religious man but I believed absolutely what she said.

Dirk chose the right moment and he stood up. "Now, look here all of you. It's time you went back to your home. I've contacted the man in your house and he's waiting for you." He saw Marieke's questioning face and my curiosity and then he explained. "Oh yes, you don't know, do you? The Town Mayor is a Major J.G. Robinson. He's Canadian and a really good man." He turned to look at me. "Kapitein Cohen, perhaps you ought to meet him." The look on his face told me that he understood the niceties of military etiquette. "He's based in the stadhuis. *It's a short walk from here. I really wouldn't advise going in your jeep at this time, the streets are rather full."*

I could see why he had been so closely involved with the Resistance. "Thank you, mijnheer Haan. *I'll walk." As they all sipped at their coffee, I stood up.*

Frank van de Meer spoke warmly. "Simon, we've enjoyed meeting you and you're very welcome to come to our home later. I'll make contact with Lottie and let you know when you can meet her."

They all shook hands and Marieke and Aukje kissed me on both cheeks. The first kiss from a woman since I'd left England.

I left the hotel and walked through the crowds. I saw little as my head spun with the thoughts of my family and what had happened to them. I should have felt anger but instead there was a burning desire to find the swines who'd done such a thing. My legal mind said justice but my heart said revenge.

The stadhuis *was busy. Uniforms everywhere; pale-faced civilians clutching sheaves of papers. Armed men guarding the entrance saluted me as I entered. The language was English but the accent was Canadian. I showed my identity card to a lieutenant and he waved me to a chair.*

"The Major shouldn't be long, Captain. He's just making sure there're no Germans left in the town."

"I thought they'd all gone?"

"Yea, you're right there. The only Germans round here are the ones in the prison. It's the collaborators we're worried about. The Dutch are taking revenge and their Resistance groups are trying to stop them. We're telling everybody that executing collaborators is murder and will be severely dealt with." With a huge grin, he added, "Personally, I can't blame them. If the bastards had treated me like that over five years, I'd shoot 'em on sight."

A door opened and the lieutenant rose from his seat. Framed in the doorway stood a man, standard uniform, khaki tunic, carefully creased trousers and shiny boots with neat gaiters. Four medals on his chest and Canadian shoulder flashes. Older than I'd expected, with a clipped military moustache and a calm face. A voice with a drawl edged with tiredness.

"Good day to you, Captain Cohen." Emphasising the 'h' in Cohen. "Do come in." I followed him through into a magnificent room. A room of the Dutch 'Golden Age'. Long nosed portraits of Frisian burghers with pale,

watery blue eyes. Two enormous chandeliers cast a warm yellow glow over the gleaming wooden floor. Overall was the aromatic fragrance of polish and candle wax.

The major saw me looking around. "Yea, a great place to have an office. All Town Mayors have the best accommodation." He turned to a rumbling coffee pot set on a small electric heater. "Coffee?"

"Please," I answered, unsure whether to sit down.

"I'm Major Robinson of the Royal Canadian Dragoons. Recently given the job of Town Mayor." A broad smile lit up his face. "Do sit down. We don't stand on ceremony here."

"Thank you, sir." I sat down on the biggest chair I could find.

Passing to me a delicate porcelain cup of steaming coffee, he sat down behind the desk and looked at me curiously. "What the hell is a Dutch officer of the Princess Irene Brigade doing here in Leeuwarden? I know for a fact that your nearest unit is at least a hundred kilometres away."

I explained and, this time, I missed nothing out. Whilst I was talking, he took a pipe from his tunic pocket and tapped it on the desk. Without filling it, he placed it in his mouth and sucked it contentedly.

"That's a remarkable story, Captain," he said. "And you've met Frank van de Meer?"

"Yes, sir."

"What do you think of him?"

Realising this man's position, I answered carefully. "I met the van de Meer family and I was very impressed with all of them. Frank van de Meer has a great inner strength that has carried all his family through terrible experiences. I think he must've worried the Germans. He was with another man called Dirk Haan."

Placing the pipe carefully on the table, Major Robinson shuffled some papers. "Dirk Haan and Frank van de Meer controlled most of the Resistance activities in Friesland. They're very brave men but bloody stubborn. They want to take over the administration and use their own police. I'm afraid that's only possible when all the Germans have been captured and collaborators have been arrested. Personally, I'll be glad when the locals can take over, I'm a soldier not a politician." Sucking heavily on his pipe, his green eyes looked into mine. "I hear you say that you're Jewish? ..... Jesus, they've had a bad time. Nothing but bad news. Are you sure there's only this one lady called Lottie Cohen left from your family?"

"As far as I can tell, sir."

His face softened. "I'm sorry that such a thing has happened to you." The major pursed his lips. "And now, what can I do for you?"

Remembering what Frank van de Meer had said, I made my request. "Sir, I'd like to interrogate Hauptsturmführer *Edvard Müller."*

The Major's face split into a grin and he threw his head back and laughed. A deep belly laugh that echoed around the ornate room. "Müller, Jesus Christ. ...... You want to talk with Müller? .... Captain, you're welcome to him." And then his face calmed. "He's a real bastard, believe me. He was in charge of the whole shooting match, arrest without trial; torture; murder but never by his own hand. He also signed the orders for the transports for the Jews to Westerbork and then on to the death camps." I was all ears. "God knows how many he's killed. He won't admit to anything and hasn't said a word since he was thrown in prison. It was only by sheer good luck that Müller was caught by young van de Meer." He leant over the table, percolator in hand. "More coffee?"

"No, thank you."

"He's in the civilian prison guarded by my men and the Resistance. I daren't leave him alone, or else they'd find some way of killing him." Filling his own cup, he sat back in the high chair and thought for a moment. "And you say that the Allies are going to charge the Nazis with war crimes?"

"Definitely, sir. Already a list has been drawn up and the charges are prepared."

"What will they be charged with?"

"Probably crimes against humanity."

Whistling quietly, he nodded. "I'll agree with that idea. And then you'll shoot the bastards?"

"Probably hang them."

"Much better. Only honourable men die by firing squad. Captain Cohen," he said. "I think you may be here a little longer than you think."

"Yes, Major, you're probably right." I felt the conversation was over and I rose from my seat. Placing my beret back on my head, I took one step backwards and saluted.'

With his eyes closing, Richard just managed to close the file and place it on the floor. Sleep came easily as the gentle rolling motion of the ship combined with the effects of the brandy and the good dinner. He dreamt of his father and the family and an imagined face of Jan Bildt floated in front of his eyes. White hair, a sharp face with a cold smile. Only the head and shoulders, no body or speech. The night went very quickly and the chimes of the ship's announcement system woke him up. Within a minute, he sat bolt upright with a blinding headache, for Richard, most unusual.

He groped for the light switch. The brightness made him blink. He forced himself to cross the cabin and turn on the shower. The water sluicing down his body woke him up and he revelled in the tingling needles of hot water. A quick shave and he pulled on a clean set of clothes.

The short walk along the corridor to the dining room centred his thoughts. All the time, he kept searching for the writer of the message. Several people wished him good morning and he nodded back to them. As he passed the pursers' office, the woman who had passed on the message from the previous night beckoned him to the desk.

'Good morning Mr Cooper. I wanted to let you know that the man who left the message just asked after you.'

Richard felt the hairs rising on his neck. 'Are you sure?'

'Oh yes. I recognised him straight away.'

'What exactly did he say?'

'It was about five minutes ago and he said, "Give Mr Cooper my kind regards."'

Richard had lost his appetite. 'What did he look like?'

'Oldish, late sixties early seventies, I'd say. Thick, grey hair. A blue jacket and trousers and, oh yes, ... he was wearing a polo necked pullover. By the sound of his voice, I'd think he was German or east European.'

'Thank you very much. If you see him again could you find out his name?' She nodded. Richard slowly made his way for breakfast carefully watching everybody that came near him. He ate little as all the time his brain worked overtime trying to work out who was watching him.

The ferry crept along the Hook of Holland breakwater and turned right into the Europort dock. Richard stood on the deck and watched the ferry manoeuvre into its berth. Within ten minutes of docking, the rear cargo doors were already grinding open. With the request for drivers to return to their vehicles ringing in his ears, he made his way to the car deck. Opening the rear hatch of the MG, he threw his bag onto the rear seat. The voice surprised him.

'Do you know you've got a puncture?' said Tom, standing at the side of the MG. 'Front nearside.'

Richard dashed along the side of the car and, sure enough, the tyre was flat to its rim. 'Shit!' he shouted, loud enough for other drivers to turn round and stare.

Tom grinned. 'I saw it as soon as I came to my cab. Don't worry. I'll get my jack out and we'll change it in five minutes.' As he spoke, he was already crawling under the trailer. Richard lifted up the rear access hatch for the spare. Quickly, Tom had the jack under the front suspension and the MG was lifted off the deck. Richard slipped on old gloves, yanked out the wheel and rolled it forward. The wheel was quickly changed and pushed back into the boot.

'I know a small garage in Brielle just near the ferry,' said Tom. 'Go into the town and it's behind the main street. They'll fix it for you.'

'That's great. Tom, thanks a lot.' Just as Richard was about to secure the wheel, he saw that the dust cap was missing. Now that worried him, he was a stickler for dust caps. After securing the wheel, he walked back to the front of the car. Dropping to his hands and knees, he soon found what he was looking for and dropped the valve cap into his pocket.

Climbing back into his cab, Tom called down, 'We'd better move. Most of the other cars have already gone. Just follow me off the ship. Brielle's only fifteen minutes away. Nice to have met you, Richard. .... Best of British.'

Normally Richard never failed to enjoy the thrill of arriving in Europe but this time, he was so apprehensive that he drove off the ship without a second thought. No customs, no immigration and straight onto the main road.

Brielle was somewhere he had always intended to visit. At eight in the morning, the town was quiet and few people were about. It was one of those bright September mornings with the waiting chill of the winter and a sharp sun casting long, clear shadows.

Richard found the small garage tucked away behind the narrow main street. He drove the MG through the big doors. Stepping out of the car, he explained his problem to the man waiting at his side. The man pulled out the spare wheel. Smiling, he said something in Dutch and connected the airline to inflate the tyre. Dropping the wheel into a trough of water they watched for the tell-tale trail of bubbles; nothing.

'Sorry, *mijnheer*,' he said in precise English. 'You don't have a puncture. Not even a slow.' Shaking his head, he added, 'You can't trust anybody these days. Some hooligan on the ferry must've let your tyre down.' Richard said not a word but he knew that the mystery man on the ferry had been responsible for trying to stop Richard identifying him and his car. Shaking his head, he kept asking himself the question, why?

'Thank you. How much do I owe you?'

'No charge,' the man replied. 'Please come again, I'm always open.' Richard slipped his hand in his pocket, took out the valve cap and screwed it onto the spare tyre. Politely, he said his thanks and reversed the MG out of the garage.

Something made him glance to his left. A small, two-storey, grey building with boarded-up windows. Richard stopped the car and stepped out onto the cobbled street. A traditional Dutch gabled roof. As wide as a house and flush with the narrow pavement. Staring at the front face of the house, he saw what had caught his eye. On a small, stone plaque were inscribed the simple words,

> *'The first Jews settled in Brielle around 1700.*
> *In 1871, in this place, a synagogue, ritual baths*
> *and a school were built. In 1942 all members of the*
> *families Cohen, Gazan, Katan and Philipse were taken*
> *to concentration camps and the synagogue was closed.*
> *Of the 21 people taken, none ever returned. Their names are*
> *remembered in a monument in the Brielle Town Hall.'*

It hit Richard hard and tears streamed down his face. Standing proud of the grey plaster, the faint outlines of the original stone window frames could still be seen. With his finger tips, Richard touched the carved hollows of the words. 'So many people, so many families,' he said aloud. Turning, he walked to the side of the building. Following the dusty path, he found the rear of the synagogue. Piles of old timber, decaying brickwork and a door sealed with a rusty padlock. There was nothing left of the people who once worshipped here.

Richard drove on, trying to settle his confused thoughts

TWENTY-FIVE

The winter worsened as did conditions in the camp. The crematoria had stopped but the killings continued. Late one afternoon, Willi Hossler called out the familiar orders.

'*Alle antreten, alle antreten!*'

Groups of *Sonderkommando* came out of their barracks and made their way to the crematorium courtyard. Willi, with a group of guards faced them. Pulling up the high fur collar of his warm greatcoat, he stamped his shiny jackboots on the hard ground to try and keep his feet warm. He nodded to *Oberscharführer* Moll, a man well known for his brutality.

'Swines!' were Moll's first words, rubbing heavily-gloved hands together. 'This morning you've something to do which will keep you warm all fuckin' day.'

Benjamin Blum knew all about Moll's sadistic sense of humour and yet he was curious, everybody knew the crematoria had stopped their deadly work. The men looked at each other and feared the worst.

'All of you, follow me!' Turning on his heel, Moll walked away from the freezing earth. The men needed no second bidding and they trudged after him and the other guards. Moll stopped at the barbed-wire perimeter fence and signalled the guard to lift the barrier.

"Canada II" was much bigger than "Canada I". 30 barracks in neat rows with secure doors. Benjamin had never entered this area and he was nervous, expecting death or at least to witness it. Moll stopped and shouted to the twenty or so inmates in front of him.

'Here we store and use what filth you've given us.' His sharp laughter echoed around the wooden buildings. 'Today you can help us to dispose of some of your unwanted shit.' Pointing to Benjamin Blum with the handle of his whip, he shouted. 'You, you fuckin' scum! .... Yes, you! Open the door of that fuckin' barrack.' And he threw a bunch of keys at Benjamin's feet. Picking them up and keeping his head down, he ran to the heavy doors. The lock turned easily and he pulled open the door.

It was dark inside and for a moment he froze. He heard Moll hissing in his ear, 'The light, you swine. The fuckin' light!' Benjamin reached to his left and found the switch. Pulling it down, the inner floodlights came on with a dazzling brightness. The men behind him gasped with shock and astonishment. Benjamin shivered and bit his lip to avoid crying out.

Everything in the wooden building stood out in pin-sharp detail. A stacked and organised warehouse. Everything was neatly labelled and the racks were piled high to the roof. The other inmates gathered around him with open mouths and staring eyes. Moll watched them, tapping his jackbooted foot on the floor.

'All right, swine!' He screamed. 'Take everything off the shelves! Carry it outside and fuckin' burn it!' Reaching into his greatcoat pocket, he pulled out a gold cigarette lighter and threw it to the earthen floor.

Benjamin jumped and reached down for the lighter. The man nearest to him, grabbed the first wooden box and dragged it towards the door. It contained photographs. Black and white, sepia, yellowing. Large posed portraits; family groups; smiling babies; holiday snapshots; some in cardboard frames, most of them loose. Old Jewish patricians with curling black locks. Jewish mothers with arms round posed children. Pretty girls. Charming children. Weddings, parties, bar mitzvahs, meals together. Smiling faces, stern faces. That one box contained cameos of all Jewish life. It was one of at least a hundred such boxes and it took two weak inmates to pull the heavy box to the door. And then there were Jewish bibles. Heavy Torah scripts. The gold and silver ends of the heavy parchment scrolls had long since been torn free. Another hundred boxes bulging with ancient scrolls and papers.

'Burn the fuckin' lot!' screamed Moll, using the lash of his whip to urge the men on.

Benjamin ducked his head and darted behind the first rack of shelving. Peering into the boxes, his heart and his eyes were heavy. A crate of decorations and medals, inscribed with every language of Europe. Ten boxes full of passports. He picked one up and stared at the dark blue cover. "*Koninkrijk de Nederlanden-Paspoort.*" Flicking it open showed the pretty face of a young girl. Black hair and a stern chin. Her eyes stared right back at his. "*COHEN, Rebecca. Date of Birth-11th June 1929. Place of abode-Leeuwarden, Province of Friesland. Distinguishing marks-none.*" He flicked over the pages, one or two immigration controls stamps. One said, "*Deutschland-Sept 1st '36*" and Benjamin thought to himself that Rebecca Cohen, whoever she was, had not received a stamp in her passport for entering Auschwitz-Birkenau. Raising the passport to his lips, he gently kissed the photograph and whispered a short prayer. He dropped it back on top of the others. For a few precious moments, he was alone with the personal and precious things of everyday family life. Walking further down the passageway, he stopped between the racks and peered into boxes.

Marriage certificates, thousands of them. Birth documents, prayer books, holy objects. A massive box full of wooden crucifixes. Diplomas, degrees, bills, receipts, letters and the ephemera of everyday life. It was all here and more. Benjamin Blum had forgotten how to cry. Moll's screaming voice made him turn and quickly walk back the way he had come.

Outside the barrack, the heap of photographs and the impedimenta of Jewish life rose higher and higher as men upended box after box.

'Where's the bastard with the fuckin' lighter?' screamed Moll.

Still clutching it in his hand, Benjamin crouched below the mound of fluttering and slithering pictures. 'Light it, swine!' shouted Moll. 'Light it!' Fumbling with the small wheel, he tried to make it turn. The whip lashed across his back and he felt its thong cut through the thin material of his clothing. Eventually, the wheel turned and he caught a whiff of the petrol and then the spark of the flint made the wick light. Shielding it with his hand, he reached forward on his knees and held it to the nearest photograph. It was a picture of an old woman with a stern face and, as the flame began to flicker, he saw her frown as she burnt. Within a minute, the chemicals on the photographs caused the pile to burn intensely. Benjamin crawled away. Most of the inmates stared at the fire, watching a hundred years of history go up in smoke. They managed to burn the contents of a few crates and boxes and then Moll's interest turned elsewhere.

Benjamin walked in a daze back to his barrack. As a prisoner doctor, he had certain privileges and the main one was to survive longer than the rest of the *Sonderkommando*. He knew the group of men that had helped to burn their history would now die.

Willi Hossler watched the flames on the paper pyre roar into the sky. Walking away from the men, he made his way back towards the crematoria. A peculiar sight met his eyes and he paused to examine his own men. They had heavy steel containers strapped to their backs and they waited in a row until he walked past them. Moll appeared at his side.

'*Obersturmführer*, permission to proceed?' Willi nodded, avoiding eye contact for he saw what was about to happen.

Moll just grinned and the first guard stepped forward towards the group of *Sonderkommando*. His back was to the floodlights on the nearest guard tower and he looked like a hooded shadow with the face hidden. Pointing the short length of pipe in his hand, the flame gulped out with an incandescent roar. Within a few seconds the remainder of the flame-throwers formed a half-circle and the tongues of pure white heat played over the men that writhed and wriggled to escape. There was no escape and the flames concentrated and the men died horribly. No screams. In twenty seconds, it was all over.

'Stop!' yelled Moll and there was a silence.

Willi held a white handkerchief over his nose and stepped back from the smouldering heaps that had once been men.

'You!' shouted Moll to Benjamin Blum. 'Get some help and take this fuckin' filth away from here. Take them to the forest and let the others burn them.'

Inmates emerged from the barracks and lifted the charred bodies onto trolleys. Benjamin followed them as the guards opened the barriers and allowed the procession to disappear into the woods where smouldering funeral pyres waited.

'*Herr Obersturmführer.*' Moll threw up a casual salute. '*Doktor* Mengele sends his compliments and has ordered us to a "Selection" on the Ramp.' He turned, and Willi followed him past the darkening earth where men had died. Past the closed gates of the crematoria. Past inmates, standing near their barracks, heads down.

He was used to the sound and hardly heard the whistle of the transport as the locomotive clanked and chugged onto the Ramp. Mengele waited, boots gleaming and dressed as immaculately as ever. At his side stood Rolf Müller. There was a stillness over the scene and, even though the locomotive was still in motion, nobody moved.

Mengele nodded. 'Good evening, *Obersturmführer* Hossler.' A faint smile crossed his face. 'This time just a small transport.' There were five wagons and no guard carriage. The inmate workers dashed forward and slid open the doors. 500 Slovakian Jews; men, women and children stepped down on to the Ramp. They waited, holding their heavy baggage, staring at the scene before them.

Through the open archway to the right of the brick tower, a black staff car roared out of the early morning mist and skidded to a halt on the Ramp in front of the officers. The rear doors swung open and two men stepped out. They wore the uniforms of the *SD* and each carried leather brief-cases. Small men but with the puffed-up importance of underlings with a mission. Striding towards the *SS* officers, they chorused, '*HEIL* Hitler!' The fatter man had a voice harsh with a Hamburg accent. '*Herr Hauptsturmführer* Mengele. I have orders here directly from Berlin.'

Mengele waved them to one side of the Ramp. 'I've been expecting you.' Glaring down at them, he extended a gloved hand.

The man undid the heavy brass buckles and reached into the case. The grey envelope was sealed and he handed it across with his left hand and saluted with his right. Mengele ignored him and broke the seal. Withdrawing the single sheet of paper, he scanned it, nodded and pushed it into his trouser pocket. Pausing for a moment, and placing his hands on his hips, he turned to face Rolf and Willi. His expression was of contemptuous acceptance and, in a voice pitched low, he said, 'Gentlemen, we're ordered not to continue with any more exterminations or any killings whatsoever.' He tapped his pocket. 'This order comes direct from the *SS* Head Office for *Reich* Security in Berlin. We must obey the order.' Lifting his head slightly, he said softly to Rolf. '*Doktor* Müller, take these people to the hospital and make sure they're fed and medically treated.'

Rolf was deeply shocked. He had never heard Mengele ever give such an order on the Ramp or at any time since he had known him. 'I beg your pardon, *Doktor* Mengele,' he said.

Mengele replied, with an edge to his voice. 'I said, *Doktor* Müller, take these people to the hospital and make sure they're fed and medically treated.' He turned and walked back towards his office.

Willi and Rolf looked at each other and Willi spoke first. 'It's just what I said. It's the end of the line.' Rolf nodded and, crooking his finger, called Moll to his side. Turning, he said loudly, '*Oberscharführer*, take these people to the hospital barracks.' Moll stared back and, for a moment, Rolf thought he was going to question his order.

'*Jawohl, Herr Hauptsturmführer*.' Snapping to attention, he threw up his arm. '*HEIL* Hitler!'

The two men from Berlin watched the train leave, climbed back into their car and drove off along the Ramp and out through the main entrance. Rolf watched the chattering people leave the Ramp and then he spoke to his friend. 'Willi, I'm a doctor and I've work to do. I'll see you later in the mess.' Without waiting for a reply, he followed the Slovakians towards the barracks, hands deep in the pockets of his greatcoat.

It was late in the morning and Rolf walked, head down, against a biting easterly wind towards his office. As he turned the corner, he was surprised to see the *Kommandant's* black car parked outside the wooden building. Striding up the steps, he pushed open the door. His nostrils smelt the pungent odour of Dutch cigars and he knew that *Sturmbannführer* Richard Bär was somewhere in the block. The orderly rose from his chair, nodded and pointed to Rolf's office.

Bär stood near the window and turned when Rolf entered. The red and black swastika armband shone out in the drabness of the room. His voice was silky smooth.

'Good morning, my dear *Hauptsturmführer*. How are you today?'
Rolf clicked his heels, it was most unusual for the *Kommandant* to visit his officers in their place of work. 'I'm fine thank you, *Sturmbannführer*.'

'Do you mind if we share a glass of your cognac?' said Bär, waving his cigar towards the glasses on the table.

'Of course.' And Rolf walked round behind his desk pulling open the drawer. He filled up two glasses and passed one to the *Kommandant*.

Bär raised the glass to his lips. '*Prost*, and here's to our future.' He downed the contents of the glass in one massive gulp and then sucked at his cigar until the tip glowed. Rolf sipped at his glass and waited. Bär cast his narrowed eyes over Rolf's face. 'No doubt you've heard about the order from *Reich* Security?'

'Yes, *Sturmbannführer*.'

'Mengele has not seen the full text of that order. He has only seen the part that applies to the halting of the exterminations. I have the full text of the telegram.' Reaching into the pocket of his greatcoat, he pulled out a flimsy slip of paper. 'The order's dated November17, 1944 and comes directly from the *Reichsführer* himself.' Bär crushed out the cigar in the bottom of the brandy glass. 'So you see, Müller, everything has to stop. We have to destroy all evidence of what's gone on here and then we have to leave. I know you've already started getting rid of records. Groups of workers are being taken by transport or by marches to other camps in Germany.' Tapping his jackboot on the floor, he suddenly faced the window and stared out across the neat lines of barracks.

Rolf thought for a moment, giving him time to empty the glass. '*Sturmbannführer*, thank you for telling me about the orders. May I ask ....?' He was quickly interrupted.

'Müller,' said Bär. 'I've told you because you're a good and trustworthy officer. Not once have you complained about your work here. You've not taken the, ... shall we say, ...' He took a deep breath and exhaled, '"Gifts" from the Jews.' Bär turned. 'Your brother officer, Hossler, knows about explosives. He will be responsible for destroying the crematoria.' Bär moved away from the window and made his way towards the door. 'Oh, by the way, Müller, two more things.' Again, he reached into his pocket. 'There's a letter waiting for you in the mess. Because of security, I had to read it. It's from a *Fraülein* Ulrika Hannsen.' Bär watched surprise pass across Rolf's face. 'I presume she's the girl who was lucky enough to be selected to mate with you for *Lebensborn*.' Raising his eyebrows, he smiled. 'Am I correct?'

'Yes, *Sturmbannführer*. That's her name.'

'She sounds wonderful.' Bär reached into another pocket. 'The second matter concerns a small, personal gift.' He pursed his lips. In his hand, lay a small, black pouch. Pulling loose the draw strings, he leant across the desk and spilt the contents onto the blotter pad. The diamonds glittered and sparkled and formed a shimmering heap. His eyes watched Rolf's face. 'Let's say it's a gift for, ... "services rendered to the *Reich*."'

Rolf touched them and they felt cold and, at the same time, hot. '*Sturmbannführer*,' he spluttered, 'I really couldn't accept this. I really couldn't.'

'Nonsense, my dear Müller. These are interesting times. Let's say that one day you may be able to help me as much as you've helped the work here at Auschwitz.' With the back of his hand, he pushed the diamonds across the pad. 'Of course, you could add them to that rather nice necklace that Glumbik gave to you some time ago.' His eyes reflected the gleam of the diamonds.

Rolf knew he was trapped. 'Thank you. I accept them with pleasure.'

TWENTY-SIX

'The civilian prison in Leeuwarden is located in the middle of the town. A brick-built, towered place with pinnacles and buttresses as though it was pretending to be a chateau. I was obviously expected because as soon as I walked across the small drawbridge the guard on the main door saluted and walked towards me.

"Kapitein *Cohen?*"

"Yes," I replied.

"Please follow me." He turned on his heel and I walked after him.

I'd been in quite a few prisons over the last few months and this one was no different. As I walked down a short corridor, the same sour smell of bodies and strong disinfectant washed over me. I duly followed the guard down a series of bleak corridors, each blocked by steel barred gates. All the cells were empty with wide-open doors.

"Not many customers?" I enquired.

"Only one, kapitein," he called over his shoulder, "and that's the bastard you're going to meet."

"'Is he guarded?"

"No," he grunted, unlocking a door at the top of a steep flight of stairs. "Who the hell wants to rescue the swine? You're welcome to him. He hasn't said a word since the Resistance brought him in." He stopped before a studded wooden door and checked the peep-hole. "I think he's asleep. Oh, by the way, kapitein, can I have your pistol please." I nodded and unbuttoned my holster. He took my Webley and slipped it into his belt. "Don't worry about Müller. He's manacled hand and foot. I'll be right outside." Selecting a huge key from a ring at his side, he jammed it into the lock and, with a slight squeak, turned the key. The door swung open silently.

The cell was small and lit by a shaded single light bulb sunk into the ceiling. My eyes grew accustomed to the light and I saw white walls and a stone floor. The door closed behind me. The man lay on a steel bed hard against the far wall. He'd propped himself up with his head in the angle formed by the corner. Although the face was in deep shadow, I could feel him watching me. He was dressed in black SS uniform, devoid of any rank insignia. Thick socks with no boots. I waited and watched for any signs of movement. His head lifted and the light cast his face into strong outline.

About my age and good looking with intense cold blue eyes. A dark stubble on his chin but the head was held up and tilted slightly to one side. He moved on the bed making it creak and the chains rattle. Then there was a long silence and neither of us moved or spoke.

I decided to break the silence. "I'm kapitein *Cohen of the Princess Irene Brigade." I stopped and let my words sink in. Another silence and I added, "I'm here for you to answer some very important questions."*

The movement of his body began in his shoulders; they began to shake. Then his chest trembled and, finally, he laughed. It was a laugh that came from the belly and it radiated over the whole of his body, then it abruptly stopped. With a rattle of chains, Müller climbed off the bed and spoke. It was a deep, strong voice and it surprised me because he spoke in English.

"Jesus Christ, I don't believe it." The accent was perfect. "I rot in this cell for three days and don't speak a word to anybody and they send a Jew to question me. A fucking Jew." He stared at me. Two blue eyes looking into two brown. Neither of us dropped our guard.

My first question was quite simple. "Are you SS-Hauptsturmführer *Edvard Müller?"*

A smile played across his lips. "Why are you here to question me? I demand ....."

"You're in no position to demand anything. In fact, I'm surprised you're still alive. In most towns I've been in recently, the Resistance have shot anybody in the SS*."*

Shrugging his shoulders, he crossed his legs and let one swing backwards and forwards. "The Geneva Convention clearly says ....

"Stuff the Geneva Convention."

"You're an Allied officer and you're bound by the Convention," he snapped back.

"I'm here unofficially. If I wanted to, I could leave and they'd shoot you anyway." The leg stopped swinging.

"Why should I answer any questions? Particularly from a Jew."

All the time the man was trying to get the upper hand by asking me the questions and I wanted to beat him at his game. "Because there's nobody else and, anyway, I'm a lawyer as well as an officer."

"What difference does that make?"

"In all probability you'll not be shot but put on trial for war crimes. Then they'll hang you." That seemed to quieten him.

"War crimes? I'm guilty of nothing."

"The illegal occupation of a free and independent country."

"The Dutch members of the Nazi party, they begged us to take control."

"Theft of property from the individual."

"All property is property of the Reich."

"Stripping of Dutch state assets."

"All assets are the property of the Reich." He became exasperated and his voice was harsh "These are ridiculous questions and I refuse to answer them."

I knew exactly what he was trying to do and I didn't rise to the taunt. "....... Shooting innocent civilians and torture."

He remained rock steady and his voice took on an official tone. "They were not innocent. They were terrorists against the Reich."

"And execution without trial."

"Terrorists do not deserve a trial."

I waited for a full minute and we stared at each other. Then I threw my strongest question at him. "What about the removing of all civil rights from the Jews. What about imprisoning them?" I felt my voice rising. "What about transporting them against their will? What about sending them to extermination camps? What about killing countless families, men, women and children?"

The leg began to swing again. "My dear, kapitein. You don't understand. As a Jew, you cannot understand. I will explain." I gritted my teeth and swallowed hard. "Jews are the eternal enemy of the German people and the Führer has decreed that they must be exterminated."

"Why?"

He held up one finger, like a schoolmaster. "The Führer decreed that all Jews must be exterminated. Only by your extermination can Germany be free."

"Müller, the Reich no longer exists." The supercilious smile on his face was beginning to annoy me.

He tapped his head with two fingers. "In here, the Reich will live forever, Whatever you say or do, it will live forever. After our glorious Wehrmacht conquered Holland in May 1940, we began the systematic anti-Jewish legislation. I won't bore you with the details."

"Bore me," I said, quietly.

Taking a deep breath, Müller spoke in a voice that had all the arrogance of the SS. "As you Jews are sub-human, untermenschen, we took away all civil and human rights. Jews were ousted from all official positions and their movements were forbidden unless we said so. Jews were not allowed to attend public theatres or other places of entertainment. We issued them with special identity cards and all Jewish children were expelled from schools. They couldn't use telephones and we stopped them using bicycles." He was in a world of his own and I watched him pouring out what he had done. "We *were in control in Holland much more than in any other occupied country and you know why? Because we were in control from the moment of the Dutch defeat. And, unfortunately for you, sixty percent of the Jews lived in Amsterdam and we were easily able to round them up. Here in Friesland, it was easier still, because there were only 852 to find. I think I got most of them." I bided my time. Müller paused for a moment and shifted his position. "There was no room for tenderness or weakness. Even now, we're still dealing with Jews." The smile on his face, as he stared up at me, was an attempt to goad me into some sort of action; I didn't respond. "Anyway, what possible interest do you have in what happened to the Jews of Leeuwarden?"*

I took a step nearer him and chose my words carefully. "I am a Jew of Leeuwarden. You transported the whole of my family to Auschwitz on September 13, 1944. The only survivor is my relative, Lottie Cohen. We'll both testify at your trial in the due course of time and, by God, I'll make sure you hang."

Müller rose to his feet and I was pleased to see he was shorter than me. His voice rose, "If there are only two Cohens left then I nearly succeeded, didn't I?"

I'm not a man to lose my temper but I did. Then I hit him. One punch in the mouth and I heard the teeth crunch. As he went down and, as the manacle stretched taut, I kneed him in the balls and he grunted. He lay on the floor and writhed in silent agony.

Feeling my knuckles, I said, "Not bad for a fucking Jew, eh?"

I turned and the door opened. The guard looked at Müller on the floor and smiled at me. He chuckled. "Good one, Sir and I didn't see a thing."'

TWENTY-SEVEN

Richard drove fast, all the time watching out for the highly efficient Dutch traffic police. He travelled up the E-22, the European Green coast road that led him north and towards the massive Afsluitdijk. A dead-straight, twenty mile long barrier separating the North Sea from the IJsselmeer lake.

Richard decided to stop at the Monument Café. A small place with a tower, built to commemorate where the builders of the two sides of the opposing dikes had met. The wind was a cold easterly and after the womb-like warmth of the car, the chill hit him hard. Bending his head, he ran down the steps into the café. One or two people drinking coffee and little happening. Richard ordered a glass of Grolsch beer and settled down into a corner seat. Pulling the map out of his pocket, he laid it out over the table. The bright colours shone back at him. With his finger, he traced out his planned route and quietly said it out aloud. 'Right, over the Afsluitdijk .... Into Friesland .... Into Leeuwarden. And I must see if that prison's still there.' His finger followed the road. 'I'll keep off the *snelweg* and keep to the minor roads. Through Sneek.' He paused and took a long pull of beer from the glass. 'By God, that's good ....' Another mouthful. 'I'd better give Lottie a call.' Placing the glass on the table and the map in front of him, he looked for the number he had written in the blue of the IJsselmeer Lake. Pulling his mobile phone out of his pocket, he punched in the numbers. She answered immediately.

'*U spreekt met mevrouw Cohen.*' The voice was calm and she spoke Dutch with the slightest trace of a German accent.

'Hello, Lottie. It's Richard Cooper speaking.

The voice changed and she spoke precise English. 'Oh, Richard, it's so nice to hear from you.'

Richard was refreshed by her enthusiasm. 'Me too, Lottie. I should be with you in about an hour and a half.'

'Fine, that's wonderful.'

'I've got your address. Where exactly do you live in Oudemirdum?'

'Oh, it's quite easy. Come in from the main road and through the village and then the first turning on the left. It's the third house on the left. I'll put the flag out for you.'

Richard laughed. He had been a little worried about meeting this old lady but her voice and manner came confidently down the phone. 'Thank you, Lottie, I'll see you later. Good bye.'

'Bye, Richard.'

Switching off the phone, he emptied the glass of beer, left some money and dashed up the steps to the MG. The roads were quiet but the strong head-wind drove hard against the car. The rain started and it came down in sheets, lashing the windscreen. The metronomic tick of the wipers was hypnotic but Richard kept up his concentration by searching the horizon for the rim of the land to appear. Ten minutes later and the first church spires rolled into view, then the trees and finally houses. Magically, the rain stopped and the wind dropped. The sign told him "Provincie Friesland" and the next sign told him "Leeuwarden 23 km". He drove on, singing to himself.

Richard slowed down and negotiated the big traffic island to the west of Leeuwarden. Wending his way down narrow cobbled streets, Richard arrived into the town centre. A quick look at the map and he pulled into a parking place opposite the prison and thought for a minute. Reaching over to his case on the seat at the side of him, he withdrew his father's file. He found it quickly and read out the right passage. "The civilian prison in Leeuwarden is located right in the middle of the town. A brick-built towered place with pinnacles and buttresses as though it was pretending to be a chateau." Richard smiled and stared at the prison. He couldn't resist. Opening the door, he stepped out of the car and, glancing in each direction, walked across the busy road. It was just as he expected.

The drawbridge mentioned by Richard's father had been replaced by a disabled access ramp. There was no other sign of change and the building exuded a penitent gloom. Glancing upwards, Richard saw a TV camera watching him. He couldn't resist smiling at it. Before he could turn to go back to the car, small door near the main entrance swung open. He was faced by a middle-aged man in the dark blue uniform of a prison officer.

'*Ja, meneer. Kan ik u helpen?*' His face seemed friendly enough.

Richard smiled, 'Oh yes, good morning. I'm sorry my Dutch is not very good.'

The man asked the obvious, 'Englishman?' Richard nodded a reply. '*Ja,* I speak the English.' Only a little.' With his thumb and forefinger he pulled at his nose. There was a pause. '*Meneer*, can I help you?'

'Not really, no.' He opened Simon's file. 'You see my father visited here during the war and I was just interested.'

The man nodded. '*Ja*, the war.' He glanced at the file. 'My father was prison officer during the war. In here, in this prison.' He patted the heavy wooden door.

Richard took a wild chance. 'Were there any Germans imprisoned in here after the end of the war in May '45.'

Scratching his nose, the officer replied, '*Denk ik wel*, ... *ja*. There was just one German. I think he was *SS*. *Ja*, My father told me about him. He knew him.'

Richard carefully explained about the last few pages that he had read in his cabin the night before. Traffic roared past behind them and the man occasionally had to raise his voice.

'*Ja, meneer*, it could have been your father that met my father.'

'What happened to the SS man in the prison?' asked Richard.

He drew the side of his hand across his throat. 'Dead, *meneer*. He was put on trial in 1945 in The Hague and then executed. He was, how do you say....... ?' He pulled an imaginary noose at the side of his neck.

'Hanged?'

'*Ja*, dat's the word, 'hanged'. As he finished speaking, the bleeper at his waist buzzed. Shrugging, he said, 'Sorry, *meneer*, I have to go back to work.'

'Thank you very much,' said Richard, extending his hand. 'You're English is very good.'

Beaming and shaking hands, the prison officer replied. 'Thank you. I learn it from the TV.' Richard then understood the reason for the slight American accent.

The drive to Oudemirdum was without incident. Even though it was autumn, the fields were a deep, luscious green. The dead flat Frisian landscape stretched away from horizon to horizon. Neat houses, carefully manicured ditches and fences gave a feeling of orderliness that calmed the nerves. Black and white Frisian cows lifted their heads and lowed as the car passed by. The weather had brightened and a cloudless, stunningly blue sky gave a pin-sharp feeling to the day.

Oudemirdum was a small village. A single street at its centre and, at the far end, a brick-built church on top of a mound. Richard pulled up near the gates of the church and remembered Lottie's directions. He drove on past two small shops and then turned left. The house was set back from the others. Typically Dutch, brick-built, with a high sloping roof and large windows. Lottie had been as good as her word and Richard smiled when he saw the long fluttering pennant hanging from the flagpole in the neat garden. Unsure where to park, he stopped for a moment and examined the short drive. Shrugging, he drove up it and parked near the front door. As he stepped out of the MG, the door opened. He expected an old lady, instead an attractive young woman dressed in jeans and a red jumper walked towards him.

She held out her hand. 'Good morning, you must be Richard Cooper. I'm Marieke Johnstone.' She gave a huge smile. 'Nice car.' Her English was good.

It took Richard a few seconds to regain his composure. 'Yes, I'm Richard …. but I don't quite understand. ………' He paused and then grasped her hand. It was warm and her grip was almost masculine.

She laughed. 'Oh, you mean Lottie? She's just gone to the shop, she'll be back in a few minutes.' Staring over his shoulder, she said again, 'That really is a nice car. Is it an MG?'

Richard smiled and warmed to this young woman. 'You're right, it is an MG, an MGB GT.'

She bent over and ran her hand over the smooth, sloping wing. 'Does it go fast?'

He laughed. 'Everybody asks that question. No, not really. About a 150 kilometres an hour. And sometimes, that's fast enough.'

She straightened and a pair of startlingly blue eyes looked into his. 'So you're Simon Cohen's son?'

This woman kept asking questions and Richard kept answering them. 'Yes, I am.'

'Wow, I've heard about you.' Before he could reply, she clapped her hands. 'At least my mother talked of you.'

'Your mother,' said Richard, searching his brain.

She sighed with an exasperated look. 'I'd better explain. My father is Richard Johnstone. He used to be a Wing Commander in the Royal Air Force during the war. My mother is Aukje Johnstone. She was Aukje van de Meer before she married my father.'

Snapping his fingers, Richard said, 'I've got it now. You're the grand-daughter of Frank van de Meer, the man who saved Lottie's life?'

'That's me. I'm Marieke. My mother named me after my grandmother.' They stared at each other. Suddenly she brushed past him and pointed down the narrow road. 'Oh good, here comes Lottie.'

It was a sight to behold. Atop a huge Dutch bike sat a thin, old lady. Her body switched from side to side as her legs pushed the pedals around like pistons. There was something majestic about the way she and the bike approached the house. Quickly, her head lifted and she waved. Within a minute, she turned into the short drive, lowered one foot to the ground and stopped.

'Hello, Richard,' she said, slipping her other leg across the frame and leaning the bike against a tree.

An imposing woman, hair as white as snow and tied back with a bright orange hair-band. She stood motionless with her head cocked to one side. Bright brown eyes in a very interesting face. There was an inner light about it that gave the complexion an ageless quality.

'Hello, Lottie,' Richard replied. She leant forward and allowed him to kiss her on each cheek.

She threaded her arm through his. 'Now, what are we standing out here for? It's chilly. Come on, let's go into the house.' She led him to the front door and he stood to one side to let her through.

The house was just as Richard expected it to be. From the hall, several panelled doors led off in different directions. Lottie opened one of them and he followed her through. A big room, stretching the full length of the house. At the front, a huge window, with potted plants on the sill. The wooden parquet floor was partly covered with Persian rugs scattered in places closest to deep leather chairs and ornate Dutch furniture. Everything was of the finest quality and in the best possible taste. A large mahogany table with matching chairs occupied one end of the room.

The aroma of fresh coffee wafted in from the kitchen somewhere at the back of the house. Richard noticed it, and he waited politely, wondering what to do next. Lottie led him towards the front window.

'Richard, do sit down,' she said with a smile and waved him to a high-backed chair. She guessed his thoughts. 'Don't worry, we'll get your bags later.' Lottie lowered herself onto an antique chaise-longue. 'Have you had a safe journey? What was the crossing like?'

They made social talk for several minutes and Richard soon realised that he liked this old woman. There was something very special about her. He heard Marieke humming something to herself in the kitchen and then the conversation stopped. He saw Lottie looking closely at him.

'Now,' she softly, '.... please tell me about your family.'

Richard explained quite simply about Jane and their children. He spoke for about five minutes. Nodding, she waited until he had finished.

Pausing for a moment, Lottie said quietly, 'I'm sorry, Richard, more questions. Please tell me how Simon died?'

Slowly and carefully, Richard told her how it had happened and he saw tears running down her cheeks. Producing a delicate linen handkerchief from her pocket, she dabbed at her face. 'He was my only living relative, you know. But, I have to tell you, we weren't very close. In fact, I'd only met him a few times. Still, ... he was family. But the family was so big and, your father left for England at such an early age, that I lost all contact with him.' She smiled. 'Anyway, I'm so glad you're here with us. .... Thank you for making contact with me.'

Richard leant over and squeezed her hand. 'Simon never really wanted me to know what had gone on during the war,' he said. 'And, as you know, he changed his name and dropped his faith.'

'That's quite common and I quite understand,' replied Lottie, carefully folding her thin arms. 'But once a Jew, always a Jew.'

Marieke walked into the room carrying a tray. She carefully laid the table and dropped cross-legged onto the carpet. She poured out the coffee into exquisite, Delft- blue porcelain cups. 'Help yourself to milk and sugar.'

'Thank you very much,' he replied and reached forward to pick up his coffee. 'Lottie,' he said, turning to face her, 'I'm so glad to be here.'

She nodded her reply. 'It's my pleasure.'

'Please, can you tell me a little more about what happened to you and how Marieke's grandparents saved your life? That is, if it's not too upsetting.'

Lottie took the cup of coffee from Marieke's outstretched hand. 'It's no problem. …. Before I say anything, Richard, I must say how much I appreciated the very kind gift your father left me in his will. I just couldn't believe it. I don't really need the money. But, no doubt, I'll find something to spend it on.'

Richard laughed. 'It was Simon's wish and I agree with him, it couldn't have gone to a nicer person.'

Lottie nodded and composed herself. 'It's quite a simple story really. I think I'll just sit back and let Marieke tell it to you. Would you mind, Marieke?'

'Not at all,' she replied, 'I've told it so many times.' She leant back against Lottie's chair, her long legs stretched out on the carpet. 'My grandfather and grandmother, Frank and Marieke van de Meer were Mennonites and great pacifists. Holland was forcibly occupied in May 1940 and they were faced with a practical moral dilemma. How do you resist the Nazis, when you're a pacifist? Eventually, my grandfather helped to form an organisation called the LO. It was composed mainly of church people and they helped to hide Jews and other groups.' Pride crept into her voice. 'Do you know, out of the 120,000 Dutch Jews, we hid 23,000 and 20,000 survived the war and that's more than any other country in occupied Europe. …. Lottie and her family had always been very great friends of the van de Meers. She refused to go into hiding and that's typical. She's so stubborn.' Marieke glanced at her. 'Anyway, Lottie worked for some time at Westerbork. You know what that place was?' Richard nodded. 'Eventually, her papers came and she was called up to report to the railway station. She was determined to go and, even though my grandmother tried to stop her, she left with her suitcase for the short walk to the station. Frank was really crafty. He told one of his friends, a Captain Schaaf, to travel in his barge along the canal near to the station at about the time the train was due to leave. This meant that the bridge had to be raised and Lottie missed the train.'

'I was furious,' said Lottie, frowning. 'Still to this day, I can remember the smile on Frank van de Meer's face.'

'All of Lottie's family had already gone,' continued Marieke, 'and she was determined to follow them. In those days people assumed you just went out to the east for labour and then returned. Frank and Marieke knew that something was wrong and they wanted to stop Lottie going. They'd already hidden dozens of people and, because of their friendship with the Cohen family, they were determined to save her.' She took a long drink from the cup. 'Just before Lottie was due to catch the next transport, she fell ill and was taken into hospital.'

'That,' interrupted Lottie, 'I can really remember. I lay in bed wearing my yellow star on my night-dress and nobody was allowed near me because I was Jewish. I felt awful and then the next thing I knew, Marieke van de Meer was standing at my side.'

'Lottie, …….. I thought I was telling the story?' grinned Marieke. 'They got her out but only by telling her that the Nazis would get them all if she refused. She was hidden with a family in a village and there she stayed until liberation in 1945.'

'Yes, indeed,' said Lottie. 'I remained hidden for two years. Without Frank and Marieke van de Meer, I would not have survived. I'm the only member of my family still alive. That was, apart from your father.'

'Does it worry you, …. surviving?' blurted Richard, biting his lip. 'I'm sorry, I mean ……..'

Lottie raised her hand. 'Oh, don't worry. It was a long time ago. I lost my first husband at Auschwitz and my second husband died five years ago. Frank and Marieke remained very good friends but they had to get on with their lives just as I did.'

'Are they still alive?' asked Richard.

Rubbing her forehead with her hand, Lottie smiled. 'Frank died fifteen years ago because of a weak heart; the war finally killed him. Marieke van de Meer is still alive but only just. She lives in an old people's home about thirty kilometres from here.'

'And your parents, Marieke?' asked Richard.

'Oh yes,' she said, 'My mother is so active. She belongs to just about every women's group in Leeuwarden. My father is still a local councillor and always thought he should have been a member of parliament.'

'And I hear he was decorated?'

'Yep, that's right as well. He got a DFC and some other medals.'

'He was given the Dutch Resistance Cross by Queen Wilhelmina,' said Lottie, stroking Marieke's hair.

'Well, my mother and my father and my uncle got that medal as well.'

'A very brave family, really,' said Richard, draining his cold coffee and placing the cup and saucer back on the table. Richard watched them. There was a pause in the conversation and he wanted to talk about his father's past. 'Lottie, may I ask how many Jews there're left in Leeuwarden?'

She closed her eyes for a moment. 'There used to be about seven hundred. I think there are only three or four now. I rarely see anybody. There aren't even enough to form a *minyan.*' She saw Richard's questioning face. 'A *minyan* is a minimum of ten people. Enough for a service in the synagogue.' Lottie talked for a few minutes and then sighed. 'Richard, could you explain exactly why you're in Holland and what this man wants? .... What's his name?'

Richard had been avoiding the main reason for his visit, worried about the implications. 'He's called Jan Bildt. I think it's a Dutch name.' Lottie nodded and then he went on to tell her about Simon's papers. They listened in silence and, occasionally, Lottie moved on the chaise-longue. When Richard stopped, the questions began. Lottie first.

'Had you no idea about your father's background?'

Richard shrugged. 'Not really, just before he died he began to talk about it. Particularly when it was close to September 4.'

'That date is so important?' said a grim faced Marieke. The atmosphere in the room changed and Richard saw Lottie's eyes close. They suddenly snapped open.

Lottie rose slowly to her feet. 'On September 4, 1944, the Cohen family, apart from myself, was transported *en masse* from Leeuwarden station to Westerbork transit camp and from there, on to Auschwitz.' She walked towards the wall nearest to the front window and beckoned.

Framed in black ebony, the letter it contained was fading with age. Unhooking it off the wall, she turned to face Marieke and Richard.

'Turn on the lights, please.' Marieke leant over and pushed the switch. Like an actress on a stage, Lottie was bathed in a strong white light from a wall-mounted spot. 'This,' she said, pointing to the frame, 'is the letter calling me to Westerbork. Perhaps, Richard, you'd like to read it?'

Stepping into the circle of light, he took it from her hand. On the yellowed paper, the typing was in jerky old letters. He read it aloud.

'Mevrouw L. Cohen,

(born. 11 - 6 - 1908)
8 Perkstraat
Leeuwarden.

CALL UP!

The German labour authorities inform you that on
Tuesday, 4 September 1944, you must report to the work camp
at Westerbork.
You may take with you the following articles:

> 1 suitcase or rucksack
> 1 pair of work-boots or shoes
> 2 pairs of socks
> 2 sets of underwear
> 2 sets of bed linen (sheets and pillow-cases)
> 2 shirts
> 2 pairs of underpants
> 2 woollen blankets
> 1 pair of overalls
> 1 complete set of cutlery
> 1 drinking beaker
> 3 handkerchiefs
> 2 towels
> 1 pullover

On Tuesday 4th September 1944, you must, at precisely
06.35 hours, report to the main railway station for processing.

The Burgermeester of Leeuwarden.

Herman Wilders

J 1064'

The letter hurt him, and for a moment, he was speechless and then he
felt Lottie's hand on his. 'I don't know why I keep it,' she said. 'Probably
because it's something I can't throw away and, anyway, Frank van de Meer
made the frame for me.' Making a quick decision, she returned the frame

back to its hook and turned to face Richard. 'But first, you must be hungry. Marieke will help you with your bags and show you to your room.' As she brushed past him, he saw tears glistening in the corners of her eyes.

It was starting to drizzle as Marieke led him out of the house. To the left was darkness and she saw his glance. 'It's the IJsselmeer lake. Only about ten minutes from here.' Dark clouds scudded across a rising moon and Richard shivered. He opened the boot and heaved out his case.

'What can I do?' she said, arms folded.

Richard grinned. 'Can you grab that travel case off the front seat? .... That's all really.' He paused 'What about dinner?'

'Don't worry about that,' she called over her shoulder, as she passed into the house and began to climb the stairs. 'I'll check with Lottie.' The stairs were very steep and Richard remembered that this was the way in all Dutch houses. 'Here we are,' said Marieke, brightly, waving a hand, 'the guest room.'

A good sized room. Fitted carpets and heavy velvet curtains. Everything was neat and tidy. Tall windows with a clear view. A tall, mahogany, antique wardrobe filled one wall and next to it was a half-open door.

'That's the WC and the shower. Or what do call it in England? The toilet or the loo ...... or something?'

'Toilet is fine.'

'OK.' And then she stood and faced him again with arms folded.

He dropped his bag onto the floor and quickly pointed to a small picture over the bed, a whirl of colours and action. 'Nice copy of a Chagall.'

'It's not a copy.'

Leaning closer, Richard sought out the signature and touched it with his finger tips. 'Are you sure?' he said, incredulously.

'Oh yes. It's genuine,' smiled Marieke. 'And that one over the bed is also genuine. ..... It's a Matisse.'

Richard shook his head. 'That's unbelievable.'

'Yes, Lottie's family were very well off. They emigrated from Germany before the war and managed to bring most of their wealth with them.'

'I thought the Nazis looted Jews of all their belongings?'

Marieke looked at him. 'You're right. But remember, Lottie's family weren't transported until quite late in the war. They managed to hide most of their things.'

Richard was curious. 'Where did they hide such things as these?' Waving his hand at the paintings.

'You name it. .... They dug holes in the ground. Knocked down walls, hid things and bricked them up again. Left goods with friends. Some of it was lost but some of the Jews that survived managed to collect most of their precious things when the war was over.'

'And Lottie?' asked Richard.

'My grandfather and grandmother built a secret cellar into this very house. It used to be a summer house for the Cohens. I'll show it to you some time.'

Lottie's voice called up the stairs. 'Richard! Marieke!'

'Coming!' and she walked across the room. At the door, she turned and smiled. 'Come down in five minutes.'

Throwing his case onto the bed, he unzipped it and removed his clothes ready for the hangers in the wardrobe. Humming, he couldn't resist looking at the Chagall. It drew his eyes closer and gave him pleasure. Pulling out his mobile, he phoned home. Jane answered immediately.

'Richard, darling, good to hear from you. How's everything?' Her voice was steady.

'Fine, Jane, everything is fine. Lottie's a wonderful person, full of life.'

'And tomorrow, it's off to the see this man Bildt?'

'Yes.'

'You know what I think about the whole thing. Just be careful, ... please.'

They chatted for a few minutes and then Richard said, 'All right, I'll call you tomorrow night. ...... I love you.'

'I love you too,' she replied.

With a sigh, he put the phone back in his bag. Looking down at his clothes, he decided to change and selecting a pair of grey, cotton trousers and matching pullover, he walked over to the mirror. It took him a few minutes and he glanced in the long mirror making sure that he was neat and tidy. Using the silver-backed brush on the dressing-table, he brushed his hair back into a semblance of a parting and nodded. Slipping on a pair of silk socks and soft suede shoes, he left the bedroom and walked carefully down the steep stairs.

Turning left, he stared at another painting near the door to the living-room. No signature, a French park scene, full of gaiety and innocence. He knocked gently on the kitchen door and walked in. The aroma of cooking hit him in the face and then he realised how hungry he was. Lottie and Marieke stood casually near the big cooker.

Lottie smiled at him. 'I've got an idea. Marieke, why don't you let Richard drive you out to Laaksum, have a breath of fresh air and then come back. By then, dinner will be ready.'

'I really couldn't,' said Richard, shaking his head. 'I must help you with dinner.'

Lottie waved a wooden spoon menacingly. 'Nonsense, I might be 86 but I'm not helpless.'

'Come on,' said Marieke, collecting a long, woollen cardigan off the chair.

'I give in,' smiled Richard, holding up his hands and helped Marieke to put on the cardigan.

He opened the car door and she climbed in. Walking round to his side, he noticed that a half-moon cast a dampish yellow glow over the flat landscape. The engine started with a throaty roar.

'Fantastic,' shouted Marieke, squirming in her seat.

Reversing out of the drive onto the road, he slipped the MG into first gear and put his foot hard down. The car responded and, with a little wheel-slip on the wet road, they drove quickly down the narrow deserted lane.

'We're going to Laaksum,' she said. 'It's a rather special place.'

'Why is that?' asked Richard, concentrating on the road ahead.

'It's a small harbour on the edge of the IJsselmeer. During the war it was used by the Resistance as a place for smuggling food and people.'

'People?'

'Yes, people. Jews from Amsterdam were brought across the lake by boat and hidden in Friesland. When the British and American bombers returned from their raids on the Ruhr many of them were shot down by the night fighters from the big *Luftwaffe* base near Leeuwarden. The Resistance picked up the crews and ferried them across the lake to Laaksum and then to ......' She stopped in mid-sentence. 'Turn left here. Careful now! It's very narrow.'

He did as he was told. The narrow road climbed quickly to the top of the dike and he braked firmly to a stop as it abruptly ended at the side of the IJsselmeer. He switched off the engine and waited. Without a word, she opened the door and climbed out. Richard came to her side and together they looked out across the flat expanse of the lake. The water was inky black and lapped gently against the side of the short breakwater.

'I love it here,' whispered Marieke. 'I come here a lot and so does Lottie. It means so much to my family.' Her eyes shone at him. 'Into this tiny harbour, were brought dozens of crashed Allied airmen and they were sent down the escape line to safety. .... Jews, food, weapons, everything came through here.'

Richard said nothing. The night was absolutely still. Nothing moved, even the water was quiet. He could see the silhouette of several sailing boats against the clouds. Behind him were two dark patches of shadow showing small houses built on top of the dike. A single light shone out through a partly closed curtain.

'Right, Richard, that's enough,' she said in a loud voice, making him jump. 'Let's go back for dinner.'

When they arrived the front door was open and Marieke was through it before Richard had time to lock the car.

'Do come into the living-room,' called Lottie.

She wore a long, black silk dress that contrasted sharply with her white hair. It was a dress in an old style but suited her perfectly. High necked with a beige ruffle round her throat. It was loose but flowed with a ripple that only silk can give. There was a touch of rouge on her cheeks and the faintest trace of lipstick. She sat on her chaise-longue with her small feet primly together. A single brooch at her neck gave off the sparkle of diamonds.

'Lottie, you look wonderful. If I'd known we were dressing for dinner, I would've … .'

She raised a hand. 'Don't be silly, Richard. I love an excuse to wear nice clothes. Please relax, we're not a formal family. How was the drive to Laaksum?'

'Fine, thank you.'

Lottie touched his hand. 'Would you like to pour us a drink, please? It's over there in the cabinet.'

'Of course,' he replied and, with a smile, he rose to his feet. Just as he walked across the room, Marieke, wearing a very short black dress, gave a little cough and walked in from the hall.

Hand on hip, she cocked her head and laughed. 'Mine's a dry sherry, please, *meneer* Cooper.'

'Charmed, *juffrouw* Johnstone.'

Opening the cabinet, he found a good selection of drinks and filled three glasses. Delivering them to Lottie and Marieke, he sat down in a tall wooden chair. Richard heard the back door open and glanced at Lottie.

'It's the lady from next door,' she said. 'She's going to serve dinner for us.'

A snowy-white, damask table-cloth. On it lay three places, each delineated by shining silver and crisply folded napkins. Crystal glasses glittered in the soft light from a tall, seven-branched candlestick.

The woman entered the room and nodded towards Richard. '*Goede avond, meneer.*'

Richard rose and helped Lottie to her feet. She took one arm and Marieke the other and they walked together across the room. He held a chair for each of them.

'The English have such delightful manners,' said Lottie, settling herself into the chair. 'Richard, please pour the wine.'

He picked up the bottle on the table and, after examining the label, said, 'This is really good. "Chateau Léoville Barton '64", excellent.' As he spoke, the woman returned, carrying a silver soup tureen which she carefully placed in the centre of the table.

Lottie leant across and removed the lid. 'Tonight we have pea soup. The only bit of Dutch cuisine that tourists know about.' She ladled out the thick soup into three bowls just as Richard filled the glasses. *'Eet smakelijk.* Enjoy your meal.'

Curiosity made Richard ask the question. 'Lottie, you have some wonderful paintings. Where did they all come from?'

'Ah,' she said with a grin, 'my family have always loved fine paintings. Particularly the French impressionists. I managed to hold on to most of them. Even through the war.'

'Don't you get worried about somebody stealing them?'

Lottie dabbed her lips with a napkin. 'Paintings are there to be looked at, not locked away. They're well insured and I like having them around. They're like old friends.'

'I like the Chagall,' said Richard.

'It's twin is in your father's study,' she said, with a mischievous smile. 'That is, if he still has it?'

Richard dropped his spoon with a clatter. 'Really, so that's where it came from. Is it genuine?'

'Yes, indeed. I sent it to him. One of my family knew Chagall.'

Richard shook his head. 'History is strange and it keeps repeating itself.'

Lottie was silent for a moment. 'Richard, there's one thing that the Nazis did take from me.'

'What was that?'

'A van Gogh.'

'You had a van Gogh?' Richard said, incredulously.

'Oh yes. My grandfather bought it in Paris from van Gogh's brother. Like a damned fool, I left it in my bedroom in my house in Leeuwarden. When I returned, most things were still there but the van Gogh had gone.'

'This is amazing,' said Richard. 'I mean, ... What was it? .... Who took it?'

'It was a self-portrait. Van Gogh painted it in 1887 in Paris.' Lottie shook her head. 'I always thought that swine Müller had taken it. But I couldn't prove a thing. God knows where it is now.'

'Unbelievable,' said Richard.

For a few minutes they ate in silence and then Lottie looked up. 'This man Jan Bildt. You said earlier, he lives in Kekerdom.'

'The fax is a Kekerdom number but his letter says his house in Bimmen. It must be a small place, because I couldn't find it on the map,' replied Richard.

'Bimmen?' Lottie looked up with her spoon in her hand. 'You can't find it because Bimmen's not in Holland, it's in Germany.'

Richard frowned. 'If you'll excuse me, I'll get the fax and my map.' Walking to the hall, he found his case. The letter and the fax were clipped together with his father's thick file, he picked them both up, and returned to the dining-room. Handing the fax to Lottie, she took it and laid it on the table. Richard unfolded the map and placed it at her side.

'Yes, indeed,' she said, scrutinising the map and the fax. 'If you look here,' and with the point of her silver knife, she traced a road, 'you can see Kekerdom, Millingen. There's the German border, and there's Bimmen, about three kilometres into Germany.'

'That's strange,' added Richard. 'I was sure he lived in Holland. And his name is Dutch, isn't it?'

'Oh, yes,' added Marieke, with a deep frown, 'very Dutch.' She looked him straight in the eyes. 'Richard, why did he give you the impression that he was Dutch and lived in Holland, when he obviously lives in Germany?'

He shook his head. 'I haven't the faintest idea.' The woman came into the room and cleared away the soup.

'I think,' said Lottie, smoothing a crease from the table-cloth, 'that he wants you to think that he's Dutch. If you thought he was German and lived in Germany then you may not have wanted to meet him.' Not waiting for a comment, she slowly read the first letter from Jan Bildt.

TWENTY-EIGHT

Willi spoke to Rolf as he supervised the packing of yet more crates. 'Heard the news?'

'No Willi, I've not heard the news,' he replied, patiently.

'Christmas leave permits have been issued.' He waved a piece of paper. 'I've got mine and, Rolf, there's one for you. I saw the envelope on the adjutant's desk.'

'If you're not too busy,' said Rolf, sarcastically, 'perhaps you could collect mine?'

'A pleasure,' grinned Willi and left.

The winter of 1944 was cold and everybody felt its icy grip. Parties of prisoners were still force marched from Birkenau but their numbers were decreasing. Rolf was due to leave from Auschwitz station on a special SS train. This time, a bus took twenty officers and their baggage. Willi and Rolf were amongst them.

'Who are you going to see in Berlin,' said Willi with his usual bluntness. 'The wife or your *Lebensborn* bit of stuff?'

They sat in a compartment to themselves and Rolf had tried to sleep. 'Mind your own business.'

'Still touchy, aren't we?'

'It's got nothing to do with you whom I see.' Rolf kept his eyes tightly closed.

'All right, I get the message.' Willi settled comfortably into the corner seat.

Twice the train stopped at stations and they managed to grab something to eat and drink. The journey took twice as long as normal and Rolf hated every minute. With gritty eyes and aching limbs, he glanced out of the dirty window. The train clanked to a halt. He heard the tramping of boots and loud voices. Glancing through the window, he saw the sign "*BERLIN-Schlesischer Bahnhof*" Struggling to his feet, he tapped Willi with his boot. 'Wake up, we've arrived.'

Willi stretched and yawned, he had slept for most of the journey. He peered out of the window. 'Not the normal place of arrival for us supermen,' he said grimly.

The reason was explained as the conductor shouted down the corridor,

'TERMINUS! TERMINUS! GET OFF HERE AND MAKE YOUR OWN WAY INTO THE CITY CENTRE!'

Rolf hauled down his suitcase and then he felt Willi's hand on his arm. His friend's face had a serious expression and he spoke very quietly. 'Rolf, we may not meet again.'

'What do you mean?' asked Rolf, frowning.

'There're strong rumours that the Allies'll be crossing the Rhine after Christmas. My family and house are on the Rhine. I want to get back to them before the Allies get there.'

Rolf stood still. Outside the train, and in the corridor, was the hustle and bustle of movement and shouted words. 'That's desertion,' he said, staring hard at his friend.

Willi shook his head. 'No it's not. It's survival, and this time my family comes first.' He grasped Rolf's hand. 'One final thing, my friend.' He fished a piece of paper out of his pocket and gave it to Rolf.. 'Here's my address and phone number. It's a farm near Emmerich. If you ever want any help, then just phone or drop in.' Giving a quick laugh, he left the compartment. There was tap at the window and Willi's grinning face stared at him and then disappeared into the crowd.

Rolf gathered up his case and, glancing in the mirror, left the train. The station was packed. Stepping onto the street, he was greeted by the bombed desolation that was Berlin. Shaking his head, he searched for a taxi. There was not a vehicle in sight and, with a shrug, he set off on foot. Rolf was not sure where he was going. He was torn between two addresses. Opposite him, across the shattered road and on a dirty wall, he saw the painted words "BIER". Making a quick decision, he walked over to the entrance and opened the door. A large hall full of swirling cigarette smoke and the smell of bodies. It was packed full. Several faces glanced up at him but nobody said anything. Normally, when an SS officer entered, people would have respectfully nodded their heads. He pushed past men and women and reached the bar. Placing his case on the sawdust covered floor, he attracted the barman's attention.

'Yer?' said the sweat-stained man.

Rolf swallowed his temper and avoided the normal courtesies. 'A beer.'

The man glared and dropped a nearly-full, stone *stein* onto the wet bar. Rolf grabbed it and took a long pull at the glass, welcoming the refreshing tang of the watery beer. He looked over the rim at the people around him. A lot of uniforms and a mixture of officers and men, something that normally never happened. Nobody acknowledged him and that pleased him, for Rolf wanted to be alone with himself. Putting the drink back on the bar, he delved into his tunic pocket and pulled out the letter from Ulrika Hannsen.

The handwriting was clear and she had used blue ink. For a moment, he held the letter to his nose and sensed a fragrance. Holding it in his hand and hidden from the man next to him, he read it.

'Apt 8
23 Seydlitz Strasse
Berlin.

15th October 1944

My Dearest Rolf,
I've wanted to write to you ever since we last met. I've had time to think about what we said to each other on that last night. I realise that what you do, must upset you. As a doctor, I'm sure you try to help people all you can, after all, you're only doing your duty. I'm so desperately sorry for what I said to you, I must have hurt you so much. I blame it all on the war. It causes so much suffering and misery.
When we met, it was the first time I'd been involved in Lebensborn. I'd been a member of the National Socialist Women's organisation for many years. When I was twenty-one, I was asked to take part in Lebensborn. At first, I was worried but then the organisation explained that it would help me. Rolf, I want to talk about everything. Perhaps when you next come to Berlin, we could meet? I'm sure we can become better friends.

Yours with love,
Ulrika Hannsen.'

Rolf took another swig at the beer and re-read the letter. He remembered the night with her so well. But, most of all, he remembered her body. That last memory made up his mind and, emptying the *stein*, he threw down some money on the bar and quickly left.

In the pitch black of a street without lights, he started walking. Sometimes it was a scramble as he climbed over piles of rubble and the neatly stacked blocks of stone and bricks. The smell upset him, it was the smell of burning and death. He made his way towards the city centre and found *23 Seydlitz Strasse* quite easily.

Before pushing open the heavy door, he checked his wristwatch; twelve thirty. Stepping into the darkly lit hall, he walked up the stairs. Apartment 8 was on the top floor and, as the escalator was out of action, Rolf found himself out of breath by the time he reached her door. He pressed the bell in one long steady burst; no answer. He tried again. This time, he heard some movement. The door opened a fraction and he saw a face in the gap. Then it opened wider and there she stood with mouth open.

'Rolf, is it really you?' she said, incredulously.

'It's me.'

She was dressed in a white night-dress, high-necked and hanging loosely. 'What a surprise.' There was a soft smile on her face. 'I think you'd better come in.'

Rolf walked into a short hallway and placed his bag on the carpeted floor. A single light bulb shone down from the ceiling. Ulrika stood absolutely still with a hand resting on her waist. Her face, devoid of any makeup, was pale, although there was a flush of red on her neck. She looked him up and down and a yearning returned.

'You look tired,' she said. 'Let's go and sit down.' He followed her but not to the living-room, straight into her bedroom. She turned to face him. 'The water's hot, I'll start your shower.' She turned and walked back into the hallway.

'I thought the water was off,' he muttered.

She frowned at his knowledge. 'Not in this area.'

Rolf thought for a moment, then removed his greatcoat and pulled off his jackboots. The sound of the shower came down the hall and, within a minute, she had returned. Brushing past her, he smelt a fragrance that was not man-made.

The shower was steaming hot and he stepped under the stinging needles. As he turned off the water, he looked around him. It was a woman's bathroom and he saw the pink towels and the neat curtains tied back with a bow. The sight of her underclothes hanging from a line on the wall excited him. Reaching for the brassiere, he touched the silken material and it aroused him. Grabbing a towel, he wrapped it around his waist and pulled open the door.

A single candle lit the bedroom. Flickering shadows jumped up and down the wall. 'I'm here, Rolf,' Ulrika said, huskily. She lay on a double bed, stark naked. For a moment Rolf waited and stared down at her. Her long pale arms opened and he dropped the towel and fell to her side. Ulrika enveloped him and she whimpered as he thrust into her. It was over quickly and Rolf grunted with excitement and relief as his sperm pumped endlessly into her. For him, it was the end of a nightmare that had began months ago in his flat and had continued when he had first met Ulrika. He thought that it was the relief that he was finally leaving Auschwitz.

'Thank you,' he whispered into her ear.

'There's no need to thank me,' she replied, breathing fast.

They both slept and it was the sound of sirens that woke them up.

'Into the cellars,' shouted Ulrika, sliding out of the bed.

'I'm not moving. The bastards can bomb the hell out of me but I'm not moving.'

'Please, Rolf, please. It's dangerous.'

'No.' He stared at the ornate plasterwork on the ceiling.

'Damn you,' she said, grinning from ear to ear and slipped back into bed.

There were no bombs and ten minutes later an "all clear" sounded. They lay together and Rolf asked the first question. 'Are you still with *Lebensborn*?'

She sat up, resting her elbow on the fluffy pillow. A white breast with an aroused brown nipple swung enticingly close to his arm. 'I'm still registered with them but I've heard nothing since we last met.'

For the first time for months, Rolf felt a glow over his whole body. His eyes watched the nipple move through a small arc, left to right and back from right to left. Without thinking, he reached out and cupped the breast with his left hand. Her blue eyes settled on his.

Ulrika laughed and ran her hand through his hair. 'I really don't know how they finally sent me to you.' She stopped as Rolf removed his hand from her breast and slipped it gently between her legs. Her eyes opened wide. 'How did they select you?' she said, hoarsely.

Watching her eyes change, he moved his fingers slowly up her leg. 'All SS men are hand-picked,' he whispered, 'and, naturally, we have the best blood.'

'And the best bodies,' Ulrika replied softly, moulding hers to his.

Later, Rolf slept like the dead and, then with a jerk, his eyes clicked open. It was not Ulrika's steady breathing that had woken him but something else. A shadow had passed over his sleeping brain. A great blackness like a threatening thunder cloud. Glancing around the room, he saw the shapes cast by the hall light through the gap under the door. He had to escape out of the darkness. A sense of panic gripped him and he snatched the sheet to one side and stepped out of the bed. At the door, Rolf turned and stared back towards her. Her slim body remained motionless. Opening the door wide enough for him to slip through, he closed it gently behind him.

His heap of clothes in the bathroom were exactly where he had left them. Without a thought, he picked them up and began to dress. As he slipped his tunic around his shoulders, his nostrils caught the whiff of something on his clothes. Pausing for a moment, Rolf breathed in deeply. He thought and then realised what the smell was. It was impregnated into the material; it was the stink of Auschwitz.

Grabbing his bag, Rolf left the apartment and walked into the darkness of a Berlin night. Rolf had no idea where he was walking to. There was no sign of dawn and the lamp posts stood at drunken angles with shattered bulbs. The darkness pressed in on him and he just walked and walked, occasionally tripping over rubble and then stumbling to a halt. The voice made him jump.

'What's the matter, *Hauptsturmführer*, are you lost?' There was a man leaning against a stone wall.

Rolf stopped and peered through the gloom. He was unsure what to say. The man gave a toothless grin and Rolf could smell his stinking breath two metres away. Trying to walk past him, the man suddenly reached out and caught his arm in a vice-like grip.

'I said, are you lost?'

Rolf freed himself. 'Leave me alone, you fool,' he snapped back.

The man gave a cackling laugh that echoed around the bombed buildings. 'Me a fool! Ha, just look at you, an *SS* officer lost in the ruined capital of his glorious Third *Reich*.'

Rolf stopped and stared hard at the man in front of him. Tall but stooped, with a thick mop of tangled, greasy hair that hung to his shoulders. There was a haunted look about his eyes and Rolf quickly saw that they did not blink. Then he also saw that the man wore a dirty, black army greatcoat.

'Why are you wearing *SS* uniform?' he said with a rising anger.

The man threw up a mocking salute. '*HEIL* Hitler! *Hauptsturmführer*. .... Because I am fucking *SS*.' He bowed low. '*SS-Sturmann* Hans Horsch at your service.'

'You drunken swine!' shouted Rolf. 'You're a deserter!'

The man's eyes glittered and his voice lowered. 'I'm a deserter and I'm fucking proud of it.'

Rolf fumbled with the flap of his holster. 'You swine! I've a good mind to shoot you now.'

The man took a step nearer and raised his hand. 'Shoot me will you? .... I've shot more men and women and children, than you've had fucking hot breakfasts.' He placed his hand over his heart and touched Rolf's arm with the other. 'Go on *Hauptsturmführer*, shoot me. Put your gun right here,' he pointed to his chest, 'and pull the trigger. Do it now!' His voice took on a pleading quality. 'Only God knows how much I want to die. I've used the gun so much, now you use it to kill me.'

Removing his Luger from its holster, Rolf clicked off the safety catch and pointed the gun at the man's head. Then curiosity overtook anger. 'What do you mean, you've shot women and children?'

The man's face changed and his lips formed a thin line. His shoulders straightened. 'Ah, Ah, …. I knew you'd be interested in the killing. After all, we are fuckin' *SS*.' Rolf lowered his gun but kept it at his waist. The man continued. 'I was a soldier in the *Einsatzgruppen* in the East. I'm sure you know what duties we carried out for the *Führer* in the *Einsatzgruppen*? I was assigned, with my group, to Poland, close to the city of Lodz. We lived a good life, plenty of free women and as much as we could drink. Oh yes, only the best for us. Cognac by the case and the women were superb, absolutely superb. We lived in houses that were once owned by Jews. My God, they know how to live. ….. My job was not soldiering, it was slaughtering.' He paused for a moment and reached into his pocket. Rolf lifted the Luger and then lowered it. The man dragged out a half-filled bottle, pulled out the cork and took a long swig. He offered it to his comrade. Rolf shook his head. The man stared at a point somewhere over Rolf's shoulder. 'The local *SD* and *Gestapo* rounded up all the Jews. Then we marched them to a place outside the village and we made them dig the pits themselves. And the surprising thing is that they did dig the pits and they never complained. They were like sheep to the slaughter. My job was simple. My comrades made the Jews line up in a row on the edge of the pit and then, on a given order, they knelt. I walked along the back of the row and shot them. I was good at my job and I used a gun just like yours.' and he pointed at Rolf's Luger. 'The only problem is, having to reload after eight shots. That really slowed things down a bit. And I never missed. I aimed at the base of the neck and the force of the shot made the Jew fall forward into the pit. The whole thing was very efficient. I could kill two hundred and fifty in two hours.' His face lifted, 'Do you know, every time I tried to drink myself stupid but I never managed it. With a woman I could get as drunk as anybody but never with the killing, …. never.' He took a quick gulp from the bottle. 'Another strange thing, *Hauptsturmführer*, is that I can remember the face of every person I killed. When I stop drinking this stuff,' he raised the bottle, 'then I see them all. Each face passes in front of me like an old-fashioned slide show. Men, women, whole families. Beautiful girls, achingly beautiful and I had to kill them because they were Jews. What a fucking waste!' Another swig. 'I didn't shoot babies or very young children. Oh, no, that was a waste of expensive ammunition. They were thrown into the pit before their parents were shot. That way they always watched their children and kept quiet. They died of suffocation when the pits were covered over.' He stopped talking and, as the first light of the dawn seeped over the buildings, he stared hard at Rolf and his voice dropped to a whisper, 'How did you do your killing, *Hauptsturmführer*?'

Rolf's heart was beating fast and his breath caught in his throat. 'By gassing and Phenol injection,' he said, in a whisper. Not knowing why he answered.

The man nodded. 'That's the easy way. No blood, no mess. Mine was more direct and more, shall we say, personal. .... *Hauptsturmführer*, do you sleep well at nights? Do you hate the dark? Do you find that you can't fuck a woman properly?'

Rolf remained motionless, unable to move a muscle, let alone speak.

The man stood stock-still and shook his head. 'I see my questions have meaning. Perhaps, one day, you'll end up like me?' With his free hand, he reached deep down into his other pocket. Rolf jumped. 'After killing three thousand two hundred and forty seven men, women and children, the glorious *Reich* gave me this.' He waved the ribbon and its medal in front of Rolf's face. 'The fucking Iron Cross, Second Class. As soon as I saw yours, I knew you were a murderer, just like me.' Leaning back against the wall, he took a last swig from the bottle and hurled it over Rolf's head. It smashed to pieces against a pile of rubble.

'And now, *Hauptsturmführer*, you can kill me.' Turning, he raised a gnarled dirty finger and pointed at the base of his neck. 'Just here. Between the third and fourth vertebrae.' There was a silence as Rolf stared at the man's back. The silence lasted for a full minute and then he turned. There was a lopsided smile. 'I told you so, *Hauptsturmführer*. Gassing is too easy. At the very least, you can give me the bottle of cognac that you've got in your case.' Their eyes locked.

Rolf said, 'How do you know ....?'

'The *SS* always provide the best for their murderers.' The toothless smile was wolfish.

Bending down, Rolf opened the case and found the bottle. Thrusting it into the man's extended hand, he watched him wrench off the cork and drink deeply. In the harsh light of the dawn, Rolf examined the man and, in a gulp of awful realisation, saw himself.

TWENTY-NINE

Richard drove hard down the motorway to Nijmegen. Clutching his map in one hand and steering-wheel with the other. Quickly, he negotiated the traffic island at the southern end of the Nijmegen Bridge and then another three kilometres and he saw the sign for Kekerdom and Millingen leading along to a much smaller road. Only another eight kilometres and he was there.

"Kekerdom", the sign read and the road dropped off the dike into a nondescript sort of place. A village with a main road and no shops that he could see. Richard wondered where the fax had come from in such a small place. Without realising it, he was lost, the road a dead end. Reversing, he turned the car round and headed back to the other road. Frustrated, he pulled up outside the first house and stopped the car. It was a pretty building, white walls and a low, tiled roof. Stepping over a flower trough, he knocked at the door.

A youngish woman answered and he asked politely, 'Excuse me, I'm sorry I don't speak Dutch. Is this the right way to Millingen?'

Smiling, she replied, in English, 'That's all right, I speak English, my sister is married to an Englishman.' Leaving her house, she pointed down the road. 'Straight down, turn left at the junction and that goes into Millingen.' Glancing at his face, she said, 'Are you looking for anywhere in particular?'

Richard remembered the address. 'Yes, it's a place called Bimmen. Is it far from Millingen?'

'You can't miss it. Past the old border post and near an old church with an onion dome.'

'Thank you very much,' he replied and walked back to the MG.

She was exactly right and the road wound its way through the small town of Millingen. The road narrowed and the blue sign said simply, 'DEUTSCHLAND' and he was in Germany. Slowing down, Richard kept an eye out for the church. Before he had time to think, it appeared on his left; he stopped. Turning to his right, he knew instinctively that the building was the farm he was looking for.

An old L-shaped edifice in farmhouse baroque so loved by rich German landowners. Screened by tall poplar trees on each side, it stood back from the road. Pale cream washed walls with the lintel stones and cornices picked out in a darker brown. A tower dominated the angle of the 'L' linking the two main buildings. The onion dome of the church was repeated on top of the tower. Over the farm lay a feeling of calm and there was not a soul in sight. Richard saw the short cobbled drive leading from the road to the farm and, with a shrug, he drove down it.

As he stopped the engine, the wooden double fronted doors of the farmhouse opened. A man came out. Obviously some kind of servant, short and dumpy, he wore a black suit and incredibly shiny black boots. With an immobile face, he inclined his bald head and waited. Richard nodded and looked around.

'Good afternoon. You must be Richard Cooper?' The deep voice made him jump.

The same height as Richard but older, probably in his seventies. The thick grey hair was cut short and he held himself erect and ramrod straight. The hand that Richard grasped was cool.

Richard paused for a moment. 'Yes, I'm Richard Cooper and you must be Jan Bildt?'

Dressed in a soft blue woollen pullover with a silk tie knotted in exactly the right place between the collars of a starched white shirt. Grey linen trousers with firm creases. It was the face that drew attention. Tanned skin shaved absolutely smooth. High cheek bones with dark hollows below the eyes, which gave some indication of age; or an illness. With the welcoming smile, the lips were partly open showing perfectly white teeth. Blue eyes looked hard into Richard's. There were no laughter lines. Bushy eyebrows neatly trimmed.

'Yes indeed, I am Jan Bildt.' The English was crystal-clear and word perfect. 'May I welcome you to "*Grosse Bauernhof*". Please come into my home.' Letting go of Richard's hand, he waved him through the ornate doors.

Richard took in the high-ceilinged hall. Subtle lighting showed off the features. A high, carved wooden fireplace. A black and white tiled floor with a huge wooden staircase that dog-legged itself up the far wall. Paintings adorned the plaster walls. It was a large hallway with arches leading off down long corridors.

'Richard, I know you've had a long journey.' Richard was unsure of the familiarity. 'So, I've provided some light refreshment in the library. Do follow me.' He walked slowly away down the nearest corridor with his guest following at his side. Richard took in everything, the size of the house; the feeling of calm and Jan Bildt. He was not what he had been expecting but the man fitted perfectly with his surroundings. Just as they arrived at an imposing door, it opened. The same servant stood to one side and gave a slight bow.

'Thank you, Hans,' said Jan Bildt. He turned to Richard and smiled. 'Please help yourself.'

It was indeed a library. Floor to ceiling with books. Modern hardbacks lined one wall and the other held heavy tomes. The smell of linseed-oil soaked leather bindings. It was all beautifully done. A huge mahogany table on which were placed three earthenware plates filled with food. Chunks of brown bread. Slices of thick sausage and sliver-thin pieces of fruit all laid out like clock numerals on the circular plates. Richard was hungry and he waited politely.

Jan Bildt waved his hand, 'Please.' Picking up a matching plate, Richard walked round the table and collected food. As he slipped the first slice of food in his mouth, he watched Jan Bildt. All the time, Richard was trying to establish exactly why he was eating with a total stranger.

'There are soft drinks and wine on the table near the window,' said Bildt. 'with two bottles of a light Hock. Just nod to Hans and he'll pour out a glass for you.' Richard could not resist, he nodded. Wearing spotless white gloves, Bildt's servant selected a delicate, long-stemmed glass and half-filled it. He passed it over to Richard.

Turning to Bildt, Richard raised the glass. 'Cheers.'

'*Prosit*,' replied Bildt.

Richard wanted to know about this man and, just as he swallowed the first mouthful of excellent Hock, Bildt beat him to it.

He walked over to the mullioned windows, causing his body to be in silhouette. 'Richard, I know exactly what you're thinking. You're thinking, "what the hell am I doing in this house, with this stranger, so far away from my home and my family?"'

Before he could continue, Richard interrupted, which caused some surprise. 'I must say straight away,' he said firmly, 'That all this could've been dealt with in a much easier way.' He pushed his points home. 'If you've information about my father, then you could've posted it to me or, indeed, visited me in England.' Richard sipped again at his glass and waited.

Bildt placed his glass down carefully on the window ledge. 'I can only apologise for my methods.' He took a deep breath. 'I rarely travel. My doctor says it's not good for me. Also, the information that I have, concerns the war. In Germany, we still have many worries about the war. The documents I possess, like me, do not travel well. Such papers are best kept under lock and key in my home rather than having them exposed to other prying eyes.' Walking away from the window, he refilled his plate. 'I also wanted to meet you. .... May I refill your glass?' Without waiting for an answer, he motioned to the servant and Richard's glass was filled.

Richard wanted to like this man. However, there was something about him that caused a deep worry. 'I've never heard of you, in fact my father never mentioned anybody by your name,' he said.

'What about your mother?' Bildt said, quietly, watching Richard's face. 'After all, she is German.' Richard made no comment. 'I would think that by now you're reading your father's diary and notes?' It was said with such aplomb that Richard nearly dropped his plate. The man's knowledge made him angry.

'Yes, I am and how the hell did you know about that?'

Bildt shrugged and swallowed a slice of sausage. 'It's logical, I suppose. I know he kept notes.' Richard let him continue. 'When people write about the war and what happened and particularly when they held such important posts as your father, then what they write has a great deal of importance.'

'The war happened a long time ago,' said Richard.

'You talk as a comparatively young man. But remember, you were born after the war ended. You were not directly involved.'

Richard sipped at his glass. 'I think having a German mother and a Dutch Jewish father involves me somewhat.'

'*Touché*,' nodded Bildt with a frown. He changed the subject. The polite smile flashed across the room. 'I presume you'd like to stay for the night?'

On the journey down, Richard had been unsure as to whether he was going to stay at the Millingen Centrum Hotel or with Bildt. But, in all honesty, he was finding this man fascinating and he wanted to know more about him. 'I would be delighted to stay here,' he heard himself saying. 'But I don't want to put you to any inconvenience .... .'

Bildt clapped him on the shoulder. 'No difficulty at all, Richard. .... Look here, I live in this old house alone, that is apart from Hans.' He put his glass down. 'It's not a problem. I'll get your bags taken from the car. If you give Hans your keys, he'll put the car away for you.'

'That's very kind but I'd prefer to ......'

'Of course, ... I quite understand. Your MG is special. Just follow Hans and he'll show where to put your car.'

Richard walked back down the corridor and Bildt made small talk about the weather. Hans had the rear hatch open and was collecting Richard's bags. He pointed through the archway under the domed tower and said something. Richard did not understand.

From the doorway, Bildt called, 'Go through the arch and turn left. It's the first building.'

Richard drove his car slowly over the cobbles and through the arch. Everything was as Bildt said it would be. Once inside the old stables, he stopped the engine and climbed out of the car. Glancing down the length of the building, he was surprised with what he saw. A wonderful collection of classic cars. A lot of Mercedes, with a sprinkling of Rolls Royce. As he walked down the long row, he saw six Jaguars, ranging from a rare "C" type, passed a magnificent "D" and then four "E" types. Every one of them was in perfect condition. The voice made him jump.

'Not a bad collection, is it?' Jan Bildt stood casually inside the last stable door.

'Wonderful,' said Richard, amazed at the surprises that this man kept producing.

'You see, we have much in common,' said Bildt and Richard nodded. 'Hans has taken your case up to your room. It's such a pleasant evening. Perhaps you'd like a walk on the estate before you go to your room?'

Richard felt instinctively cautious but he could hardly refuse. What he really wanted to do was to find out about his father and so he answered politely. 'A pleasure, Mr Bildt.'

'Please call me Jan. All my friends do.' They walked past the end of the farmhouse and through a screening circle of massive oaks. Bildt stopped and waved towards the buildings. '"*Grosse Bauernhof*"', he said, expansively, 'has been here for nearly three hundred years. Of course, the estate used to be much bigger but over time, a lot of the land has had to be sold off.'

'How long have you lived here?' asked Richard as they walked onto a concrete road.

'Since just after the war. Property was at quite a good price in those days. The place was almost a ruin. The Americans had used it as a billet and they had not taken care.' Fields stretched away towards the undulating skyline. Small woods and coppices dotted the landscape. 'Over the years, I've managed to buy back some of the land but I'll never be able to return the farm to its old status.'

There was little sign of any activity and Richard wondered just what this beautiful land produced. He was curious. 'What crops do you grow?'

Jan Bildt stopped and plucked a berry from a bush. 'I don't grow a great deal of anything really. Europe pays me a lot of money not to farm my land. I make what money I need from pigs.'

'Pigs?' said Richard, incredulously.

Bildt chewed and swallowed the berry. 'Oh yes, pigs. I've got thousands of them,' pointing with his finger into the distance. 'They're over there. Fortunately, the wind's blowing in the right direction. On some days the smell gets pretty bad. The locals complain but then I employ most of them. The Dutch are the worst. Before my phone went ex-directory, they were always phoning about the smell.'

'Is that why your fax number is in Holland in Kekerdom?' said Richard, very quietly.

Bildt stared. 'That's clever of you.' He shrugged his shoulders. 'I like my privacy and I'll do anything to protect it.' There was a change in his demeanour. He stopped walking and turned. 'It's getting a bit chilly now. …. Let's return to the house.' As dusk approached, they walked back down the road.

The main doors opened, as though Hans had been watching them approach. Giving that same jerky bow, he stood to one side as they walked through into the hall.

Bildt paused. 'Richard, I'm sure you're tired after your journey. Perhaps you'd like to take a shower and rest. Please remember that my home is your home.' Hans took his long coat. 'The gong will sound at seven-thirty and I've invited one other guest.' Before Richard could ask the question, Bildt gave a polite smile and beckoned to his servant. 'Hans, do take Mr Cooper to his room.'

Hans set off across the hall towards the stairs. Richard followed him. Each tread creaked slightly and he could not help looking down at the hall below. Jan Bildt stood motionless and his expressionless face followed Richard's every step.

At the end of a long corridor, the servant opened a stout wooden door. Richard stepped into the room.

A large living space dominated by a massive, open-hearthed fireplace. The burning logs crackled in the draught from the closing door. A high, ornate plaster ceiling with a superb brass chandelier hanging dead centre. Richard walked across the wooden floor to the window. Moving the heavy curtains to one side, he glanced down into the darkness, trying to work out where he was.

The room was well-furnished with comfortable chairs and a long sofa. In the corner stood a roll-top desk and then he saw a small door half-hidden in the oak panelling of the corner of the room. Stepping round the largest chair, he opened the door and stepped into the bedroom. Another big room, with a four poster bed standing squarely against the longest panelled wall. A tall cupboard was open and Richard saw his clothes hanging neatly on hangers. His empty suitcase lay open on a wooden trestle and he noticed his shoes had been carefully polished. He phoned his wife.

Rebecca answered and gave a squeal of delight when she heard Richard's voice. 'Dad, ... it's so good to hear from you.' And then she hesitated and her voice changed. 'Are you all right. I mean, ... are you safe?'

'Stop worrying, Rebecca,' he replied laughing. 'I'm absolutely fine and there're no problems. Now, please, can I speak to Jane.'

'See you, Dad.'

'Hello, darling. How are you?' Her reassuring voice sent a warmness through his heart.

'I'm absolutely OK. In fact, I'm sitting in my own room and feeling quite at home.' In fact, he wasn't but he wanted to allay any fears for his wife.

'What's he like, this man, Jan Bildt?'

'Utterly charming,' replied Richard, stretching his legs. 'Not at all what I expected. He's a very rich pig farmer.

'A pig farmer,' shouted Jane.

'Yep, a pig farmer.'

She hesitated. 'Have you found out anything about your father?'

Richard pondered his answer. 'Bildt knows something, I don't yet know what.'

'And you're staying the night?'

Richard smiled. 'Listen, I'm staying here for the night. Stop worrying, I'm being well looked after. There's this butler, he's really spooky and I'm having dinner here. In fact, I find the whole thing really interesting.'

Jane caught the tone of his voice. 'Well, I'm relieved and how was Lottie Cohen?'

Richard told the story of his meeting and explained about the family that they had never met.

'I see and you're coming back on the ferry tomorrow night. Is that still your plan?'

'Yep, I should be finished here after breakfast ....'

'With lots of bacon?' interrupted Jane.

Richard saw the joke and laughed. 'Yes, darling, with lots of bacon.' They chatted for several minutes and then the conversation was over.

Richard knew there would be a drinks cabinet somewhere and he quickly found it. The tall chest of drawers in the corner were not really drawers. A good selection and he poured himself a large measure of brandy and quickly downed it. Glancing at a carriage clock on the desk, he realised that he had thirty minutes left before dinner. Dashing to the large bathroom, he turned on the water, threw in some soap crystals from a glass bowl and began to undress.

Lying in the hot refreshing water gave him time to relax. 'I'll have dinner with this man and his friend,' he thought, 'and then I want him to tell me exactly what he knows about my father.' After washing in the rich lather, he drew himself out of the bath and began to towel himself vigorously. Within five minutes, he had slipped into a clean shirt and knotted on a bright silk tie. Just in time, the sound of the distant gong echoed through into his room. Humming to himself, Richard opened the door and walked down the corridor. He passed half a dozen doors and all were solidly closed. Paintings of bewigged men and elegant ladies lined the walls and underfoot the long carpet stretched forever. Eventually, he arrived at the top of the stairs and paused to look down.

Jan Bildt was waiting and he glanced up when Richard started down the stairs. What surprised Richard most of all, was that Bildt was dressed in a full dinner suit and a damned good one at that. Beautifully cut and made from silk. The starched shirt had a bright red bow at the top and an equally dazzlingly red cummerbund at the waist. He radiated wealth and good living.

'Good evening, Richard,' he said, warmly. 'I hope you've had a rest.' He saw the glance. 'Oh, yes, the dinner suit. I'm sorry but when my friend comes we always dress for dinner.' Wringing his hands, he was genuinely concerned. 'Please don't worry. Just forget about it. It's my bad manners.'

Richard held up his hand. 'It really is no problem.'

'Ah, excellent,' Bildt replied, clapping hands with perfectly manicured fingers, 'I'm glad you understand. Let's go and have a glass of sherry before dinner.' As he walked away, Richard caught a waft of a very expensive cologne.

They walked together through another door that led to an ante-room. Glass cabinets full of delicate porcelain. On a beautiful veneered table stood a decanter and three glasses. The ever-present Hans hovered. Bildt nodded and two glasses were carefully poured out.

'*Prosit*,' said Bildt. His blue eyes glinted.

'Cheers,' replied Richard.

Bildt downed the glass in one gulp and, without looking, held it out to be refilled.

Richard asked a question that had been beckoning since he had spoken to Jane. 'Mr Bildt......'

'Jan, please.'

'May I ask if there's a lady of the house?'

Looking at him with a steady stare and a slight lifting of the shoulders, Bildt replied quietly. 'There used to be but she is no more.' He let that sink in. 'Sometimes other guests come to stay here but as I said earlier, I like my privacy.'

From the corner of his eye, Richard watched Hans move across the room and open a pair of double doors. Turning slightly, he saw a large, square polished table lit by a huge silver candelabra; three neatly laid places for dinner.

Bildt looked at his watch. 'My good friend is a little late. Do take a seat.' Richard folded himself into a comfortable chair. Almost as he was about to speak, Hans scuttled across the room and left to go into the hall.

'It's pork for dinner, cooked in a special "*Grosse Bauernhof*" way.'

'I thought it may be pork,' said Richard, mischievously.

Bildt's eyebrows lifted and then he smiled. 'Ah yes, the British sense of humour and, of course, you're right, I eat a great deal of my pork.'

Their conversation stopped as a man walked into the room. Richard did not recognised him.

'Good evening, Mr Cooper.' The English was quite good.

'Good evening,' replied Richard, rising to his feet.

'Ah yes,' added Jan Bildt. 'Richard, may I introduce my very oldest *kamerad* and good friend, Willi.'

To Richard, the name meant nothing.

THIRTY

Rolf fought with his conscience. Torn from Ulrika's warm bed and feeling depressed and worn out, he was unsure whether or not he should visit his wife. The deserter in the street had shaken his normally firm composure as had many other events of the past few weeks.

Pushing his way through the streets, it took him an hour to find his apartment. Cursing the whole Allied Air Force, he struggled up the stairs. The front door hung off its hinges. With a kick of anger, Rolf knocked it to one side. Dropping his suitcase to the floor, he walked a half-pace sideways and looked at himself in a long cracked mirror. Shaking his head, he said aloud, 'Rolf Müller, you look a God awful mess.' He was right. His riding boots were gouged and covered in mud and dust. The long, green greatcoat was stained with grease and smudges of burnt timber. It was his own face that made him stare. Although he was a young man of twenty-eight, he looked twice that age. Grey skin drawn tight across the cheek bones. Pale lips drawn into a thin line and the eyes, the eyes. Gone was their sparkling blueness, replaced by sunken hollows with pin-prick, black pupils.

Walking down the hall, Rolf saw the black greatcoat hanging on a bent hook. The rank epaulette made him frown, the silver and gold of an *SS-Oberführer*. And then it hit him. Turning, he kicked open the bedroom door. There she was, Angela's naked white body astride a fat, white pig of a man. Torn between shooting him and killing her, Rolf chose to do nothing but stand and stare. The door crashing open stopped her at the precise moment of orgasm. With a scream of half-pleasure and half-surprise her head whirled round, sending her lank hair swirling round her shoulders.

Recognition was instant. 'You bastard,' she screamed. 'What the hell are you doing here?'

The man under her, saw Rolf's uniform and tried to sit up; he could not. 'Did you hear me?' she shouted.

An iciness spread over him like a cold shower. 'Don't let me stop you, Angela. You're obviously enjoying yourself.'

The white pig found his voice and snarled, '*Hauptsturmführer*, what the fuck are you doing here?'

Rolf walked calmly across the bedroom, unfastened his pistol holster and removed the Luger. Gripping the butt until his knuckles whitened, he pushed it closer to the man's face and then finally into his mouth. Leaning over him, he said softly, 'My name's Müller and I'm this whore's husband.' He clicked off the safety catch and pulled back the hammer. The coldness in his voice stilled them both. 'I'm not going to kill you because she's not worth it. Enjoy yourself while you can. The war's nearly over and we've lost.' While the gun made the man gag, Rolf, with his other hand, grabbed his wife's long hair. Forcing her head back, he filled his mouth with a ball of angry phlegm and spat it full into her face.

Standing back, Rolf's gaze swept round the room. On her dressing table, lay the diamond necklace. With a vicious twist, he removed the muzzle of the revolver from the pig's mouth causing a grunt of pain. Stepping back from the scene, Rolf turned, swept the necklace into his pocket and strode towards the door. Hearing movement behind him, he swivelled, brought the Luger up to his waist and fired two shots. One bored a neat hole in the headboard above the bed. The other shattered the mirror on her dressing-table, sending a shower of glass across the floor. Walking through the open door, Rolf turned into the lounge. The drinks cabinet was half-open. He took the two bottles of spirits and stuffed them into his pockets. At the end of the hall, he collected his bag and left the apartment.

Rolf's head was clear. As he walked back onto the cracked pavements of the *Friedrich Strasse*, he knew exactly where he was going. On the *Wilhelmstrasse* was a small officers' club, strictly for the SS. Rolf had stayed there before. The rain still poured down and it took another thirty minutes to arrive at the entrance. Turning the heavy handle, he stepped inside. A corporal leapt to attention.

'Good morning, *Herr Hauptsturmführer*.'

'Morning,' replied Rolf, breezily. 'I want a room and I want my uniform cleaning and pressing.'

'*Jawohl, Herr Hauptsturmführer*.'

The room was standard officers' with a tiny shower. Rolf stripped off and, before he plunged into the shower, somebody arrived and removed his uniform and boots. The stinging hot water hit him hard and, gasping for breath, he soaped his body vigorously and revelled in the pleasure of being clean. There was a quiet knock at the door.

'Come,' called Rolf.

The orderly entered, laid out the uniform and boots on the bed and left. Rolf slipped back into his clothes, straightening his shoulders and felt like a new man. Opening the door, he marched down the corridor to the stairs. Within a minute, he was in the bar.

Blue smoke, a darkened room, drunken laughter, shouts and a heaving crowd of uniformed men. Rolf felt immediately at home and plunged into their midst. He knew nobody and nobody knew him. It was the best excuse to get blind drunk and it took him about an hour.

The next thing he remembered was somebody shaking him. '*Hauptsturmführer*, there's a message for you.'

The headache was blinding and, held his head in an intense grip.

'I'm sorry but the message is important.'

Opening his eyes, Rolf saw a steward holding a grey envelope. As he moved, his stomach heaved and emptied its contents over the bed. 'Jesus Christ,' he shouted, 'leave it on the table.'

'But, *Hauptsturmführer*, I was told that you had to read it and give an immediate reply.' The man looked scared and wrinkled his nose as the stench of vomit. Fumbling, he drew out a sheet of paper. 'It's marked URGENT,' he said, 'and says that you must report to your unit immediately. You're to report to *Templehof*. Your plane leaves in two hours.' Placing the orders and the envelope on the table, he fled.

Rolf groaned and flashes of light seared across his eyes. There was another wrenching heave in his bowels. Trying to sit up, he only succeeded in falling off the bed. When his stomach was finally empty, he crawled into the shower. Somehow he turned it on and lay in the corner as stream of icy cold water showered on to him.

The repeated knocking at the door forced him to stand up. By grasping every protuberance he could see, Rolf arrived at the door. Turning the handle, he opened it a fraction. A lieutenant stood in the corridor.

'*Herr Hauptsturmführer*, your transport for *Templehof* airfield arrives in fifteen minutes.' Rolf nodded and closed the door.

His uniform hung neatly on hangers and the boots were shinily clean. As he succeeded in drying himself, he wondered who had put him to bed. There was a clean white shirt and he managed to slip it over his shoulders. Then he was ready. Pulling open the door, he managed to walk down to the reception desk. The lieutenant grinned up at him.

'Feeling a little better now, *Hauptsturmführer*?'

'No, I most certainly am not,' he grunted.

'I hope you've had a good stay here, sir?'

'Stay. Stay where?' Rolf glanced at his wrist-watch. 'I've had about six hours and that's all.'

The lieutenant smile again, 'Sorry, you've been here nearly two days. You slept solidly for over thirty hours.'

'Unbelievable,' grunted Rolf.

A uniformed old man came through the door. Giving an old fashioned

Wehrmacht salute, he announced. 'Transport for a *Hauptsturmführer* Müller.'

'That's me,' said Rolf, wearily.

His transport was an ageing lorry minus its canvas top. Rolf sat in the front with the driver, who said not a word as the lorry bucked and heaved its way across rubble and partially filled-in bomb craters.

Templehof was almost deserted. Two aircraft stood in hangars and the concrete taxi areas were a mass of filled-in holes. The lorry pulled up outside the once magnificent front entrance and Rolf climbed down. The driver leant over and threw the bag down to him. With a belching blue exhaust, the lorry stuttered off back into the rain.

The waiting hall was half-full of miserable looking men in uniform and Rolf thought this was probably how he looked. Outside, the cloud base was low and Rolf hunched into the corner of the hall. Thinking that the aircraft would not be on time, he sat on his case, leant against the wall and pulled down his peaked cap. Sleep came quickly and he dozed.

'*Hauptsturmführer*, please wake up.'

Opening his eyes, he saw a man looking at him.

'Sir, your flight's on final circuit now.' The man darted back into an office.

Shaking himself, Rolf rose unsteadily to his feet and peered across the airfield. He heard the aircraft before he saw it and then it skimmed low out of the clouds. Without any change in direction, it flew straight onto a short runway and taxied quickly towards the hangar. A battered *Junkers* 52 lumbering along on one of its three engines, oil patches streaking its fluted aluminium sides.

Jerking to a stop, the engines idled over and a door flew open. A crewman beckoned Rolf and he walked across the short strip of concrete to the aircraft. As he climbed up the steps, the noise from the radial *BMW* engine was deafening and he held his cap with one hand and gripped his suitcase with the other.

The flight droned on and on and the roar of the engines did nothing to help Rolf's throbbing headache. He was puzzled by his own behaviour. Earlier he had been drunk. This was something that normally did not happen and he could not understand why. Eventually, he drifted into a restless sleep.

The *Junkers* landed bumpily at a small grass airfield some distance from Krakow. Rolf climbed wearily into the back seat of the waiting car. The journey took over an hour and it was dark when he arrived at Birkenau. Bright arc-lights still glared out over the bleak countryside and a frost made them sparkle like diamonds. The mess was nearly empty and a solid wave of tiredness passed over him.

He was just about to walk to his room when a steward looked up from the reception desk. 'Excuse me, sir. It is *Hauptsturmführer* Müller, isn't it?' Rolf nodded. 'There's a message for you, *Hauptsturmführer*.' And he handed over an official grey envelope. Rolf stuffed it in his pocket.

The cold night air hit him in the face and he took a deep, refreshing breath. Determined to walk to his quarters, he set off down the footpath to the barracks. A full moon made everything clear and sharp. As he trudged along, he stopped and stared across the road towards the barbed wire fence that stretched away into the distance on either side of him. Nothing moved but something was different, something was missing. It took Rolf a full minute to work it out and then he snapped his fingers with the realisation; it was the sounds and stench of the crematoria. Gone was the roar of the flames and the stink of burnt flesh. It made Rolf sniff the air, all he could smell was the frost and his own body. Stamping his feet on the ground, he strode on to his room.

The sight of his spare uniform hanging in his locker made him strip everything off and go for a shower. Before he climbed into his narrow bed, Rolf tore open the envelope. A standard message, a simple instruction telling him to report to the adjutant's office first thing in the morning. Rolf fell asleep quickly but not before noticing that the shriek and clank of the night time transport trains were no more.

Arriving at the headquarters building, he knocked on the office door and waited.

'Come in.'

The adjutant looked up from his desk. 'Do sit down, Müller.' He continued scribbling something. Eventually throwing his pen down, he said, 'Thanks for reporting back. Did you have a pleasant leave in the wonderful capital of the *Reich*?' The comment was made with a thin smile and a raising of the eyebrows.

Rolf sighed. 'It wasn't a good leave. In fact, it was awful. Berlin's a ruin.'

'I know,' replied the adjutant. 'I was there a week ago and it only gets worse.' He stretched his arms above his head. 'How's your wife?' Rolf just shook his head. The adjutant nodded. 'I know what you're saying, Müller. It's happening to many of our men as well. I'm lucky, I'm not married. Anyway, thanks for following your orders and returning to Auschwitz.'

Rolf sat forward in the chair. 'Why was I ordered back early?'

The adjutant shrugged his shoulders. 'All SS personnel from concentration camps on leave have been ordered back.'

'Why?' asked Rolf with some irritation.

The adjutant chuckled, 'Because, my dear Müller, many of our SS brothers are deserting. Fleeing from the sinking ship. Taking anything they can get and just disappearing.' Tapping his fingers on his the desk, he shook his head. 'The *Reichsführer* said he would look after all of us. I'm beginning to doubt his word.' Throwing back his head, he laughed. 'A few weeks ago, I would have been shot for saying that. But now, who knows?' And then his face became more serious. 'And what about you? Do you have somebody else you can go home to?'

'Yes,' replied Rolf, without thinking. 'I do have somebody.'

'At least you have a profession. I'm just a killer who pushes paper work. What future is there for the likes of me?'

'You're a damned good administrator,' replied Rolf.

'I somehow don't think the Allies will recognise my qualifications.' He pulled open a drawer and took out a bottle and two glasses. 'A pity, because I've followed my orders to the letter and obeyed my superiors.' He filled the glasses and pushed one across the table. Rolf shook his head. 'In two days it'll be Christmas 1944 and it'll be the last one for us here at Auschwitz.'

'What's happening now?' asked Rolf.

The adjutant refilled his empty glass and slugged it back. 'The Russian army is only fifty kilometres away. The whole of Germany is moving away from somewhere to somewhere else. God knows where we're going to.'

'What do I have to do?' asked Rolf, wearily.

His adjutant shuffled some papers. 'Check the final arrangements for the destruction of Crematoria V and III. And keep an eye on some of the NCO's, a lot have left already. If they try to leave here without permission, shoot 'em.' He cast his eyes to the ceiling. Rolf, feeling the meeting was over, began to stand. 'Müller,' and he stared Rolf straight in the face, 'you're one of the few people I can depend upon, thank you.'

Rolf did his job in a Birkenau that was over half-empty. As he walked to the place where the burial pits had been emptied and the rotting bodies had been burnt, he saw columns of inmates leaving through the main gates. Long rows of people dressed in rags and most with no footwear. Constantly the still air was punctuated by screams of terror, the shouts of the guards and the baying of dogs. For a moment, he watched them and not one lifted his eyes from the frozen earth to the blue sky above.

Christmas Day was an orgy of drinking and women. Rolf kept well away from it. He wrote several letters to Ulrika and posted them, unsure whether they would ever arrive. The day after Christmas he tended to some of the SS who had been injured in a chance air raid that hit some of the SS barracks.

These were indolent days for Rolf. Sometimes he stood out in the cold air and watched the great fleets of American and Russian bombers unload their cargoes on nearby industrial targets. At night, he heard the ever-increasing rumble of Russian artillery. On New Year's Day Josef Mengele returned and Rolf knew that something was going to happen.

Mengele had gone to the Crematorium and ten minutes later Rolf found him. He was standing talking to a guard. When Rolf approached, he turned. 'Rolf, good to see you again.' He tilted his head and smiled. 'I need to talk to you. Let's walk.'

The snow had stopped and the ground was thick with the previous heavy fall. It was a cold day but the wind had dropped and the snow seemed to cover up what this awful place really was. Mengele made sure they were out of earshot of anybody near the Crematorium. They walked along the road at the side of the Ramp and Rolf waited for Mengele to speak.

'Rolf, later today I'll be leaving Auschwitz, never to return. Auschwitz is finished.' He gave a hollow laugh. 'The Russians are only thirty kilometres away and if they jumped on a train, they'd be here on the Ramp within an hour. Everybody is heading west and I advise you to do the same, as quickly as possible.' He stopped and caught Rolf's arm. 'I'm telling you this because I have a place in my car for you. You're welcome to accompany me. I've made special arrangements.' He removed his hand.

Rolf thought for a moment and quickly made up his mind. 'Doktor Mengele, I'm flattered that you want to help me. But I must turn down your request because I have my orders.'

Mengele smiled. 'Yes, my dear Rolf, I quite understand. But we SS doctors are special. There will come a time when what we've learnt will be welcomed by the world. Whole new branches of medical science will be opened because of our work here at Auschwitz. In ten years, people like you and I will be much in demand.' He sighed. 'You have one hour to change your mind.' Rolf stiffened as Mengele embraced him and the sickly cologne came to his nostrils. Mengele released him and strolled away. Rolf watched the figure walk down the side of the Ramp, neither looking left nor right. It was January 17, 1945 and the receding figure walked through the arched railway entrance and disappeared.

Daily the sound of the Russians drew ever closer. For Rolf, it was a time of limbo. He was torn between fleeing or waiting for the promised evacuation of *SS* personnel. His final order came, the blowing up of the intact Crematoria V. On a signal from him, it was the Jewish labourers that blew it up. As Rolf watched, he was quite surprised to see an inmate that he recognised. A desperately thin Benjamin Blum walked towards him and stared him full in the face.

'*Doktor,*' he said, softly, with a strange light in his eyes, 'is it not most apt that Jews built these places, died in them and that finally we destroyed them?' Rolf was speechless and then Benjamin Blum turned and left.

With the man's face sealed into his mind, Rolf walked back to the main entrance to the camp. Behind him, burning fiercely, twenty-nine storehouses containing looted clothing and personal belongings. When he arrived back at the mess, an unusual sight greeted him. Dozens of cars, lorries and vehicles of all sorts were parked haphazardly on the snow covered grass area. Bright lights everywhere and men running around. He ran into the mess reception hall and stared about him. Suitcases, piles of clothes, documents. Packing-cases lay in jumbled heaps. Overall, the noise of panic.

As Rolf arrived, *Sturmbannführer* Klein sat on a huge leather case drinking a bottle of champagne. An experienced *SS* officer with a sense of humour out of keeping with his surroundings. His face always had a dazzling smile and he was a well known ladies man.

'Müller, it's time to go,' he shouted. 'Transport's waiting. The stewards have packed all your belongings and your cases are here somewhere,' and he laughed and belched at the same time. 'Perhaps you'd like to travel with me? I need some company.'

'Where are we going to?' said Rolf, already searching for his bags.

'Fuck knows. Anywhere, apart from this shit-hole. The Reds are five kilometres away and they could be here within the hour. You'd better get a move on.'

Rolf ran back to his quarters, lifted the floorboard and breathed a sigh of relief when he saw the bag containing the necklace and the diamonds. Slipping them into his pocket, he ran as fast as he could back to the mess.

It took Rolf ten minutes to find his case. Clipped to the top of it was a sheaf of papers and he recognised his new orders. A crescendo of gunshots came through the open door of the mess. He looked up.

'Don't worry about it,' said Klein, smiling at him. 'The last guards are just shooting a few more Jews. Let them know we're still about.' And he winked. Rolf stayed with him until their transport was ready.

It was a huge black staff car complete with a general's pennants flying on the sloping wings. There was no driver. 'Only the best for the *SS*,' shouted Klein. 'I'll drive. I love driving, especially when I'm pissed.' Rolf threw the bags into the massive boot and climbed into the front seat. 'Let's have a look now.' Switching on the ignition, Klein tapped the fuel gauge. 'Yep, we've got fuel.' He flipped open the glove compartment. 'And maps. Sort 'em out, Müller.'

The Mercedes engine burst into life at the first pull of the starter. Klein slipped the big car into first and pulled away from the mess. A steady stream of vehicles turned left from SS administration buildings and made their way west. As they passed the arched entrance to Birkenau and bumped over the railway tracks, all the lights within the camp went out and there was total blackness.

THIRTY-ONE

The dinner was magnificent. Candles, the very best of German wine and charming hosts. Richard deliberately drank little. The two men were obviously close friends and, when the brandy arrived, Richard asked the questions.

'Jan, may I ask when you and Willi first became such good friends?'

Bildt tilted his head to one side and paused before answering. 'During the war, Willi and I served together in the army. Nothing serious, we were just soldiers in the *Wehrmacht*.'

'The *Wehrmacht*,' said Richard. He now wanted to check out something that had been floating through his mind since he had met Lottie. 'Not the *SS*?'

'Oh, no,' replied Willi, drawing deeply on a fat cigar, 'the *Wehrmacht* were not *SS*.'

'For a short time,' interrupted Bildt, 'we were attached to the *Waffen-SS*. Just administration on the Eastern Front.'

'In Russia?' said Richard, feeling that something was not quite right.

'Poland, actually,' Bildt added. Swirling the brandy in his glass, he looked Richard straight in the eyes. 'That was only for a few months, and then we rejoined our *Wehrmacht* units.'

Richard searched his brain. 'I thought when you served with the *SS*, it was for life?'

Jan Bildt caught Richard's line of thought and laughed. 'Ah, yes, of course, Richard. You're a historian. May I ask what period?'

'Modern European.'

'Yes, indeed. That accounts for your knowledge of the German army.'

'I know a little,' said Richard, feeling his hackles rise.

'By "a little" and, knowing the British liking for the understatement, I presume you know a great deal more than you say?'

'Probably,' replied Richard

'Mmm, I see.' And Jan Bildt placed the glass on the table and folded his arms.

Richard changed tack. 'Thank you very much for a superb dinner, I enjoyed it greatly.'

'Your company gave me great pleasure and Willi was looking forward to meeting you again.'

'*Ja*,' said Willi, 'I'm sorry for the intrigue on the boat.'

'What?' said Richard sharply.

'*Ja*, I was on the boat to make sure that everything was all right for your journey.'

Richard felt a rising anger. 'I suppose you let my tyre down?'

Willi shook his head and opened his hands. 'Your car tyres? No, ... nothing at all.'

Richard did not believe him.

They retired to a room adjacent to the dining-hall. Tall windows looked out over a floodlit avenue of trees. A log fire glowed in the big hearth. Richard was immersed in a soft chair. The brandy inside him had mellowed the thirst for what he wanted to know but he could not wait any longer.

'Earlier, I asked what you knew about my father. Now, I would like to know, ... please?'

Willi carefully stubbed his cigar out in the silver ashtray and rose to his feet. 'I think, Jan, that the time has come for me to depart. These things that Mr Cooper wishes to know, are private.' He turned to Richard, who, for a moment, thought he was going to click his heels. 'If you'll excuse me, Mr Cooper?'

'Of course,' replied Richard.

Willi did not shake his hand but merely inclined his head and left the room. Richard waited.

Jan Bildt sat erect in his armchair. He looked the picture of a wealthy landowner but there was something else about him that was difficult to describe. Richard noticed this and felt the mood of the conversation change. Bildt placed his still glowing cigar on the ashtray and then he steepled his fingers and touched the tip of his long nose.

He spoke very quietly, almost in a whisper. 'Richard, I asked you to come to my home because I had to tell you something that is very important. It's so important that I find it very hard to bring myself to say it. It's something that's been locked away inside me for fifty years. What I am about to say will change our lives forever.' He stopped talking and, with a forefinger, wiped a bead of sweat off his forehead.

Richard had no idea what he was talking about. 'Perhaps you'd better tell me about it,' he said, with not the faintest idea what he was going to hear.

Jan Bildt uncrossed his legs, rose slowly from the chair and, for the first time, showed his age. He crossed the room and stared through the window into the blackness at the end of the avenue and then straightened his back and turned. In a strong voice, he said, with his startlingly blue eyes never leaving Richard's face, 'Simon Cohen was not your father.'

'What?' exclaimed Richard, half out of his chair.

'No, because I am your real father.'

THIRTY-TWO

Rolf chose the quietest route away from the fleeing convoys of cars and lorries. Avoiding built-up areas but all the time heading north west, always north west. The night was still and cold. The heavy Mercedes held the road well, although at times it slid across the icy surface and lurched into rutted tracks. Klein drove the car aggressively and sang loudly as he kept the speed up. After an hour, they met their first obstruction.

'What the hell's that?' Klein shouted, skidding the car to a halt.

'I don't know,' answered Rolf, peering through the dirty windscreen. Ahead of them were the dim rear lights of a lorry. Pulling out his Luger, Rolf opened the door. 'It looks like a marching column. …. It could be the Russians. I'll stand on the running-board and you drive ahead slowly.'

The lorry moved to one side and then Rolf saw what it was following. A column of hundreds of people. He recognised their tattered rags; the blue and grey stripes of Auschwitz. The lorry's headlights cast a hovering cone of light over the trail of misery. They were not people, they were emaciated skeletons staggering, crawling and grovelling along a frozen, snow-covered track. Above the sound of engines came screams of pain, shouts of the guards and, occasional gun shots. Rolf saw one *SS* guard casually place his pistol against the neck of a woman on her knees and shoot her. The inmates stepped over the body and moved slowly forward. Klein drove the car steadily ahead for twenty minutes and then the lead vehicle came into view. As he stared inside, he saw the unmistakable outline of Josef Mengele.

'Don't stop,' shouted Rolf and climbed back into the car. He turned to Klein. 'Where're they going to?

'The concentration camp at Grosse Rosen,' answered Klein.

'In God's name, why?'

'Hiding the evidence, just as the *Reichsführer* ordered,' replied Klein grimly, gripping the huge steering wheel even more tightly. The car droned on, driving on sidelights when the moonlight allowed. Eventually they found a major road and several times Rolf stopped the car and scrutinised the map.

'Where are we, Müller?'

'We're past Breslau and on the main road to Berlin.' Klein took some sandwiches out of a bag. Offering one to Rolf, he enquired, 'I presume we both want to go to Berlin?'

'Why not? I can't think of anywhere else to go to.'

Klein swallowed a chunk of bread. 'We should really report to SS Headquarters. But I think I'll take a couple of days leave. .... And you?'

'Yes, I'll take a day off and then I'll decide what to do. I think Berlin is going to need every soldier it can find.'

Klein stretched and started the engine. 'Fuck Berlin. It'll soon be every man for himself.' They accelerated back onto the road. 'By the way, Müller, have you brought any insurance with you?' He gave a cunning smile.

'Insurance? .... What do you mean?'

'Jesus,' he retorted, 'you professional men. What I mean is, do you have any goods, ... any "things" that you can use to save yourself and prepare for the future?'

Rolf thought of the diamonds and the necklace. 'Yes, ... I do have one or two "things".'

'Thank Christ for that. I thought you weren't a complete idiot.'

There were no road signs and road checks appeared. Once or twice papers were checked. The sight of the staff car and the SS officers inside were sufficient. The Auschwitz administration had done its job well and there were no problems.

As they drove closer to the centre of the city, it became more difficult to make progress. Eventually, they were pulled over to the side of the road. An elderly sergeant saluted them and shouted, '*Hauptsturmführer*, you can go no further by car. You must drive to the next road and turn left into the *Wehrmacht* barracks and park your car.'

The gardens of the barracks passed by and were replaced by a jumbled collection of wrecks. Klein parked at the far end of the disorganised mess and then locked the car. He offered his hand and Rolf shook it. 'I'll leave my name and address at the *Adlon* Hotel. If you need me, that's where you'll find me. Good luck in the future.' They went their separate ways.

Rolf had already decided to go to *Wilhelmstrasse* and it was a short walk to Headquarters. Most of the once magnificent buildings were in ruins, however, he soon found the entrance to the basement. Stepping past the guard, Rolf walked down a short corridor and spoke to a man sitting behind a large desk. They stared at each other. 'I'm reporting in as ordered,' said Rolf wearily. 'Here are my travel orders,' and he placed his papers on the desk.

The man looked up and nodded. 'Thank you, *Hauptsturmführer*. Please take a seat for a moment.' Scanning the papers, he walked away from the desk and through an open door. It closed silently behind him. Rolf waited for twenty minutes. The corridor was constantly busy and there was nobody he recognised. Eventually, the man returned.

'Please follow me.' He beckoned Rolf after him.

The door led to steps which went downwards through several levels. The man stopped at another door and knocked quietly. Opening it, he stood to one side. An ante-room with antique furniture and rich carpets. An officer clicked his heels.

'Good afternoon, sir,' he said. '*Gruppenführer* Schultze will see you now.' Rolf was surprised and attempted to brush the dust off his uniform. The lieutenant noticed Rolf's worry. 'It doesn't matter, sir. Everybody coming from the front is in a bit of a mess. The *Gruppenführer* is quite used to it.'

'I'm not,' snapped Rolf and walked through the open door.

The decor of the room was extravagant. Everything was too much and Rolf recognised bad taste when he saw it. But nothing could deny the brooding power of the man behind the ornate Louis XIV desk. Standing stiffly to attention, Rolf stared fixedly ahead at Hitler's portrait on the wall above Schultze's chair.

'Sit down,' said Schultze softly.

Rolf eased himself into the high-backed chair opposite the desk.

'You've travelled directly from Auschwitz?' The cold eyes gimletted into his.

'Yes, *Herr Gruppenführer*,' replied Rolf.

'We're brother officers of the SS. Don't keep saying, "Yes, *Herr Gruppenführer*." "Yes, sir", will be fine.'

'Yes, sir.'

'Good, ... now, tell me what happened at Auschwitz.' Rolf told his story.

'Was all evidence of the Final Solution destroyed?'

Rolf was wary of this man and his power. 'Yes, sir. Records were either removed or burnt. Inmates were marched away to other camps.'

'Was Auschwitz-Birkenau empty when you left?' Rolf watched him taking notes.

'No, sir. In my judgement, there are hundreds, if not thousands, of inmates still remaining.'

Schultze sighed, throwing his gold pen on the desk. 'My God, what inefficiency. No wonder Himmler's worried.' Leaning back in his enormous throne-like chair, he stared hard at Rolf. 'What were your feelings about your work at Auschwitz? I hope you're not one of those weaklings that I hear too much about?'

Rolf felt a trap. 'Well, sir. I obeyed my orders and carried out my duties.'

Schultze chuckled, 'Don't we all, my dear Müller, don't we all.' He picked up a sheet of paper and scanned it. 'You'll be attached to the staff here at the Headquarters and there is much work to carry out at the *Reichsbank*. Work that will be beneficial to both of us.' His smile was of pure greed and he paused for a moment as his mind wandered off elsewhere. Folding his arms, he watched Rolf with his cold eyes. 'We are pleased with your work, *Hauptsturmführer*. You have indeed carried out your duties and what's more, you're the first SS officer from Auschwitz to report here for duty. Your accommodation will be at the *Maikaefer* Barracks on *Friedrich Strasse*.' He pushed an envelope across the desk. 'And yes, ... with immediate effect, you're promoted to *Sturmbannführer*. My congratulations, *Sturmbannführer* Müller.' His extended hand felt cold and clammy. 'This meeting is now over.'

Rolf jumped to his feet. 'Thank you, *Herr Gruppenführer*. Thank you very much. *HEIL* Hitler!'

'*HEIL* Hitler, Müller.'

The one good thing about his promotion meant that at the barracks he was provided with a larger room. With a sudden pang of worry, Rolf delved into his suitcase. He always carried any money and other important items in leather wallets. He sighed with relief when he saw the pouch holding the diamonds. The plain handkerchief was tied in a knot. Swiftly he undid it. The necklace slipped into his palm. With a grunt of pleasure, he re-wrapped it, placed it back in one of the wallets and pushed it into the corner of his tall cupboard. The room was comfortable and soon he had stored everything neatly away. A hot shower finally cleared the exhaustion of the journey and, almost before he had towelled himself dry, there was a quiet knock at his door and he called out for the person to enter.

A corporal stood in the doorway, holding Rolf's uniform in one hand and a collection of envelopes in the other. '*Herr Sturmbannführer*, here is your post.' He handed over two envelopes.

'Thank you,' replied Rolf. Inwardly smiling at the sound of his new rank. A glance at the covers showed him where they had come from. The brown envelope was dated three weeks previously and was addressed to him care of SS Headquarters. One had his name with no stamp and the other one made his heart pound as he recognised the neat handwriting; Ulrika Hannsen. Holding Ulrika's envelope in one hand. and his SS dagger in the other, he carefully slit open the flap and the censor's seal. Taking out the letter, he held it to his nose and the perfume made his testicles twitch. Rolf read it aloud.

'Apt 8
23 Seydlitz Strasse
Berlin.

15th December 1944

My darling Rolf,

Since we last met, I've written a dozen letters and thrown them all away. When I awoke on that morning and found you had left me, I cried for an hour. I thought at first that it was because of me that you'd left but then I realised you must've had a great deal on your mind. My bed is now so lonely and every night I sleep with my arms around a pillow, longing for it to be you. My body yearns for you in a way that I've never felt before. Every day I hear of deaths and I pray to God that it won't be you. I love you, Rolf Müller, I don't care what you do but I love you. I'm lonely for you and so is my bed. I don't know whether this letter will find you but when it does, please come to me my darling. PLEASE COME TO ME before I go crazy.

Ever loving you,

Ulrika.'

Rolf knew exactly where he was going to later that night. The next envelope had no censor's seal and he ripped it open. It contained a tightly folded sheet of paper. Three words in capital letters.

'NOW SAFE - WILLI'

'You clever bastard, Willi Hossler. I bet you're somewhere with that wife of yours,' thought Rolf.

The grey envelope was official and bore the *SS* stamp and seal. Rolf read it through once and then again.

Rolf slowly dressed. Pulling on his jackboots and, carefully removing a lose thread from his new collar insignia, he left his room and strode down the stairs and past the reception desk.

He walked because travelling by car was difficult. He picked his way over the ruins of his capital city and it made him curse aloud. There was the stink of escaping gas and burning timbers. With an eye and an ear seeing and listening for air raids, he wended his way towards *Seydlitz Strasse*.

It was not as he had left it. The whole apartment block had vanished to be replaced by a shoulder high pile of rubble. Rolf stared in amazement and then realised that Ulrika may be lying underneath this pyramid of brick. There was nobody in sight and a stillness lay over the area. He ran down each side of the block, at the far end, a low wall remained standing. Built from old stone, it was solid and well built. In the middle, stood an open door. He dashed through and down a flight of brick steps into the cellars. He stared around him and then stopped, letting his eyes become used to the gloom. Ahead, two electric lights flickered and showed him the way.

He walked on. More movement and he recoiled; rats. Fat, big, with gleaming yellow eyes and he heard the leathery patter of their feet. His nose wrinkled with the sharp stench of human excreta and urine. He heard voices and he hammered on a heavy door. It opened a crack wide.

'What do you want?' The man's eyes gleamed in the faint light. Rolf repeated his question. The crack widened. 'There was a woman living five doors down. I don't know whether she's still there.'

'Where's that?' said Rolf, anxiously.

'Turn left past the roof fall.' The door slammed shut.

He found it. The last door was splintered and he saw the flash of a light through a hole. He tapped on the panel. No answer. He kicked it with his foot.

'Who is it? What do you want?'

Rolf recognised the voice and shouted loudly, 'It's me, Rolf. Let me in.' There was the sound of bolts being drawn and the door slowly opened. She fell into his arms and he felt her body heave.

'Thank God, you're safe,' she sobbed. 'Thank God, you're safe.'

Rolf looked over her shoulder. A cell of a room. A tattered carpet on the floor. A few sticks of furniture and a bed with blankets in an untidy heap. Two half-burnt candles provided the only light. A smell of body sweat and rot. Gone was the fragrant, beautiful young girl.

Rolf eased her away from him and saw the tear stained eyes and the straggled hair. 'What happened?' he asked, gently.

'About three weeks ago,' she said, hesitatingly, 'there was a big raid. It went on for hours. I went to the cellars with nothing and I still have nothing .... apart from these disgusting clothes.' Tears streamed in dirty rivulets down her face. 'I lived in the corridor with some other people and then I found this room after somebody else had died.' Her eyes, big and open, stared up at him. 'I had to drag their dead bodies from here and leave them in the streets.' She burrowed into his shoulder.

'How did you eat?... Where .... ?'

'I pee in a bucket down the passage. The rats follow me. I hate them. Most days the soup kitchen comes past and then I eat. When it doesn't come, I don't eat.' She swung away from him and dropped on to the bed.

Rolf made up his mind very quickly. 'Ulrika, stand up and come with me.' He saw her mouth begin to open. 'Do it now, ... please.' Scrabbling around, she found some old army boots with the soles hanging out. Slipping them on, she stood at his side and her hand crept into his. Looking down at her, Rolf, very gently pushed a lank strand of hair out of her eyes and wiped away a tear. 'Don't worry, Ulrika, everything's going to be all right.'

Six months ago, if Rolf had walked down the avenues of Berlin with a woman looking like Ulrika on his arm, he would have been arrested by the *Gestapo*. Now, nobody cared a damn or gave them so much as a second glance. Most of the time, she stumbled and then he carried her. They crossed the *Unter den Linden* and reached their destination.

The *Adlon* Hotel stood on the corner of *Pariser Platz* and *Wilhelmstrasse*. Although pock marked by shrapnel, it was still standing and, through its glass doors, he saw shining lights and people. The finest hotel in Berlin. Without a pause, he held open the door for Ulrika.

'No,' she whispered, 'I can't go in there.'

'You damned well will,' grunted Rolf.

The lobby was full of people. Officers of all ranks, most of them with gold and silver braid. Women in glittering jewellery and fine clothes. A blue haze of cigar smoke. Pulsating music. As they walked together across the deeply carpeted floor to the reception desk, people suddenly noticed them. Rolf felt eyes staring at him and the crowd parted like the Red Sea.

The manager emerged from his office and met them at the desk. Without hesitation, the words came tumbling out. '*Sturmbannführer*, we have no rooms available.'

'Shut up,' replied Rolf, in a menacing whisper. 'I want a room for my friend here and I want it, ... NOW!'

The manager drew himself up. 'The *Adlon* Hotel is full. I have no rooms.'

The crowd was hushed and one or two women giggled. Rolf took a step closer. He opened his mouth and was about to raise his fist.

'She can have my room, Rolf,' drawled a voice across the lobby. 'I'll sleep in a broom cupboard.' *Sturmbannführer* Klein in full *SS* mess uniform leant against the door to the restaurant, a cigar in one hand and a glass of champagne in the other. All eyes turned to him. 'Congratulations on the promotion, Rolf. Well done.' Walking across the lobby, he placed his hand on the manager's shoulder, making him flinch. 'Empty my room and fill up the bath for this young lady.' The manager paused. The grip tightened. 'Do it now,' ground out Klein. '..... And quickly.'

'Yes, *Herr Sturmbannführer*.' The manager turned to the clerk and whispered something. The crowd carried on with its revelry as though nothing had happened.

THIRTY-THREE

'You're a bloody liar,' shouted Richard. 'You're a bloody liar.' His body began to shake and, for a man who was usually calm, he balled his fists.

Jan Bildt was utterly immobile. 'I completely understand how you feel and ……'

'How the hell can you?' A rage rising like bile.

Bildt stood with hands behind his back. 'It's been a long and difficult time for me. I've waited fifty years. Every day, I've wanted to contact you.'

'Tell me exactly what you mean ……. and say it bloody quickly.' Richard shook with anger and he spat out his words.

Bildt remained calm. 'Its a long story. …. A long story.'

'Just a sentence will be enough and then I'm going to walk right out of here, pack my bags and leave.' Squeezing the back of the chair until his knuckles turned white, Richard waited.

Bildt took a deep breath. 'After the war, Simon Cohen married the only woman I ever loved and that woman bore my only child. You are that child. It's as simple as that.'

Richard rarely swore but he did so now. 'Why the fucking hell should I believe you, a fucking German?' Trying to compose himself, he banged his fist on the chair in frustration.

'This "fucking German" is your father,' snapped Bildt, 'And that means you're German, one hundred per cent German. You were never even half a Jew and I bet you never really felt like one anyway.'

Richard took a half-step forward. Bildt never flinched. Then it hit Richard and it hit him hard. 'My mother was your, …….. your woman?'

'Yes …. .' Bildt's face was expressionless.

Richard faltered. 'But she met my father in the ruins of Berlin. She was a refugee.'

'Exactly and she didn't lie.'

Richard's mind whirled. 'I'm leaving here now and, when I've found out the real truth, I'll be back. …. With my solicitors.' Still shaking with anger, Richard strode across the room, opened the door and rushed into the hall.

In three minutes, he was packed and ran down the stairs two at a time back to the hall. Bildt was waiting.

'I'm sure we'll meet again,' he said, quietly. Richard ignored him.

Pulling open the heavy front doors, Richard walked brusquely out into the courtyard and along to the stables area. The garage was already open and Hans waited quietly near the car. Richard avoided any eye contact. Throwing his bags into the rear, he slid into the seat and turned the starter. The engine failed to fire. Again he tried; nothing.

'Shit' he shouted. Striding round to the front of the car he raised the bonnet and peered into the engine compartment. Now Bildt was standing next to his servant.

'Trouble, ' he said, softly. Richard glared at him and, for a moment, thought that these two men had something to do with the problem. Jumping into the car, he turned the key and the engine fired first time. The bonnet catch clicked home and Bildt nodded.

Richard reversed the MG sharply, causing Bildt to jump out of the way. Sliding on the night-damp cobbles, he accelerated hard and sped down the driveway back onto the main road. He roared along until the street-lights of Millingen slowed him down.

At the far edge of the village, he stopped and, with his head over the steering-wheel, began to plan his next move. With a deep sigh, he made up his mind. 'I'm going home,' he said, 'And I'm going home now. .... Direct to Dover. .... Non-stop to Dover.'

Jamming the car into gear, he made his way back along the pitch-black roads to Nijmegen.

Richard drove steadily and fast. Although he travelled through the night, he felt no tiredness. The events of the last twelve hours jumbled and jumped through his brain. At times, he shouted aloud and he drove with the radio on full volume. He hit Calais in early morning and the ferries were empty. Driving straight on board, he parked and made his way to the cafeteria. Thankfully, he ordered a coffee and breakfast. The crossing was rough, with winds piling up on the bow making the empty ship seesaw in the waves. It did not help the breakfast and, even though he was a seasoned traveller, the constant motion made him sea-sick and the contents of his stomach emptied over the slippery deck.

Feeling dreadful, Richard drove his car off the ferry. His head whirled round and round and he felt sweaty and dirty. After clearing customs and immigration, he turned left out of the dock and climbed up the steep access road and over the cliffs. A Little Chef cafe loomed up in front of him and he pulled into the car park, not for food but to use his phone. Jane's voice cheered him up.

'It's Richard.'

'What is it?' Her voice was full of concern. 'What's the matter? Why are you phoning now?'

'Something's happened. I can't tell you over the phone.' He watched his hand trembling

'Oh, my God,' she shouted. 'It's something to do with your visit to Bildt. I know it is.'

Richard heard her heavy breathing. 'Listen, Jane, it is something to do with Bildt, ... '

The interruption was direct. 'Are you hurt? Oh, please tell me you're not hurt.'

'Listen, I'm quite all right. I've driven all night and had a bloody rotten crossing but I'm OK. I should be home by midday. Please wait in for me.'

'Richard, what's it all about? You've got to tell me something. You've got to.'

He tried to speak calmly. 'All right, all right. .... It's something to do with my mother and my father and it's something I've got to talk to you about. Now, please calm down and I'll keep in touch.'

'Yes, Richard,' she said with a voice full of emotion. '........ I love you.'

'And I love you.' He switched off and went to wash his face.

The remainder of his journey went without mishap. There were the usual hold-ups on the M6 north of Birmingham and that did nothing to help his frustration and bubbling anger. This anger, and coffee every hour, kept tiredness away.

Eventually at midday, he pulled into the drive of his home. She was waiting for him. Running to her, he flung his arms round her. She kissed him full on the lips.

Unlocking herself from his tight embrace, she said, eyes wide open, 'Darling, are you all right?'

He looked straight into her eyes. 'We must talk, ...now.' He glanced through the open door. 'Are the children home?' Jane shook her head. Taking her roughly by the arm, he led her through the house to the living-room. 'You'd better sit down,' he said firmly. 'Because what I'm going to tell you is unbelievable. .... Absolutely bloody unbelievable.' Jane sat at his side and waited. Trembling, Richard found it hard to speak. Placing his back firmly against the sofa, he composed himself. In his mind for the last fifteen hours, he had thought through what he was going to say but still it came out in a blurt. 'This Bildt bastard told me that he is my father and not Simon.' His throat locked and he nearly choked.

'Richard, what on earth are you talking about?'

Shifting on the sofa, he tried to gain control of his tired emotions and the words came out in staccato bursts. 'Simon's not my real father. ..... He says, he's my father.' Richard's hands swept to his head. 'Oh, my God, if it's true, ... if it's true, ... then my whole life's a mess.'

Jane saw her normally calm husband begin to cry; he rarely cried. Slipping her arm round his shoulders, she pulled him close. 'Oh, my darling, tell me all about it.'

Biting his lip, Richard began. 'Bildt lives in this fantastic house. It's a farm with acres of land. An utterly charming man, suave and very sophisticated.'

'How old is he?' asked Jane, leaning back into the comfortable sofa.

'Probably in his late seventies,' replied Richard, staring fixedly at the carpet. 'Tall, thick grey hair and a prominent nose. He had blue eyes, ... just like me. The more I think about those eyes, the more I see them staring at me ...... Jane,' he hesitated and turned to face her. 'I've got blue eyes.'

'So has your mother,' she answered, quickly.

Richard nodded, 'Yes, I've been thinking about her. Sabina must know about it. I've got to talk to her, ... today.' He began to rise from the sofa. She pulled him back.

'Not yet, not yet,' she said. 'Just relax and talk about it.' Stroking his hand, Jane kissed him gently on the cheek.

Richard tried to calm his throbbing head. The sight and smell of his own home helped somewhat but still an anger seethed deep within him. He lay full length on the couch and pushed his jumbled thoughts into some semblance of order.

'Richard, hang on,' Jane said, standing and quickly walking out of the room. She returned several minute later, carrying a tray. Setting it down on the small table, she poured out two cups of tea.

Richard explained everything, leaving nothing out and Jane did not interrupt. It took him twenty minutes to recount exactly what had happened and then he sat back with a flushed face and tightly-clasped hands. Jane watched him. 'Well,' he asked, tensely, 'what do you think?'

She pursed her lips. 'Richard, I honestly don't know what to think. But one thing is for sure, you've got to talk to your mother.'

'All the time that awful thought has been going through my mind and I just can't bring myself to face it.'

'Do you believe what he says?'

'It sounds so ridiculous that I have to believe it.' Richard shook his head. 'My God, I, ... I wish I'd never gone. But, if all of this is true, then I've got to get to the bottom of it.'

Jane poured out the tea. 'Richard, I'm with you all the way.' She paused, taking a sip of tea. 'What shall we tell the children?'

'Everything,' replied Richard, without hesitation.

Jane nodded. 'I would recommend caution, because, if Bildt is your father, then it has implications for their relationships with their grandmother. Remember, they're still recovering from the death of their grandfather.'

Richard quickly drank half the cup of tea. He was much calmer and their discussion helped him to think more rationally. Removing her hand from his, Jane ran her fingers through her hair, a self-conscious mannerism that he knew so well.

'What is it?' he asked.

'Well, ... you're back home. You've had a shock and you're tired. The children are due home in two hours.' Her green eyes stared into his and she reached out and touched his forehead. It was a physical contact that threw them together. Jane held his head close to her shoulder and she whispered into his ear. 'I've been so worried about you.' Jane looked at him. 'What shall we do now?' she said gently. 'Where do you want to begin?'

The practical side of Richard's nature, surfaced. Holding Jane tightly for a moment, he said firmly, 'First, I want a hot shower. Then, a change of clothes and then, ... please let's talk again?' He took a deep breath.

Richard felt a lot better. His head was clearer and there was a sense of purpose in his stride as he left the living-room and walked to the stairs. Being home gave him strength. The bedroom held Jane's distinctive smell. An odour that was not a perfume; it was something special. For a moment, while he undressed, he held it in the back of his nasal cavities and found it stimulating.

The shower refreshed Richard and when he returned to the bedroom, he towelled himself hard, savouring the pleasure of being at home. The bed invited him and, quite naked, he fell onto it. Staring at the familiar things around him, he did not hear the bedroom door open and then suddenly Jane stood at the side of the bed.

'Hello, darling.' Her voice was husky and her green eyes were wide open.

No other words were necessary. She pulled her loose sweater over her head and dropped it to the floor. He saw the swell of her breasts over the lacy blue bra and felt instantly aroused. With a flick of her wrists, she flipped undone the belt of her skirt and pulled down the zip at the rear. He welcomed her with open arms.

'Shit,' muttered Richard, as he undid her bra, 'why does travelling always make me randy and, after all that's happened?'

'You stupid man,' she whispered. 'It's nothing to do with travelling.'

He welcomed her into bed. 'How can I do this after what I've just gone through?'

'Shut up,' she whispered.

It was her that guided him and revelling in a mixture of pure love and deep lust, their sex was natural, measured and unbelievably enjoyable. They orgasmed together, enjoying their act of intimacy.

A fully dressed Jane looked down at him and then sat on the bed. 'Feeling better?'

'Absolutely, it's the best medicine I could have had,' said Richard, stretching.

She gave a cat-like grin. 'I've been thinking. I really want to know more about what Simon did because I believe the answers to some of your worries may lie in what he's written.' She frowned. 'Richard, we've got to sort this thing out together. If you remember, you read out some of the notes to me and I want to read more.'

Taking a deep breath, Richard focused his thoughts. 'Mmm, a good idea. And, I've decided that I'm going to see my mother tonight. No pre-warning, no phone call. I just want to know, from her, what the hell is going on.' Richard squeezed her hand and threw back the bed clothes. Jane smiled, kissed him on the cheek and went downstairs. He quickly dressed in jeans, a warm shirt and sweater. Staring at his face in the mirror, he saw the dark shadows under his eyes and shook his head.

A hot coffee was waiting in the kitchen and he began to talk. 'There's something about Bildt that I can't put my finger on.'

'What do you mean?' asked Jane, sipping at her drink.

'The house is full of expensive things and he dresses in the best clothes. It's a huge place and he lives in it by himself.' Richard swallowed a mouthful of coffee. 'He must be a wealthy man to have that sort of lifestyle.'

'Any sign of a woman's touch?' said Jane.

'Nope, there was no sign of a woman anywhere. There's something else as well. A close friend of Bildt's, a man called Willi, was on the ferry. He said that he'd been keeping an eye on me.'

'Now that's weird,' said Jane. '…. He actually followed you?' Richard nodded. 'And it seems as though they were comrades in arms, from what you said earlier?'

'Yes, the *Wehrmacht*,' nodded Richard.

'What's the *Wehrmacht*?'

'It's the German name for the combined navy, army and air force.'

Jane stared hard at him. 'Was the *Wehrmacht* part of the *SS*?'

The coffee mug hit the table. 'Shit,' grunted Richard. 'That's exactly what I thought and I asked him about it, but he denied it.'

Jane pursed her lips. 'There's always something in the news about war criminals and the Nazis. I just put two and two together.'

Richard's thoughts and emotions tumbled together. 'If he is my father, …. if, …. then he could be *SS* and he could be a war criminal.'

'Steady, steady,' said Jane, carefully. 'We mustn't jump to conclusions. I'm sorry I said such a thing. After all, there were thousands of German soldiers after the war who just went back to their normal lives. Just the same as Simon did.'

Richard stepped down off the stool and paced around the kitchen. 'Yes, yes, I know about all that. But, this man, …. this man, has something about him that I can't get hold of. Why didn't Bildt just write me a letter himself rather than going into faxes and third parties?'

'If you think about it,' said Jane, curiously, 'perhaps Bildt was so worried about the whole thing that he couldn't do anything until Simon died. And, even then, how else could he have approached you?'

Richard tapped his forefinger on the kitchen table. 'Maybe he wasn't allowed to leave the country. Maybe he isn't telling the truth. What about the old copy of my birth certificate?' He threw his hands into the air. 'Oh, shit, shit. ….. I wish I'd ignored the whole thing.'

The front door opened. Placing a warm kiss on his lips, she stepped back and said quietly, 'Richard, let them settle.'

David came in first, all of a rush, and dashed towards him. 'Hi, Dad, great to see you. Did you get me the Bon Jovi CD?'

Shaking his head, Richard tussled his son's hair. 'Sorry David, I had no time.'

Rebecca quietly stood in the doorway, flicking her long hair away from her eyes. She stared hard at him for a moment. 'Hello, Dad. …. How are you? You look worried. Was it a bad journey?'

Richard put his arm around her shoulder. 'I'm fine, thanks.'

Rebecca frowned at him. She felt their mood. 'What's wrong?'

Her parents glanced at each and nodded. Richard told the story as clearly as he could and waited.

It burst out of David like a torrent. 'It can't be true,' he said angrily, straightening on his stool. 'Simon was your father. How dare this man Bildt lie about our family? He must be lying. ….. He must be!'

Rebecca waited for David to subside. 'Dad,' she said, slowly and deliberately, 'if, …… I say, …... if, what this man says is true, then you're German and David and I are half-German. Is that right? ……. And, it means that Simon was not our grandfather.'

'Yes,' replied Richard.

'It has to be proved,' added Jane cautiously. 'Richard and I have not yet seen any direct evidence.'

Between every sentence, there was a paused silence, as each member of the family tried to work out the consequences of Richard's visit to Bildt. Richard opened his mouth to speak and was interrupted by the phone ringing.

'I'll get it,' said David, jumping up. Whilst he was away, nobody spoke. He returned, holding a piece of paper. His spoke softly. 'Dad, it's a fax for you.'

With a feeling of dread, Richard took it from David's hand. The message was simple enough and he read it to himself, thought for a moment, and then read it aloud.

'"Grosse Bauernhof"
Deutschland
Fax: 00 49 438644

Dear Richard,

I'm assuming you have arrived home. I'm so sorry that I have caused you so much heartache and anger, it was not my intention to do so. You must be thinking about what I said and how it can possibly be true. It is true and I can easily prove it.

Please speak to your mother as soon as possible. Maybe then, you can visit me again and we can discuss our future relationships. I've always known that I had a son and I always knew it was you. I could do nothing until Simon Cohen died. As far as I know, he's been a loving and caring father and I will thank him forever for being just that. I am not a young man and neither am I well but I do want to spend some time with my son, your wife and my beautiful grandchildren before I die. Your mother cared for me in the very difficult times at the end of the war. I have not seen her for fifty years. Willi, over those years, used to occasionally visit England and tell me how things were. The last time he came, was when Rebecca was born. He was present at her Christening and he told me she was a beautiful baby.

Yours very sincerely,

Jan Bildt.'

'It's creepy,' said Rebecca, her eyes wet with tears.

'I think it's disgusting that he's had us watched,' said Richard, indignantly. 'Just imagine, over the last twenty years, Bildt must've known exactly where we lived and what we did. ..... I can't believe it.'

'Dad, it must be true,' said David. 'I mean he wouldn't have gone to all this trouble, if it wasn't true.'

'I've thought about it in the same way,' said Richard. He rose from the sofa and began to walk about the room.

'This man must love you,' added Jane slowly, causing Richard to look at her. 'Yes, ... think about it. For fifty years, he's known about you and wanted to see you. Now, he wants to do what he can for you. I know it hurts when you think of Simon. But .... I really believe you have to see this man again.'

'What about Grandma?' Rebecca said quietly. She sat composed, with her hands crossed neatly on her lap. She turned to face Richard. 'Dad, are you going to see her and talk about what's happened? Perhaps she can tell you more.'

'Don't worry, I'm going to see her.'

'She's still our grandmother,' said David, with a raised eyebrow. '..... Isn't she?'

'Oh yes, she's definitely your grandmother and she's still my Mother.'

Richard sank back into the sofa. 'Right,' he said firmly, 'let's give ourselves a shake. I'm going to pour a drink.'

'Aren't you driving tonight?' asked Jane, as Richard filled up a whisky glass.

'Nope, you can take me.' He turned. 'David, some ice, please.'

'Right, no problem.' Rebecca followed her brother out of the kitchen. It left Jane and Richard standing together.

'They took that well,' said Richard.

'So did you,' replied Jane.

The children returned and they all talked for half an hour and then Jane spoke. 'If you don't mind, I want to read Simon's notes for a while. I'll be in the study.'

'That's fine,' said Richard.

Jane was used to speed reading, it was part of her job. She found Simon's notes fascinating and totally absorbing. The depth of his experience surprised her. For as long as she had known him, she had always thought that he had been just a junior officer. What she read, did not help to clarify the situation, in fact, it only confused her even more. That did not please her, in her profession, clarity of thought was an essential skill.

THIRTY-FOUR

The room at the *Adlon* was perfect. Whilst Ulrika lay in the hot bath, Rolf walked back down the stairs to buy her some clothes. The shops in the lobby were open but there was little on the shelves. He bought what he could, a dress, lingerie, and make-up. As he walked back though the busy lobby, Klein was waiting for him.

'Everything all right?'

'Thanks for the room. It was very good of you.'

'No problem,' replied Klein, waving his cigar. He winked and dropped his voice. 'We Auschwitz brothers must stick together in our times of need. …. By the way, I assume the young lady is not your wife?'

'You're quite right.'

'Very nice, very nice. Does she have any friends?'

'Not that I know of,' said Rolf, frowning.

Klein scratched the tip of his nose. 'Have you been paid yet?'

The question surprised Rolf. Because he had not been paid for a month and the impending bill from the *Adlon* was already worrying him. 'No, I haven't. Why?'

'Don't worry about it,' answered Klein, breezily. Reaching into the deep pockets of his riding breeches, he took out a fat envelope. 'Here, take this ….'

'Really, …… I, …. eh …. couldn't.'

Klein laughed. 'Nonsense, there's plenty more where that came from. Anyway, in this bloody war, I like to see people enjoying themselves. Oh, by the way, if I were you, I'd move anything of value that you have at the barracks. There were *Gestapo* searches in there this morning.' Clapping Rolf on the shoulder, he walked away wreathed in cigar smoke.

When Rolf returned to Ulrika's suite, she was sitting naked at the dressing-table, staring in the mirror. She turned. 'Hello, darling. …. What the hell's happened to me?' She was emaciatingly thin and as pale as death.

'It's called war, Ulrika, …. war. It affects us all.' Staring at her body, he placed the boxes on the bed.

Squealing with delight, she ran across the room. Ulrika began tearing open the packages and holding each item to her body. Rolf found her every movement thrilled him and he kept touching her as she spoke.

'How did you know my sizes? Everything fits so perfectly. .... Black underwear, ... gorgeous, you devil. You're wonderful.' With small exclamations of pleasure, she tried on each item.

She ran into his arms and her long blonde hair flowed over his green uniform. 'Oh, Rolf, my darling Rolf, I love you so much ... but I'm exhausted.'

'I know,' he said softly, into her ear.

She ran her hands over his face and, with her fingers, traced the dark patches under his eyes. 'I think it best if we just rest tonight and see each other tomorrow. .... You don't really mind, do you?'

He ached for her. 'Ulrika, I quite understand. Don't worry, you'll be quite all right here.' He felt himself saying these things and yet he just wanted to drag her into the bedroom and make love to her. His hand crept to her breast and cupped it softly.

Rolf slept for fourteen hours, although he was awake every hour. The nightmares were becoming worse and they were always about the same thing; Auschwitz. When he slept in daylight there were no nightmares. They returned only in the darkness. He always awoke with a cry on his lips and lathered in sweat. It was the sound of the midday air raid that finally made him jump out of bed.

His written orders instructed him to report directly to the *Reichsbank*. Everything in the enormous building was on a grand scale and there was not a soul in sight. In the dead centre of the marble entrance hall was a star-like pattern of alternating colours of marble. Rolf stood in the exact centre spot and then he heard the echo of footsteps. Down the upper dog-leg of the stairs a small figure appeared. Rolf watched him walk down the last steps.

Doctor Walther Funk was fifty-four years old. Minister of Economics and President of the *Reichsbank* since 1940. Round shouldered, with a stomach barely hidden by a well-cut, dark grey suit. Clasping his thin hands together, he slowly advanced towards Rolf. A round, smooth face with thinning grey hair. A soft voice with just a trace of a lisp.

'Good morning, *Sturmbannführer*. How kind of you to be on time.' He did not offer his hand.

'My pleasure, *Herr President*,'

The smile was lop-sided. '*Doktor* Funk will be fine.' He turned back towards the stairs and then paused and said softly, 'Please follow me.' Funk walked though a huge doorway leading off the entrance hall.

They walked together down a narrow passageway until they reached a heavy steel door. Rolf watched him. Funk produced a bunch of keys on a steel chain from his pocket. Two keys opened two locks and the door swung noiselessly open.

Funk turned and gave a thin smile. '*Doktor* Müller,' he said, 'I've brought you down here to show you exactly what work you'll be carrying out.' He rocked backwards and forward on small feet in black shoes. 'Behind me is the main vault of the *Reichsbank*. The German national gold reserves are kept in here and other, shall we say, ... "assorted deposits".' He smiled at his own joke. They both watched the door swing open.

A huge cellar of a place with a central walkway and galleries on both sides. Cages made of steel bars delineated sections, each carefully labelled. There was a smell of carbolic and something else. Some of the cages contained immense stacks of gold bars. Other sections held neatly tagged canvas sacks. At the far end of the passage were boxes of assorted sizes stacked in precise rows like a warehouse. The atmosphere was cool and there was a distant hum of ventilators.

'Do you find it interesting, *Doktor* Müller?' said Funk, softly. Rolf nodded. 'Let me show you round.' As they stepped forward, two older men in black overalls appeared from a small office to the left of the vault entrance. Clicking their heels, they stood to attention. There were gold bars stacked 5 metres long and a metre high. Funk smiled. 'This section contains gold worth $500,000,000.'

Rolf stared about him, speechless and let Funk ramble on.

'Let's go to Section 17. I'm sure you'll find that of great interest.' Humming something to himself, he moved on. Funk waved his hands this way and that. 'The sections we are passing now, contain the total German paper money reserves.'

One of the men picked up a bag and loosened the draw string. He handed it over to Rolf. Inside were smaller dark blue velvet pouches and Rolf knew instantly what they contained. The man upended one over Rolf's extended palm. A torrent of diamonds, all of exactly the same carat. In the bright lights of the vault, they shimmered and sparkled like living things.

Taking a deep breath, Rolf said one word, 'Wonderful.'

'Ah, ... ah,' said Funk, with a slimy grin. 'diamonds are my favourite as well.' Rolf allowed the stones to trickle back into the pouch and he remembered his pouch hidden in his quarters.

Funk stood erect, thumbs pointing downwards. 'My dear Müller, Section 17 is one that needs, shall we say, ... "Special Treatment."' He chuckled at his own joke. The door swung open. A collection of tea-chest sized boxes. Rolf recognised their markings. Funk watched his face. 'Ah, ... I notice you've seen these boxes before.' He turned to the man and waved his finger.

Producing a small jemmy from his overalls, the man levered off the lid. Rolf peered in, knowing what he was going to see. 'Gold dental fillings,' said Funk. 'These have not yet been smelted.' The box contained a jumbled heap of gold teeth and fillings. Funk smiled, 'I understand Müller, you know about how these objects are processed? Wasn't there a learned paper written on the subject?'

Rolf thought for a moment as he searched his knowledge. 'Yes, indeed, *Doktor*. In 1940, a Victor Scholz published a doctoral dissertation called, "On the Possibilities of Recycling Gold from the Mouths of the Dead.". The dissertation was carried out with the approval of the Medical Department of the Stomatolgy Institute of Breslau University.' Rolf watched Funk's face as he spoke. 'When the Jews have been gassed, their bodies are searched for gold and precious metals. Other Jews search anuses and vaginas.' He saw Funk flinch and Rolf wanted to see him flinch again. 'They use crowbars to wrench out the gold teeth. Sometimes they do it before they're gassed. Last year we employed 40 prisoners in this work. The torn-out teeth are then soaked in muriatic acid to remove scraps of tissue and bone. Usually, inside the crematorium, the gold is melted into small gold bars and then sent to you here in the *Reichsbank*. The first shipments arrived in November 1942. I can clearly remember that during May last year, we took 40 kilos of gold from Jewish mouths. These teeth,' and Rolf poked them with his finger, 'must have left after we destroyed the crematoria. Otherwise, they would have arrived as ingots.' He took a step closer to Funk. 'Vaginas were the favourite place for hiding diamonds. Half of the diamonds in here will have been found in Jewish cunts.' He waited for the reaction.

Funk stiffened and his face lost its compliant expression. 'Ah, … *Doktor* Müller, I see you've had a great deal of experience. It's that experience we want to use here at the *Reichsbank*. Your task will be to ensure that these ….,' he waved a podgy hand over the contents of the wooden box, '"things" are properly processed. Smelting is necessary to remove the gold from the amalgam base. I want them cast into small ingots.'

'Small ingots?' asked Rolf.

A slight flush came over Funk's face. 'Yes, small ingots. Easier to transport.'

'I understand,' said Rolf, raising an eyebrow.

Funk took a deep breath and his eyes narrowed, making his face appear even fatter. 'Have you heard of *Aktion Reinhardt*?' he said, quietly, ensuring the assistants were out of earshot.

Rolf searched his memory. 'No, *Doktor*.'

'*Aktion Reinhardt* was begun in 1942. All proceeds from the camps are shipped here and transferred into a special account for the *SS*.'

'And gold teeth,' added Rolf.

'Yes, gold teeth. Although I must say that that small amount of gold only amounts to a tiny part of the proceeds from the concentration camps.'

'What exactly is my work?' enquired Rolf. 'I know nothing about banking or business.'

'Don't worry. You're a trusted and highly recommended *SS* officer. You will have to account for and check the gold bars that are melted here in the *Reichsbank*. Transhipments occur every week and you'll be responsible for the crating of the gold and the loading onto the transports.'

'Where does it go to?'

Funk nodded and a smile crossed his lips. 'Both myself and Deputy President Puhl are also Directors of the Bank for International Settlements in Switzerland.'

'Switzerland?' exclaimed Rolf.

'Yes, Switzerland. The Bank was set up after the First World War to provide the Allies with reparations paid by Germany. The gold goes to the Swiss National Bank and to other neutral countries.'

'What's the gold used for, *Doktor*?'

'Another good question. It's a well-known fact that Germany cannot win the war. We're surrounded on all sides and soon Berlin will fall. From now on, German business and industry must realise that the war cannot be won and that Germany must now take steps in preparation for post-war commercial activities. The money in the accounts of the Swiss banks is ready for that investment to take place.' Funk grinned and licked his wet lips. 'There is another connection with your work at Auschwitz-Birkenau. One of the *Reichsbank's* directors is Hermann Schmitz, head of IG Farben.' Funk paused to see if Rolf could make the connection.

'IG Farben?' Rolf tugged at his ear lobe and then snapped his fingers. 'The suppliers of *Zyklon B*?'

'Precisely,' smiled Funk, 'and their shares went up when Auschwitz was fully operational.'

Rolf shivered as Funk touched him on the shoulder. 'You, *Sturmbannführer* Müller,' said Funk with pride in his voice, 'are now part of the new *Reich*. Through the use of our wealth, we will rise again and conquer, not militarily but economically. We we'll live in a new capitalist world and that is the only way we'll survive.'

Rolf was motionless. He was suddenly involved in an unseen future. From the mouths of murdered Jews to the Fourth *Reich*, all in a space of six months.

THIRTY-FIVE

When Jane dropped Richard at Sabina's house, she kissed him on the cheek. 'Try not to hurt her,' she said softly.

He nodded. 'I want some truth from her. This whole thing has gone on for far too long.'

The car drove away, leaving Richard standing alone on the drive. A chilly night made him shiver and he realised that he was tired. Pausing for a moment, he stared up at the house he had known so well as a child. Then, he made up his mind and walked to the front door. He pulled back the horse-shaped door-knocker and let it fall. Through the stained-glass windows of the front door another light came on and he waited. His mother's familiar silhouette came down the hall and Richard's heart beat faster.

'Who is it?' called Sabina.

'Richard.'

The bolt was drawn back and the lock turned.

She looked him up and down and her voice was full of welcome. 'Richard, you're back. .... Why didn't you phone? ... Do come in.' Stepping over the threshold, he closed the door behind him. Sabina opened her arms and held her son tightly. Letting go of him, she looked into his eyes, and he saw fear. 'Let's go into the morning-room. I always have the fire lit in there.' He followed her. Richard sat in the old winged chair and she looked down at him.

'What can I get you?' she asked, quietly. 'A cup of tea, coffee or something stronger?' There was genuine pleasure on her face.

'Tea'll be fine.' He tried to rise and she gently pushed him down.

'Richard, wait here. I won't be a moment.' He watched her slowly walk across the room. His eyes closed and then Sabina returned.

'I've used your favourite Earl Grey,' she said, sitting in the chair opposite the table. All the time, her blue eyes kept glancing at his face. She passed him the porcelain cup and saucer and settled back into the cushioned chair.

'How was your journey?' There was a slight tremor in her voice.

Richard stirred his tea. For twenty-four hours, he had rehearsed exactly what he was going to say but it came out as something completely different.

'Mother,' a title he rarely used, causing her head to lift, 'I stayed with a man who told me he was my father.'

Sabina took a deep breath and carefully placed the cup and saucer back on the table. Slowly rising from her chair, she turned and walked towards the open fire. Gripping the head-high mantle-piece, she stared into the glowing coals. For a full minute, she remained motionless and then turned to face her son.

'What was the man's name?'

'Jan Bildt.'

Shrugging her thin shoulders, she asked another question. 'How old is he?'

'I would think about seventy-five or so.'

'Please tell me more about him?'

Richard told her exactly what had happened, word by word and minute by minute. She did not interrupt. When he stopped, she walked away from the fireplace and returned to her chair. Richard patiently waited but he so desperately wanted answers.

'Oh, my dearest son,' she said, quietly. 'I knew it would all come out. This is a day I've dreaded, ….. dreaded for fifty years.' Wiping a palm over her forehead, she bit her lip.

'I think, Sabina,' said Richard, slowly, 'you'd better tell me everything.'

She composed herself and looked him straight in the eye. 'It's absolutely true. If this man is whom I think he is, then possibly, he is your real father.'

'I thought as much,' muttered Richard, nodding.

'I don't know what went on. It was war-time and things happened so differently.' Her eyes closed and she clasped her hands tightly, resting them on her lap. She spoke in a hushed voice. 'My real name is Ulrika Hannsen. I changed my name to Sabina when I came to England with Simon.' Richard quietly interrupted.

'What is Bildt's real name?'

Sabina's eyes stared at the floor. 'His name is Rolf Müller.'

'Müller, Müller,' mused Richard, '…. I've heard that name before.'

'If you've been talking to Lottie Cohen, then you probably have.' Her face was absolutely still and her unblinking eyes lifted up to look at him.

'Yes,' he said, with his face beginning to flush, 'you're right. The head of the SS in Leeuwarden was called Edvard Müller. I presume there was a connection? …. His brother?'

'Yes,' she answered, in a whisper.

'If Edvard Müller was SS, then was his brother also SS?'

Sabina lied, knowing full well what the awful circumstances would be. 'No, …. he was in the *Wehrmacht*.'

Richard sighed loudly and leant back in his chair. The tea had already gone cold. He spoke with a rising anger. 'Just tell me exactly what happened.'

With moist eyes and a tremor in her voice, she began. 'I worked as a secretary in a law office. In the early days, life in Berlin was wonderful. Lots of handsome young men from all over Europe came to Berlin and I enjoyed myself. When my parents were killed in an air raid, it hit me very hard. As an only child, I was used to loneliness but when they'd gone, life was no longer exciting and I drifted in and out of relationships. I'd been a member of the German National Socialist Womanhood since I was eighteen. I never thought they would give me any help but they were there when I needed them. In 1944, they told me about an organisation called the *Lebensborn* Project. At that time, I had no idea what it was all about.' She sighed. 'I soon learnt.' She shook her head. 'My God, I learnt very quickly.'

'What was the *Lebensborn* Project?'

'Himmler proposed the scheme and he established it in 1935. Its aims were to support large families and to care for and look after expectant mothers.'

'Seems quite noble to me.'

'There were other considerations.' Her voice settled. 'It was also to care for the children of unmarried mothers.' Richard made no comment. 'Later, there was the more important primary aim of matching genetically and racially pure males and females. In that way, Himmler said that he would be able to secure Germany's future. The children produced would be born out of marriage and, under *Lebensborn*, this was morally acceptable.'

Richard fidgeted in his chair and Sabina stopped talking. 'Was I a result of a *Lebensborn* …….. "matching"?' he asked, with a racing heart.

His mother looked at him with moist eyes. 'Yes, Richard, I think you were.' He shook his head. She swallowed hard. 'In 1944, life became increasingly difficult. Several times I lost my job, particularly when offices were bombed. Berlin was a nightmare. Eventually, I was persuaded to take part in *Lebensborn*. I had to report to a specialist in the city centre. For an hour, two doctors examined me. They measured every part of my body, on the inside as well as the outside. They physically hurt me and I cried whilst they carried out their examination. I felt degraded and I still dream about it, even today.' She paused and wiped her eyes. 'Then I had to go and meet this man. He explained about the need for me to produce a racially pure Aryan child. He had a file in front of him and it was all about me. He read out parts of it and I never knew that they'd so much written about me. And they'd checked if I had any Jewish blood. They'd even found out about my mother's asthma when she was a little girl.' She shook her head.

'How did you first meet this man, Rolf Müller?' All the time, his mind was bursting with questions.

She gave a quick nod. 'I received a letter telling me to report to the local National Socialist Womens' office. When I arrived, I was shown to a room and told to wait. After a few minutes, a man came in and sat down behind a big desk. Then he told me what I had to do. It was so unusual that I remember it all quite clearly. He wanted me to go away for a weekend to meet an SS officer and other important people. He showed me photographs of a castle in Kallinchen not far from Berlin and then said that I was to have my own room and the best of everything. He told me I was to go to the *Wertheim* store on the *Kurfürsten Damm*, the best department store in Berlin, and buy whatever clothes I needed; money was no object.' She gave a quick smile. 'The *Wertheim* store, Richard; only the very richest people shopped there. He gave me an envelope, which I knew contained money, he said it was for "expenses". Richard, can you imagine what this man was offering to me? Berlin was in ruins. I'd hardly any money and no future. The opportunity was just unbelievable and I accepted it.' Her face became more animated. 'Shopping was a dream come true. I bought things that I'd never thought of owning. The evening dress was French and fitted me perfectly. Dark blue silk, cut low and very special.' Her eyes closed for a moment as she searched her memory. 'When the man asked me about my period, I was embarrassed. He explained that everything had been arranged for me to go away on the fourteenth day of my ovulation; my most fertile time. You know, I didn't really care. I'd previously had one or two affairs and I certainly wasn't a virgin.' Richard shuddered. 'My "chaperone", as he called my partner, was a Rolf Müller. He was a young man from a good family and had carried out special duties for the *Reich*. He showed me a photograph and Rolf was as handsome as I thought he would be.'

Richard had tried to keep quiet. 'Sabina,' her eyes showed concern, 'did Simon know about any of this, ... this *Lebensborn* thing?'

'No, never. It was something I never told him.' She cocked her head to one side. 'The man from the Project then told me what would happen if I became pregnant. *Lebensborn* would look after everything. There were special homes where I would be cared for. He explained that individual needs and feelings had to be subordinated to the needs of the state. The new order had to be racially pure. I remember the words so clearly.'

'That sounds like racist clap-trap to me.'

'You're quite right. At the time, and when you were living in Nazi Germany, it all seemed perfectly reasonable and quite acceptable. If you were approached by *Lebensborn* and turned them down.' Her hands fluttered to her face. 'Well, ... I heard of young single women, like me, who just disappeared without trace.'

'Did they expect you to have children?'

'Oh yes, it was the prime purpose of the Project. And, what's more, they wanted us to keep having children. The state rewarded women with the Honour Cross if they had large families.'

Richard wanted straight answers. 'Did you know who Jan Bildt really was?'

She shrugged her shoulders. 'Let's say, I had an idea.'

'Why didn't you tell me before I made this journey to Holland?'

'Richard, ... oh, Richard,' she replied, with moistening eyes. 'You may remember that I tried to warn you not to go, but you did insist.'

Now the questions came flooding out.

'Did this man Müller ever see you after I was born?'

'No.'

'Did Müller know that you bore his child?'

'Yes.'

'How did he know?'

'I wrote one letter with a birth certificate.' Then suddenly her eyes filled and she began to cry. Great blobbing tears rolled down her cheeks, causing rivulets of mascara and face powder. With hunched shoulders, she frantically tried to find a tissue from up her sleeve.

Richard froze and, for a moment, watched his mother cry. In a way, he wanted her to be upset. By not rushing to her side, he wanted her to understand his feelings. In the end, his deep love for her forced him to reach in his pocket for a handkerchief. He stood up and walked towards her. Although Richard dabbed at her eyes, the tears still rolled out. He could feel her wracking sobs and it distressed him.

'Mother, mother, please stop crying.' He stared hard at her face. 'Why the bloody hell didn't you tell me about all this?'

Sabina shook her head and looked down. 'I couldn't. I was ashamed of myself.' Her head lifted. 'It's so wonderful when you call me Mother. Why I ever allowed you to call me Sabina, I'll never know.'

Richard touched her arm. 'Should I call you, ... Ulrika?'

She stiffened. 'I left Ulrika Hannsen behind fifty years ago. I don't ever want to bring her back.' Gently, she pulled herself away from him and returned to her chair. Looking at him, she said firmly, 'Simon was the only man I ever really loved. He was the perfect husband. He cared for me and loved you. That was all I could ever ask of any man.'

'I know,' said Richard, quietly, dropping back into his chair, his anger calming by the minute.

Taking a deep breath, she composed herself, hands clasped again neatly on her lap. 'I want to tell you about Rolf Müller. Do you mind if I do that?' Richard shrugged. 'A Mercedes picked me up from my apartment and I was taken to Kallinchen. My room was out of this world.' Richard watched her eyes become dreamy as she relived the occasion. 'I bathed in a bath with gold taps and scented water. My dressing table was filled with the most expensive French perfume. Oh, Richard, Richard .... that dress, that wonderful, wonderful dress. I had all the underclothes to go with it and the make-up. Somebody came to do my hair and then I was ready.' She stopped for a moment, savouring the memories. 'When I walked down that grand staircase, everybody was looking at me. It was probably the most exciting moment in my life.' She stared hard at the fire. 'I saw Rolf Müller for the first time at the dinner-table. Rolf was such a handsome man.'

'Still is,' muttered Richard.

'Eh, ... yes,' she said, unsure how to respond. 'He had blue eyes and blonde hair, just like me. I don't remember what was for dinner and I can't remember much of what we said to each other. We stood out on the terrace for a while and then left the others. We drank champagne and nothing else and it went straight to my head.' Richard opened his mouth to speak and Sabina held up her hand. 'Before you ask, that was not when you were conceived.'

'How often did you see him before you met Simon?'

'Several times. On one occasion, he saved my life. That's something I'll always be grateful for. Berlin was continually bombed and he found me, fed me and made sure I was safe.'

The fire had burned down to a dull, red glow. Richard felt Sabina's tiredness and the events of the day had made him weary. His mother carefully watched him. 'Sabina,' he said,' I think I've heard enough for one night and I need to think about what you've told me.'

'Richard,' and she spoke in a whisper, 'I can't ask for your forgiveness but I can ask you to try and understand what happened?' He saw the worry in her eyes. She seemed to have visibly aged.

He sighed. 'I may find it in my heart to forgive you but I can't understand why you never thought of telling me, particularly after Simon passed away.'

Brushing her hand across her forehead, she licked her lip and replied, 'I'll be more than happy with your forgiveness. I think we'll have to talk again.'

'Yes.'

Sabina composed herself. 'Richard, are you thinking of going home now? .... I mean you're tired.' There was real concern on her face.

Richard thought for a moment and then made a decision which surprised him. 'Would you like to come home with me and stay for the night? You'd be more than welcome.'

Putting her hand to her mouth, she shifted uncomfortably in her chair. 'Oh dear, ... oh dear. Will it be all right with Jane?'

He nodded. 'She won't mind.' He rose from his chair. 'I'll go and phone and tell her we're on our way.'

As Richard walked from the living-room, he paused for a moment and squeezed his mother's shoulder. Closing the door quietly behind him, he reached for the phone on the hatstand in the hall. Jane answered and he carefully explained.

'Oh darling, it's no problem at all,' she said, quickly. 'When you'd gone, I really felt for both of you. I'll make some coffee and phone for a taxi.'

Sabina collected a few things from her bedroom and Richard waited for the taxi. For a moment in the hall, they stood together.

THIRTY-SIX

On most nights, Ulrika welcomed him back to their room at the *Adlon* but the war and the work sapped his energy.

Most of the time, Rolf spent in the gloom of the bank's vaults or in the dark streets on the way back to his barrack. But, on this particular day, the early morning was bright and sunny and Rolf paused to look through the windows on the first floor of the bank. Hardly a cloud in the deep blue sky. It was almost as if there was a hint of a long-awaited spring.

It was the heaviest single bomber raid on the city that had ever been attempted by the Allies. They dropped high explosives, incendiary bombs, fragmentation shells and land mines. Berlin was a paradise for the American bomb-aimers. The massed bombers dropped a total of 2,267 tons of bombs on the administrative heart of the beleaguered capital of the *Reich*.

The city was ravaged and Rolf was directly in the middle of it. The raid lasted three hours. One notable building seemed to be the prime target. The *Reichsbank* took direct hits on every part of its ornate structure and Rolf felt every one of them. When the first bombs fell, he was with the office workers in the old vault used as an air raid shelter. The women screamed as the whole tomb-like structure shuddered. Rolf's head shook as the bombs' percussion waves painfully echoed and re-echoed around the confined space. Squeezing into a corner, his eyes sought light or anything that he could see; there was only inky blackness. Bodies brushed past him and the screams went on and on. His imagination travelled to another chamber and, for a terrifying moment, he thought he detected a whiff of *Zyklon B*. Then he panicked and a great sucking scream rose into his throat. Clenching his fists until his hands became numb, Rolf eventually gained control.

The raid was over. By crawling round the cell-like vault and scrabbling with both hands, he managed to turn the heavy door latches and he was the first out. He climbed quickly up the stairs to a circle of sunlight above. Rolf stopped to stare. The enormous solid edifice of the *Reichsbank* was no more. Dusting down his uniform, he searched for a reference point.

Funk stood in the centre of his huge office. The massive ornate desk was upturned and badly damaged. There was a bleeding scratch on his cheek, making a trickle of blood darken his white shirt.

'Gentlemen,' said Funk to his assembled staff, 'we must protect the vaults as soon as possible before any further raids take place.' He turned to Rolf. '*Sturmbannführer* Müller, get all available bank staff and move bullion and other materials into the smaller vault and do it quickly.'

'Yes, *Herr President*.' Rolf snapped his fingers and several men stepped forward. They rushed back down the stairs and climbed into the ruined central section of the bank. It took him two days to move everything to safety. When his task was complete, he walked back up to Funk's office. The President was still there, engrossed in a deep conversation with other men. Maps were spread out on the uprighted table. A few words were spoken and then finally, Funk looked up. 'All right, gentlemen, we are agreed.' The heads nodded. Taking a gold pen from his pocket, he pointed to the large map. 'At this time, the Americans and the British are almost at the Rhine. The Bolsheviks are a 100 kilometres from Berlin. Our duty is to secure the future of Germany. Therefore, we're taking the wise decision to move the *Reich* reserves to a place of safety.' He laid his pen across the map. 'The Merkers potassium mine is 320 kilometres south-west of Berlin. Inside its galleries and shafts, we will store the reserves.' Standing back from the table, Funk waited for a reaction.

He turned to Rolf, '*Sturmbannführer*, you must arrange the transport trains.' As Funk glanced at his watch, Rolf understood why he personally had been placed in such a responsible position. A man who had worked in the death camps was a man who could be trusted.

Rolf had enough time to call at *Obersturmbannführer* Eichmann's department to arrange the transport. Eichmann was not present in his office but one of his officers was and Rolf received a surprise when he saw who was waiting for him.

'My dear Rolf.' Klein extended his hand. 'We meet again. Is it to rescue damsels in distress?'

'I think not,' replied Rolf, with a frown.

The office was sumptuously furnished with the very best of antique pieces. Klein half-filled two crystal glasses with whisky and, as Rolf explained his needs, passed one across. 'I know you don't need the trains for Jews,' he said, 'because there aren't any left.' He laughed at his own joke and took an almighty swig from his glass. With a jackbooted-leg draped over the corner of a superb mahogany desk, he eyed Rolf up and down. 'My dear friend, I know you're working at the *Reichsbank* for that queer, Funk. I know this morning that the bank received a direct hit from an American B-17 and therefore, ……..' He stroked a forefinger up and down his gleaming boots. 'It has to be the gold.' Again that laugh. 'I can see by your normally expressionless face that it's the gold.' Another mouthful of whisky. 'Let's see now and I'm guessing, that'll be a total all-up weight of about a hundred and fifty tons. And that, Rolf, as they say, is a lot of fucking gold.'

Rolf was impatient. 'Klein, can you get the transport?'

He waved his hand and grinned. 'No problem, no problem. Let me think now. The German railways used to charge us, that is the SS, about two *Reichsmarks* per Jew for transport to the camps. That's why Eichmann used to make the Jews buy a one-way ticket. …. Everything at a profit. Let me think now,' and his grin became even wider. Klein squeezed the side of his nose between thumb and forefinger. 'Two bars of gold will cover all the trains you'll need. Delivered to this office tomorrow and, of course, I'll give you an official receipt.'

Rolf swirled the whisky round the glass and then carefully placed it back on the desk. He said, shaking his head, 'Klein, I'm never quite so sure whether you do all this for the *Reich* or yourself.'

Klein stretched, slowly rose to his feet and saluted. '*HEIL* Hitler! Everything I do is for the glorious *Reich* and my beloved *Führer*.' He laughed. 'Or what's left of it. Bye, see you tomorrow.'

Rolf felt dreadful. His face was drawn with tiredness and his uniform was filthy. For a moment, as he walked down the broken pavement, he was tempted to just go back to his quarters and sleep but then the single light over the *Adlon* Hotel beckoned and he gave in. The doorman nodded and Rolf pushed his way past the crowds in the lobby. The noise and music was deafening. Slipping off his greatcoat, he slowly climbed the stairs. With his key, he opened the door to Ulrika's apartment. There was no response when he called out her name. Shrugging his shoulders, he walked through to the bathroom and turned the taps full on. Within a minute, his clothes were in a crumpled heap in the corner and he was lying in the hot, soapy water. After the noise of the air raid, the total quietness of the bathroom was immensely satisfying. He dozed for a few minutes and then gave himself a vigorous wash. His third spare uniform was hanging exactly where he had left it three days previously. A quick check in the mirror, to make sure that his hair was perfectly in place, and he left the apartment.

Rolf found her in the lobby sipping tea with another woman.

Ulrika's eyes lit up. 'Rolf, I'm so glad to see you. I was really worried after the air raid this morning.'

'Everything's fine,' he replied, as he looked at her face. 'How about dinner?'

'Wonderful. …. Give me two minutes and then I need to change.' She pulled at the sleeves on the dark blue dress.

'Not necessary, Ulrika,' answered Rolf, touching her hair and glancing at the woman. 'You look fine. I'll wait in the bar for you.'

The bar was packed and there was an air of excitement and gaiety. Rolf ordered a glass of beer. It went down quickly and he signalled the waiter for another one. Rolf peered towards the double doors and then, suddenly, she was at his side, whispering into his ear.

'Hello, Rolf.' And she kissed him full on the lips.

'Come on, Ulrika,' he said, grasping her hand. 'Let's go to the restaurant.' Pushing their way out of the madness of the bar took several minutes.

A magnificent room with a small ensemble playing soft music. The guests were a mixture of uniforms sprinkled with civilians. The maître d' stepped away from his small table and, when he saw Rolf and Ulrika, gave a respectful bow.

'Good evening, sir, madam. Your usual table?'

'Naturally,' replied Rolf, 'and a bottle of your Bollinger.'

He gave a polite cough. 'Sorry, sir. We're out of Bollinger. But we do have the odd magnum of Pol Roger.'

'That'll be fine,' said Rolf, as Ulrika took his arm. The maître d' led them to a quiet corner where a table for two was already laid.

Candles flickered away and Rolf felt the warmth of her thigh against his leg. Her hand crept into his. The champagne arrived and Ulrika giggled with delight. The cork popped and the two tall glasses were filled. As they drank deeply, the menu appeared and Rolf held one to share between them. 'Ulrika,' he said wearily, 'I've had a busy day and I'm really hungry.'

She ran her hand down the side of his leg. 'I feel just the same, my dearest. I'll have whatever you're having.'

Rolf ordered and the waiter refilled their glasses. They sat close, making small talk about work and the war. Rolf watched her face. From the corner of his eye, he saw a familiar figure and began to rise from his chair.

'What is it, Rolf?' said Ulrika.

'My brother.'

'What?' she said, with a look of surprise.

In the formality of the restaurant, they shook hands. Edvard Müller, in full *SS* mess dress, nodded and smiled.

'We meet again, little brother,' said Rolf.

'We certainly do.' Edvard's eyes wandered towards Ulrika. 'Are you going to introduce me?'

'Sorry, …. of course.' He gave a half bow. 'Ulrika Hannsen, may I introduce my brother, Edvard.'

She coolly looked him up and down and then held out her hand. Clicking his heels, he brushed his lips over her fingers. 'I can see the family likeness,' she said, with a broad smile. 'Would you like to join us?'

Ulrika saw the two men exchange glances and then Edvard said, 'Thank you *Fraülein*, I have urgent business to attend to. Maybe another time.' He smiled. 'I know it's the height of bad manners but I must have a private word with my brother. That is, if you could please excuse him for a few minutes?'

'Of course.'

The two men inclined their heads and walked quickly to a quiet corner of the restaurant. She watched then engaging earnestly in conversation. Then, finally, Edvard placed his hand on Rolf's shoulder, then glanced towards Ulrika, waved, and left.

As Rolf returned and pulled up his chair to the table, she said, 'I didn't know you had a brother.'

He smiled. 'There's lots of things you don't know about me.'

Holding hands across the table, Ulrika frowned. 'Tell me, Rolf, why is that woman over there staring at us?' She nodded to the other side of the restaurant.

'Who do you mean?' replied Rolf, squinting through the cigar smoke.

'She's sitting with a man at the table near the piano.'

The heat waves distorted the woman's face and, when he moved the candle, the face came sharply into focus. Rolf's heart gave a surging leap of anger. The woman recognised Rolf and rose from her seat. She wore a startlingly red dress, cut very low and she walked slowly across the polished floor with a tantalising sway of her hips. Men stopped eating and looked up to watch her. As she came closer, her partner came more clearly into view and then Rolf recognised him. It was Klein.

'Who is it, Rolf?' whispered Ulrika. 'She seems to know you.'

'She's my wife.'

'What!' she retorted.

Angela stood directly in front of the table and, with her hand on her hip, said in a loud voice, 'Well, my dearest. Who are you with tonight? Is she the *Lebensborn* whore, or somebody you picked up off the street?' She sucked deeply at a cigarette.

Rolf felt Ulrika begin to rise to her feet and he pushed her down with the palm of his hand. Several other guests turned in their seats, watching the spectacle unfold. Feeling his wife's eyes boring into his, he said quietly, 'Don't make a fool of yourself, Angela. I'm dining with a friend.' Out of the corner of his eye, he saw an obviously drunk Klein lurching across the floor.

She said coldly, 'You talk about me with men and look at you. You lying swine. You're no better that the rest of the men in this city.'

Rolf rose to his feet just as Klein arrived. 'Just go away and leave me alone,' Rolf said, in a voice that was deadly calm.

'That's just what you'd like, isn't it?' She leant over the table and pointed her finger straight into Ulrika's face. 'This little whore'll soon learn what you're really like.' Straightening, she smoothed her silken dress so it clung to her breasts and then stared into Rolf's face. 'I don't need you any more because I can have any man I want.'

Klein propped himself against a chair in front of the table. 'Hello, Rolf. What's happening here? What do you think of my girl? .... Isn't she gorgeous?' His eyes closed as he drank deeply from a glass.

'This "girl" happens to be my wife,' said Rolf so quietly.

'Oh really.' He laughed, slapping Angela on the rump. 'Well she's a damned good fuck, whoever she is.'

Rolf boiled but felt utterly helpless. 'Enjoy your meal, Klein and you're welcome to her.'

'You fucking pig,' she shouted at the top of her voice. 'I owe you something.' Clearing her throat like an old woman, she spat a ball of phlegm full into Rolf's face. Stiffening, he nearly lost control and lifted his hand to strike her.

'Don't,' said Ulrika softly, grasping his arm.

'Oh, the whore fights does she?' snarled Angela.

'Steady on, there's a good girl,' muttered Klein.

She whirled round. 'You SS, ... you're all the same. You may get away with killing Jews but you can't get away with treating me like that.'

It was her final comment that instantly turned Klein stone-cold sober. 'That's enough,' he said sharply and, with a deft flick of his wrist, he grabbed Rolf's wife and dragged her away from the table.

Rolf sat down and tried to calm his anger. Some of the other guests stared with curiosity and some with downright disgust. As they turned back to their food, Rolf tried to speak but the words stuck in his throat.

'Darling,' said Ulrika, calmly, 'drink some more champagne.' He did as he was told and drank two whole glasses before he could coherently utter a word. Just as he opened his mouth, Klein appeared at the table.

With a stony face, he gave a quick bow. '*Sturmbannführer* Müller, as a fellow SS officer and, I hope, as your friend, I humbly apologise for what was said to you this evening. I hope you can accept my apology. ' At attention, he waited for Rolf's response.

Rising from his chair, Rolf looked at Klein's face. 'I accept,' he said, calmly.

Klein clicked his heels and nodded. 'Thank you, Rolf.'

As Rolf sat down, Ulrika pushed her glass away. With blazing eyes, she hissed, 'I didn't know you had a wife.' Why didn't you tell me? Why did I have to be so humiliated?'

He thought for a moment and sipped at the lifeless champagne. 'It was over long before I met you. We had irreconcilable problems. I thought it wasn't necessary to tell you because I thought it didn't matter.'

'You silly man.' And her anger partially subsided. 'Please take me out of here?' she said. 'I can't face these people.'

Rising to his feet, Rolf pulled her chair back and she took his hand. They walked arm in arm across the floor of the restaurant looking neither left nor right.

THIRTY-SEVEN

Richard paid the taxi and, with his mother, walked to the house. Jane opened the front door. 'Sabina,' she said, 'I'm glad you came back to stay with us.'

'It's kind of you to invite me,' she replied, slowly removing her coat.

Jane led them down the hall, into the living-room and they sat down in their usual places.

Sabina looked at them both and fiddled with the belt of her dress. She was the first to speak. 'I know I should've told you both about this thing but I couldn't do so whilst Simon was alive.' Shaking her head, she spoke firmly but there was a tremor in her voice. She looked at Jane. 'Do the children know about it?'

'Yes,' Jane replied, expressionless.

'Where are they? Please can I speak to them?'

Richard shook his head. 'They've gone to bed, Mother. They've had a hell of a day.'

'Oh, yes, of course.' Wiping away a single tear from each eye, she composed herself. 'I really don't know what to say.'

Before any of them could say another word, the phone rang. 'I'll get it,' said Richard. He took the call in his study. 'Hello, Richard Cooper speaking.' There was a pause and, for a moment, he thought it was Bildt. The voice that spoke back to him was instantly recognisable.

'Oh, hello, Richard. This is Lottie Cohen speaking. I'm sorry to call you at this late hour. It's just that I was wondering how your journey was?'

With a brief moment for thought, Richard replied, 'Lottie, nice to hear from you. It was an interesting journey, very interesting indeed.'

'Did you meet this man Jan Bildt?' she said in voice edged with concern.

'Oh yes, I most certainly met him.'

'What was he like?'

Richard went on to explain and she did not interrupt. When he stopped talking, he heard Lottie take a deep breath.

'It's an amazing story, Richard and one that must greatly upset you. Is your mother sure about the name, Rolf Müller?'

'Absolutely.'

'I'm so sorry for you.' He could feel the sadness in her voice and something else he could not quite fathom. 'Can I help you in any way at all?' she asked.

'I am upset,' he said. 'In fact, I'm very angry about the whole thing. Lottie, ... I really don't know yet whether you can help. I'm absolutely exhausted and I need to sleep on it ... and, I've got to try and help my mother.'

She paused. 'Richard, who's going to help you?'

'Don't worry about me. My family are being really supportive. Listen, ... can I call you back tomorrow?'

'Please do. .... Good night and good luck.'

'Bye, Lottie.' The phone clicked dead.

As he walked back into the living-room, Jane looked up and, out of Sabina's view, gave a nod and a smile of reassurance.

'Just a friend from work,' said Richard, sitting down next to his mother.

Sabina looked tired and Jane placed her hand on her shoulder. 'Why don't you go to bed?' she said, gently. 'The guest room is ready. .... Look, we'll talk about this tomorrow.'

'Tomorrow? ......' replied Sabina, falteringly.

'Tomorrow,' said Jane. 'It's Saturday.'

She rose unsteadily to her feet. 'Oh, yes, I'd forgotten. I just lose track of time.'

'Come on,' said Jane. 'I'll help you,'

'Oh dear. It's been a very difficult evening for me.'

'It has for all of us,' added Richard, shaking his head and with an anger still deep within him. 'Good night and sleep well.'

Forcing himself to relax back into the sofa, he tried to collect his thoughts. The last twenty-four hours had proved to be the most difficult time in his life. With closed eyes, the images of Jan Bildt kept flashing through his mind and then his mother's face came jumping into focus.

'Richard,' Jane gently touched his shoulder, making him jump, 'let's go to bed.'

Laying in bed, Richard quietly stared at a pattern on the wallpaper. Jane came out of the shower and, slipping into her night-dress, crawled into bed at his side.

'That was a hell of a couple of days,' she said, nestling against his shoulder. Her mind was teeming with questions and, before sleep, she wanted some answers. 'Damn it,' she said, softly.

'What's the matter now?' he said, with some irritation. She climbed out of bed. 'Jane,' he called out, 'where are you up to?'

'I'm going for Simon's diary.' At the door, she turned. 'I'll read it in the study and then you can sleep. Goodness knows, you need it.'

'Oh damn it, bring it in bed and we'll read it together.'

She laughed and he lay back with half-closed eyes. As Jane carried the file to the bed, a loose sheet of paper slipped out. It fluttered to the floor and she bent down to pick it up.

Richard saw her movement. 'What is it this time?'

'I'm not sure. It's different to the other document.'

'Pass it over.'

Sitting up in bed, Richard whistled. 'Listen to this.

'To Majoor Simon Cohen. Thank you for your kindness.

Artur Seyss-Inquart. 16 October 1946.'

'Who was Artur Seyss-Inquart?' said Jane, peering at the yellowing piece of paper.

'Artur Seyss-Inquart,' whispered Richard, 'was Hitler's Commissioner in the Netherlands.'

'Why was he thanking Simon?'

Richard shook his head. 'God knows, and the more I get involved in this affair, the more worrying it becomes.'

Carefully, he placed the scrap of paper on to the table at the side of the bed.

She began reading.

'I though a lot about my family and I still couldn't believe they were dead, even though all the evidence so far pointed to that awful conclusion. There wasn't a great deal for me to do in Leeuwarden. Most of the Germans were being sent back to the fatherland, strangely enough, via Westerbork. Now, that I found a strange quirk of history.

One night I couldn't sleep and so I decided to visit Müller. I wanted to meet him again because the man fascinated me. He was in exactly the same cell as before and hadn't changed one bit. The arrogance was still there. There was a silence that I was determined not to break. After a couple of minutes, there was a sharp inhalation of breath. "What the hell is happening outside this place?"

"The Third Reich has had its day and the Russians are at the Reichstag."
That shocked him. "They've promised to take Hitler and parade him through the streets of Moscow before they execute him."

Müller had no answer and then, with a rattle of his manacles, he rose to his feet. He must have been looking after himself, as his prison-pale face was shaven smooth. His voice was calm.

"What's left for me?"

"With what you've done, Müller," I said, "I would think a quick trial and then the Dutch will hang you and good riddance I say." I felt tiredness wash over me. What he said next stopped me dead.

"Not everybody died in the camps."

I forgot my reticence. "What did you say?"

He took a deep breath. "Yes, it's true. Jews were transported to camps all over the Greater Reich." And then he paused, knowing he had my interest. "Many will have survived." Another calculated pause. "It's possible that some of your family may still be alive."

As much as I hated asking this man for anything, I had to ask. "How can you be sure?"

He shrugged his shoulders and kicked his stockinged foot against the bed. "My brother knew about the camps. I used to meet him quite often. I know how the system works."

I was sure it was a trick. "The war is over Müller and your brother is probably dead or at least a prisoner of war."

"I know my brother,' he said softly. "He's clever and he's got friends in high places. If anybody can avoid being taken prisoner, then he can. And another thing, Jew." He was goading me. I ignored him. "We Germans are the world's finest record keepers. I bet, in your investigations, you've found stacks of documents and records by the millions. All stamped, sealed and stored?"

Of course he was absolutely right. I'd been amazed at the sheer quantity of paperwork. Every building used by the Nazis had been packed full of files.

"Now you're interested, aren't you?" Müller sniggered again. A little habit I found increasingly irritating.

"What do I do to find out if my family are alive or dead?"

"It's quite simple. You just follow the records. First, check in Westerbork, because nearly all the Dutch Jews were transported through there. In the main offices in the camp you'll find the lists. All the names of the people being sent to the concentration camps will be there."

"The death camps have been liberated."

"If that's true, then it's not a problem. Copies of individual records were kept in Berlin. Just look them up."

I fell into his trap. "Where?"

"I know exactly where they are and there are no more than five people alive who know their location."

"Why should you know?"

"Because, Jew, my brother told me where they were and," he tapped the side of his head, "I've got a very good memory."

"And I suppose, you murdering bastard, that you want me to take you there, so you can show me."

"Not necessarily. I need approval from the highest German official in Holland and I doubt whether you'll ever get that. Or, I may just change my mind before they shoot me."

"Shoot you, Müller. Oh no, it's the rope for you and even that's too quick." I'd really had enough and, after shouting for the guard, I left Müller to his thoughts.

When I awoke in the morning, there were two messages for me. The first one was simple, orders telling me to report to Brigade HQ in Groningen. The second message was an invitation to the van de Meers' house for dinner.

At their house, there was one person in the waiting group that I'd wanted to meet.

"Simon Cohen," Frank said quietly, "this lady is Lottie Cohen." There was no handshake, she merely leant forward and kissed me on both cheeks. She was younger than Marieke van de Meer, slightly built, with long black hair framing a very beautiful face. Lottie spoke Dutch with a strong accent and just a hint of German, particularly in the vowels. As she spoke, she tilted her head to one side.

"Simon," she said, softly. "I've waited a long time to meet you again. You're my only living relative." The way she said it, so matter of fact and so simply, made my emotions give a great surge and I just threw my arms around her. Frank smiled and led us through the front doorway into the house. I walked down the hall into the living-room.

"Mevrouw van de Meer, ... "

"Marieke, please."

"Marieke, thank you for inviting me to your home."

"It's our pleasure,' she replied, pushing her fingers through her long blonde hair.

"What's going to happen to the Nazis?" asked Lottie, sitting down on the sofa and curling her slender legs under her.

"There'll be war trials in all the occupied countries," I replied. "For the Nazi leaders, bigger trials will be held somewhere in Germany."

"Will we have to be witnesses?" asked Marieke.

"Yes," I replied. "Although, in most cases evidence will be given through sworn statements."

Aukje brought in a tray of coffee and placed it gently down on the small table in front of me. She filled each cup, pointed at the milk and lumps of brown sugar and nodded. I reached forward and stirred the coffee.

"What about Müller," asked Marieke, her forehead creased with a frown.

"What will happen to him?" She sat primly upright and I could see the anger burning in her eyes.

"He'll be tried and punished?"

"The death penalty?" Marieke said. *"Will he be executed?"*

"Yes," I said quickly. *"There'll be the death penalty when needed."*

"The man deserves to die," said Frank, looking me straight in the eye.

His comment surprised me because I knew he was a pacifist. *"You know Müller has a brother?"* I said. They all looked surprised. *"His name is Rolf Müller and he was a doctor at Auschwitz concentration camp in Poland."* I felt Lottie stiffen and, as I turned to face her, she visibly paled.

"Oh my God, no," she gasped. *"It's not possible. How can coincidence play such a trick on us?"*

"What's the matter, Lottie?" And I felt myself staring at her.

"The Müller here in Leeuwarden sends my family to Westerbork. The trains were then sent to Auschwitz. When they arrived, the other Müller was waiting for them." There were tears in her eyes. *"Simon. It sounds like a plot hatched by the devil."* Her brown eyes stared intently into mine. *"..... You've got to find him. You've got to bring him back here for trial in Holland. It's your duty. This is something you must do."*

They all looked at me. My coffee had gone cold and, for a minute, I was unsure what to say, so I said little.

"We trust you to do what is right," said Frank, leaning over to fill up my cup.

"He'll dealt with by the due process of law," I heard myself saying, letting myself off the hook.

By the end of April 1945, most of Holland was liberated but in the west of the country, the Germans still held vast areas of land. 'Fortress Holland' as Hitler called it, was to be fought over to the last man. There were all sorts of rumours of a last-ditch battle by the Germans.

The visit to my HQ just outside Groningen was only a matter of reporting what I had been doing in Leeuwarden. I was honest with my commander and I explained what Müller had told me about the records and my family. He told me I could have two weeks to find out what I could and he agreed that I should take Müller under armed guard to Berlin. But he had to be returned to Leeuwarden to stand trial in Holland.

I had a driver and a jeep all to myself and I knew exactly where I was going to; Westerbork. It's an easy drive only 40 kilometres south of Groningen. As we drove down the long narrow road leading to the main gates of the Westerbork Transit Camp, we both stopped talking and the driver slipped *the jeep into a lower gear. Just before we reached the gates, I nudged him to stop.*

A huge, half kilometre square of sandy soil with high barbed-wire fences all around. Tall watch towers at each corner, with another half-way along each side of the square. I'd seen enough and nodded. The jeep approached the main gates. There were Canadian armed troops on guard and, as we stopped, they unslung their rifles. One checked our passes and identities. The others hovered around us and smiled.

"What ya here for, sir?" The guard gave some semblance of a salute.

"I need to speak to your CO."

"Yea, sir. .... See that tall building?" I nodded. "He's in there."

As we drove through the gates, I saw a mixture of people. On one side of the road a crowd of families, some smiling, some sitting in dejected groups. On the other, men in tattered black and green uniforms, standing in orderly columns guarded by heavily armed Canadian troops. We braked to a stop and watched.

A women dressed in a long, brown coat saw us and walked across the road. Although the sun was warm enough, there was a chill wind blowing straight at her. She huddled down into the coat and pulled up the collar.

The khaki uniform of the Princess Irene Brigade is the same as that of the British Army and she assumed we were British or Canadian. Her face was pale and drawn but there was a sparkle in her eyes. She looked down at us in the jeep. "Hello, how are you?" she said in English with a Dutch accent. "Do you have cigarette?"

I didn't smoke but I always carried a few packs of Players Virginia. I found one and opened it. Her face lit up. I offered her one and said, in Dutch, "Help yourself." The people behind her began to take an interest and slowly rose to their feet.

She was surprised. "Are you Dutch? I thought you were Canadian."

I pointed to the Dutch shoulder flashes and explained who I was. My words must have carried in the wind because the people began to slowly walk towards us. Within a minute, we were surrounded. There were men and women of all ages and children and even babies. The two packs of cigarettes just disappeared. Somebody patted me on the back and then it started. Shouts, cheers and everybody talking at once. I knew they were happy. Then there was a man in uniform at my side.

"Hi there," he said in a soft Canadian accent. "I'm Captain Tex Jones of the Canadian Forces and CO of this God forsaken place. What can I do for you?" I stepped out of the jeep and saluted. The crowd moved to one side and quietened. I introduced myself and showed him my orders.

"Jesus," he said, "if you want to look at records, then there's hundreds of thousands of 'em." He pointed to a long wooden barrack. "In there, ... they're all stacked up. Help yourself. I've gotta bottle of Scotch in my office when you've finished. You and your driver are welcome to join me."

"Thanks Captain." I was conscious of the hovering, gaunt looking crowds. "Who are these people?"

He smiled. "They're your people." He nodded and grinned. "With a name like Cohen, they're most definitely your people .... Ask 'em."

A hundred faces looked at me and then the woman, a cigarette in each hand, walked towards me. "Kapitein,' she said, 'we are the last Jews in captivity in Holland. The Canadians came here and liberated us." She waved her cigarette towards the Captain. "Many have gone back to family or friends. We're waiting for the west of Holland to be freed and then we'll also leave. Some have nowhere to go."

I asked her, and I already knew the answer. "Were people transported from here to Auschwitz?"

She paused for a short time and I felt the other people drawing closer. "Yes, ...' And she spoke so softly, 'to Auschwitz-Birkenau, to Mathausen, to Dachau, to Treblinka, to Buchenwald, to Sobibor, to Bergen-Belsen, to Ravensbrück, to Majdanek, to Theresienstadt, to Gusen, to Neuengamme, to Sachsenhausen, to Torhen, Flossenburg, Ebensee, Chelmno, Tuttlingen, Schömberg, Schörzingen, Spaichingen, Günskirchen, Stutthof, Lagedi," and then she abruptly stopped, took a deep breath and looked at me. "Shall I continue?" There was an absolute silence and even the wind had dropped.

"Are there that many places?" I said, incredulously.

"Yes and many more." Her gaunt cheeks hollowed, as she took a long drag at the cigarette. "Are you a Jew? Your name sounds Jewish."

I nodded and told her my story, everybody listened and you could have heard a pin drop.

It was one of those days that you remember for the rest of your life. I stood in a lonely place where, over three years, my people had been forcibly moved from life to death. I was surrounded by Jews who had escaped death. I felt their warmth and sadness even though they said not a word. I was unsure what to do next, not wanting to move. The woman slipped her hand into mine.

"Come on, Simon Cohen," she said with a wan smile. "Let's go and find out what happened to your family.'"

Jane stopped reading and carefully placed the pages on the bed. 'Richard, this hurts me and I can't take in any more. I've got to have some sleep.' Richard's eyes were half-closed and he sighed.

'What's the matter, darling?' she said, carefully placing the file on the floor.

Richard put his hands behind his head. 'I'm sure that the Rolf Müller in the diary, is the same as the Rolf Müller that my mother knew. It can't just be a coincidence. It must be the same man who claims to be my father.'

Jane pulled up the quilt over her shoulder. 'It's a question only Bildt can answer.'

'I know it is.' Richard sighed. 'The whole thing is very confusing. ....
It's as though I'm travelling on a journey that was pre-ordained. Simon goes to Holland, I go to Holland. Simon looks for a Müller, I look for a Müller. Rolf Müller knows my mother, I know my mother.'

Jane lay in his arms. 'Let's sleep on it.'

'If I can,' replied Richard, touching her hair.

'What do you mean?'

'Sleep is difficult. I go to sleep and then I keep waking up. It's because of this Bildt thing.' Switching off the light, he closed his eyes and held her close.

A gentle knock on the bedroom door forced them to awake. 'Come in,' called Jane, glancing curiously at the bedside clock.

Richard stirred and reached for the light switch only to find that the day had dawned. 'What time is it?' he said.

Sabina walked into the bedroom carrying a tray with a teapot and two cups. 'It's half-past ten,' she answered, quietly, pouring out two cups.

'Ten thirty,' exclaimed Richard. 'I can't believe it, I feel as though I've been asleep for five minutes.

'Exactly twelve hours,' said Jane, reaching for a cup and saucer. She looked up at Sabina. 'Thanks for the tea. Did you sleep well and how are the children?'

She smiled. 'I slept a little and they're fine. They were up early and we managed to talk about things.'

Richard balanced a cup and saucer in his hand. 'Did you talk about last night?'

Sabina pushed away a wisp of grey hair. 'Yes indeed and they asked me some very interesting questions.'

'And?' said Richard, with the cup almost to his lips.

'David and Rebecca understand what's happened and they wanted to talk about it.' She paused. 'We've laid the table for breakfast and it'll be ready in five minutes.' She looked at them questioningly. 'Is that all right?'

Jane was the first to slip out of bed. 'That's fine. No problem.'

Their children were already dressed and waiting in the kitchen. Rebecca smiled. 'Morning.'

'This is very good of you,' said Richard, in amazement.

Rebecca rinsed the pan of eggs under the cold tap and said over her shoulder, 'We thought it would be a good idea. After all, it's Saturday and Grandma is here.'

Jane raised her eyebrows and settled comfortably into a chair. 'You ought to do this every day.'

'No way,' muttered David.

The eggs were placed neatly in their cups and the toaster popped its contents onto a plate.

'Coffee everybody?' said Sabina but there was an edge to her voice.

It was Rebecca who asked the most important question. 'Dad, what are you going to do about this man Bildt? Or are we,' Richard nodded at the "we", 'just going to forget the whole thing?'

Placing his knife and fork on the table, Richard glanced round at his family. 'I've thought about it and I want to see this thing through. I owe it to Simon and to all of us. I want to meet this man and I want the complete truth from him. …. At the moment, I don't think he's telling me everything.' He looked towards his mother and she just stared back. Richard shook his head. 'I'm not so sure whether I'm British or German, or whether I'm Jew or gentile.'

'David and I as well, Dad,' commented Rebecca. 'It means a lot to us.'

'I'm sorry, I know it does and that's why I'm going back there.' David screwed up his face. 'What's the matter, David?' asked Richard.

'This may sound stupid.' he looked at his father. 'But if you aren't British and Simon was not your father, then does it mean that you and Mum are not married? It could mean that Rebecca and I, well …… you know, …… illegitimate?'

Richard kept his face absolutely straight. 'Don't worry, David. My name is correct and our marriage is quite legal. I'm still your Dad.'

'Phew! Thank God for that.'

'This time I want to come with you,' said Jane. 'This time, I want to meet Jan Bildt.'

'You mean, Rolf Müller,' said Rebecca quietly.

Jane folded her arms. 'To me, he's still Jan Bildt until I've met him. And …. What about you, Sabina?'

She answered slowly and deliberately. 'It's fifty years since I last saw him. I never want to see him again.'

'Richard,' said Jane, with some irritation, 'I think we ought to go back and see him as soon as possible. Maybe we can leave tomorrow night?'

He nodded, his brain working out the schedule and its implications. Jane was, as usual, quite correct in her judgement. 'Just what I was thinking,' he said, 'and you're absolutely right. I want you to come. We'll go together.' She smiled across the table at him.

Breakfast was finished and they cleared the table. Richard, remembering his promise to call Lottie, retreated to the study. The phone rang three times and then it was answered.

Sabina, sensing that Jane and Richard wanted to be alone, picked up her handbag and said to Jane, 'Listen, I really ought to go to the shop in the village. I can quite easily walk. I'll be back in half an hour.'

'David and I'll come with you, Grandma,' said Rebecca grabbing David's arm.

Jane nodded. 'No problem. See you all later.'

Lottie took some time to answer the phone and her voice was firm and confident.

'Richard,' she said, 'thank you for calling me back. How are you after last night?'

'Everything is OK, thank you,' he replied. '….. Listen, Lottie, Jane and I are thinking of coming to Holland on Monday to see Bildt. Do you mind if we call in to see you?'

There was a pause and then she replied cautiously. 'That's all right with me and you're both very welcome to stay if you want to. But ……' and she hesitated, 'may I speak honestly?'

'Of course.'

'Since we last spoke, I've had time to think. You remember telling me that Bildt's real name was probably Rolf Müller? …. Was he SS the same as his brother?'

'No, Sabina said he was in the *Wehrmacht* and Bildt said the same thing.'

'Richard,' there was worry in her voice, 'I'm sorry but I can't believe what your mother's telling you. Because, it would be very unusual for one brother to be SS and the other to be in something else. It's all to do with blood and family'

He was puzzled and there was a stab of anger. 'What's your concern about Rolf Müller?'

There was a hesitation that came down the phone and her voice trembled slightly. 'Edvard Müller in Leeuwarden was directly responsible for the transporting of our family to Auschwitz and, therefore, I know in my heart, that he sent them to their deaths.'

Richard remembered Simon's notes. 'And you think that Rolf Müller's work is definitely connected with that of his brother's?'

'I'm sorry,' she said, 'but it seems logical.'

Richard had settled the thoughts about Simon and his mother. The last twelve hours with his family had helped him to logically explain what had happened. Lottie's new ideas and his father's notes did not help.

'What do you suggest I do next?' asked Richard.

Lottie sighed. 'This morning, I gave some thought as to how I might help. Have you heard of a man called Simon Wiesenthal?'

'Yes. Isn't he the man who found where Adolf Eichmann was and had him kidnapped and taken to Israel?'

'That's him. He has lists and records of virtually everybody who was in the SS and what they did.'

Richard felt an emotional pit yawning in front of him. 'Look here, Lottie, I appreciate your help. But what use will it be if I do find out Rolf Müller was in the SS?'

'Richard,' her voice was steady, 'If your real father was in the SS and, remember, he is Edvard Müller's brother, then he was certainly involved with the Holocaust.'

He felt all the nagging worries of the last couple of days come flooding back. 'What you're really saying is that my real father could be a war criminal?'

'Yes, that's exactly what I'm saying.'

'Lottie, that thought has been at the back of my mind for some time. But I just can't bring myself to think about it.'

'You owe it to Simon and to your friends in Holland. Remember, you're now the custodian of Simon's history and that carries enormous moral responsibilities. I think you ought to go and talk to Simon Wiesenthal in Vienna. I can arrange for you to see him. .... If you want me to?' Lottie stopped talking and Richard knew it was up to him.

He knew she was right and unhesitatingly gave her the answer. 'Lottie, thank you. Please arrange it and as soon as possible.'

There was elation in her voice. 'Thank you, Richard. Thank you. I'll phone you back later.'

After placing the phone back on its hook, Richard stood stock-still with his mind, yet again, whirling in questioning circles. Eventually, he made his way upstairs to shower and dress. Jane was sitting in front of her dressing-table.

'Where's Sabina?'

'She's nipped out for a while. I think she wants us to be alone.'

'She's right,' replied Richard.

Seeing his anxious face in the mirror, she said, 'What's the matter now? You look as though a bomb has dropped on you.'

He threw himself onto the bed. 'You're not far from the truth. I've just been talking to Lottie.'

'What did she say?'

Richard carefully explained.

'It puts another complexion on things completely.' She turned round to face him. 'Now, you've got to see it through.'

'It could hurt my mother. .... It means, she's still not telling the truth.'

'Oh hell, Richard,' she snapped back, 'just think about it. She's kept it secret for fifty years. At best, she's what she says she is and at the worst, she's a liar. It's now time for your future and our children's and, come to that, mine. Come on, you've got to sort it out.'

'It's going to be hard and I'm not sure what I'm going to find.'

For the first time that day, Jane's patience broke. Jumping up from her chair, she spun round. 'Richard Cooper, why the hell are you always so damned calm about things? Here we are with a major question mark over our family and you say it's going to be hard.' Her eyes blazed and she stood, hands on hips. 'Of course, it's going to be hard, bloody hard. Why do you think I want to be with you? .... I'll tell you why. To make sure that we find out once and for all.' Richard took a step back and then Jane calmed a little. 'Anyway, you might need a good lawyer,' she added, with just a ghost of a smile.

'You're right. Now, I'm going to get dressed. There's a lot to do.'

Lottie was as good as her word and, later in the afternoon, the phone rang. Richard took the call in his study.

'Hello, Richard. It's Lottie here.' Without hesitating, she began to explain. 'I've spoken to Simon Wiesenthal's office and he can see you tomorrow, Sunday at 2 o'clock in his office in Vienna. His apartment is in the suburbs, just get in a taxi and ask for the Documentation Centre on *Salztorgasse*.'

'Thank you,' he replied.

'Can you make it?' He's a busy man you know. The next time he could see you is months away.' She paused for a moment.

'It's no problem. Jane and I are going together.'

There was genuine pleasure in her voice. 'Richard, I'm so pleased. Perhaps when you've met him, you and Jane could come here and tell me what's happened.'

'Lottie, that's a great idea. I may want to go on and see Bildt later. But first, I'll hear what Simon Wiesenthal has to say.'

'Just give me a couple of hours warning before you come and Marieke will collect you from the airport at Schiphol.'

'I could hire a car.'

'It's absolutely no problem at all. Marieke would love to help.'

Richard thought for a moment. 'Lottie, I'm pretty certain in my own mind that Jan Bildt is my real father. If it's true, then it means that you and I aren't related.'

She chuckled. 'Yes, I've been thinking about that as well. Don't worry, we've been family for fifty years and nothing can change it, not even a man like Bildt.'

'Thank you.'

'Bye. Keep in touch.' And Lottie hung up. Richard sat back in his chair for a moment and then started to organise what he had to do.

After a few phone calls, he booked two seats on a British Airways flight to Vienna for ten thirty in the morning and called Jane. She walked back into the study.

'Where are we going?' she said, with a grin.

'Vienna to meet Simon Wiesenthal.'

Sitting down opposite him, she said curiously, 'Hmm, now that's interesting. Tell me about him.'

Folding his arms Richard, searched his memory. 'From what I can remember, he's a Jewish man in his eighties and originally came from Poland. He was imprisoned in the Nazi concentration camps during the war. Wiesenthal survived, as did his wife, and then he set up some sort of organisation based in Vienna to seek out war criminals. I think he also runs a documentation centre with files and information on Nazis. He also had a lot to do with the hunt for Adolf Eichmann and Mengele.'

Jane nodded. 'Eichmann, I've heard about, because his trial in Israel is standard reading for law students. .... Who was Mengele?'

Richard folded his arms. 'An *SS* doctor at Auschwitz. He carried out medical experiments and supervised the gassings.'

'My God, Richard,' there was a look of worried concern on her face, 'what the hell are we getting into?'

'I'm not so sure,' he answered, shrugging his shoulders. 'But we can't stop now.' Richard bit his lip. 'One thing, Jane. Please don't tell Sabina or the children we're going to Vienna tomorrow. Tell them we're going to see Lottie'

Jane smiled and smoothed away an imaginary crease from her skirt. 'I agree. It's better she doesn't know. .... I think I'd better go and do some packing.'

He stared through the window.

'What's the matter?' she said, putting her arm round his waist.

Pulling her close, he kissed her gently on the forehead. 'I know I've got to see this through but it scares the shit out of me.'

'I'll let you into a secret, Richard. It scares me as well.'

THIRTY-EIGHT

Rolf managed to see Ulrika twice a week and then only for fleeting moments. The *Adlon* was the usual hive of reckless activity. As he walked in through the revolving doors, a middle-aged woman jumped out from behind a tall potted plant, making him jump with surprise. '*Sturmbannführer* Müller,' she said in a whisper, eyes darting all around the lobby.

'Yes, ... who the hell are you?' For a moment, Rolf thought she was a beggar of some sort and then he noticed the nurse's uniform under her long coat.

'My name doesn't matter,' she whispered. 'I must talk to you urgently, ... in private.' She looked over Rolf's shoulder. 'Is there somewhere we can talk without being heard?' Seeing him frown and hesitate, she took his arm. 'It's urgent, *Sturmbannführer*. Very urgent.'

He sighed irritatingly and nodded. 'All right, follow me.'

The hotel had several small meeting-rooms. She nervously followed him in to one of them. 'What is it? What do you want?' Rolf said, impatiently. 'Come on now, hurry up'.

Leaning towards him, she said quietly, 'I bring a message from *Doktor* Mengele.' Rolf had been standing, now he closed the door. Hearing the name Mengele brought back unforgettable memories.

'Where is he?' he asked.

She shrugged her shoulders. 'I don't know. He asked me to find you and give you this.' Reaching into the pocket of her coat, she withdrew a small packet. 'I'm sorry I didn't find you earlier, *Sturmbannführer*, I had great difficulty in locating you.' She pressed the package into his hands and then stood up. 'I've done my job,' she whispered. 'Now I must go.'

Rolf was curious. 'Why did he give the package to you?'

The woman's face turned crimson. Before she could answer, she walked past him and was gone.

The package was wrapped in strong paper and sealed with waxed string. There were two envelopes and he selected the smallest one first. Opening it, he extracted the single sheet of paper and immediately recognised Mengele's neat script.

'My dear Rolf,

This letter, I am sure, will come as a great surprise to you. I hope you've remembered our great work that we achieved together. I'm now working as a doctor in a field hospital between the American and Russian lines. I will leave Germany as soon as is practically possible. I do not want to live in a conquered and despoiled Fatherland.

I want you to ensure that our medical records are safe. They will be invaluable for the new Germany. Our research is of great commercial and medical value. The records are stored safely in two railway wagons. One of the last things I was able to achieve was the safe moving of these wagons to a railway siding now in part of the Reich occupied by the British. They are identical to the ones that were used for the transports to Auschwitz. Their precise location is indicated on the map in the other envelope. The special wagons are marked above the buffers with a red letter "M". They're not hidden because they're in the middle of hundreds of other wagons and nobody will search them all. However, people being what they are, they'll probably smash some of the wagons for firewood. The documents are hidden behind wooden panels at the ends of each wagon. As well as the records, there are some gifts that will ensure your well-being for the foreseeable future. (Do remember, our names are on those documents.)

Now, I have shared my legacy with you and I trust you will use it wisely for the benefit of the Fourth Reich.

Your colleague,
Josef Mengele.'

Placing the letter carefully back in the envelope, Rolf pushed it into his pocket. The other document was a tracing of a map showing a railway line somewhere near a small German town near the Dutch border. Rolf smiled when he remembered Willi's address. Or perhaps Mengele was cleverer than he thought.

The letter came as a surprise to Rolf. He had been trying to put Mengele and the death camp at Auschwitz as far away from his consciousness as possible. The letter brought it all flooding back. It occurred to him to forget the wagons and their contents but Mengele's sentence, "Do remember, our names are on those documents", stuck in his mind.

Rolf stood near the bar in the *Adlon* finishing off a glass of beer. From the corner of his eye, he watched Klein pushing his way across the crowded floor. Since the episode with his wife, Rolf had seen little of him in the Hotel.

Klein bellowed to the barman, 'Two more beers and be damned quick about it.' Settling onto a stool, he waited for Rolf to speak.

Rolf couldn't help smiling. 'Why is it, Klein that when the city is in ruins and the Russians are only two hours away, you can still smile?'

'Ah, ah,' and he laughed loudly, 'it's because I'm the supreme optimist. Whereas you, my dear Rolf, are always the absolute pessimist.' The beer arrived and he downed the half-litre. 'Same again, barman.' His smoothly shaved face became serious. 'Have you heard from your wife?' Rolf shook his head. 'The last I heard of her,' continued Klein, 'was that she'd left Berlin.'

'Who with?' said Rolf, with an expressionless face.

'I don't know, Rolf. I'm sorry, I don't know.' They both sipped at their beer. Klein changed the subject. 'What plans are you making for leaving Berlin?'

The question made Rolf smile again. 'Klein, you're always making plans for leaving? First it was Auschwitz and now it's Berlin. Just where the hell do you think we can go to?'

Klein took a deep breath. 'Listen, my friend. We in the SS are chosen people. We'll be well looked after, *Aktion Reinhardt* made sure of that.'

Rolf asked sharply, 'What do you know of *Aktion Reinhardt*?'

'When you work close to the *Führer*, you know about most things. At Auschwitz, you I and helped to gather in the proceeds of the Final Solution and soon we'll be able to use it. The special account we have in the *Reichsbank*.' He chuckled. 'Will help us out of this miserable place.'

'I know,' said Rolf, softly.

'You know? Really, sometimes Müller, you're a bit of a dark horse.' Klein nodded. 'Anyway, back to leaving Berlin. Already, some have fled the sinking ship.'

Rolf frowned. 'As I said, where are people going to? There's nowhere in Europe left to run to.'

Klein smiled his most charming smile and swirled the yellow beer round his glass. 'South America, my dear friend, South America. Argentina seems the most attractive place and there are ways and means of getting there. Would you like me to book you a place?'

'No, thank you. I've got a job to do.'

'You never change, Rolf Müller. You're typically SS, always following orders.' He leant across and touched Rolf's arm. 'Just remember that you and I have worked in the camps and we've personally been responsible for the deaths of thousands, if not tens of thousands.' He sat back. 'Yes indeed, the Allies'll be looking for the likes of us.'

'I was a doctor following my orders.'

'Shit to that. Get out while you can and don't leave it too late. Remember the Russians nearly caught us at Auschwitz and I'm bloody sure they'll catch us in Berlin. And there's something else,' his face became serious, 'get your girlfriend out as quickly as you can.'

The singing began to subside as civilians and soldiers made their way to the restaurant. Klein saw Rolf glance at his watch.

'Are you dining here tonight?' said Klein.

'Possibly, ... I wanted to see if Ulrika was in her room.'

'Don't worry about it, Rolf,' Klein said turning on his stool. 'Right now, she's coming into the bar.'

There was a smile on her face and Rolf knew that tonight, he would be staying in her room and not back at his dreary quarters.

THIRTY-NINE

Sabina thought they were going to visit Lottie, as did David and Rebecca: they all seemed happy enough with the lie. Richard and Jane drove to Manchester Airport and left the car in the long-stay car park. Quickly checking in, they passed through passport control into the departure lounge. It was a Sunday morning and fairly quiet. There were few passengers. Jane bought them a drink and Richard ambled off into the bookshop. She settled down into the deep cushioned seats of the bar and waited for him.

Later he found her and sat down. 'Guess what?' Richard's face wore a huge grin. 'Look at this book I've just bought.' He carefully withdrew it from the plastic bag. 'It's called "Simon Wiesenthal - A Life in Search of Justice" by Hella Pick. Now isn't that a strange coincidence?'

Taking it from his hand, she looked at the stern old face staring back at them from the dust jacket and looked up. 'I can't believe this is the man we're going to visit.' Putting the book down on her lap, she passed Richard his drink. 'I've been wondering. Why you didn't finish reading Simon's notes?'

He sipped at the drink. 'I'm going to but I'm worried about what I might find.' Richard took another mouthful.

'I understand,' said Jane. She began flicking through the pages of the book and glancing at the photographs. 'If you don't mind, I want to look at this.'

'No problem,' smiled Richard. 'Will you excuse me for a minute?' He walked away and Jane watched him curiously before turning over a few more pages. Five minutes later, he returned. 'I hate sharing books and so I've bought another copy.' Jane shook her head, grinned and, silently, they read together.

After twenty minutes, Richard leant over. 'Jane, we're being called for boarding.' He nodded towards the green TV screens.

She closed the book with a snap. 'He's quite a man, isn't he? I can't wait to meet him.' They walked to the gate and waited patiently. Jane turned to Richard and squeezed his hand. 'I've flown dozens of times but I still enjoy flying. It's always so exciting.'

The plane was only half-full and they chose to sit towards the rear of the fuselage. The take-off was as smooth as ever and soon the in-flight meal arrived. They ate together, immersed in Simon Wiesenthal's story. The steward removed the mess of the meal and, as the aircraft droned on, Richard carried on reading. He was tired but the book gripped him. Occasionally, he glanced sideways and saw Jane was equally engrossed. It was the sheer guts of the man that impressed him. Never giving in and never stopping the search for justice. Occasionally, he flipped back to the front cover and stared at Wiesenthal's photograph.

The journey took two hours. It was the gentle descent that made them look up. The fasten seat belts sign came on and they nodded at each other. The steward checked everything and, within ten minutes, the aircraft was parked neatly at the end of a telescopic ramp.

'Here we are,' said Jane, expectantly.

'Yep,' smiled Richard.

After collecting their baggage, they walked out into the bright fresh air of a Sunday morning. Outside the terminal, they did not have to wait long. A white Mercedes taxi pulled up in front of them and Richard opened the door. The driver scuttled round the side and put the bags into the boot. 'Hilton International, *Am Stadpark, bitte*,' said Richard, as the driver returned to his seat. The roads were quiet and the driver made no comments. The hotel reception was expecting them and the check-in formalities were quickly completed.

'Jane,' said Richard, as their baggage was whisked away, 'let's go to see Wiesenthal straight away. Time is a bit short.'

'Fine,' she replied.

'All I need is a pen and my notepad.' He checked the pockets of his blue Crombie overcoat. 'OK,' he breathed, 'let's go.' Jane took his arm and they nodded to the doorman for a taxi. 'There's one thing, Jane.' She glanced at him. 'The Knight's Cross certificate has been worrying me. I don't want to mention it when we go into the meeting.'

She squeezed his arm. 'Don't worry, darling.'

They found another taxi and Richard helped her into the back seat. '*Salztorgasse, bitte*,' said Richard, quietly.

The driver looked over his shoulder. '*Salztorgasse*?' he called. 'For Wiesenthal?'

'*Ja, danke*,' replied Richard, with a surprised look.

The journey took about ten minutes. Richard paid the man and stepped out of the car. Jane slid out after him. He stared around as the taxi sped away and observed his surroundings. 'Not very impressive is it?' he said.

A rather run-down back street full of high concrete faced buildings and there was not a soul in sight. The entrance to the Documentation Centre was in no way special. A narrow entrance with a wheeled dustbin blocking the steps. Richard pushed it away and stepped into the gloom. Clutching his hand, Jane followed him up the flight of stone steps.

Unsure what to expect, Richard took things slowly. There were several doors to the left and the right, all with name tags and securely closed. Eventually, he came to another door. He knocked quietly. The peep-hole was obscured for a moment and then the door opened.

A smartly dressed woman looked at him and smiled. 'Mr and Mrs Cooper?' Her English had only a slight accent.

'Yes, that's right,' replied Richard, returning the smile. 'We made an appointment through a *mevrouw* Lottie Cohen in Holland.'

'Oh yes, please come in.' They stepped through the door. A short, dimly-lit passage and walls lined with photographs and certificates. 'Follow me, please.'

There was that unmistakable smell of dusty documents and old newspapers which made Jane wrinkle her nose; a smell that lawyers knew well. The woman turned and smiled again as she led them into a large room stacked from floor to ceiling with box files. In the middle of the boxes stood two desks, littered with documents.

'Mr and Mrs Cooper, if you would like to wait here a moment,' she said. 'I'll see if Mr Wiesenthal is ready for you.' Picking her way carefully round open boxes of documents, she walked across the room towards an open door. A moment later, she returned. 'Please come through.'

A small room. Two windows looked out into a vertical wall of other apartments, little light came in. Books lined two walls. On the third wall, more framed pictures and citations. The far end of the room was dominated by a huge map. Richard's eyes flickered across its title. "GERMANY UNDER HITLER'S DICTATORSHIP 1933-1945". Small black swastikas indicated the location of concentration camps and other places of death. Below it, against the wall, leant a red plush sofa that had seen better times. It was heaped high with magazines, more books and folded newspapers. In the centre of the room stood a small, brass coffee table. Two equally worn red armchairs were placed strategically on each side. Dominating everything was Simon Wiesenthal.

For a moment, the room was absolutely silent. Three pairs of eyes surveyed each other. He was taller than Richard expected, a little over six feet. The man did not look his age. Slightly stooped and wearing a sports jacket that hung loosely from sloping shoulders. Grey trousers with neat creases and shiny black shoes. A conscious scan of the man's outer everyday shell took only a split second and then the attention was immediately drawn to the face. Powerful but with reflections of a deep inner strength. A bald, dome-shaped head helped to set off the long, jowly jaw. The peppercorn moustache, neatly trimmed to give the lips a firm line. The voice seemed to fit the man perfectly and he spoke careful English with a heavy Polish accent.

'A pleasure to meet you, Mr and Mrs Cooper.' Handshakes were exchanged. 'Do sit down.' There was only one chair and both men stood to one side to let Jane sit. The secretary appeared with another chair for Richard. Their host waited near his littered desk.

'Thank you, Mr Wiesenthal, for finding time to meet us,' said Richard, trying to sum up the man before him.

Raising his hands in an expression that was so Jewish, he replied, 'It's my pleasure Mr Cooper. When Lottie Cohen phoned me yesterday, she caught me at a rather fortunate time.'

Richard hesitated. 'I gather you know Lottie?'

With a delightful chuckle, Simon Wiesenthal answered the question. 'Oh, yes. She's one of those very rare people that life throws up from time to time.' He answered the next question before Richard could even say it. 'She's helped me in the past with information concerning the Dutch Nazis. I've never had the pleasure of meeting her but I would think she's rather special?'

Richard responded. 'Yes indeed. I recently stayed with her and she's a wonderful woman.'

'Mrs Cooper,' Simon Wiesenthal turned to Jane, 'I understand you're a lawyer and that your husband is a headmaster, two noble professions.'

'Thank you,' smiled Jane at her charming best.

Crossing to his desk, he sat down and, folded his arms. 'Now, ... I hear from Lottie that you want to know about a man called Rolf Müller?'

'Yes, please' replied Richard.

Simon Wiesenthal rubbed a long forefinger across his chin and the brown eyes settled onto Richard's face. 'Mr Cooper, before I say anything, I must ask you to tell me about your connection with this particular Nazi.'

Jane reached out and held Richard's hand. Then he told the story. Occasionally, Wiesenthal made a scribbled note and his head lifted to nod or shake but he did not interrupt. It took Richard twenty minutes to explain and then he relaxed back into the chair.

'You, know, Mr Cooper,' said Wiesenthal softly, after a moment's pause, 'you're the third *Lebensborn* child to walk into my Centre in as many weeks.'

'Are there many?' asked Jane.

He nodded and pursed his lips. 'Oh, yes, a few. But Mr Cooper is the first British *Lebensborn* that I've ever met. .... What the Nazis did will never go away. In twenty years there'll be none of them left.' He chuckled. 'I'll certainly be long gone before then. But now we're starting to deal with the children of the survivors; the children of the perpetrators and the children of the *Lebensborn*.' His eyes closed and, for a moment, he was somewhere else. Taking a deep breath, Simon Wiesenthal smiled and said firmly, 'Now this man, Rolf Müller.' With his long fingers, he pushed papers hither and thither across his desk and then found what he was looking for. 'Ah yes. *SS-Sturmbannführer* Rolf Ernst Müller, sometimes known as Hermann Schmidt. I've never heard him use the name Jan Bildt.'

'*SS*?' exclaimed Richard.

'I'm sorry,' said Wiesenthal, 'didn't you know he was *SS*?'

Richard frowned. 'Both Bildt and my mother said he was *Wehrmacht*. I was not sure. .... Who do I believe?'

He cleared his throat. 'Definitely *SS*. His brother was *SS Hauptsturmführer* Edvard Müller. Head of the *SS* in Leeuwarden in northern Holland from 1940 until 1945.' Leaning across the table, he held the file between finger and thumb. 'Is this photograph a true likeness? I know it's a bit old.'

Richard craned forward. It was in black and white taken at a three quarters view. The peaked cap was set at a rakish angle and there was no mistaking the skull and cross bones deaths' head badge set above the shining peak. The young face had a handsome half-smile and the expression was unmistakable, Richard had seen the older version three days previously at the "*Grosse Bauernhof*".

'Yes, that's him.'

'Ehm, yes,' said their famous host, '... let me see now,' and he laid the file carefully in front of him. 'Rolf Ernst Müller, born in Saxony, June 11, 1918. His parents were both doctors. He did well at the local grammar school and attended medical school for five years and, under the auspices of the *SS*, graduated early as a doctor in 1942. After the *SS* training centre at Bad Tolz, he was posted to the medical section at Auschwitz-Birkenau.'

'Auschwitz? Oh my God,' gasped Richard, his face going pale. 'I half-suspected it. How can you possibly know all this? And how do you know it's true?'

Simon Wiesenthal nodded and a tired smile crossed his lined face. 'Mr Cooper, every day I'm asked that same question. I'm sorry but it's very simple. In these three rooms, I have the records of many Nazis and other people connected with the Holocaust. If they're not in here, then they're in the German Records Centre near Stuttgart. And, what's more, the Americans have copies of all records and further information in Washington. So you see, this file in front of me,' and he tapped it with a bony finger, 'is a copy of the genuine thing. In fact, it was faxed to me during the night from the Yad Vashem Memorial Centre in Jerusalem. The Nazis were meticulous record keepers and I've never doubted their paperwork.' He waited for a moment for Richard to compose himself. 'Would you like me to describe his duties at Auschwitz?' Richard nodded dumbly. 'Right, ... the SS doctors were a very special group of men. Their prime task was to select people for the gas chambers as they arrived at the camp, usually, may I add, on special transport trains.'

Richard held up his hand. 'Excuse me, Mr Wiesenthal, my father, or should I now say, my stepfather, has told me many times about the transports to the death camps.'

Simon Wiesenthal was an infinitely patient and considerate man. He knew it was important to let his guests talk. 'Would you like to tell me what your father told you?'

Richard began and repeated the story that he had heard from Simon's lips only a few weeks previously. Again Wiesenthal took notes and the brown eyes constantly switched from Richard's face to Jane's.

'You said the Cohen family were transported from Westerbork on September 4, 1944.' Clearing his throat and, with a sniff, he said, 'Now that's interesting. .... Ah yes, the *Rampe* at Birkenau. It was the unloading point for Jews and the other so called subhumans.' He watched Jane shudder. 'I'm sorry, Mrs Cooper but that's what the Nazis called Jews, Gypsies, homosexuals, Jehovah's Witnesses and other minority groups.' He paused for a moment and cleared his throat. 'The SS doctors waited for the guards to form the people from the transports into columns, normally five a breast. They had something about people being in five's. The doctors then glanced at each person and sent them, either to the right for life, or to the left, for gassing and death.' He opened another file. 'In fact, I have here a photograph showing exactly how that took place.' He came round from behind the desk and placed the photograph on the brass table. A black and white grainy image showing groups of people standing on sandy ground. Long shadows cast over wooden barracks. Several men in SS uniform stood casually by. A smiling officer, with arm raised, stood opposite the head of the queue.

'Mr Wiesenthal,' said Richard in a trembling voice, 'surely that man standing in front of the group is not my father?'

He shook his head. 'No, no, certainly not. This picture was taken by an unknown SS man in 1944. Probably in Autumn by the look of the trees.

The officer standing at the head of the queue is *SS-Obersturmführer* Heinz Thilo. He was another camp physician at Auschwitz from October 1942 until the camp was liberated in January 1945. He died of natural causes in 1947.' With a slim pen, Wiesenthal pointed at the centre of the photograph. 'If you look carefully, you can see that Thilo's hand is pointing to the left. It means that the old man in front of him is on his way to the gas chambers.'

Jane had kept silent but now she began to talk. 'Did all the doctors take part in these selections?'

'Yes.'

'Did they have to?'

Simon Wiesenthal pursed his lips and the thin moustache quivered. 'Now we get to the point. They were serving members of the SS. They were Hitler's elite and sworn to follow orders to the letter. Some of the Auschwitz doctors were worse than others. Josef Mengele enjoyed selections and never missed one whilst he was a camp physician. Some of them claimed to be more lenient, although I've never believed that fact. You ask a member of the SS whether they had to do it and they'll always say they were, "following orders". Everything they did was an order from Hitler himself. In cases appertaining to the Holocaust, that defence has been dismissed.'

'Theirs is not to reason why, theirs but to do and die,' said Jane quietly.

'With the SS, that was exactly correct.'

Jane gave a half-smile and sighed. 'The obedience of a soldier is not the obedience of an automaton. A soldier is a reasoning agent. It is a fallacy of widespread consumption that a soldier is required to do everything his superior officers order him to do. The subordinate is bound only to obey the lawful orders of his superior.'

Simon Wiesenthal looked up in surprise and smiled. 'Ah, ah, Mrs Cooper, only lawful orders. I see you've been doing your homework.'

Richard turned round and glanced at his wife. 'I didn't know you'd been reading about this.'

She smiled grimly at both men. 'It was one of my dissertations at law school. I've been brushing up.'

'You are of course, Mrs Cooper, referring to the *"Einsatzgruppen* Case" tried by the American Military Tribunal?' A similar half-smile passed across his lined face.

'Yes, and there's also the precedent of the ………'

'Excuse me,' said Richard, patiently. 'You two may share similar legal interests but I'm here to find out about my father.'

'Of course,' said Wiesenthal, nodding. 'I quite understand your worries.

But the morality of the Holocaust will effect your understanding of your father's actions.'

'Are you absolutely sure that the man who says he was my father was involved in these selections?'

The domed head inclined. 'Absolutely sure. There was no way in which an *SS* doctor at Auschwitz could not be so involved.'

'What else did he have to do?' asked Richard, and all the time Simon Wiesenthal's answers struck home.

'When the selections had taken place, the people were marched to the gas chambers. They were gassed and the doctor in charge had to check whether they were dead.'

'How?' There was a slight waver in Richard's voice.

'Usually by feeling for a pulse in the neck.' Wiesenthal touched a point below his ear. 'Normally, they only checked maybe, ... one in a hundred.'

'A hundred?' said Jane, incredulously.

Simon Wiesenthal spoke very quietly, almost in a whisper. 'At Birkenau in 1944 they could gas and cremate 15,000 victims every 24 hours and that's only a rough estimate.' Jane shook her head. 'The Auschwitz doctors played a key roll in the whole process of death.' He took a deep breath and sat back in the old chair. 'For the *Reich*, they legitimised all deaths. When the main camp at Auschwitz was opened, all inmates were medically inspected by doctors. Deaths were certified by doctors. The cause for death on the certificates was usually something like, "shot whilst trying to escape", or "succumbed to bacterial infection". Later there were no examinations of any kind, only selections on the *Rampe*.' His soulful brown eyes rested on Richard's face. 'I'm sorry to say your father was a doctor that fell into the latter category.'

'Mr Wiesenthal,' said Richard, softly, 'I know I have to accept your word on these matters but ......,' he hesitated. 'How, in God's name, did he ....?'

The interruption was so gentle, 'Mr Cooper, I know exactly what you're going to ask me. It's a question that I'm asked every day and one that I ask myself every night and God's name doesn't come into it.' He opened his hands and shrugged. 'I don't have the complete answer. It's something that you,' his eyes flickered across to Jane, 'and your family will now have to live with for the rest of your life and for all coming generations.'

'Yes,' Richard replied tersely, 'thoughts about my family have been going through my mind. But I would like you ..... personally, to please try and answer my question.'

He leant over his desk. 'It's a very difficult question to answer. You have to look at both Judaic and German history. Let me simplify things for you and try and explain the German reasoning.' Holding up his hand like a school teacher, he began to count on his fingers. 'Firstly, the Jewish character. Deep within the German psyche, the Jews were always a degenerate race. Physically deformed, when compared with the Aryan. For generations they had interbred and were therefore of poor stock. Secondly, Jews were evil and therefore a threat. Thirdly, Jews were extreme and were not capable of any logical thought. Fourthly, all Jews wanted to destroy Germany and were entirely responsible for their own actions. Put all these facts together, and Hitler did that in *Mein Kampf*, and the only logical answer for the *Reich* was to eliminate the Jews and thus the "final solution" was envisaged.' For a full minute, the people in the room sat in silence.

'Mr Wiesenthal,' said Jane. 'How on earth could a man who was a doctor just leave home in the morning and then go out and kill people? It was not only against his Hippocratic Oath, it was criminally illegal?'

'Mrs Cooper, you speak from a legal viewpoint that has had over fifty years to assimilate the Holocaust.'

'Excuse me again,' said Richard, impatiently. 'I'm not really interested in the legality of the Holocaust.'

'Or the illegality?' said Jane.

'Mr Cooper, I know what you're asking me,' said Wiesenthal. 'You want to know about your father, don't you?' Richard nodded. 'Well, I want to tell you a little about your stepfather Simon Cohen.'

'You know about him?' exclaimed Richard.

He smiled as the conversation changed tack. 'Oh yes, he was a junior lawyer at the Nuremberg War Trials and did a great deal to bring some of the Dutch Nazis to justice. He assisted in the trial of Seyss-Inquart, the *Reichs* Commissioner for the Netherlands.'

'If that's the case, Mr Wiesenthal,' Richard reached into the pocket of his overcoat and pulled out an envelope. 'How do you explain this? It contains a slip of paper which fell out of my father's diary.'

Taking it from Richard's hand he scrutinised the yellowing piece of paper. 'It looks genuine,' he said carefully, 'and it looks like Seyss-Inquart's signature.' Simon Wiesenthal returned the document and took a deep breath. 'I have no idea what that message means, or what it's about.' Richard placed it back into the envelope. 'There's another thing. Jan Bildt mentioned a man called Willi. I know it's a long shot but it may link in with Müller.'

'The name Willi, I seem to remember from somewhere.' Rising to his feet, he called softly, 'Rosemarie, here a moment, please.' She entered the room and nodded at Richard and Jane. 'Check the name, Willi something. I think you may find him in the Auschwitz SS lists.' She quietly returned to her office and he sat down.

Clasping his hands, he said, 'Mrs Cooper, I'd like to return to your question about being a doctor at Auschwitz. Talk to any SS doctor who worked in the death camps and they all become uncomfortable when you mention the Hippocratic Oath. For most of them, they believed that the *Führer* Oath took priority. In fact, the conditioning was so powerful that they actually believed that the Jews were subhuman and therefore exempt from the Oath.'

Jane shook her head. 'But surely at the war trials, the ethics of these oaths were taken into account when sentences were pronounced? I thought the Nuremberg Trials made it very clear what contributed a war crime and from there the doctors were classed as having committed crimes against humanity.'

'Ye-es, Mrs Cooper, you're quite right. It took some time for the names of the doctors to be recognised. Many of them had already made elaborate plans to escape from Allied hands. Mengele was the prime example. The American Military Tribunals found some of the doctors guilty and they were executed. The tribunals were held not only at Nuremberg but also in other places where crimes had been committed. For example, at Dachau in 1946. There were also British Tribunals held at Lüneburg and Belsen. One of the most important trials, as far you're concerned, began in Frankfurt on December 20, 1963 and lasted twenty months. They were called the, "Auschwitz Trials" because they involved men who had worked at Auschwitz-Birkenau.'

'Were they doctors?' asked Richard, biting his lip.

'Some of them, yes.' Simon Wiesenthal slowly turned in his seat and scanned a shelf full files. Finding the one he needed, he pulled it down and laid it on the desk. His voice was matter of fact. 'Four SS doctors were on trial. Franz Lucas, accused of taking part in selections on the *Rampe* and of supervising the insertion of *Zyklon B* into the gas chambers. He was charged with complicity in joint murder on 4 separate occasions of at least 1,000 persons. Willi Frank, also accused of taking part in selections and using *Zyklon B* in the gas chambers. He was also charged with the joint murder on 6 occasions of at least 1,000 persons. Willi Schatz and Victor Capesius had the same accusations made against them.'

'Were they found guilty?' asked Jane.

Turning over a page, he replied, 'Yes, Lucas was found guilty and sentenced to 3 years and 3 months hard labour. Frank was found guilty and given 7 years hard labour. Capesius was given 9 years hard labour. Schatz was acquitted.'

For the first time, Richard became angry. 'I don't believe it. How the hell can you be found guilty of such crimes and be given such trivial sentences? What kind of justice is that?'

Simon Wiesenthal carefully closed the file. 'You have to realise that, at that time, Germany was sick and tired of war crime trails. One of the Frankfurt prosecutors actually said, "The majority of the German people do not want to conduct any more trials against the Nazi criminals." Even Bonn's Minister of Justice pleaded that the "Murderers amongst us" be left in peace.' Simon Wiesenthal folded his arms and his face was expressionless.

'I think it's utterly disgraceful and I can't understand the verdict of the court.' Jane said coolly, although her face had paled.

'Mrs Cooper, I don't want to upset you.' Unfolding his arms he leant forward. 'There have been no war crimes trial in Britain since the war and yet there are many *SS* murderers living in your country.'

Richard had calmed but what he heard, again upset him. 'I don't understand. How the hell do you know that?'

'It's quite simple really. The Germans pay war pensions to 459 people in Britain. Some of those are ethnic Germans but most come from countries that used to belong to the Soviet block. Remember that Poles, Ukrainians Romanians were in the *Einsatzgruppen* extermination units. The German Government insists that no foreigner can claim if they are guilty of crimes against humanity. But I doubt if they cross check against their war crime records. In 1986 one of my assistants gave a list of 17 names of known Nazi war criminals living in Britain to Margaret Thatcher, who'd just returned from a visit to Israel. When she saw the evidence, she was furious and then, only after several years, was the War Crimes Bill passed by Parliament.'

'What are you really trying to tell us?' said Richard, trying to work out the direction of the discussion.

Simon Wiesenthal smiled. 'Your father, Müller, is quite obviously an untried war criminal. Even in the 1960's, you can see what totally ridiculous sentences guilty *SS* doctors were given. Things have not greatly changed.'

'Then why do you continue in your search for these Nazi criminals?' said Jane

He nodded and tapped a finger on the desk. His voice steadied. 'We must never ever forget what happened. We must always seek justice for the sake of the victims and to set examples for the future. We must always seek out these criminals whether they be old, rich or protected by others.'

'And my father?' Richard's face was pale.

'I realise you've not told me where he lives.' He shrugged his shoulders. 'It doesn't matter. You said his name's Jan Bildt. All I have to do is to pick up the phone and ask directory enquiries. Within a minute, I would have the number and the address. …. No, Mr Cooper, …. Müller is not going anywhere.' He rose to his feet and walked round from behind his desk. 'What happens to *SS-Sturmbannführer* Rolf Ernst Müller is entirely up to you. I know you want to see him again, because you want to ask him if all this,' he waved his around the room, 'is true? You want to believe me but you also want to confront him.' He stared down at Richard and his face was not unfriendly. 'You want to see what his answers are to your questions.' And then his voice softened. 'I want you to decide if he is guilty or not guilty. Then, no doubt, you will let me know what to do.'

Richard's head dropped. Jane leant across and gently held his hand. His head lifted and he spoke very quietly. 'Mr Wiesenthal, what would you suggest we do next?'

The secretary returned to the office with three files. Simon Wiesenthal opened them one by one. 'Mr Cooper, there are three officers with the first name, Willi. They are, Langen, Sobek and Hossler. Hossler was a known friend of Müller's. Can you remember if Müller mentioned his friend's last name?'

Richard shrugged. 'No, not at all. At the time, I thought it was strange but I thought no more of it.' Simon Wiesenthal closed the files.

'Before you go to your father,' he said. 'I would like you to meet a man who knew him. He was in Birkenau whilst Müller was there. He saw what he did and he's already made statements to that effect. His name's Benjamin Blum and he was a prisoner doctor at Auschwitz. He's an old man now,' a slow smile spread across his face. 'just like me. He lives in Budapest, because that's where he was born.'

'Budapest,' exclaimed Jane. 'That's some way from here.'

He shook his head. 'No, it's not. You can catch an express train from here in Vienna and be there in two and a half hours.' Richard and Jane glanced at each other and nodded. 'If you wish,' he continued, 'I could phone Doctor Blum later today and ask him if he'd meet you?' He left the question hanging.

'Yes,' Richard replied, quickly. 'We certainly would like to meet him.'

He leant against his desk. 'May I suggest that in Budapest you stay at the Hotel Gellért. It's a nice old place and only a few minutes walk from Doctor Blum's apartment.'

Richard glanced at his watch. 'That's an excellent suggestion and one that we'll take up.' He rose to his feet and turned to help his wife. 'Mr

Wiesenthal,' he said, 'you've given us a great deal of your time and understanding and I must thank you for your help. Now, I think Jane and I will have to leave you.'

A gentle smile spread over the old man's face. 'It really has been a pleasure and I'm here to help.' He grasped Richard's hand firmly. 'Believe me, I know what you're going through. The truth is never easy to accept and it will take time to even understand what you've heard today. Or, you may never ever understand it. …. Please be careful.'

FORTY

On that particular night, Ulrika was delicious in bed. Her orgasms were never ending and each time he found it harder to satisfy her. Every time he lay back to catch breath, she was on him again. The air raid sirens moaned and he thought the bombers would bring him some welcome relief. But, no, she just pulled him back down and mounted him like some Venus on heat. The pounding and percussion of the exploding bombs excited her even more and he tried desperately to control her writhings. As the final ebbing whine of the "All Clear" faded away, she collapsed on top of him.

In the middle of the night, he awoke with a start and then he remembered. Slipping out of bed, he padded across the floor to his briefcase. Flipping off the catch, he searched into the corners and found what he had so carefully placed there earlier in the day. In his palm, the diamond necklace was icy cool.

The light from under the bedroom door was enough to see her outline. Pushing the sheets back away from Ulrika's slim body, he stared down at her for a moment. Slowly and gently, he placed the necklace across her neck and, with his finger, gently touched her lips. She stirred and muttered something. Rolf let his finger run down the curve of her neck to her left breast. Toying with her nipple, awakened her with a rush.

'What's the matter?' she said, with open eyes. Her hand reached up to her neck and she grasped the necklace. 'What is it?' she cried. Rolf switched on the bedside light. 'Oh, my God, I don't believe it,' she cried. Holding the diamond necklace in front of her, she sat up and Rolf watched her nipples awaken with excitement. 'Is it for me? …. For me?' she said, incredulously.

'All for you, Ulrika. All for you.'

'Diamonds,' she whispered. 'They're magnificent. But why? …. Why?'

'Stop asking "why?" They're for you. I'm giving them to you to look after for both of us. They'll guarantee our future.'

She frowned. 'Where did they come from?'

He laughed. 'Ask no questions and you'll be told no lies. Just enjoy them and be happy.'

Ulrika played with the necklace and fondled it first in one hand and then in the other. Rolf reached across her body and her head dropped down as he fastened the catch in the nape of her neck. The biggest diamond swung low and nestled between the half-moons of her breasts.

'Fantastic,' she whispered huskily and pulled him down on top of her.

They both slept a deep, dreamless sleep. Rolf was the first to awake and, with a sense of panic, he glanced at the fingers of his luminous watch. 'Damn,' he muttered, throwing the bed clothes to one side. Stepping out of bed, he strode towards the bathroom. Turning, he glanced back. Ulrika's slim body lay curled in the foetal position, her breasts cast short shadows onto the silken sheets. The swooping curves of her small buttocks showed other shadowy recesses. Rolf paused and felt an instant pang of desire. Sensing pure lust, he clenched his fists and turned back to the bathroom. The icy cold needles made passion disappear and he cried out.

The cry must have woken her, because as he left the bathroom, she was sitting up in bed. In that perfectly feminine way, she had the sheet pulled up over her breasts but he could see erect nipples jutting through the clinging texture of the silk.

'Good morning, Rolf,' she said huskily. 'Did you sleep well?'

'Perfectly,' he replied and used the towel to punish his desire.

'Why don't you come back in bed for just five minutes?' Her eyes pleaded and the silken sheet dropped just enough to catch his eyes.

'Do you know what you're doing to me?' he grunted. Grabbing his clothes and yanking them on.

'I love you in riding breeches,' she said with a smile. 'They make me think of riding horses and long legs and movement. Come back into bed and ride me, ... please.'

With his city collapsing around him, he almost wanted to give in and let her take-over. His iron-hard discipline took over. Slipping on a shirt, he walked over to the bed and leant over her. 'Ulrika, there's plenty of time.' His hand crept under the sheet and cupped her breast. Increasing his grip, made her squeal with pleasure.

'You swine, Rolf Müller,' she cried. 'You bloody swine.' He kissed her full on the lips and felt her wet tongue sneak into his mouth and twine itself around his. At last, he unlocked himself and stood back.

Throwing on his tunic, he began to fasten the heavy buttons. 'Today, I'm going to find out how the hell we can get out of Berlin.' That surprised her.

'Thank God,' she said. 'I've been wanting to ask you for weeks but I know how difficult it is for you.'

He shrugged his shoulders. 'The Golden Pheasants are already on their way.' He saw her frown. Rolf laughed. 'That's the Berliners' name for the top Nazis who leave.' Collecting his cap, he gave the peak a final polish and set it firmly on his head. With a habitual tug, he set it at the correct *SS* rakish angle. Waving goodbye, he unlocked the apartment door and stepped out into the corridor.

On this day on April 13, 1945 the contents of the *Reichsbank* were to be moved south. Rolf's duties were to make sure that the greater part of the wealth of the fatherland was transported safely away from the city and to the waiting trains. At two different stations in the southern suburbs, the trains, codenamed *"Adler"* and *"Dohle"*, waited. Powerful Krupp locomotives steamed up to the correct boiler-bursting pressure. They paused, wreathed in blasting white steam as the engineers kept the gauge needles just below the limits. The raw power was needed as tons of banknotes and precious objects weighed much more than the usual lighter, human loads.

At the *Reichsbank* two separate convoys of massive trucks were almost loaded. Four steel helmeted guards were perched on top of each vehicle with two tripod-mounted, MG 34 machine guns resting on steel frames; their fields of fire covering a full circle. Open topped lighter and speedier trucks, full with guards, were parked between each load-carrying vehicle. The roar of diesels and the softer chug of the escort cars clamoured into the morning air. Blue and grey smoke wafted into the faces of the men that lined the loading area. Nobody spoke as the steel doors and the canvas flaps were finally closed and sealed.

Rolf glanced up and down the rows of vehicles, received the saluted signal from the sergeant and then blew his whistle. The piercing shriek broke the excited calm and the drivers gunned their engines. More smoke filled the air and then the lead *Kübelwagen* carrying Rolf and his NCO's drew away, followed by the rest of the convoy. The journey to Berlin-Michendorf and Berlin-Lichterfelde-West railway stations would normally have taken thirty minutes; this time, it took over an hour. The vehicles were forced to continually stop and start as they negotiated piles of rubble and huge bomb craters. Diversions sent them down narrow streets that, as often as not, ended up in dead ends. Most of the time Allied bombs rained down and buildings around them collapsed into dust. Tongues of flame licked at the convoy and the guards dived down into the cover of their vehicles.

Rolf saw not a living soul as his car constantly sought the most direct route south. His uniform was covered in dust and torn in several places. He used his hand to scrape caked dust off his goggles and, eventually, he threw them away. It took another 15 minutes for all the convoy to arrive at the station where the *"Adler"* train waited and an hour to unload the boxes and bags. *"Adler"* had two wagons into which was loaded half of the total available wealth of the *Reich*, 250,000,000 *Reichsmarks* and 105 bags of foreign currency.

Rolf dashed down the empty platform and waited for two Mercedes staff cars to arrive. Behind him, stood a *wagons-lits* carriage fully provisioned for a long journey. The waiting steward looking strangely out of place in white gloves and dark green livery. With klaxons blaring, the two cars swept onto the platform and braked to a halt. Rolf saluted, as *Reichsbank* President Walther Funk stepped out, followed by his assistant, *Doktor* August Schwedler. Another man climbed out of the other car and walked straight up to Rolf. *Reichsbank* Director Hans Alfred Von Rosenberg-Lipinski was the civilian in overall charge of the evacuation of the bank.

'Müller, how did everything go?' he asked, tersely. 'Did we lose anything?'

'Everything went perfectly, *Herr Direktor*. The remainder of the convoy should arrive at Berlin-Michendorf within the next ten minutes.' Both men ducked as another bomb exploded outside the station.

' ...... And the gold Müller? What about the gold?'

'No problem at all, sir. The convoys left the city as arranged. They'll meet you as arranged, spot on time.'

The Director thumped Rolf on the shoulder. 'Excellent my dear Müller. Well done. Your duties are now finished. Report directly to the *Führerbunker*. Good luck.' Rolf watched them scramble into the guarded carriage. Funk grasped Rolf's hand, shook it and clambered up into the coach. Before Rolf had time to signal to the engineer, there was a massive blast of steam and the train began to pull out of the station and soon it vanished noisily into the early morning mist. Rolf turned back to the cars and waved them away. The incessant bombing had stopped and there was an uncanny silence. Striding back to the *Kübelwagen*, he climbed over the door and nodded to his driver. The convoy had already started the drive back to Berlin and Rolf wearily followed them.

The task that he had so ably completed, and the night before with Ulrika, had exhausted him. Returning to his barracks, Rolf ate a lunch that was hardly edible. At least in his spartan room there was a clean change of clothes and that, with a shower, made some of his vigour return. He walked to *Reichs* Chancellery not noticing the desolation. The ruins of his city had no further effect on him.

The day he joined the staff at the *Führerbunker* was a day that Rolf remembered well, it was Friday April 13, 1945. He entered the underground catacomb of passages and rooms via the entrance from the Foreign Office corridor. The first thing that struck him, was the stench of human sewage and unwashed bodies. The atmosphere was totally different from when he had last visited. To Rolf, it seemed as though he was re-entering a barrack block in Birkenau. *SS* guards of the *Leibstandarte* Adolf Hitler Regiment saluted and checked his documents. Unsure of his duties, he reported directly to *SS-Obergruppenführer* Max Juettner, the officer in charge of the Bunker. Juettner was sitting alone in a guard room off the main corridor that divided the bunker. He hardly looked up from a pile of files.

'Ah, …. yes, Müller.' Then he looked up and his eyes stared hard into Rolf's face. 'There's sod all to do here. Just keep out of the way and salute when you have to. Make sure the guards roster works properly and well, …. you know ……' his hand fluttered in the air. 'Look busy.' His head dropped back to the files and Rolf knew he had been dismissed. Snapping up a salute, he turned and walked out of the room. The corridor stretched away in front of him. Narrow with chairs and sofas arranged haphazardly along walls dripping with moisture. The leaders of the *Reich* passed him by and raised not a flicker of interest. One visitor surprised him; it was Klein.

'Hello, Rolf,' he said, with grin. 'I heard they'd put you down here. All the faithful ones end up in the Bunker.' He wore a muddy leather greatcoat and his boots were filthy. He noticed Rolf's glance. 'Yes, I look a real mess. If I'd come in here like this a month ago, I would probably have been shot.' Then his face became more serious and Rolf knew there was something wrong. 'Sorry to have to tell you this Rolf, but the *Adlon*'s been hit.' Rolf jumped out of his chair.

'Ulrika, is she …..?'

Klein put his hand on Rolf's shoulder. 'Don't worry, she's all right. I found her with the rest of the guests. They've been evacuated.'

'Are you absolutely sure she wasn't hurt?'

'Really, don't worry,' Klein replied, shaking his head. He quickly checked his watch. 'I'd better be on my way. I'll see you later at the barracks.' He began to walk back towards the steps at the end of the corridor and then turned. 'Bring a few bottles,' and he gave a huge wink and then snapped his fingers. 'Oh, ….. by the way.' He returned and grabbed Rolf's arm. Pulling a piece of card from his tunic pocket, he said, 'Do you like classical music'

Rolf stopped and turned. 'Eh, yes. …. Of course.'

Klein laughed. 'At least there's some people in this damned place that still enjoy a bit of culture.' He took a deep breath. 'Tomorrow at 5pm in the Beethoven Hall, the Berlin Philharmonic Orchestra will give its last concert. You and Ulrika can have my ticket.' Without waiting for an answer, he pushed the ticket into Rolf's pocket and strode away.

FORTY-ONE

The journey from Vienna to Budapest on the *Avala* Express took just under three hours. As the train sped across the low Hungarian foothills, the conductor came and checked their tickets and Richard tried to doze.

'Darling.' Jane's hand shook his arm. 'Do you mind if we read from Simon's diary?'

'Not at all,' he replied with a smile. Reaching over to his travel bag, he took out the file and handed it across.

'Right,' she said, taking a deep breath, 'where were we? Ah yes. .....'

'The woman led me across the muddy tracks to the wooden barrack. "Who are those other people over there?" I asked, pointing to the sullen groups under guard.

"They're NSB," she replied, surprising me by spitting on the ground. "Dutch Nazis waiting to be sorted and dealt with. We never speak to them." Then she strode off, suddenly stopping near a single railway line. The shiny rails glinted in the sun light. She stooped and ran her fingers along the harsh, cold steel and then looked up at me. "Our people came in here and then left. You know, Simon Cohen, over 70,000 Dutch Jews have travelled along these lines and we're the only ones that've remained in Westerbork."

"How do you know that none survived?"

She shrugged her shoulders and pinched out the cigarette-end. Her answer was logical. "Where are they?"

The door to the barrack was unlocked. Pushing it open, she walked into the dark interior and clicked on the lights. A whiteness illuminated everything.

"My God," I heard myself saying. Row after row of neat wooden shelving. All stacked from floor to roof beams with files and ledgers. The polished wooden floor gleamed. Not a bound spine out of place, not a speck of dust to be seen. Every one numbered and labelled. "What the hell is this place?" I asked.

"Central records," she said, brusquely. "I worked in here for three weeks. I was so good, that they sent my family away and left me here." She watched my face. "When were your family transported and what were their names and addresses?"

I gave her the details and she walked slowly down the first aisle towards the far end of the barracks. At one point, she stopped and turned. "Cohen's of ... Leeuwarden did you say?" She saw my nod. Reaching up to the top shelf, she pulled down a ledger. Glancing at the number on the spine, she opened it. "September 4, they left Leeuwarden. ... The Cohens. ... The Cohen's. ... Ah, yes, here we are. Transported from Leeuwarden to Westerbork September 4, 1944. Left for Auschwitz on September 11. This means they would have arrived at the camp on the morning of September 13, 1944."

September, September, September. That month kept running through my mind. It was September 1939 that I last saw my parents. September 1944 when I returned to Holland and now September when my family arrived at the Auschwitz death camp and September when they were murdered.

The woman pulled at my arm. "Did you hear what I said, Simon Cohen?" She pushed the ledger into my hands. "Read it for yourself"

The bound volume was heavy. Beautifully bound in a black leather with gold numbering on the spine and the front. The pages were neatly divided into columns and the writing was in clear, black Gothic script. Names, addresses, occupations. Fresh, clear pages made from best quality paper. I mentally checked all the 42 names. Yes, they were all there. Listed by date of birth and date of departure The ledger suddenly became heavy in my hands and I wanted to hurl it to the floor. The names began to blur and then, just in time, she took it from my hands.

"Are you all right?"

"Yes, ... thank you." My head cleared. "It's just so hard to believe."

She smiled with understanding. Gently taking the ledger out of my hand, she held the top corner of the page between forefinger and thumb and then tore it from its binding. The sound of the tearing echoed down the racks of ledgers. "Take it," she said, eyebrows raised. "'It's yours."

I wanted to get out of the building and away from this awful place. Jamming the paper in my pocket, I pushed past her and ran down the aisle, my nailed boots echoing back from the ledgers of death.

The fresh air made me stop and shake myself. I walked alone along the railway lines, with the woman following me at a distance.

The driver saw my mood and climbed into the jeep. The engine started immediately, something it had never done before. The Canadian Captain emerged from his office and waved. I couldn't talk to him and I certainly didn't feel like a glass of his Scotch. At the gate, the barrier was closed and one of the guards waived us down. I was tempted to drive through it. The jeep stopped.

"Sir," the guard called out. "There's an urgent message for you."

The Captain ran to the jeep holding a piece of paper. "Sorry, Cap'n Cohen.

I know you're in a hurry to get out of this cursed place but this message looks urgent." He passed the flimsy over to me. *The message was quite simple.*

"URGENT stop. REPORT WITH IMMEDIATE EFFECT TO ACHTERVELD stop THERE TAKE ORDERS FROM LT. KOLONEL CAS VAN HOUTEN, CHIEF OF STAFF FOR PRINCE BERNHARD stop 1130HRS 29 APRIL 1944 stop".

I tapped the driver on the arm and he engaged first year. Before I could do anything, the woman leant across and kissed me gently on the cheek.

"Find and kill the Nazi murderers," she whispered in my ear.

The roads were fairly clear and neither if us spoke for a good half-hour. We didn't stop. My driver had estimated five hours to Achterveld but we made it in four. It was difficult to talk over the sound of the engine and that gave me time to think. Müller was right. I knew my family had left Leeuwarden and now the piece of paper in my tunic pocket, proved that they had left Westerbork. I had to see him again and find out where the Auschwitz documents were located. The change in engine note made me sit up. Then it all started to happen.

Achterweld was a typical, Dutch village. A cobbled street, a largish church at one end and open flat fields at the other. One or two decorated gabled houses and a couple of empty shops. There were military everywhere. We parked near the church. A second lieutenant with Princess Irene shoulder tabs waved us down.

I said, "What's going on here?"

He began to explain. "Well, sir, on April 22, Montgomery stopped the Canadian advance into Holland. ... In the west of the country our people are starving. ... Eisenhower sent a message to Seyss-Inquart making a proposal about food transport and Seyss-Inquart accepted. ... There was a meeting here yesterday and there'll be another meeting tomorrow with the Allies and the Germans."

"How were the Germans represented?" I asked.

"Reichskomissar Seyss-Inquart, and some others." Then I heard a door open. I turned and saw Prince Bernhard. He came straight to me and extended his hand.

"Kapitein Cohen, I presume. We meet again."

I took in the General's rank badges, the ready smile and the overall feeling of a man relaxed and at ease with himself. Round steel spectacles clipped firmly round his ears and the handshake was firm. He wore British serge battle-dress and a peaked cap that I remembered from our last meeting. "Th ..... thank you, sir," I managed to stutter. "What exactly do you want me to do?"

"Kapitein, *at the next meeting, I want you to shadow Seyss-Inquart. Sit as close as you can to him and make notes about anything unusual that he does."*

"Sir," *I said conscious of the fact that I was interrupting him.* "May I ask ... why?"

"Kapitein, *I've seen your personal record. What you've done in the background is greatly appreciated. I know you're a highly qualified lawyer and that you were involved in the early discussions on war trials for the Nazis. Your own family have perished because they were Jewish."* He paused *for a moment.* "Seyss-Inquart is on the list of wanted war criminals and I want to gather every tiny piece of information that we can use in the case against him." *Leaning forward, he placed his arm on my shoulder and said softly,* "How was it at Westerbork?"

I explained and he listened. Occasionally, he brushed a hand across his brow and sometimes he closed his eyes but, he listened. Looking up, he said softly, "When tomorrow's meeting is over you can go and get this man Müller, take him to Berlin and find out what's happened to your family. Collect all the evidence you need. Use your family as an example of how to catch these murderous swine."

I remember mumbling something and thanking him and that was all. I felt his hand on my shoulder and he said, "Oh, and there's one other thing. You can't come to a meeting as a captain. With immediate effect, you're promoted major." *He grinned.* "The last time we met, I promoted you. If I meet you again, I'll probably have to promote you to colonel." *He turned and was gone.'*

'Richard,' said Jane. 'This is incredible. Are you sure you had no idea that your father was involved at this level during the war?'

Richard shook his head. 'None at all. I thought he was just an officer with a law degree. Yes, I knew about the van de Meers and Lottie but I had no idea about Seyss-Inquart. It's all very worrying.' He sighed.

'Why worrying?' said Jane, placing the file gently on the small table.

'The note from Seyss-Inquart. Perhaps Simon really did something to help the Nazis.'

'Don't be silly.'

'Well, remember,' Richard said, staring at the file. 'After the war he was no longer a Dutch citizen and he never explained to us what really happened.'

Jane turned round and squeezed Richard's hand. 'Don't you think Bildt being your father has a lot to do with this?'

'I don't know. Why didn't Sabina tell me everything?'

Jane let go of his hand. 'She had her reasons as much as Simon had his.'
'I've noticed one other thing,' said Richard.
'What's that?'
'You no longer refer to Simon as my father.'
'Neither do you.'
The train rolled swiftly on and they dozed for a while. After twenty minutes, Jane nudged him. 'I've been thinking,' she said. 'Have you spared any more thoughts for your mother?'

Richard stretched, giving him time to wake up and gather his thoughts. The words came out with a surprising vehemence. 'Deep inside, I'm so angry with her. She must've known what Bildt was up to and she's not seen fit to tell me. It's as though there's never been any trust between us.'

'Have you thought that maybe she was scared of admitting the truth,' said Jane. 'She's had to live with this for a long time.'

'Yes, I know all that. Wiesenthal has almost proved to me that Bildt's a war criminal responsible for the deaths of thousands. Although I still can't believe it. And, what's more, …. he's responsible for the murder of nearly all of the Cohen family.' The train hit a bend and Richard steadied himself against the arm rest. 'Jane, you do realise that he was the *SS* doctor on the Ramp who selected my family on that night in September 1944?' She nodded slowly. 'I want to confront him with what I know. I want to accuse him of mass murder. When I see his reaction, then I'll decide what to do with him.' Richard sighed and reached for her hand. 'I just can't believe the awful coincidence of the whole thing. For years, Simon told me the story of how his family were put into a train and transported. Yesterday, I heard about the man who sent them to their deaths. That man is my father. If it was a novel, nobody would believe it.'

'Richard,' she said softly, 'There's yet another awful coincidence, probably one you haven't thought of.' She folded her arms. 'In the same way that Müller had the power of life and death over your family, now you have the same power over him.'

Richard pursed his lips and pulled at his ear lobe.. 'I hadn't thought about it quite like that.'

They settled back into their seats and the train travelled smoothly on.

The narrow strips of family vineyards slowly gave way to the sprawling outer suburbs of Budapest and the train slowed. The smoothness of the welded rail joints departed and the clackety-clack of jointed rails made Richard sit upright. Jane reached for her handbag and Richard gathered their coats and luggage.

At Keleti Station, Richard stepped down from the air-conditioned comfort of the first-class carriage and the hurly-burly of Budapest hit him smack in the face.

'Wow,' muttered Jane, clutching on to her handbag.

Richard carried their suitcase and guided her down the platform. 'Look.' And he pointed. 'Taxis.'

'Better than walking,' laughed Jane.

The taxi was a battered Lada with blue smoke belching from its exhaust. The driver leapt out and grabbed their baggage. He said something that neither of them understood. Then he spoke English.

'American?'

'No, English,' replied Richard, bundling Jane into the narrow, board-like back seat.

'Ah, English. Very nice,' muttered the driver, sensing a good tip.

'Hotel Gellért, please.'

'Hotel Gellért, very nice.' Then he rammed the Lada into first gear and sped off down the road.

Budapest enveloped them. There were trams on one side, trolley buses on the other and taxis of all shapes and sizes. Their taxi took them over the fast flowing Danube. Richard twitched as the car lurched in and out of a deep pothole and then it braked screechingly to a stop. A doorman pulled open the door and waited for Jane to slide out of her seat. In a flash, the driver had the boot open and the luggage on the trolley.

For a moment, Richard paused and looked around him. The Gellért was one of Budapest's most famous old Art Deco hotels. They walked into a soaring lobby with a high domed ceiling and a circular balcony floating around the first floor level supported by impressively thick marble columns. In the centre of the lobby, and directly below the dome, a small fountain played, stared at by a lone, bronze nymph. Deep leather chairs stood on the marbled floor..

'Good afternoon, sir, may I help you?' Behind the reception desk, the dark suited man was genuinely polite.

'Good afternoon,' smiled Richard. 'Mr and Mrs Cooper. We have a reservation for tonight.'

He smiled and checked the computer screen. 'Yes, Mr Cooper. My name is Lajos Imre. A reservation made via the Wiesenthal Documentation Centre in Vienna.' He signalled to the porter. 'That will be suite 407.' The registration form slid across the desk. 'Please fill this in sir and sign it.'

'Thank you,' replied Richard, gathering up their passports and key. They made their way across the lobby to the lifts. The hallways to the rooms were deeply carpeted and the porter had the door open and waited for them. He placed their bags in the small entrance hall and waved them through into the lounge. Receiving Richard's tip, he nodded a smile and left them alone.

Jane removed her coat and threw it onto the sofa.

'I feel guilty,' said Richard, quietly.

'Why, darling?'

'I'm enjoying being here with you. It's very special and yet, I'm here to speak to a man who saw my father murder people.'

Jane placed her hands tenderly on Richard's face and kissed him full on the mouth. 'You mustn't think like that. You can't begin to carry your father's crimes on your shoulders. Life is here to be lived to the full. Simon would not've liked you to live with that worry.'

Richard returned the kiss. 'Jane, you're probably right but it still concerns me.' He smiled. 'Come on, let's unpack and have a drink.'

Within twenty minutes, they were back downstairs to the bar. A smallish place with a curving bar and matching upholstered seats. One or two other guests nodded their way as they sat at the bar. The blonde woman serving the drinks smiled at them, flicking her long blonde over her shoulder, she said, 'Good evening. My name is Viktoria Grenzel. Can I help you?' They ordered two drinks.

'This is really very nice,' said Jane. 'I wish we could do this sort of thing more often.' Jane moved closer and Richard felt her warmth.

'Under different circumstances, yes,' he replied.

Their wine was almost finished when the receptionist found them.

'Excuse me, Mr Cooper,' he said, politely. 'There's a man waiting to see you at the desk.'

Richard was surprised. 'Thank you, Lajos. Did he give you his name?'

Reaching into his breast pocket, he took out a visiting card and passed it to Richard.

Richard glanced at the oblong of white card. 'Please ask Doctor Blum if he would like to join us.'

They both rose to their feet, as the receptionist returned, accompanied by another man 'Mr Cooper, this is the gentleman who was asking for you.' He smiled and returned to his desk.

'Hello, Doctor Blum. I'm Richard Cooper and I'd like you to meet my wife, Jane.'

Benjamin Blum was thin almost to the point of emaciation. He wore a loose fitting dark blue suit and matching suede shoes. A lick of white hair was smoothed back over a balding head. A proud face with brown eyes that carried the same haunted look as Simon Wiesenthal's. The voice was low and firm and he spoke very precise English.

'Good evening, Mr and Mrs Cooper. It is very nice to meet you.' He extended his hand and Richard shook it, followed by Jane.

'Do sit down, Doctor Blum,' said Richard. 'May I get you something to drink?'

'Thank you, that is very kind of you.' He hesitated for a moment and stared at the shelves behind the bar. 'A small Scottish whisky would be nice, please.'

Jane smiled. 'Doctor Blum, it's very good of you to come and see us here.'

With a polite chuckle, he replied, 'I hope you don't mind me coming straight to the hotel?'

'Not at all,' said Richard, 'We were going to call you anyway.'

Taking a small sip at his drink, he smacked his lips. 'I like whisky. It's one of my little pleasures in life. Oh dear, I don't have many left. Well now, … that is enough about me.' He took a deep breath. 'I hear from Simon Wiesenthal, that you would like some help.'

'Did Mr Wiesenthal say what sort of help we needed?' asked Richard.

Benjamin Blum shook his head and took another sip. 'No, not really. He said that you wanted to know about a doctor at …… at Auschwitz.' Richard noticed that as he said the word "Auschwitz", the hand holding the glass trembled and he carefully gripped it with his other hand. 'Perhaps, you could tell me exactly what you would like to know?'

Richard told his story simply. It took about fifteen minutes and whilst he told it, Benjamin's glass was refilled. He listened carefully.

'Mr Cooper,' Benjamin Blum said quietly, 'I have the greatest sympathy for you because both you and your family are cursed with something that was not your fault. Before I tell you about your father, let me tell you about my family. I was born and educated here in Budapest. I was a happy young man from a good Jewish family. I decided to go and start a general practice in Slovakia. It was the biggest mistake I ever made. In 1942, I was taken by the *Gestapo* and ended up in several camps and then Auschwitz. I was one of those people who survived Auschwitz and the Russians liberated me in January 1945. I managed to return to Budapest and then I sought out my family.' He shook his head and brushed away a single tear. 'As you know, the Hungarians were part of the Axis powers and, for most of the war, Hungarian Jews were exempt from deportation. Later, the Nazis murdered 200,000 Hungarian Jews. I'm the only survivor from the whole of my family.' He stared at Richard and his head tilted to one side. 'It seems, Mr Cooper, that you have two fathers. One is dead and one is still alive - I have nobody.' Sitting back in his chair, he drained the whisky from the glass.

Jane and Richard looked at each other, impervious to the other people in the bar. 'Did you marry?' asked Jane, gently.

'Yes, I did. My wife was killed in a road accident. There were no children.'

The bar was filling up and their quiet conversation was interrupted by happy people wanting a pre-dinner drink. Richard turned his head. 'Benjamin, perhaps we could go back to our suite. I could order something to eat?'

Benjamin nodded. 'That would be very nice. Very nice indeed. I normally eat by myself.' Placing the glass on the table, he rose to his feet and reached for his long overcoat. Jane took him by the arm and helped him down the steps away from the bar. The lobby was busy as guests left for the Budapest night life. Whilst they waited for the lift, Benjamin looked around him. 'You know, Mrs Cooper,' he said softly. 'The last time I came into this hotel was when I graduated in 1938. We held a party in the restaurant and I remember every minute.' The lift doors opened and he stepped inside. 'I've never been in here since.' He turned and looked hard at Richard's face. 'Do you know why?'

'No,' said Richard.

'Because during the war it was used by the Germans. They took over every room. I was glad when the Russians took it.'

'I'm sorry,' said Jane. 'Richard and I could take you somewhere else.'

'No, no, my dear. Don't worry about it. It's changed, …. and anyway,' he shrugged his shoulders, 'it's good to lay bad memories to rest.' Making their way down the hallway, Richard opened the door to their suite. They walked through into the room and Jane took Benjamin's overcoat.

'Please sit down. May I get you another drink,' said Richard. 'Maybe another small Scotch?'

'Please.'

Benjamin Blum settled himself comfortably into the deep armchair. 'Now, Mr Cooper, you would like to know about Rolf Müller?'

'If it doesn't bother you,' replied Richard. 'Yes, I would.'

He began slowly and his eyes kept moving slowly from Jane's face and back to Richard's. '*Herr Doktor* Rolf Müller. A leading member of the medical department of Auschwitz-Birkenau Concentration Camp. I saw him nearly every day.' Slowly, he brushed his few white hairs back over a pale bald head. 'And you say he's still alive?'

'Yes, I met him a week ago in Germany.'

'In Germany? ..... I suppose that's not unusual. Many of the camp doctors practised for years after the war. ..... I was a prisoner doctor, an unusual species of subhuman in the death camp hierarchy. There were many like me. Some collaborated with the Nazis and helped them. They were tried after the war and some were executed, some were put in prison.' For a moment there was a new spark in his eyes. 'I'm sorry, I deviate from your father. .... Müller was typical SS. He carried out selections and killed like the rest of us so called doctors.'

'Killed?' asked Richard.

'Oh, yes. I helped him to kill by phenol injection and by other means.' He saw Jane's glance and turned to face her. 'Inmates had phenol injected straight into their hearts. It was quicker than the gas chamber and most of the inmates who had to take part in the medical experiments were murdered in that way.' She reached for whisky bottle and refilled the glasses. 'Müller was efficient and very careful. He hardly spoke to anybody and kept himself to himself. A handsome man and always immaculately dressed. That made him seem worse. He worked closely with Mengele. I met most of the SS doctors and the worst was Josef Mengele. He was the coldest murderer I have ever known. It was the eyes, you know. When those eyes looked at you, you knew they were the eyes of the devil himself.'

'Did Rolf Müller ever kill with his own hands?'

Benjamin Blum seemed surprised by the question. 'Oh, yes, of course. I mean he didn't strangle people with his bare hands or shoot them like some of the guards did. He killed them medically and scientifically.'

'How many?'

He lifted his hands. 'Only God knows. I personally saw him kill dozens. But then there were the selections on the *Rampe*.' He pronounced it the German way, as though he did not want to soil the English language. 'Every time he directed somebody to the left, he was condemning them to death. Therefore, logically, he was responsible for the deaths of thousands, if not hundreds of thousands of people.' He swallowed a mouthful of whisky and put the glass back on the low table. Jane refilled it and nodded. 'He escaped you know, as did Mengele. He left just before the camp was liberated. I saw him several days before he left and he spoke to me.' He smiled. 'Now that was unusual. You see, he knew that I'd been watching him. Most of the time, I was just another prisoner. But towards the end, he realised that I would make a perfect witness for the Allies. I'm surprised I'm still alive.' He rubbed his chin. 'I'm surprised Müller is still alive. Most of them are dead or they just disappeared. Where did you say he was living?'

'In Germany near the Dutch border.'

'And you say you actually met him?'

'Oh, yes, I most certainly met him.'

'Mmm, ... you do realise, Mr Cooper that Müller is a war criminal and, as yet, he's not been caught.' He paused before asking the next question. 'Are you going to report him to Simon Wiesenthal and the German authorities?'

Richard had half expected the question. 'I don't know yet. It's something I have to think about.'

Benjamin Blum's eyes narrowed. 'Don't think too long because, if you don't, I most certainly will. .... For fifty years I've had nightmares about Auschwitz. Most of them have been about the medical experiments I was forced to carry out. I can still see every face and I remember precisely what happened. I don't want to remember but, when I close my eyes, it's like a never ending film. You know, Mr Cooper, they say that some people only dream in black and white and others dream once a week.' He took a deep breath and closed his eyes. 'Believe me, I dream every night in full glorious colour, with stereophonic sound and I can even smell Auschwitz. I can touch it. I relive every second of what happened. That's the reason why I know exactly what your father looks like.' He stopped talking and his eyes opened wide.

A thought passed through Richard's mind. 'Doctor Blum, do I look like my father?' He felt the tired old eyes looking at him.

'Maybe around the nose. You're his height and there is something in the way you hold yourself. May I ask, ... what is your profession?'

'I'm a headmaster.'

He smiled. 'I somehow knew you weren't a doctor. Teaching is much respected here in Hungary.' There was another pause. 'I want to say to both of you, that you have my sympathy. You must find living with this knowledge very difficult.'

Jane answered the question. 'Doctor Blum, we do worry about it. But we have the support of our family. It's much harder for you because you have nobody.'

'Thank you,' he said, politely. 'Since I left Auschwitz, I've never practised medicine. I've had odd jobs here and there and I did receive some compensation from the German government. I didn't like it because it was dirty money. I manage but I do get lonely.' He sighed and then said, 'Apart from the killing, I have something else in common with Müller.'

'What's that,' asked Richard.

Benjamin Blum pulled up the loose left sleeve of his jacket and unbuttoned his shirt at the wrist. 'We both have tattooed numbers.' Dark blotchy blue and etched deep into the skin was the number **35866**. Richard and Jane stared at it. 'It's my badge of honour,' said Benjamin, touching it lightly with his fingertips.

Jane reached for the phone. 'Doctor Blum, may I order something for you to eat?'

He touched the tip of his nose and sniffed. 'Thank you, that's very kind. A sandwich would be fine, I'm not a big eater. I suppose it's because I live alone.' Jane placed the order.

There was a silence and Richard thought about the old man in front of him. For the last two weeks Jan Bildt had been a mysterious shadowy figure but now he was a real person with a real history and with people that knew him.

'Benjamin,' said Richard. 'What was Müller like compared with the other doctors?'

He closed his eyes, as though he was searching a card index file. 'As I said, Mengele was the worst. The rest could only be better than him. Some of them tried to help in small ways. A little extra food here, or a quick death there. Müller was as straight as he could be. He always followed orders and he spent lot of time with Mengele but that was because Mengele respected him as a doctor.'

'How did he escape?'

'At the end, the SS panicked. Most of them fled to the west. Mengele took with him a train load of medical records. God knows what happened to them.'

There was a knock at the door and Jane excused herself. 'Doctor Blum,' said Richard, 'at Auschwitz did you know of an officer, who's first name was Willi? I'm not sure of his second name but it could have been, Langen, Sobek or Hossler.?'

He nodded. 'Yes, I know the name Hossler. He was SS, not a doctor. In charge of one of the sections at Birkenau. He was a murdering swine just like all the others.' His sharp eyes looked at Richard's face. 'He was Müller's best friend.'

'Willi Hossler,' said Richard, 'if it is the same person, is now living near Müller and is obviously a close friend of his.'

'I'm not surprised,' commented Blum. 'Towards the end I saw them together. The SS always helped each other.'

Jane pushed the trolley across the room and carefully placed a plate of sandwiches on the table.

'Tell me, Mr Cooper,' said Benjamin, selecting a plateful of food, 'did Müller look rich?'

Richard swallowed a mouthful of chicken. 'Yes indeed, very rich. His farm was more like a small chateau and beautifully furnished.'

'Lots of paintings and silver and gold ornaments?'

He frowned. 'Yes, there were. How did you know that?'

'They would all be loot from the Jews. The warehouses at Auschwitz held enough stolen goods for all the SS to be millionaires. No doubt, Müller had his share. My family lost everything, everything. When I came back, I had to start all over again.' The whisky was having its effect and Benjamin Blum became more voluble. 'Have you heard of Adolf Eichmann?' Before Richard could nod a reply, Benjamin rushed on. 'In 1944 Himmler sent him here to deal with the Hungarian Jews and we all know what that meant, don't we? Eichmann was the architect of the scheme to trade the freedom of Jews for trucks. I still can't believe it.' He took another gulp of whisky and a mouthful of sandwich. He looked hard at Richard. 'Quite often Eichmann used to stay in this hotel. It's rumoured that he had a suite on the fourth floor full of women and drink.' Leaning forward, he whispered, 'It could be this very room .... This very room.'

Jane shivered. 'May I pour you a cup of coffee, Doctor Blum?'

He blinked and caught her meaning. 'Oh, yes please. I'm so sorry. At times I do get a little worked up.'

'Milk and sugar?'

'Yes, please.' He leant back in his chair and turned slightly to face Richard. 'You mentioned *Lebensborn*? I've heard about it, although I've never met anybody who knows anything about it. Would you mind telling me what you know?'

'No problem, Doctor Blum.' Then Richard went on to carefully explain exactly what he knew.

'I'm so sorry, Mr Cooper. I didn't know just how involved you were with everything. I mean, ... and you only found out two weeks ago?'

Richard gave a hollow laugh. 'Yes. Two weeks ago I thought I was half-Jewish with a German mother. Now I'm probably full German with a Nazi war criminal as a father.'

Benjamin nibbled carefully at a cheese sandwich. 'I thought I'd heard everything about the Nazis but your story is quite fantastic. And you say your father was a Dutch Jew?' He did not wait for an answer. After munching away the final sandwich, Benjamin Blum folded his arms and said, with conviction, 'Justice without revenge is what Simon Wiesenthal says and I agree with that completely.'

'Don't you feel any hatred?' asked Jane.

He nodded. 'That's a normal question that I'm frequently asked.' He smiled and somehow the earlier shadow had gone from his thin face. 'At first, I felt like killing every German that existed. That emotion soon fades away and it's replaced by a need to understand why it happened.'

Richard nodded. 'I feel that as well.'

'There is no complete explanation for what people like your father and thousands of other people did. No doubt, you will find out that he had a perfectly normal childhood and loving parents. The idea that all SS were criminally insane human beings is not true. They only became like that when they put on the uniforms and went to the SS training schools. Mr Cooper, your father was one of those people. He was totally conditioned and could do nothing else.'

'He could have resisted,' said Jane, quietly.

'Impossible to do that. Any people who opposed Hitler were either killed or put into concentration camps. If Müller had made the slightest objection to what he had to do, then within twenty-four hours he would have been on the Eastern Front. Oh, no, he had no more choice than me and he was bound by his oath of allegiance to Hitler.'

The conversation suddenly stopped and there was an awkward silence. The plates and the whisky bottle were empty. The draught from the half-open window caused the temperature in the room to fall rapidly. Richard felt it, shivered and stood to cross the room.

Benjamin shook himself. 'Mr and Mrs Cooper, I really must go home.' Pushing his bony hands against the arms of his chair, he levered himself upright. 'It has been very interesting to meet you and I hope I have been of some use.'

Jane took his arm and smiled. 'Doctor Blum,' she said, 'it's been very interesting for us as well. And you've been a great help.'

Richard walked towards the door and then suddenly Benjamin Blum stopped and turn to grip Richard's shoulder. His eyes bored into Richard's head. 'Mr Cooper, have you ever been to Auschwitz?'

'No,' Richard replied.

'Whilst we've been talking,' continued Benjamin, 'it has occurred to me that you should visit that awful place. Since I left it on February 4, 1945, I've never returned. In four months, it's the fiftieth anniversary of my departure. I've never really wanted to go back.' The bony hand bit deeper into Richard's shoulder. 'After meeting you both, I would consider it a great honour if you and your wife would accompany me back to Auschwitz.'

Jane surprised her husband. She leant across and kissed Benjamin Blum gently on the cheek; he blushed. 'Benjamin, thank you for asking us. It would be a privilege for us to go with you and we'll be in touch as soon as we return to England. But are you sure you don't want to go with your friends?'

'Oh dear, no. I don't believe in all these journeys of remembrance. What is there to remember?' He nodded his head. 'Yes, this will be the only time that I will ever return to Auschwitz and I would like it to be with you and your husband.' He let go of Richard's shoulder and smiled. 'After all, Mr Cooper, we may be strangers. But you are now part of the Holocaust and your family will be, ... forever.'

Richard led him back to the lobby and gently placed him in a taxi.

The meeting with Benjamin Blum exhausted them. They showered and went straight to bed. 'Darling,' said Jane, with her head on the pillow, 'I really don't know what to say.'

Cradling her head in his arm, Richard pulled her close. 'Let's not say anything and sleep on it.' Gently, he kissed her. 'I love you.'

Before they left the hotel, Richard sent a fax to Bildt. Almost before he had time to check-out, the clerk handed him a return message. It was simple and to the point.

'"Grosse Bauernhof"
Deutschland

My Dearest Richard,
I am delighted to hear from you at long last. You and your charming wife will be more than welcome to visit my home the day after tomorrow.

Kindest regards,

Jan Bildt.'

The half-empty KLM flight to Amsterdam left dead on time and, as it banked away from Ferihegyi Airport, Richard looked down at the Danube dividing Buda from Pest. His eyes caught the white stone of the Gellért shining up in the late afternoon sun and he had a fleeting second to try and guess where Benjamin Blum lived.

Jane was perfectly relaxed. 'After listening to that old man,' she said. 'I knew you'd want to go to Auschwitz.' She thought for a moment. 'Richard, can you imagine what he must have gone through? I mean, ... it's a story so terrible, it defies explanation.'

'Do you know what upset me more than anything?' said Richard and Jane shook her head. 'It was when Benjamin said to me that we are now part of the Holocaust. Simon's family history used to upset me but this ever unfolding story is really affecting me.'

Jane dozed for a moment and then shook herself. 'Time for a little more reading, I think. Can you pass me Simon's file, please.'

Richard rose from his seat and reached up into locker. Pulling down his flight bag, he found the file and handed it to Jane.

With the soothing drone of the engines in her ears, Jane relaxed into the seat and opened the file. She read quietly and Richard was able to sit back and close his eyes.

'We met in a school hall. A long table lay down the centre with chairs aligned down each side. Every place had a place-name. Seyss-Inquart's seat was directly opposite the American, General Bedell Smith. To his right, sat Prince Bernhard and, on his left, the Canadian, General Galloway. I was allocated a chair directly behind the Prince's left shoulder. Seyss-Inquart entered the meeting room.

It was the first time I had chance to see Seyss-Inquart at close quarters. He wore a grey uniform with all the usual silver braid. On his tie was the gold swastika pin, recognition that he was held in Hitler's highest regard. He was very composed. Long carefully manicured fingers lay on the surface of the wooden table. Occasionally, he nodded or pursed his lips. I watched his eyes. They say you can just a man's soul through his eyes. From those eyes, I could judge nothing, they were a pale blue and very cold. I felt I couldn't trust him. I took notes and made one or two sketches and just watched and listened. I saw him, for a fleeting second, stare at my face. It was a look that went straight through me. What made me concentrate, was the thought that this man had been responsible for the order for the SS to begin the round up of the Dutch Jews, including my family. From Seyss-Inquart to Edvard Müller, the chain was almost complete.'

'This is some story,' said Jane, stretching. Putting the file down. 'I just can't believe what happened. …. Are you sure your mother's never read it?'

Richard shook his head. 'I don't think so. Before we meet Müller, I want us both to finish reading it.'

The steward came round with the last drink before landing and Richard packed the file away into his bag. They sat together and drank the coffee, each with their own thoughts.

FORTY-TWO

Rolf found the *Adlon* a smouldering shell. It was late at night and there were no street lights left to illuminate his way and so he sat for a moment on a pile of still warm roof timbers. Eventually, he rose to his feet and began the long walk back to the barracks. Thoughts rushed through his mind, the uppermost one being Ulrika's safety and her whereabouts.

It was the early hours of the morning when he approached the gates of his barracks and saw for the first time that there were no guards. As he carefully walked along the unlit road, the silhouette of the block loomed into view. From the top floor, came clearly the sound of singing and revelry. Within the building there were only flickering candles and oil lamps. As he climbed the last step to his floor and turned a corner, he saw the reason for the noise. In one of the mess rooms were at least thirty officers of all ranks. Their voices sang at full volume and their leader was Klein, stripped to the waist. Red-faced and pouring with sweat, he reached the top note and then saw Rolf watching him.

'*Sturmbannführer* Müller!' he bellowed. 'How's life in the *Führerbunker* and how's the "corporal"? Has he given any new orders for the saving of the glorious *Reich*?'

The fact that Klein said such things in front of other officers shocked Rolf. Then he realised Klein was drunk. Undoing the buttons of his tunic, Rolf accepted a bottle of beer from a man sprawled in a low chair. Gulping down a mouthful of the tepid liquid, he watched what was happening.

With a loud belch, Klein stood at Rolf's side and said loudly, 'Come on, how's life in the shit hole?'

'Proceeding satisfactorily,' replied Rolf quietly.

'Jesus fucking Christ!' roared Klein. 'The Russians are 10 kilometres to the east and the Allies are an hour to the west and you say, "proceeding satisfactorily." My God, Rolf, I always knew you were an idealist but not plain fucking stupid.'

Pushing Klein away, Rolf said coldly, 'What else do you expect me to say? I'm trying to be loyal to my country. I swore an oath just like you did.'

Klein's sweat streaked face loomed closer to Rolf. 'Fuck the oath and fuck the *Führer*. Tomorrow morning, or should I say this morning.' He laughed at his comrades and they laughed with him. 'We're all leaving this bombed out pile of rubble that we used to call a city.' Klein's mercurial temperament took over and his face became serious. 'My dear Rolf, forget about all this oath and loyalty shit and come with us. Germany is finished.'

Finishing the bottle, Rolf looked around him. The other men were silent and they watched him carefully. Taking another open bottle from Klein's hand, Rolf took a long swig and thought carefully about his answer. He nodded and his face was expressionless. 'I agree with you that Germany is finished but the German people are not.' There was a tremble in his voice. 'I have never felt so disgusted and angry in all my life. I've served the *Führer* loyally and I've done unspeakable things.' He quickly emptied the beer bottle. Rising to his feet, he smashed the bottle against the stone wall. 'I'm saddened by it all, as I'm sure you, my brother officers, are also saddened.'

Rolf's words were simple and straight from the heart. Some men glanced at each other and others nodded. The atmosphere changed completely. Klein picked up his tunic and slipped it round his shoulders. For a moment, he looked at Rolf and then said, with a straight face, 'Rolf Müller, you constantly surprise me. I envy your loyalty and pride. I'm going to bed and the offer of escape still holds.'

Rolf shook his head. 'Thank you, Klein. I always seem to be running away from somewhere with you. This time, I'm not yet ready to go.' Refastening his tunic buttons, he said, quietly, 'Where's Ulrika?'

Klein smiled. 'I'm not so sure. They were evacuating to the nearest *U-Bahn*. She's probably down there.'

'I'll go straight away.'

Klein was incredulous. 'Don't be crazy. You've just come from there and it's pitch black outside.'

Rolf opened his mouth to answer and then they both heard the sound. Klein dropped flat to the floor dragging Rolf with him.

'What the hell is that?' shouted Rolf.

It came from the east and began as a trembling in the ground and then the windows of the barracks became brightly lit with white flashes. The sound came last of all and rocked Rolf and Klein as they lay prostrate on the floor. Waves of thunderclap explosions rolled through the building and solid reverberations shook the foundations. Then it abruptly stopped as quickly as it had began. The silence was nerve-wracking.

'That,' said one of the men, 'was the start of the Russian bombardment of Berlin.'

'How can that be possible?' asked Rolf, pushing himself upright onto his knees.

'You bloody *SS*. .... Ha, ... you've no idea.' There was a grinning smile on the man's face. 'You're listening to 152mm guns at maximum elevation with a range of 10 kilometres.'

'Are they that close?' asked Rolf, with a worried frown.

'They most certainly are,' retorted the man dressed in the grey trousers of the *Wehrmacht*. The men listened to their expert. 'Give them another couple of minutes and they'll start again. It takes the Russians that long to reload and fire.' Almost as he spoke the last word, the bombardment began all over again and they dropped to the floor.

'My God,' said Rolf almost in a whisper. 'We don't stand a chance.'

'They're aiming at the city centre. They're after Hitler and the Chancellery. The Russians'll destroy everything on the ground and then send in flame-throwers for the rest.'

'No they won't,' said Klein. 'They want Hitler and the rest of them alive.' He grinned. 'Anyway, I'll be gone long before then.'

Rolf managed to scramble towards his quarters. Hoping for a quick wash, he turned on the shower; there was no water. Cursing, he slipped into another uniform and left the barracks. There was not a soul around and still the raucous singing came from the top floor. Shaking his head, Rolf plodded on, impervious to the sounds of the continuing onslaught.

It took him an hour to return to the ruined *Adlon* and, in the light of the early dawn, he looked around for any signs of life; there were none. Sighing, he walked on to the nearest *U-Bahn*. At the top of the steep flight of steps leading down to the station, he stumbled into one or two weary looking people. Without a second glance, they made their way back to what might be left of their homes. As Rolf began to tread carefully, waves of stale air billowed up from below. Flickering oil lamps lit his way and their black smoke smeared the walls above. Litter and rubbish lay everywhere. Holding his hand over his nose, he walked down deeper into the dank depths. He had to push his way past anonymous bodies who clawed their way upwards and away from the claustrophobic platforms below.

The sight that greeted him at the bottom of the last steps, shocked him. Row after row of wooden beds stacked on top of the dirty platforms. It was the smell that hit him hard. Human excreta littered the rusting steel lines and the stink of unwashed bodies hung over everything. He searched for any sign of Ulrika and eventually, as he reached the end of the platform, he stopped and began to call out.

'IS ULRIKA HANNSEN HERE?'

He dropped off the platform and onto the track bed.

'IS ULRIKA HANNSEN HERE? .... HAS ANYBODY SEEN ULRIKA HANNSEN?'

Soon, the yellow lights of the platform disappeared behind him and he was forced to feel his way forward. Odd flickering candles showed the way and he constantly tripped over sleeping bodies. A hand pushed him in the chest and an unseen woman's voice, with stinking breath, bellowed into his face.

'What the fuck do you want?' she said, harshly. The hand grabbed his belt and, for a moment, Rolf thought she was after his gun. He pushed the hand clear and shouted back at her.

'Get off me. I'm looking for somebody.'

'Aren't we all darlin',' she replied, throatily. A candle, spluttering into life in her other hand, showed a haggard face and lank hair. Rolf recoiled.

'Have you seen a young woman?' he said. 'She was in the *Adlon*.'

'The *Adlon*? There's nobody from the likes of the *Adlon* here.'

'Are there people in all the tunnels?'

'Hundreds of 'em. There's another platform a hundred metres along. There's plenty of people along there.' Rolf felt slimy lips touching his cheek.

'Thank you, whoever you are.'

'My pleasure.'

The number of people thinned and eventually the end of the dimly-lit platform hove into view.

'IS ULRIKA HANNSEN HERE? ....' Instantly, his call was answered.

It was a faint voice. 'Rolf, ... I'm here. ..... Near the entrance to the stairs.' He stumbled forward towards her voice.

She rose from the shadows and he reached out for her. For a minute, they did not speak. Then Rolf spoke first.

'Ulrika, how are you? Are you all right?'

Via a single smoky oil lamp on the wall, he saw her face. It was streaked with sweat and dirt. 'I'm fed up,' she whispered, 'tired and scared to death but I'm all right.'

'What the hell happened?' He pushed her half away from his body and stared down at her pale face.

'When the warning sounded, none of us took any notice. Then the bombs came closer and closer and I ran towards the cellars. By then, it was too late and the whole building collapsed around me.' She took a quick breath. 'I must've been unconscious, because the next thing I remembered, was being pulled out from under a pile of timbers.'

'Oh, poor Ulrika,' whispered Rolf into her ear.

'To be quite honest,' she replied in a matter of fact way. 'I don't remember much of what happened. I've got a few scratches and a bruise on my head and that's about all. The staff at the hotel were very good. They me gave the coat I'm standing in and some shoes.'

A different kind of concern shot through Rolf. 'Did you manage to save any of your belongings?'

'None at all but I've got my bag and .... .' Then she knew exactly what Rolf meant. 'Oh, my God, ... the diamonds. I've lost them. They were in my room under the bed. ...... I'm sorry, Rolf, they've gone.'

'Shit, shit, shit,' he said angrily. 'That necklace was my insurance for the future.'

Her shoulders slumped and the relief at being found faded away. 'We can always go back to the hotel and see if they've been found.'

'Oh, yes,' said Rolf, sharply, 'I can just imagine me going up to the workers clearing away the rubble and saying, "Have you found a stolen diamond necklace, please?"'

'Where did you steal it from, Rolf?' she said, softly, staring at his face.

He made his excuses, closing his most secret thoughts. 'Don't worry about that.' He turned away, realising that people were beginning to stare. 'Come on, let's get the hell out of here.' Rolf, rather roughly, grabbed her arm and propelled her off the slimy platform and down onto the tracks. Without a word, they scrambled back towards the surface.

FORTY-THREE

It was late afternoon when the KLM Boeing approached Amsterdam. Before Richard had time to think, the runway rushed up to meet the aircraft and, with a thump, they were down. Passport and immigration took only twenty minutes. Richard smiled as he recognised the figure on the other side of the glass screen at the end of baggage collection.

'I presume the attractive young woman you're waving at is Marieke Johnstone?' said Jane, raising an eyebrow.

'How did you guess?' grinned Richard, collecting a trolley and loading onto it their baggage. Within a minute, they were out into the hurly-burly of Arrivals.

Marieke waited quietly, dressed in jeans and a navy-blue sweatshirt. She saw Jane's quick glance in her direction and nodded a greeting. 'Hello,' she said. 'Welcome to Holland. I'm Marieke Johnstone.'

'I knew you were,' replied Jane, with a smile. 'I've heard so much about you.'

'Not bad, I hope.' There was a sparkle in her eyes.

'Of course not,' laughed Jane.

Marieke's face became serious. 'I had hoped we could meet under happier circumstances. But never mind.' The two women looked carefully at each other.

They all followed her as she made her way through the busy crowds. Jane walked at her side and Richard heard them chatting. The glass doors slid open and the chill wind made him shiver while Jane and Marieke chatted on. By the time they had reached the car, they were friends.

Marieke turned to him as she fastened her seat belt. 'It's not like your MG but it goes and I enjoy driving.'

'Don't worry about it,' laughed Richard. 'I like the old Volvos.' Gritting his teeth as she accelerated away from the parking space and lunged into the motorway fast lane.

She drove expertly through the afternoon traffic and Richard settled down for the journey. He saw the motorway signs for Amersfoort and, after glancing at the map, realised that he was only a few kilometres from Achterveld, the place where Simon had met Seyss-Inquart. Again, he was following in Simon's footsteps. They made good time to Oudermirdum.

It was all new to Jane and she glanced about her as they pulled into the small village. Marieke pointed out one or two landmarks and then turned into the narrow road leading to the coast. It was nearly dusk as the car parked in the short gravel drive. Richard stepped out and opened all the doors.

'Hello, Richard,' called a familiar voice from the house. He turned and saw Lottie's smiling face in the doorway. 'Leave your bags,' she said, 'and come in. I've coffee ready for all of you.' Jane took Richard's arm and led him up the drive. Lottie stepped out onto the tiled porch. The two women faced each other.

'You're just as Richard described,' said Jane, leaning forward to shake hands.

'I hope he described me in a nice way,' commented Lottie, kissing Jane on both cheeks. She wore a long, black woollen skirt and a dark green open-necked blouse with her white hair tied up in a loose bun. Carefully extracting Jane's arm from Richard's, she took her hand and led her back towards the house. Richard heard her talking and he knew the two of them would get on well.

The living-room was full of candles and their flickering glow gave a calm, warm feeling. Lottie waved everybody to sit down and Jane sat in the big chair near the window. Then Lottie poured out cups of coffee and handed them round.

There was the usual mundane chit-chat and Richard chose the right moment to explain to Marieke and Lottie about the conversation with Simon Wiesenthal. They listened intently and, when he mentioned the gassings at Auschwitz, Lottie pulled a small lace handkerchief from up her sleeve and dabbed at her eyes. When he had finished, she wanted to know all about Benjamin Blum.

'There are plenty of witnesses to what happened in the camps,' she said. 'But I've never gone out of my way to meet anybody and, indeed, I've never wanted to. But the deeper this thing goes, then the more I want to know.'

Marieke sat forward and said quietly, 'I've a friend called Gert Koopmans, who's the curator of the Frisian Resistance Museum and I asked him what he knew about Edvard Müller. He phoned me back and told me what he'd found out.' Reaching into the pocket of her skirt, she pulled out a scrap of paper. 'Yes, …. Müller was taken prisoner and put on trial in the Hague later in 1945 and executed. However, there's one very interesting point. On May 15, 1945, he was taken from his cell to an unknown destination and returned a week later.'

'Does it say who took him and why?' asked Richard, remembering Simon's diary.

'It just said, "Removed for further questioning". A guard detail from the Princess Irene Brigade took him. It doesn't say who the officer in charge was.'

Richard caught Jane's flickering glance and made no response. 'I see,' he said 'Yes, that's interesting.'

They ate a good dinner and the stories continued. Later, Marieke excused herself. She rose from her chair and said, 'I have to go but I'll be back in the morning with my car.'

'That really isn't necessary,' said Richard quickly. 'We're going by train most of the way and hiring a car when we get to Nijmegen.'

'Wouldn't think of it,' she replied, with a grin. 'Anyway, the old thing needs a good run. Please use it. I'd be most upset if you didn't.'

'Thanks a lot,' said Richard.

He poured out a night-cap and they sat together with a Mozart CD playing quietly in the background. He was tired and needed to sleep.

'What are your plans for tomorrow?' asked Lottie.

Richard sat back in the deep comfort of the sofa with Jane at his side. 'We've decided to visit Westerbork on the way to Bildt's house,' he replied and turned to Jane and she nodded an unspoken acceptance. 'We'll drive there and then on to Millingen, see Bildt, and then stay the night in a hotel. When we've spoken to him, we'll return the car and then fly home.'

'And is that it?' said Lottie and her eyes seemed half-closed. 'Will all this come to an end when you've met Rolf Müller?'

Richard sipped the coffee and thought for a moment. 'I want to hear from his mouth whether what I've learnt about him is true. If he denies it, then I'll continue until he tells the truth. When he does admit to the truth, then I'll inform Simon Wiesenthal and let him tell the appropriate authorities. Justice can then take over.'

'What do you want to happen to him?' He could feel Lottie's eyes staring hard at his face.

The answer to that particular question had been going through Richard's mind for some time. In fact, it was a question that was beginning to cause him some sleeplessness. He sighed. 'There's some debate about whether people responsible for war crimes should now be brought to justice,' he said quietly. 'In England, the trial of Szymon Serafinowicz, allegedly a Nazi Bylorussian, was dropped because, at 86, he was too old and suspected of having the early stages of Alzheimer's Disease. There are other cases pending and, because of the passage of time, it's unlikely that any of the men and women in Britain will ever come to trial.'

'What proof do you have that Rolf Müller really committed these crimes,' said Lottie. 'All you have, Richard, is an old man who says he witnessed everything to do with Müller. Put him in front of Müller in a war crimes court and I doubt whether they would even recognise each other.' Lottie's voice was quiet and she spoke her English slowly and carefully.

'You may have a point.'

'Of course, Richard,' she said, very quietly, 'you could put your mother in court.'

'Hang on a minute,' interrupted Jane. Her cool, legal brain sifted through their words. 'Sabina's evidence, if she ever went into court, and I doubt whether Richard would ask her to do that, would only be hearsay evidence. In the light of her relationship with Müller, no court would accept her word. .... No, the only real proof will lay in documentation, only then, and when it's finally proved that Jan Bildt is Rolf Müller, will there be a strong enough case to prosecute and stand a chance of winning.'

Lottie's eyes rested on Richard's face. 'Did Simon leave any documentary evidence?'

Richard moved restlessly on the sofa and avoided her eyes. 'Yes, a file of some sort and two envelopes. I think they're something to do with deeds on the house and that kind of thing.'

'That's unlike Simon,' she replied, with a knowing look. 'I remember him as being rather fussy.' As she spoke, several of the candles spluttered out. It was a moment when the evening seemed to be drawing to a close.

'I think, Lottie,' said Jane, stretching, 'that I'm as tired as the candles. Do you mind if we go to bed? We've a long day tomorrow.'

Pushing herself out of her chair, Lottie rose to her feet. 'Of course not,' she said, with a smile. 'Sleep well. I'll call you in the morning when breakfast is ready.'

Richard linked his arms in hers and kissed her on the cheek. 'That's very nice of you and thank you for listening.'

'Oh hell, I can't get to sleep,' said Richard, turning over in the unfamiliar bed.

'It's because we're not sleeping together,' whispered Jane from across the room. Her bedside light clicked on.

'I know a wonderful way of going to sleep,' said Richard, with a grin and tousled hair.

'Oh no, not in a strange house,' answered Jane, pulling up the sheets.

'You're wrong,' he laughed. 'It's not that, that I want. It's to listen to your sexy voice reading some more of Simon's notes.'

'A good idea,' she said, pushing down the sheets. 'I was just thinking the same thing.' Leaning out of bed, she pulled Richard's bag towards her and took out the manila folder. 'I didn't know there were envelopes in the safe with the folder.'

Arranging his pillows, Richard replied, 'I never thought about them. I was only interested in the file. But there could be some real proof of Müller's guilt in the envelopes.' He sighed. 'Before you say anything, no, I didn't bring them with me. They're back in the safe at my mother's house.'

When the meeting was finished, I had an opportunity to meet Seyss-Inquart. His English was passable.

"Herr majoor, why are you here?" A high pitched voice.

"I'm here as a lawyer and as a serving officer." When I said the word 'lawyer' his eyebrows raised and he licked his lips.

"Why is a lawyer here?" he said. Now his cold eyes settled onto mine.

"I'm an expert on war crimes and I've been ordered to take notes about your activities." It worked.

Seyss-Inquart gave a ghost of a smile and his head bowed. His reaction was downright creepy. "Of course, Herr majoor, I wish to help in such ac ..... activities. How can I be of assistance?"

Standing in front of me was the number one monster in Holland. For over five years, he'd had thousands killed and tens of thousands deported to concentration camps, including my family. I knew I would never have another chance like this one, so I took it. I decided on flattery and bluff and I spoke to him in German.

"Reichskomissar, I need information from one of your SS officers now imprisoned in Leeuwarden. He won't talk to me, unless he has authority from a higher rank. Nobody in Holland has a higher rank than you, Reichskomissar."

Seyss-Inquart glowed with helpfulness and his round head nodded up and down as he made noises in the back of his throat. 'Of course, majoor, of course. In these difficult times, it is important that we all co-operate with each other. Maybe, one day you can help me?" With a churning stomach, I nodded

Turned his head, he called to one of assistants and snapped his fingers. "Headed notepaper and a pen. .... Schnell, schnell." Leaning over the table, he looked up, pen in hand. "What is the name of this officer?"

"SS-Hauptsturmführer Edvard Müller." I watched him scribble something.

With a flourish, he signed it. "Is this satisfactory? It says, "To 'SS-

Hauptsturmführer *Edvard Müller and members of the* Schutzstaffel. *You are ordered to give whatever assistance is required to* Herr majoor ...." *He paused.* "What was your name,.... Bitte?"

"Majoor .... Cohen." *His jaw dropped and the slimy smile disappeared but I had him.*

"Did you say, 'Cohen'?" *He pronounced the word as though it was a disease.*

"Yes," *I said loudly.* "Cohen, C-O-H-E-N." *The note was finished and, with a glare of contempt, he pushed it across the table towards me.*

I was amassing evidence quite well and I placed Seyss-Inquart's letter away in my file side-by-side with the page from Westerbork. My job with documents and reports was done and I had one more night in Achterveld and then I left for Leeuwarden. On the way, we stopped for fuel in a German base that the Canadians had taken over. We not only filled up the tank but we received information that neither of us could have dreamt of.

The Canadian supplies sergeant was waving his arms at my driver and I thought there was trouble. I strolled across, until I was in earshot. Then I heard the driver say, incredulously, "Are you sure he's dead?"

"Yep, the son of a bitch is stone dead." *I witnessed the sight of two grown men hugging and taking turns to lift each other off the ground.*

"Excuse me," *I said.*

"Major, sir, yes sir," *snapped the Canadian sergeant, saluting.* "That bastard Adolf Hitler is dead. Fuckin' stone dead!" *He must have seen my mouth drop.*

"Is this true?" *I asked, unsure as to whether to believe him or not.*

"Absolutely, sir. The* Führer *(He pronounced it* "Foorer") *took poison and shot himself. The Russkis found his burnt body outside a bunker. And what's more,"* he was jumping with excitement. "The other madman, fuckin' Goebbels also took poison and he's dead as well. Ain't that fantastic? ...... Sir?"

I had to believe what he said and we all shook hands and cheered. With Hitler dead, the final defeat of Germany was at hand.

I went straight on to the Hotel de Kroon . *Dirk Haan made me welcome. They'd already heard about Hitler's death and the celebrations were just beginning. I wanted to be the man who told Müller and I drove straight from the hotel to the prison.*

The guard recognised me. "Congratulations, on the promotion, majoor. I presume you've come to see Müller?"

"Does he know about Hitler's death?'"

He shook his head and grinned. "No, we just let the bastard rot. He's all yours." *He handed me the keys.*

I unlocked the door and walked in. He jumped up from his bed, saw who

I was and dropped back. I just opened my mouth and said it. "Hitler is dead. He committed suicide on April, 30."

"You're lying," he snarled.

I was in complete control and enjoying every delicious second. I rammed home the information. "He took poison and then he shot himself. It is said that his driver burnt the body in the garden outside a bunker. Goebbels also took poison." I leant against the door and looked suitably casual.

He rose slowly to his feet and then threw up his arm stiffly. "HEIL Hitler!" he shouted and a shiver ran through me. His fanaticism was not dead.

I waited for a minute. "Müller, you've had it. There's no more Reich, no more Führer. I now have more control over you than a rat in the sewers."

"So?" he said softly, staring across the cell.

"Last time I was here you said to me, that there was a possibility that my family was still alive."

"Aha, Jew, aha." His eyes lit up. "Now I see what you want." He began to laugh and it echoed around the cell. "A Jew wants something from me." Abruptly, he stopped laughing. "Why should I help you?" he said. "I'm a dead man anyway."

Reaching into my file, I produced Seyss-Inquart's letter and held it out towards him. The embossed heading stood out, even in the pale light. Taking it from my hand, he stared at the words. Once he held up to the light-bulb as though looking at a forged banknote.

"How did you get this?" The tone in his voice had changed.

"Personally from the Reichskommissar ."

He thought for a moment and re-read the letter. Looking up, he handed it back to me. His voice was pitched low. "I must obey orders. What can I do for you, Jew?"

FORTY-FOUR

After walking round the almost deserted streets for an hour, Rolf found a small hallway in an apartment block not too far from his barracks. It was dry, clean and uninhabited. When Rolf jammed the door closed it felt safe, even though they were in the dark. They sat together on a broken flight of wooden stairs.

'What do we do now?' said Ulrika, staring about herself.

'Don't worry. This afternoon we're going to a concert.'

'What?' she exclaimed, jumping indignantly to her feet. 'What the hell are you talking about? …. Here we are with nowhere to live. …. Berlin in ruins. …. The Russians only days away. No food, nothing to drink. I feel absolutely exhausted and you, ….. you …. Talk about going to a bloody concert.' She stood up and kicked a broken chair across the dusty floor. 'Rolf Müller, you amaze me.' She flopped back onto the stairs, trying to hold back the tears.

Rolf held her close, gently smoothing her hair with his hand. 'I'm attached to the *Führerbunker* and I can get hold of food and somewhere for us to live. But today, we will attend the concert.'

Ulrika shook her head. 'The concert,' she said slowly, 'how can I go to a concert in these,' she pulled at the shabby coat, 'these ….. rags?'

Rolf was pleased. If Ulrika could worry about how she looked, then she was tougher than he thought. 'Now listen, carefully,' he said. 'I want you to wait here. Don't go outside under any circumstances. I'll return within the hour with clothes and food. Tonight you'll once again sleep in a bed.'

He was as good as his word. Baroness Von Varo, in constant attendance in the Bunker, gave invaluable assistance. Fortunately, she was the same size as Ulrika and, when Rolf asked her for help, she left and later returned with a suitcase of clothes from her wardrobe.

'Thank you, Baroness,' said Rolf, clicking his heels.

'Think nothing of it, Müller,' she said, drawing deeply on a slim cheroot. 'I'd rather your girlfriend has my clothes than the Russian animals.' She opened her bag and gave Rolf a brass key. 'This is for a small apartment that I no longer have any use for. Use it for as long as you wish.' She allowed him to kiss her hand. 'In these days we all have to help each other.'

Ulrika was amazed. 'Rolf Müller, how do you do it? We've lost everything and you walk out of here, find me some beautiful clothes and somewhere to live and we're going to a concert. ….. I do love you.'

They embraced and again Rolf took control. 'Hurry up and get changed,' he said, brusquely. 'We have to leave in twenty minutes.'

At 5pm on April 12, 1945 the Berlin Philharmonic Orchestra performed its final concert. The Berlin Philharmonic Hall was relatively unscathed by the bombing. The beautiful ornate red and gold auditorium was packed full. The electricity in the hall was switched on and the stage was as bright as day. There was an air of excitement in the audience, as though something extraordinarily final was happening.

Rolf and Ulrika took their seats near the front and they waited in silence. The orchestra paused for their leader to walk on to the stage. When he did so, there was thunderous applause and he faltered for a moment, overcome by overwhelming emotion Then protocol took over and he took up his allotted seat in the violin section. The conductor, Robert Heger, strode across the stage, arrived at his podium, stared through the bright lights at the audience and then turned to the orchestra. With baton raised, he held the silence like a hammer above his head and then the baton dropped. The pounding notes of Wagner's finale from the *Die Götterdämmerung* hit the still air, sending hearts racing and emotions churning.

The strident notes froze Rolf to his seat. The music depicted the destruction of Valhalla, the death of the Gods and the final end of the world. It was an apt choice, because, as the music gripped Rolf in its crescendos and its depths, it finally made him decide to leave Berlin. There was not a single moment when the decision was made. It was logically founded on a culmination of events. At the end of the piece, there was no applause, just a prolonged silence. Then the strings of Beethoven's Violin Concerto, played by Gerhard Taschner, the brilliant twenty-three year old violinist.

The violin brought one memory into Rolf's brain. The last time he had heard the Violin Concerto was in Auschwitz. Played by a lone violinist from the Berlin Symphony Orchestra as the Jews walked to the gas chambers. At the time, he was not conscious of its impact but now it touched him so hard that he cried. Great blobbing tears rolled down his cheeks and his body shook. Then he knew why, it was not the death of the Jewish violinist that made him cry, it was the music.

Bruckner's Romantic Symphony changed the atmosphere. Rolf glanced sideways at Ulrika. Her eyes were tightly closed and she was pale in the stage lights. But still their hands were interlocked. As the last note died away, the audience rose to their feet. They applauded for ten full minutes and cheered until they were hoarse. Rolf wanted to leave but he stood motionless, locked to the floor. Then the orchestra left the stage and people turned to stare at each other. They did not know that almost every musician would leave Berlin immediately in a special coach that would take them to the Allies.

He looked at Ulrika. 'I have to leave Berlin,' he said softly. 'The Russians'll kill me if I stay.' Her face flushed and she tried to say something but he placed his hand gently over her mouth. 'I'll hide you until the Allies arrive and then I'll return.' He said the words with people flowing past him. Eventually they stood alone and the hugeness of the concert hall pressed down upon them.

Later, they walked through the city together, ignoring the wreckage around them and the constant Russian bombardment. After missing the street several times, they eventually found it. The apartment was down some steps off a narrow pavement. A small locked and barred door opened easily with the Baroness's key. It was not really an apartment, more of a windowless bed-sitter in a cellar. It had a tiny toilet and a large stone sink in the corner. There was a musty smell hanging over the simple furniture and the brick floor.

Ulrika stared about her. 'My God, this is a awful place,' she said, quietly.

'How the mighty are fallen,' breathed Rolf.

'What did you say?' she asked, craning forward to hear.

'Nothing.'

Rolf looked into her face. 'Ulrika, I have to leave you for a couple of hours. There are things that I must attend to.'

Springing away from his side, anger flashed across her face. 'What you're really trying to tell me is that you're going to escape with your rich SS friends. Leaving me here in this hole to be raped by any Russian who happens to be coming along.'

'You don't understand .... .' He tried to explain but she quickly cut him off. 'Oh, my God but I do. It's so obvious. I've got nowhere to go but you have.' She stood, hand on hips, with a fire in her eyes. 'Then I suppose you'll want to come back and screw me again, won't you? .... I'm still, ... still ..... your little *Lebensborn* whore, aren't I?' Turning her back on him, she walked across the hard floor and slumped onto the old bed.

Rolf had seen this coming. 'Now listen to me ....' She rolled away from him. 'I'm going back to my quarters and then I'll get food for you. This whole damned thing will be over within two weeks. Before then, I'll leave Berlin and then within a month, come back for you You'll have money and a store of food. Anything you need, I'll leave for you. Don't worry, just hide before they get here. Already hundreds of people are escaping to the west. The *U-Bahn* tunnels are still open and you'll be quite safe.'

She spoke quietly, with her back to him. 'If it's that safe, then why don't you stay with me and we'll escape together?'

'Ulrika,' he said, raising his voice. 'I'm *SS* and I used to work in the camps and I have an *SS* number tattooed under my arm. The Russians'll identify me and certainly shoot me. I've got to get to the Americans before the Russians get to me. I'll come back and stay with you, but until then, ….. I must leave you.'

She turned to face him and said, in a voice loaded with scorn, 'I'm an attractive woman and don't think that the Americans will be nice after the Russians have finished with me.'

Rolf banged the door with his fist. 'It's quite obvious you don't understand the strategic situation in Berlin. I do.' He opened the door. 'I'll see you in a couple of hours.' Unfastening his holster, he took out his gun and threw it to the floor. 'Use it if you have to and don't leave this room.'

'You bastard,' she whispered. He didn't hear her and the door closed behind him.

Rolf was taking a chance. The money from Klein and the bag of diamonds were still safe in his room. Removing them from the wardrobe, he pushed some of the packets deep down into an overnight bag and fastened the heavy, buckles. Glancing round the spartan room that had never really been his home, he smiled grimly to himself and left the barrack forever.

It was a bright sunny day with spring sunshine and it took him an hour to reach the Chancellery. As he ran along the deserted streets, the high-pitched screaming sound of multi-rocket launchers made him cover his ears and crouch near any available cover. By the sound of the shelling, he knew the Russians must be in the near suburbs. At the Chancellery, the guards were still at their posts and they saluted him. They checked his pass before he made his way through the eerily quiet building to the corridor entrance to the *Führerbunker*. The sounds of the bombardment faded as he ran down the winding, slippery steps into the gloom.

Leaving his bag hidden behind a cupboard, he strode along the narrow corridors towards Juettner's office.

Rolf reported to *Obergruppenführer* Juettner. He looked up from some papers. 'Ah, Müller,' said Juettner, 'I have a special mission for you and I'm asking you to do this, because you're a man that can be trusted.' He waved towards a chair. 'Sit down and I'll give you the precise details of your mission.' Rolf had no idea what was happening. Around him was chaos and the cloying atmosphere of the bunker. Outside was the wreckage of Berlin and Ulrika waiting in a dank cellar; if she was still alive. Juettner, folded his arms, leant on the big desk and cleared his throat. 'Several hours ago, here in the bunker, the *Führer* and his friend Eva Braun were married.' He's made out his political testament for the future of the *Reich*.' Rolf opened his mouth to speak. Juettner raised a finger and carried on. 'However, from this moment you take orders directly from me. Is that understood *Sturmbannführer* Müller?' The two men stared at each other.

Rolf's head whirled and he replied softly, 'Yes *Herr Obergruppenführer*.'

'One of three copies of the *Führer's* Testament is to be taken to *Generalfeldmarschall* Keitel in Schleswig-Holstein.' Juettner nodded and touched his chin. '*Oberst* Von Below of the *Luftwaffe* has been entrusted with delivering this document to the *Generalfeldmarschall*. You're to accompany Von Below and give protection. Do you understand your orders?'

'Yes, *Herr Obergruppenführer*.'

Juettner stood up and glanced at the clock on the wall. 'You'll be leaving at midnight tonight. That's in two and a half hours. Report directly to the *Oberst* at the garden entrance to the *Führerbunker*. Do you have any questions?'

Rolf had at last found his way out of Berlin and he wanted to know how he was going to achieve it. 'Yes, sir, how will we escape from the city?'

'There's a way through that has already been tried and tested. Take one small bag and a weapon.' Already Juettner's mind was elsewhere.

Rolf felt as though an enormous load had been lifted from his shoulders. After throwing up a salute, he turned and dashed back down the corridor. Collecting his bag, he ran up the staircase and back into the Chancellery. Within half an hour, he was hammering on the door to Ulrika's hiding place. For a moment, he thought she had gone and then he heard her voice.

'Who is it?'

'Rolf,' he shouted and kicked the door.

'Go away.'

'If you don't open the door, I'll kick it down.' He heard the bolt being drawn.

Ulrika faced him, dressed in a grubby long coat. Her face was dead white and her lips formed a firm, thin line. She held his gun with two hands and pointed it straight at his head.

His eyes saw the safety catch in the "off" position. 'Don't be a damned fool,' he said, sternly. 'That thing could go off at any minute.'

'I don't care.'

He took a step forward and placed his hand on the door. She stiffened and the gun's muzzle dropped to his chest. 'Just push the safety catch back on and give to me,' he said, softly. She shook her head and he saw tears running down her cheeks.

Rolf smiled his most charming smile. Quickly, at lightening speed, he pushed the gun sideways, grabbed it, and kicked the door wide open. Ulrika screamed, fell backwards, and Rolf neatly caught her.

'You swine,' she spluttered, trying to push him away.

Holding her firmly against him, he let the gun fall to the floor. Pushing the door closed with his heel, he lifted her off her feet and walked across the room. A single candle flickered in the corner and the room felt damp and cold. Rolf found the bed and lowered Ulrika gently onto the rough blankets. Stepping back, he watched her. She stared back at him, chest heaving. In the distance, there was a rumble of heavy artillery and occasionally the walls trembled. Tiny flakes of ceiling plaster fell down at each explosion. The brick floor was hard to his feet and a scrap of tattered carpet covered a worn spot at the side of the bed.

'Why?' she said drawing, her legs up under her.

'Why, ... what?' he replied.

'Why did you bother coming back here? Or did your glorious *Führer* tell you to?'

His voice was tired and he spoke slowly, clearly enunciating each word. 'I came back because I care for you. By tomorrow, Hitler will be dead and so will Germany.'

'Hitler dead?'

'Yes, dead.'

She laughed, almost hysterically. 'So you are going to leave me.'

He walked slowly over to the side of the bed and looked down at her. 'Yes, Ulrika. But I'll make sure that you survive.'

'What are you going to do?' she grated. 'Wrap me up in a parcel and send me to the first American general that walks into Berlin?'

Lowering himself onto the bed at her side, he said softly, 'What else can I do? I have to leave.' His hand moved towards hers and she involuntarily jerked but her hand remained. 'As I said, I'm going to leave you some money and something else.' He smiled grimly and his hand crept into hers. 'I want to give you something that's very special. You must only use it when all hope has gone.' Their hands closed. She looked up at him, her mouth half-open. Rolf reached into his tunic pocket and took out a small metal box. He pushed it under the dirty pillow. 'Inside there's a pill. If the worst happens, put it into your mouth and bite it.' His grip on her hand tightened and she winced. 'It's cyanide. .... Death occurs instantly. You'll feel nothing.' She closed her eyes. Another distant explosion and a flake of plaster fell. He watched it flutter through the air towards her and it fell softly onto her cheek. With his finger tip, he gently pushed it away. As he touched her velvety skin, she opened her eyes and, with her hand, reached over and pulled him down to her. Her need surprised him.

'Oh, my darling Rolf,' she breathed into his ear. 'My darling Rolf. Make love to me, it may be the last time.' Quickly they undressed each other. The candle spluttered out and there was blackness. Their place of intercourse did not matter, neither did their next hour of life. It was sex born of desperation. Quick, hard and finally satisfying. When it was over, Rolf lay at her side and breathed deeply, trying to control his heaving chest. Ulrika, perspiring heavily, touched his lips with her hand. Neither of them spoke. There was total silence.

Ulrika heard it first; a tiny scraping sound. She stiffened, making Rolf jerk awake. From behind the bed, the sound came again,. It was a patter of something moving. She rolled over and clung to him. And again that whisper of movement. Rolf bounded off the mattress and reached in front of him. Nothing he could see or touch. Remembering where the candles were, he groped his way to the table, stumbling and falling over their discarded clothes. Finding the matches first, he struck one and held it aloft. Darkness broken by a glimmering circle of light that moved as he moved. On the table, his hand found the stub of a candle and, with a muttered curse as the match burnt to his fingers, he lit it.

'What is it, Rolf?' she said to him, 'What's that noise?'

Slowly he walked across the room, waving the candle from side to side. Standing close to the bed, his ears strained to catch the sound; nothing. He turned his head and looked down. Ulrika lay in the foetal position and, in a voyeur's glimpse, he saw the tautness of pale buttocks and the curly wetness of her pubic hairs.

'Oh, my God,' she gasped. 'It's there again. Behind the bed.' Springing off the mattress, she ran to the far side of the room.

Rolf yanked the bed away from the wall. He listened; nothing. Then he saw the outlines of a metal grid let into the wall, knee-high and rusty with age. Dropping to his knees, he stared through the grill, holding the flame of the candle as near as he could.

'Rats,' he called over his shoulder. 'Just rats. I can see the reflection of their eyes.'

FORTY-FIVE

'Here's Marieke in the car,' said Jane. She rose from her seat. 'I'll let her in.'

Lottie reached across the table and took Richard's hand. Her brown eyes looked hard at his face. 'Richard, please be careful when you see him and be careful what you say. There are powerful forces at work here. As a Jew, I know what has happened to people in the past who have tried to prove the truth. Look after yourself, you're the only family I have.' She squeezed his hand and then let go, sitting back into her chair.

Marieke breezed into the living-room. 'It's a lovely day for travelling,' she announced, 'and the weather forecast is excellent.' She beamed at Richard. 'I saw your bags in the hall. I've put them in the car.'

'Thanks,' he muttered, swallowing the last mouthful of coffee.

Jane saw tears in Lottie's eyes and she walked round the table and put her arm around her waist. 'Lottie, thanks for everything. I've enjoyed meeting you and you're every bit as good as Richard said you were. We'll meet again.'

'I know,' smiled Lottie, kissing Jane gently on the cheek. 'God go with you.'

Richard enjoyed the old Volvo. They left Oudermirdum on a bright autumn day and drove steadily and carefully across the flat Frisian countryside. For the first ten minutes, they said little to each other.

'Richard,' said Jane, after ten minutes, 'how long will it take?'

'It's about an hour and a half to Westerbork. We could probably stay for an hour or so.'

'Fine,' she replied,' but now I'm going to read some more of Simon's notes. It won't put you off driving, will it?'

'No,' laughed Richard, 'not at all.'

'Eventually, in May, I had time to travel and I made my preparations. I was allocated a flight to Berlin from the airfield at Leeuwarden. I went with the driver to the prison to collect Müller. I had orders to keep him manacled and, after my visit to Westerbork, I was happy to follow such orders.

The Dakota was late and we had to wait in the jeep. Eventually, there was a drone in the sky and the aircraft appeared low on the horizon. The

Dakota landed and taxied towards us. With engines ticking over, the rear door in the fuselage opened. A pair of short ladders were hooked into place and an airman waved us in. Battered by the noise and the slipstream, we ran across the grass with our baggage and threw them through the door. The driver went back to the jeep, unfastened Müller, and dragged him out to the steps.

Müller was handcuffed to a fuselage frame. I strapped myself in and the engines roared to full throttle. The vibration and the shaking scared the hell out of me and I clung to the seat like grim death. Eventually the Dakota lifted off and levelled. For a few minutes, I sat and looked around me. We were the only passengers. There were stacks of boxes, all lashed down and secure. A miserable looking Müller sat at the end of the fuselage and some distance away from us. The drone of the engine lulled me into half sleep but my brain would not let go.

After about three hours, one of the crew came to find me. He motioned me to the flight deck and I followed him. The crew turned round to smile and the co-pilot passed me a headset. His words came across quite clearly.

"Hello, Major," he shouted above the roar of the engines. "How are you?" I nodded and gave a thumbs up. I felt very experienced. "Turn the switch on the face mask." I did and heard the pilot crystal-clear. "We're approaching Berlin. I thought you might like to see it." He pointed down through the narrow window as he turned the control column to the left.

In Antwerp, I'd seen the damage caused by the V1's and the V2's. This was something beyond my comprehension. Below me lay the neat gardens, straight roads, and the woods of suburban Berlin. The centre was very difficult to describe. The aircraft's steeply banking turn brought me directly over the top of the rubble. I could have leant out and touched it. And it was rubble; just piles of bricks, stones and timber. No building was over first floor height. Utter desolation, utter destruction, utter waste. There were people, I could see them walking along narrow roads. Then the Dakota flipped back onto the straight and level.

"Sorry, Major," said the pilot, nodding at me, "landing time. Go back and strap in, please."

As I sat down, the sight of that shattered, once great city made me turn to look at Müller. He saw my glance and our eyes met. I don't know what was going through his mind. But something made him nod and then he cast his eyes downwards. For the first time, his shoulders were stooped.

With a bump and a thud the Dakota touched down and the tailwheel dropped onto the runway. The shaking and vibrating rattled my teeth. The aircraft came to a standstill and the engines quickly jerked to a stop.

The crewman walked past me and unlocked the door. I stared outside.

There was a smell in the air that I came to know so well. A mixture of burnt timber, dust, people, and something else that only existed in Berlin. Later, I analysed it as the stink of war.

A British Bedford truck waited at the bottom of the steps, rear flap down and open, ready to receive its prisoner. Four Military Policemen in red caps saluted, two on each side of the steps.

As I stepped into a bright sunny day, their sergeant saluted me and said gruffly, "Good afternoon, sir. I'm Sergeant-major Horrocks, British Military Police. Welcome to Berlin. We're the escort for the prisoner."

"Thank you. Sergeant-major. We can manage."

There was a gleam in his eye. "Sorry, sir. I have my orders." He shrugged his shoulders. "I'm sure it'll be all right if you, sir, shall we say, ... eh, assist us."

Military protocol satisfied, I turned and nodded to my driver. Darting back into the Dakota, he reappeared with Müller and waved to the MP. Müller stood in the doorway and, for a minute, paused. With the leg chains at full stretch, he stood, head up, and looked around him. Then, with slow deliberate steps, he walked down the rungs of the short ladder. A slow smile spread over his face.

"Ah, I see it takes five people to guard me." He glanced in my direction. " So, majoor, I am still an important man."

I was prepared to ignore his continual goading but the sergeant-major was not. With crashing hob-nailed boots, he stepped smartly forward to Müller's side, placed his mouth a centimetre from his ear and shouted in that inimitable way of British sergeant-majors.

'SHUT YOUR FUCKIN' MOUTH, YOU FUCKIN' NAZI SCUM!" He took one pace backwards. "NOW MOVE TO THAT FUCKIN' LORRY! FUCKIN' DOUBLE-TIME! LEFTRIGHT, LEFTRIGHT, LEFTRIGHT!"

He made me jump but the effect on Müller was instantaneous. His eyes popped and he scrambled across the short distance from the steps and was bundled into the lorry. The sergeant-major turned to me and winked. "That sorted that bastard out, sir. I 'ate the fuckin' SS."

I wasn't sure where we going to. I sat in the front of the lorry next to the sergeant-major who was driving. Knowing how rank conscious the British are, I broke the ice by engaging in small talk. "Been here long, Sergeant-major?'

"Only a few days, sir."

"What's it like?"

"Not bad, sir. The krauts are a bit awkward. But then they'll do anything

for fags and food.' He nodded, steered down a narrow road and said, "Who's the fella in the back? Some sort of SS?"

"Yes, a Hauptsturmführer Müller. He was in charge of the SS in northern Holland."

Sucking at his lips, he jammed the gearbox into high gear. "As I said, sir. I hate the fuckin' SS. I hope we shoot the lot of 'em."

"Possibly, Sergeant-major, possibly. Where exactly are we going to?"

"Maikaefer Barracks, sir. It's an old SS place just north of the city." We had to drive through the centre and the destruction was complete.

The barracks were solid enough with a just few shell holes in the walls. It had been taken over by the British because this was their sector. I checked in my papers at the guardroom and then the lorry braked to a stop.

"Right, sir," said the sergeant-major, "here we are." He winked. "I've booked a hotel room for our guest in the back. It's where they used to torture people. When I first went into the place, it was like something out of the middle-ages." Switching off the engine, he opened the door and jumped out.

The rear flap of the Bedford lorry dropped and Müller was the first out. He found it difficult to move and the MP's didn't make it any easier. With their white truncheons, they prodded him towards the low prison building. It was an awful place. Half the lights didn't work and the tiny cells were filthy and stank of urine. I waited until Müller had been pushed through the door of the first cell.

"Sergeant-major, I'd like to spend a few minutes with the prisoner."

"Right, sir." He sucked his lips and crashed to attention. "Rather you than me. I'll look after your weapon and I'll be right outside the door."

"Thank you." I handed the Webley over to him.

Müller spoke first. He was certainly more subdued than in the prison in Leeuwarden. Leaning against the wall, he ran a hand over his stubbly chin. "You've got me here. Now what?"

"In one hour's time, I'm going to take you out." I looked hard into his face. "And then you're going to take me to where the records are." He shrugged his shoulders.'

Richard, turned off the main road. They drove down a long narrow road following small signs saying, *'herinneringscentrum kamp westerbork'*. Flat heathland with no houses and kilometres of dense woodland. Eventually, they arrived at a car park surrounded by trees. The rain had stopped and, stepping out of the car, Richard paused for a moment. Although the car park was half-full, there was a tremendous feeling of calm.

He looked across the bonnet to Jane.

'Can you feel it?' Richard said, softly.

Jane nodded. 'Yes, I can. It's so peaceful. I expected crowds and some sort of museum.'

Together, they walked towards a low, single storey building at the end of the car park. The signs informed them that this was the exhibition area of the Westerbork complex. Inside was cool and lit by soft lighting. There was a reception desk and a small shop. Richard walked up to the woman behind the desk.

'Good afternoon,' he said.

She looked up and smiled. 'Can I help you?' Richard carefully explained his family circumstances. 'You need to see the Curator. Please wait a moment and I'll find him for you.'

Visitors walked past them and into the main exhibition. Richard and Jane did not have to wait for long. A youngish man came out of a room near the entrance.

'Good afternoon,' he said. 'My name is Hans Colpa. The receptionist explained to me why you're here. Perhaps you'd like to come through to the library?' Richard and Jane rose from their chairs and followed him. The library was fairly small and very quiet. He waved them into two chairs. 'I gather that you're trying to find out about members of your father's family who were transported from Westerbork to Auschwitz?' Richard nodded. 'Do you have their names and dates of transportation?'

'Yes,' replied Richard. 'They were the Cohen family and they left Leeuwarden on September 4, for Westerbork and arrived in Auschwitz on September 13, 1944.'

'May I ask, Mr Cooper, why you need this information?' asked the curator, curiously.

Richard did not want to explain the real reason. 'It's for our family records. We're trying to trace some of the more distant members.'

Folding his arms on the table, he looked hard at Richard and Jane. 'Do you have any proof for this request. I mean, ... your name is not Cohen .... and we do have to be careful with records and confidentiality.'

Jane thought for a moment, rose to her feet. 'Please excuse me. I'll be back in a minute.' Richard knew what she was going for.

'I expected to see lots of buildings and,' Richard said, 'and, well you know ....?'

'Yes indeed, Mr Cooper,' replied the young Dutchman. 'Westerbork was completely demolished in 1971. In 1970, the official National Westerbork Memorial was unveiled by Queen Juliana. It's situated at the exact spot, during the war, where the railway line terminated. Later, in

1983, Queen Beatrix opened the new memorial centre.' As Jane returned, he looked up. 'This building is a permanent exhibition portraying the occupation of the Netherlands with special emphasis on the persecution of the Jews.' He watched Jane remove Simon's file from the flight bag.

'I think this will give you the proof you need,' she said. Thumbing through the file, she selected the relevant pages. Removing a rusty paper-clip, Jane pushed the pages across the table. The curator, fished some gold-rimmed spectacles from his pocket and hooked them round his ears. Quickly reading down the first page, he nodded and turned the page over. Then, after slowly removing his spectacles, he said, 'Fascinating, absolutely fascinating.' He tapped the pages with his forefinger. 'We have very few first-hand accounts from the period immediately proceeding the liberation. Mr Cooper, I presume you've changed your name?' Richard nodded. 'Your father had a page from one of our record ledgers?' Again Richard nodded. 'Do you still have the page. I mean with you?'

Richard shrugged. 'No. ..... I'm sorry.'

'A pity, because I see here,' the curator pointed to a note in the margin, 'it says, "kept and stored." I presume, it means that your father kept it somewhere more safe.'

Then Richard understood, at almost exactly the same time that Jane exclaimed, 'One of the envelopes. Of course. Why didn't we think of that before we left England?'

The man's face brightened. 'So you think you may it somewhere?'

'I'm pretty sure we have it at home,' smiled Richard. 'Why do you ask?'

'Here in the Memorial Centre, we have most of the records kept on micro-fiche and computer. The original records are kept at the Netherlands Institute for War Documentation in Amsterdam.' He frowned. 'Mr Cooper and Mrs Cooper, I presume that you're looking for some original record of their transportation.?'

'Yes, please,' replied Richard. 'Is that possible?'

The curator nodded and turned to his computer monitor. 'It says in the notes, September 4, 1944. ...... Let's have a look.' Images of lists passed across the screen. 'Ah yes, just as I thought.' He swung the screen towards Richard. 'Here take a look.' He pointed with the end of a pen. 'Arrival September 4, that's clear enough. I'll just count the Cohen names. ....'

'42,' said Richard, quietly.

'A moment, please. ..... Yes, 42. Just as your father said. But, and just as I expected, the page with your family names on, for the departures of September 11, is missing.' Turning away from the screen, he said, very quietly, 'You must have that missing page back in England.'

'I'm absolutely sure I have,' nodded Richard.

'Mr Cooper,' said the Curator, re-paper clipping the pages, 'If at all possible, the Memorial Centre would very much like a copy of that page.'

'No problem,' replied Richard, slipping the sheets back into their correct place with the other pages. 'As soon as I return home, I'll send the original to you. Could you please give me copies of the relevant pages for the arrival of my family at Westerbork?'

'I'll see to that straight away.' He picked up his phone and said something in Dutch, glancing at the screen to check the details. He returned the phone back onto its cradle. 'Perhaps you'd like to go to the main outdoor memorial in the woods? It's not too far from here and you can take your car.'

Richard glanced at his watch. 'We're rather short of time and …. ' The curator held up his hand.

'Don't worry,' he said, with a helping smile. 'If you're in a hurry, I'll come with you. We can be there and back in twenty minutes.'

'OK, that's fine,' agreed Richard. Taking a deep breath, he reached into his overcoat pocket. 'I'd like your advice on another little matter.' He unfolded the Knight's Cross certificate. The embossed gold glinted in the neon light. 'Is this genuine?' He pushed it across the table.

The curator's eyebrows arched in surprise. 'Now that's interesting,' he said, softly. From his desk, he picked up a magnifying glass and carefully scrutinised the signature. Biting his bottom lip, he looked up. 'It's definitely Hitler's signature and it's a genuine document. The printing, the paper, the embossing, is all absolutely right. I see it's your father's name.' He left the statement hanging.

'Yes,' said Richard. 'But how the hell could he be in Berlin the day before Hitler died. And how did he get a medal from him?'

'I have no idea.' The man shrugged his shoulders. 'Maybe your research will prove something.' There was a different light in his eyes and Richard wanted to know why.

'Does this mean that *majoor* Simon Cohen could have been a traitor?' Richard said so softly.

'Mr Cooper,' replied the curator, smoothly. 'Many strange things happened in the war. Who knows what this means? Anyway, if you look carefully, it's written as "*Major*" the same as in English. Not, "*majoor*", as in Dutch.'

Richard drove down a narrow road through woods alive with spring. Jane sat at his side. There were few people about. He did not know what to expect. They stopped in a small car park and the curator opened the car doors. They followed him through the trees to a long and narrow clearing. For a few moments, they paused. There was a railway line beginning from a set of wooden buffers and extending a hundred metres along a gravel-bedded track. At the other end, the lines were twisted up into the air like a piece of modern art. Then he understood the symbolism.

Walking alone, Richard went towards the massive wooden buffers. Around him, not a bird sang or a tree moved; he was totally alone. Gently touching the rough timbers and the solid, cast steel of the buffers, Richard bent down and placed his fingers on the cold, steel rail. Looking up, he saw Jane watching him from the far end of the track.

'This is the start of my journey,' he said softly, with tears in his eyes.

FORTY-SIX

'My God,' shouted Ulrika. 'I hate rats.'

Rolf gave the rusty grill a sharp kick.

'What the hell are you doing?' cried Ulrika, slipping on her dress.

'If the rats can get here, then we can get out,' he snapped back to her, pulling the grill out of the wall in a shower of old plaster dust. Dropping to his knees, Rolf stuck his head into the gaping space.

'This must lead somewhere and it could be a bolthole to get out of here.'

'I don't like boltholes used by rats,' she said, peering over his shoulder.

Suddenly Rolf disappeared, plunging the room into darkness. On his knees, he crawled along the narrow shaft, pushing rubble to one side with one hand and holding the candle aloft with the other. He pushed forward keeping an eye out for the rats. The tunnel kept to the same height for some time and then, eventually, it turned sharply right. He was in a chamber, as big as the room he had come from. Carefully, he dropped a metre to the brick floor.

The chamber had tunnels leading off in all directions. He stopped for a moment and examined each one in turn. It was the smells and the sounds that made him decide. The stench of raw sewage and the squeaking of hundreds of rats. Walking across the rubble-filled floor, he stooped and began to quickly walk down the sloping passage. Soon, he had to walk more carefully as the sewage began to flow between his feet. Grunting with the smell, Rolf pressed on. Then he heard another sound; the sound of human voices. Turning quickly left, he saw lights in front of him.

The sewage tunnel led to a bigger chamber. Stone-lined and dripping with moisture, it echoed with voices. Staring downwards in amazement, he saw at least a hundred people. All in small groups gathered around smoky fires and oil lamps. Fortunately, he was dressed only in his dirty uniform trousers and could have been anybody. At first, as he walked towards them, nobody noticed his presence.

He stared around and saw a group of men coming towards him. 'Where am I?' he cried out.

'You, my friend,' said one of the men, in a well spoken voice. 'Are in the fourth chamber of the central Berlin sewer system.' He waited for Rolf's reaction. 'Anything else you'd like to know?'

'Not at this moment,' replied Rolf, relaxing. The man was older but still stood erect. His coat was badly torn although well cut.

He stared at Rolf more closely. 'I see you haven't got any food or anything useful. What do you do for a living?' Rolf was about to lie and the man raised his hand. 'No ranks, no promises. Just your civilian job.'

'I'm a doctor.' The very words surprised Rolf. It was the first time since he had left Auschwitz that he had ever told anybody he was a doctor.

The man nodded and grasped hold of Rolf's arm. 'A doctor, you say. Now that's fortunate. We've a man here with a broken leg. Can you help him?'

'Yes,' replied Rolf. 'Show me where he is and I'll see what I can do.' Together, they walked past groups of people who turned to stare.

A man lay in the shadow of a huge stone pipe that disappeared into the barrel-vaulted roof. He was a bundle of rags and, as Rolf approached him, he shouted out in pain. Bending over, Rolf could smell the *schnapps*. Kneeling at his side, he pulled the blanket away from his legs. Gently, he used his fingers to feel for the break. The man screamed with pain. 'I can't see,' Rolf shouted. 'Get me some light.' Several candles were thrust forward. The scream subsided into a low moan. Rolf stared at the leg.

'How is he, *Doktor*?' Rolf revelled in the sound of his title.

'It's bad. It needs resetting and splinting. He should have the proper dressings and be taken to hospital.'

'We can obtain the dressings but a hospital may be more difficult to find,' said the man, amid roars of laughter.

'All right, all right,' said Rolf, brusquely. 'You'll have to hold him down whilst I reset the bone. It's going to hurt him. Is there any alcohol? We'll just have to get him drunk.'

'He's pissed now,' shouted a woman. 'How the fuck do you think he's survived so long.'

Rolf nodded and smiled. The injured man's hand suddenly reached up and gripped Rolf's shoulder.

'Come closer,' he croaked. 'Closer.' Rolf leant over his face. The man crooked his finger and whispered. 'You don't recognise me, do you, *Hauptsturmführer*?' Rolf jerked back in surprise and stared hard at the face before him. The man pulled him down again. 'It's me,' he said, so faintly that Rolf could hardly hear him. '*Sturmann* Horsch. We last met on the streets of Berlin and talked about killing.'

A stab of fear went through Rolf's brain. 'I remember you Horsch. What the hell are you doing here?'

He let go of Rolf's shoulder. 'Like you, surviving. ..... Now, for God's sake, fix my fuckin' leg. I don't want to die.' Heavy eyelids clicked closed over dull bloodshot eyes

Rolf fixed his leg but not before Horsch had screamed his guts out until the agony made him unconscious.

There were no thanks and he made his way in total darkness back to Ulrika. She heard him coming and he saw the light of a candle.

'What's happening?' she said in a voice edged with terror. 'Where've you been?'

Groping his way through the hole in the wall, he rose to his feet, stretched and reached for his tunic. 'Ulrika, I've found your place of safety.' Then he explained.

'In the sewers?' she said, shaking her head. 'I can't live in the sewers.'

'You can,' said Rolf opening his bag. 'It's either the sewers or the Russians.' Withdrawing a bundle of banknotes from his bag he stared hard into her face. 'Make your choice.'

Ulrika shrugged and sat on the end of the bed. 'I have no choice.' She shook her head. 'What do I do?'

Rolf thrust the notes into her hand. 'Take these and keep them somewhere safe. Use them only when you need them. …. Where's the box I gave you?' She reached into her coat pocket and held it in her palm. Rolf turned to his bag and fumbled out of her sight. 'Give me the box.' She passed it to him. Flipping open the lid, he said, 'I'm putting in here a single diamond ….'

'What?' she said loudly, leaning forward.

He held it between forefinger and thumb. The blue, cut diamond cast sparkling white flashes of light across the room. He dropped it into the tiny padded interior of the box and it nestled beside the yellow cyanide capsule. Biting his lip, he said, pointedly, 'Now, you must hide the box in the very safest place you have.'

'Yes,' Ulrika answered. 'I can put it into ….' Then she understood. 'No, …. oh no. … I can't do that. It's …… disgusting.'

'You've no other choice,' Rolf said, icily. 'That box contains your choice between life and death. Put it into your vagina, … now.' Through Rolf's mind flashed the *Sonderkommando* searches after the gassings. The *SS* in him wondered if the diamond had been there before. 'Hurry up,' he said, brusquely. 'If it embarrasses you, I'll turn away. But I can't leave you until it's safely hidden.'

She began to sob and he turned his back to her. He heard the rustle of clothes and then a small scream of pain. 'It's done,' she whispered and he turned back to face her.

'Be brave, Ulrika.' Holding her close, he tasting the saltiness of her tears. One final clinging kiss and he strode away and left her.

Rolf had time to collect supplies and weapons. Worries about Ulrika vanished as his mission unfolded. *Oberst* Nicolaus Von Below was late and, as Rolf waited in the garden near the Bunker entrance, he was able to watch Von Below come through the exit and approach him.

A typical German aristocrat. Tall, straight backed with square shoulders. The light blue *Luftwaffe* uniform was perfectly cut, although most of it was covered by a long, unbuttoned leather coat. Over his shoulder hung a bulging rucksack. The face was thin with high cheek-bones and an aquiline nose. The voice had soft upper-class intonations.

'*Sturmbannführer* Müller?' he said, quietly.

'Yes, sir,' said Rolf, saluting. The two men looked at each other. Then Von Below stuck out his hand.

'I hope you can fight, Müller?'

'I'm a doctor.'

'Hm .....'. He grinned. 'Then we make a good pair. You're a doctor and I'm a pilot. This is not going to be easy.' He walked back to the Bunker entrance and Rolf followed him. In the pale light of the corridor, Von Below took out a street map from his rucksack. 'Now listen carefully. Our escape route has been well used.' With a carefully manicured finger, he traced the route. 'With a bit of luck, through the Russian lines near *Masuren Allee*. Hopefully, near there, we'll pick up a guide from the Hitler Youth, who'll take us to *Reichs-sportsfeld*. Then, on to the bridge at *Pichelsdorf* and then take a sailing boat down the Havel Lake.' He lifted his finger and snapped the map closed. 'Can you sail a boat?' There was a quizzical smile on his face.

'A little,' Rolf replied. 'I once crewed for my brother on the Frisian lakes in Holland.'

'Good man.' Von Below slipped the *Schmeisser* M40 machine-pistol off his shoulder. 'I see you've the same weapon. How many magazines have you got?'

'Four.'

'Excellent. We can hardly take on the whole Russian army but at least we can fight back.' Lifting back his cuff, he glanced at his gold wrist-watch. 'Right, it's midnight. Synchronise the time and then we'd better leave, or that guide won't be waiting.' Throwing the rucksack over his shoulder, he stared at Rolf. 'Any questions?'

'No, sir.'

They walked briskly and, where the streets were clear, they covered each other by darting into doorways and crouching behind piles of rubble. They made good time and only occasionally saw people on the streets. Their way was lit by the star-shells that the Russians hurled into the sky every twenty minutes. Just near the Victory Column, a heavy machine-gun opened up. Bullets spattered into the stone cobbles of the road in front of them and they fell to the ground. 'Quick,' shouted Von Below. 'Behind that tree.' They waited.

'Sounds like one of ours,' said Rolf, surprised at his knowledge.

'Go to the left,' Von Below whispered. 'I'll go to the right. Don't shoot, unless you have to. ... It could be ours.'

Again the heavy chatter of the machine-gun. The rounds smashed into the tree causing splinters to fly everywhere. Rolf jerked as a thin sliver of wood cut into his cheek. Grunting with the sharp pain, he pulled off his leather glove, found the end of the splinter and yanked it out. Even in the dim light of the fading starshells, he saw blood on his hand. Then he laughed aloud. In the whole of the war, it was the first time he had spilt his own blood. Raising the *Schmeisser*, he unfolded the butt and pressed it hard against his shoulder, looking for the man who had made him bleed. Staring down the sight, he tried to steady the shaking image as it jumped up and down like a yo-yo. Taking a deep breath, Rolf forced himself to relax, still the sight wavered around in circles.

'Müller,' shouted Von Below's voice from behind another tree stump. 'What the bloody hell's the matter with you?'

Rolf lowered the weapon and grabbed hold of the tree for support. Taking a deep breath, he called back, 'It's OK now.'

'Count to five and shoot at the last muzzle flame .... and I'll come in from the back. When I shout for you, ... come running. Do you understand me?'

'Yes. .... One, two, three.' Sweat poured down Rolf's face and his body shook with fear. He heard himself counting aloud and he stared into the darkness trying to imagine where the last shots had come from. 'Four, five,' and then he lifted the *Schmeisser* and let loose a whole magazine. Thirty two rounds of ammunition blazed across the road and ricocheted in all directions. The flashes, the noise and the smell of cordite made him close his eyes and the recoil forced the muzzle upwards. When the magazine finally clicked empty, he let the weapon drop. Around him was complete silence. Then Von Below whispered through the still night air.

'Come here quick. .... Don't shoot.'

Rolf slung the *Schmeisser* over his shoulder and edged away from the tree. Trying to appear casual, although he was absolutely terrified, he crept across the open road. There was a pile of sandbags waist-high. In the discernible light, Von Below stood on the rim of the bags. Rolf arrived at his side.

'Thanks for the covering fire,' he said, softly, eyes staring in front of him. 'I don't know what the hell you were aiming at but you did the job.' He waved his weapon down into the sandbagged emplacement.

'Oh, my God,' said Rolf, staring at the scene before him. 'I didn't know they were ours.' Two boys, dressed in Hitler Youth uniforms and no more than twelve years old, lay sprawled against their machine-gun. 'Are they dead?' Rolf said, jumping into the pit.

'Of course,' replied Von Below, lighting a cigarette.

Rolf dropped to his knees. Quite automatically, Rolf removed his glove and felt for the pulse in the neck. Nothing. There was little blood. He stood up and stared at the boys.

'I didn't know .... .'

'Don't worry about it. Neither of us could have known. It's called war.' Von Below, drawing hard on the cigarette, looked Rolf up and down. 'Anyway I thought you people in the SS were used to killing people.' Without waiting for a reply, he threw the cigarette away, jumped down off the sandbags and began to walk away.

They made good progress and said little to each other but all the time, the dark image of the dead boys of the Hitler Youth stayed in Rolf's consciousness.

The next problem was making contact with their guide. In the darkness, going was difficult and, several times, they stopped to look at the map. They drew enemy fire near the *Tiergarten* railway station and managed to swing away from the Russian lines. Rolf knew the Hitler Youth headquarters well and, within three hours of leaving the *Führerbunker*, they arrived on the steps of the main entrance. Entering the imposing stone building, they found it empty.

'Is anybody here?' shouted Rolf, the *Schmeisser* cocked and ready.

Von Below grabbed Rolf's arm and pulled him to the floor. They both lay absolutely still.

'Over there,' the *Luftwaffe* officer whispered, 'there's a light showing at the far end of the corridor.' He crawled away in front of Rolf and disappeared. Quickly springing up, Von Below kicked open the door and charged into the room.

There were a dozen or so uniformed soldiers; not one older than fifteen years. Sitting huddled on the floor underneath a single oil lamp, none of them moved but they stared upwards with big eyes. The oldest one leapt to his feet with a Luger pistol in one hand and a *Führer* salute in the other.

'*HEIL* Hitler! *Herr Oberst, Herr Sturmbannführer.*'

Von Below forced a relaxed smile and put his pistol back into its holster. 'Are you the senior man here?'

'*Jawohl, Herr Oberst.*' The boy stared fixedly ahead and Rolf saw the smartness of his appearance.

'I am *Oberst* Von Below,' he said, watching his words take effect. All the boys struggled to their feet and stood to rigid attention. 'Is there a guide here to take us to Lake Havel.' There was a hesitation and then the smallest boy from the end of the line stepped forward.

'*HEIL* Hitler! *Herr Oberst.* I am ordered to carry out that duty.' In a voice squeaking with adolescence.

Rolf smiled and nodded. ' Your name?'

'Schmidt, number 3869957, *Herr Sturmbannführer.* I am to escort you to Lake Havel and find you a sailing dinghy and then take you to the other side.'

Von Below grinned at Rolf. 'Lead on Schmidt. We're in your very capable hands.' The boy saluted again, picked up a pack and a loaded *Schmeisser*, nodded to his friends and walked towards the door. They left, leaving the boys still at attention.

The boy Schmidt was like a rabbit in a burrow. Rolf and Von Below followed him through alleyways, down dark streets, across bomb-cratered fields until they arrived at the massive, looming *Reichs-sportsfeld Stadium*. Then the boy paused and, raising his finger to his lips, waved them to the ground.

'*Herr Oberst,*' he whispered. 'The most direct route is to the south of the *Stadium.*' Then he was up on his feet and running like a hare to the shadows of the building. Rolf and Von Below silently followed.

They heard the Russians rather than saw them. Roaring engines, plumes of diesel fumes, clattering tank tracks and shouting voices. Escaping them was easy. They crawled, ran and hid their way across every piece of cover. Soon they arrived at the bridge over the northern end of the lake. There was an inky blackness as Von Below, alone, reconnoitred the approaches. Apart from convoys of Russian vehicles, there were no troops on the ground. And soon, he was back to their position.

'No problems,' Von Below whispered. 'We'll go across one by one on my hand wave. We must hurry, soon it'll be daylight.' He said to the boy, 'Schmidt, how long do you think it'll take us to get to the lakeside?'

'From here, *Herr Oberst,* about thirty minutes. We can hide for a while in the sailing club.'

One by one, they ran across the road and disappeared into the spring-green scrub at the side of the lake. The boy from the Hitler Youth was right, because, exactly thirty minutes after they had left the bridge, the misty surface of the lake appeared darkly in front of them. The boy found a footpath and they padded down it. He knew exactly where it was going to. The expanse of the lake lay before them, with the ruined outlines of the club house to their right. After looking all around, they walked towards it. Von Below stared out towards the dead calm lake. A quarter moon hung motionless in a starry sky.

Taking a deep breath, he said quietly, 'Before the war I used to come here. It was a very exclusive club. I remember pretty girls, brown bodies, gay parties and, oh yes,' he laughed, 'sometimes a little sailing.' Sighing, he turned round to Schmidt. 'Show us where the boats are.'

The boy nodded and grinned. 'Yes, …. *Kameraden.*' Rolf smiled. 'The boats are hidden by the lake. Please follow me.' With the nimbleness of youth, he turned to see if they were following him. There were three boats, all partly submerged. Their masts were secured down into the hull.

'Ah, …ah,' said Von Below. 'Delta class racers. Two man crew and good in a stiff wind. No problem. Schmidt, where are the sails and the rigging?'

The boy dropped knee-deep into the water and clambered over the gunwale. 'In a box at the back, *Herr Oberst.*'

'In a locker near the stern,' muttered Von Below, ….. 'Right, let's get going.' He pulled off his boots and jumped into the water. Together, they heaved the wooden dinghy on to its side and the water spilled out. Within ten minutes, by feel, and using the wan light of the moon, they rigged the dinghy and the sail was quickly cleated and ready for raising.

'All right, Schmidt', said Von Below. 'We can take it from here. Can you make your way back home safely?'

The boy's face was crestfallen. 'But, sir, …. My orders are to escort you out of the city. I have not yet carried out my orders.'

Von Below gave a kindly grin. 'Schmidt, you've done a great job. Nobody could've done what you've done.' He shook the surprised boy's hand.

Schmidt drew himself up and beamed with delight. 'Thank you, *Herr Oberst.* Thank you very much. ….. *Auf Wiedersehen, Kameraden.*'

'Müller, prepare to cast off and make sail.'

'Yes, sir,' replied Rolf, taking up his crew position in the middle of the dinghy.

FORTY-SEVEN

They drove as quickly as possible to Millingen. It was still a three hour journey and Jane passed the time by reading. Richard had been very quiet since he had left Westerbork.

Staring straight ahead down the rolling monotony of the motorway, Richard thought for a moment. 'Since all this started,' he said. 'Westerbork is the first time I've ever been close to a place where the Cohen family actually were. Simon told me the story and we've read it in the diary but,' he banged the steering wheel, 'can you imagine what it was like to be in that place and, …. then, …. getting into cattle wagons. …. Jane, we've no idea, …. no idea whatsoever.'

The radio was on so Richard and Jane said little to each other. Eventually, Jane took Simon's file out the bag. She glanced at Richard. He nodded and switched off the radio.

'I left Müller and went for a walk in Berlin. What a God awful place it was. The damage was unimaginable. The Germans must have gone through sheer hell in the last months of the war. I had little sympathy for them. Places that I'd heard about, the Reichstag, *the* Brandenburg Gate, Unter Den Linden. *Everything was in ruins. I stopped and looked at what must have been the Chancellery. The massive stone building was still standing although there were gaps in the masonry.*

Whilst I was near the building, a couple of English sergeants walked by. We exchanged salutes and I went across to talk to them.

"Good morning," I said and they grinned.

"Morning, sir."

"This is the Chancellery, isn't it?"

"Oh yes, sir," replied the taller one. "This is the place where Adolf used to work." He noticed my interest. "Have you been inside?" I shook my head. "Would you like us to take you round? You, know, the proper guided tour, courtesy of Sergeants Rose and Jackson of the Kings Own Rifle Corps."

The humour and good will of the English Tommy never failed to amaze me. "Gentlemen," I replied, "it would be a pleasure."

We walked through the shattered main entrance into the main hall. It was just a shell, smashed statuary; the wreckage of chandeliers laying on the marble floor; roof beams at odd angles. What really surprised me was the amount of paper that littered almost every part of the floor. It blew about like confetti. I bent down to pick a file. The word "GEHEIM" in big capitals was printed clearly on the front. I opened the file.

One of the sergeants said, "Everything round here is marked 'Secret', sir." He glanced up the stairs. "Would you like to see Adolf's office?" I nodded and enjoyed the comradeship.

We tramped along a corridor, climbing over destroyed furniture. Up a flight of stairs that were wide enough for a tank. A short corridor, lit by glass roof panels. At the end was a huge, marble-framed, open doorway, doors hanging off bronze hinges. I was the first there and, as I entered the room, I stopped. A cavern of a place with broken chairs and furniture spread like match-wood over the floor. The glass in the windows was gone. A huge, half-burnt portrait of Hitler lay across a sofa. There was that same smell of burnt wood and charred paper. The two soldiers stood on each side of me.

"This was Adolf's office," said Sergeant Rose, softly. "From here, he planned the whole bloody war. He gave orders that killed millions of innocent people."

"Yes, indeed," I said, amazed at what lay before me.

A desk was the most dominant feature and it was still intact. It was the biggest desk I'd ever seen. Made from what looked like one piece of wood, it rested four square on the marble floor. Chipped here and there and with the drawers damaged, it filled the room. I felt drawn to it. Touching it made a shiver go through me. What hell had been created by orders signed on this very wooden surface.

"Look at this, sir," said Sergeant Rose, holding aloft a neat stack of documents.

'What's that?" I asked climbing over a broken chair. He'd pulled open one of the desk drawers.

"Certificates signed by Hitler." He peered at them in the half-light. "I think they're for medals. Here, sir, what do you think?" I took them from him and scanned the words. Beautifully printed in German Gothic script. The eagle clutching the swastika stood out in deeply embossed gold.

"You're right, Sergeant Rose," I said. "They're medal certificates." I thumbed through the sheets of heavy velum. "All classes from Knight's Cross with Oak leaves, to Iron Cross, Second Class."

"They're nicely done, sir," said Sergeant Rose. "Is Hitler's signature real?"

I held the paper up to the light and, removing my glove, fingered the black ink. 'Yep, I think so." The other sergeant whistled. I held onto the certificates and we looked about us.

We all felt the atmosphere. I dropped the papers onto the table and strolled towards the window. The empty window frame stretched down to the floor and I realised that it led out onto a small balcony. As I stood alone, I realised that this very balcony was the place where Hitler had addressed the crowds. For some reason. I gripped the stone balustrade and stared below me. There was not a soul in sight, apart from one mangy dog sitting in the middle of the tram line. It must have seen me move into the daylight because it lifted its head and let out a mournful howl. A sound that seemed so fitting for this place.

"Sir," one of the sergeants called. I shook myself and walked back into the room.

Wearing huge grins, they had the medal certificates laid out on the table. Sergeant Rose held a pen in his hand. "Sir, are you game for a laugh?" I felt the atmosphere in the room lift.

Without thinking, I replied, "Yes. Why not?"

"It's like this, sir." he chuckled. "We think we deserve a medal, so we're going to have an Iron Cross, first class and we thought that you'd like a Knight's Cross with Oak Leaves. Is that all right with you?"

I had to laugh. Here I was in Berlin in Hitler's study with two English soldiers and all we could do was laugh. "Sergeant Rose," I said, with a smile. "I think it's a great idea."

Chuckling away, the sergeant wrote neatly in the correct space in a flowing copperplate script. Completing the other sergeant's name, he blew over it and handed it across to him. "Now then, sir," he said. "What name is it, please?" I watched him write it out. "I'll put on it the date before Adolf topped himself, then the folks back home'll think he really gave it to you." Screwing the cap back on his pen, he handed the certificate to me. I must admit it looked very grand. **Major Simon Cohen.** *Slipping it back into my pocket, I glanced at my watch.*

"Gentlemen, I'll have to be going now."

"That's a pity, sir," said Sergeant Rose, "'cos we were going to have a look at Adolf's bunker in the cellars."

At the time, I'd never heard of the bunker and now I wish I'd gone with them. "Sorry," I said. They jumped to attention. Returning their salutes, I walked out of the room.'

Richard braked and pulled over into a parking place.

'One worry solved,' said Jane, throwing her head back and laughing. 'Just imagine, he's in Hitler's office and all he can think about is souvenirs.'

Richard shook his head and joined in with her laughter. 'It was typical of him,' he said, pulling on the handbrake. 'And then, he leaves it for us to find. …. I bet up there,' he jabbed his finger upwards, 'he's laughing with us.' Reaching over to the back seat, Richard fumbled with his overcoat and managed to pull the certificate out of the pocket. Smoothing it out on his lap, he said, 'Sergeant Rose, wherever you are. You've no idea how much worry you've caused us.'

When their laughter stopped, Richard started the engine and drove back onto the motorway. 'Read on, Jane,' he said. 'Let's see what else Simon has got in store for us.'

'It was time for Müller to talk and then I could go back to Holland. The barrier to the barracks was down and well guarded by Military Police armed with machine-guns. They checked my papers and waved me on.

When I unlocked Müller's cell door and walked in, he rose from his bed and stood loosely to attention. He was the first to speak.

"How was my city, Major?" His manner surprised me. This was not the Müller I knew.

"Your city is a total ruin. It's as simple as that."

I never even had to ask the question, Müller said it quite simply. "I'm ready to take you now to find the papers that you need."

"Where do we have to go to?" I asked him, quietly, I suspected a trick. My hand was on the butt of the Webley. He saw my hand and laughed.

"Don't worry Major. I don't want to lose my life just yet." The change in him still surprised me. "Life is full of strange coincidences," he continued. "You've brought me to Berlin to find out about the death of your family. You'll find out what you need to know without leaving this military camp." With a rattle of chains, he took a step away from the bed. I felt the hair on my neck stiffen. Müller looked coolly at me. "I give you my word as a German officer, that I will not attempt to escape."

"And I give you my word as a Dutch officer that I'll shoot you, if you even you so much as try. Anyway, I don't give a damn for your word of honour." Without turning round, I kicked the door.

"Right, Müller," I said, stepping to one side. "Lead on."

He frowned. "Major, ….. the chains? …… You have my word of honour."

I laughed and gave him a sharp shove on his shoulder. He staggered a half-pace, turned with a face that was the old Müller.

The German barracks was now quite full of British troops and we got a mixture of glances and salutes. Müller stared stonily ahead. After five minutes, we came to a particularly large building. Well-built in solid German style and four storeys high.

Müller stopped and faced me. "Fourth floor," he said, sourly. "Last room at the end."

The building was not yet taken over and our heavy footsteps echoed hollowly back at us. Müller clanked up the stairs. The top floor was as neat and as tidy as any barrack could be. It was as though the occupants had walked out a minute before we arrived. Glancing at the door numbers, Müller shuffled down the corridor until he reached the last door. Turning the handle, he walked in.

A comfortable officer's quarters with a bed, a table and two lockers. On the bed, the mattress was neatly rolled back. No indication as to the identity of the last occupant. Everything was militarily tidy and where it should be.

"Müller," I said, "If this is some sort of joke ….. ?"

"This was my brother's quarters," he said, leaning against the window. "The last time we met, he gave me strict instructions to collect copies of his papers."

Still smelling a rat, I said, with some anger, "What's this got to do with what I need?"

He nodded. "Records from the camps were kept in the camps and copies here in Berlin. I doubt whether the Russians have left anything at Auschwitz and, here in Berlin, they will have shipped everything back to Moscow. But, Cohen but," I noticed the major had gone, "my brother is not a fool. He knows how useful and dangerous such records can be." Dropping to his knees in the far corner, he stared intently at the heavy, wooden skirting- board. Placing the finger tips of both hands onto the upper edge, he pulled hard. Behind me, I heard the driver cocking his Sten. Müller muttered something in German and there was a creaking sound from the timber.

"As I thought," he grunted, pulling out an envelope from behind the board. "Rolf did not forget." He turned, stood and extracted a single sheet of paper from the envelope. Smiling, he stared at it and then laughed.

"Put it on the bed," I snapped.

Müller, still laughing threw it on the bed and stood back. It was a map and a few directions. It looked as though it was copy of an original. There were criss-crossing lines, an obvious road marked 'To Emmerich' and other dots and circles. At one point there was a cross with a figure 2 at the side. Translated, the directions said that two wagons were marked with a red letter M above the buffers. The lines were obviously railway lines and their complexity showed the size of the place.

"What's this Müller?" I said, brusquely.

There was a mocking smile on his face. "I thought my brother may have said where the documents you wanted, would be hidden. I expected a map of

Berlin and the name of an office. All you get is a map of railway sidings. If there's anything there, then my brother would have got it by now and destroyed it."

I was back at square one. My driver was quicker than me. For the first time, he spoke to Müller. Speaking very quietly, with the stubby muzzle pointing straight at Müller's chest, he ground out the words. "Why else did you bring us here?"

Müller looked disdainful. "I don't talk to the ranks."

My driver nodded and walked past him. Turning to me, he said, "Watch him, sir." Drawing his bayonet, he levered back the skirting-board. "Ah, Ah, ... I thought so." He rose to his feet, holding something in the palm of his hand. "I think you would call it a nest-egg." It was a small, draw-stringed leather bag. Slipping the string, he tipped out the contents onto the table. Two beautiful diamonds glittered in the dim light. Out of the corner of my eye, I saw Müller lunge. Quickly, I stuck out my boot, he tripped and fell into a sprawling heap. I had my revolver in his ear before he could move. He growled and then flopped back.

With my foot on his chest, I turned back to the diamonds. "Müller, how did you expect to get back for these?" He shook his head and glared back at me. "What's in these wagons?" Still no answer. I kicked him quite hard, because I'd had enough of this lying, scheming Nazi bastard. There was no answer.

I handed the diamonds over to the Provost Marshall. He was a pleasant enough man and fascinated to hear my story. The same rank as me and another lawyer. Although, he'd practised and I hadn't. We drank almost of a bottle of gin together and sat in the mess for most of the night.

"Simon," he said, half-asleep in a deep chair, "you've got rare skills that we may need in the coming weeks. If I clear it with your CO, could you stay a little longer?"

"Why?" was my quick answer.

"The war crimes trials are being arranged and we need somebody who's knowledgeable in these matters. You speak fluent German, Dutch and English and well, ... eh, ..."

"Yes?" I enquired, knowing what he was going to say.

"You're a Jew and your motivation makes you search that bit harder."

I agreed with his point. "Yep, that's fine by me. I'd want my driver to stay with me and Müller needs looking after until I can take him back."

"No problem with Müller. We've plenty of cells available."

On that night, I didn't go to bed, I slept on the couch in the mess. At dawn, a steward woke me up. Three cups of coffee later, I felt a lot better. On *that day, I interrogated half a dozen* SS *but they were no different to any others I'd met. In fact, it was all a bit boring. John Peterson, the Provost Marshall called by after my last man had gone.*

"Hello, Simon. You remember that piece of paper you gave me the other day? You know the one with the railway lines and the road on it?"

I'd given it him in the hope he could check it out for me. "Was it of any use."

"I spoke to the RAF about it." He passed it back to me. "Sorry, no go on this one. It's a plan of the railway marshalling yards at Emmerich near the Dutch border. During the first week in May, and just after the German surrender was signed, the RAF plastered it. Something about suspected ammunition and hidden tanks. Everything was totally destroyed." My heart sank and he must have seen my face. "I say, are you all right? You went sort of pale."

I shook my head. "No, it's all right. It must be the gin we drink every night." He smiled and went back to his office.

I must admit, I was depressed. Müller had raised my hopes that some of my family had survived, now I had no way of proving if it was true. I just wanted to get out of this awful building and breathe some fresh air. It was a bright sunny day and I walked and walked. I didn't see the mess of Berlin around me. I saw fresh green leaves on the few remaining trees. Children playing in the ruins. The odd horse pulling a cart and birds fluttering through the air. I really felt that the war was over and it made me realise how tired I was. I was somewhere to the north of the city centre, when all signs of people disappeared and it became very quiet. I checked my Webley because I'd heard about the occasional attack in isolated areas. Then I saw the British soldier. He was talking to somebody and then he moved to one side.

I was five yards away from her; my breath stuck in my throat. It was the strangest sensation I'd ever felt. She was a little smaller than me. Straggly blonde hair and her head was tilted to one side, rather like a bird. She wore a long, filthy overcoat and shoes with cut-out holes for the toes. She was beautiful in a special way that even now I find difficult to describe. As I walked towards her, the soldier saluted me. I was so taken by her, I ignored him. It was as though this woman and I were the only people in Berlin. She held my eyes with hers and they were a startling blue. She remained immobile as I came closer. I just stared at her face. Her lips were full and the deepest red. She smiled and inclined her head. An arm's length away, I stopped. Then I saluted.

"Good morning," I heard myself saying in German. "My name's Simon Cohen."

She smiled, showing a row of perfect white teeth. "Good morning," she replied firmly. "I'm Ulrika Hannsen."'

Jane closed the file and placed it on her lap. She turned to Richard. 'Wow, at least that part of the story is true,' she said. 'It matches perfectly with what Sabina told us.'

They were ten minutes from Nijmegen and already the massive structure of the bridge over the Waal loomed up in front of them. It was mid-afternoon and the sun was beginning to drop down low on the flat horizon.

'Is there much more to read?' asked Richard, concentrating on the narrowing motorway.

'Another ten pages.'

'I'm sure about what's in those two envelopes back in Simon's safe.'

'I bet you're thinking the railway map is in one of them.'

He nodded. 'That thought did go through my mind. But then, Simon says that the RAF had bombed it flat. Which means there's nothing left.'

'Unless Rolf Müller got there first.'

Richard flicked on the head-lights. 'You could be right. This thing is just as big a mystery as it ever was.' The Volvo rumbled over the bridge. Richard knew where he was going to and turned left around a big traffic island.

'You know your way,' said Jane, checking her seat belt.

'Yes, indeed. I had a good guide. Simon came here in almost exactly the same way, although, he came from the south.'

'How does that make you feel?'

Richard nodded. 'Really good. After the last piece you read out, I feel almost as if he wanted us to do this. I expected to find the lists of people and be able to see Müller's signature and then be able to confront him.' He shook his head. 'It's now highly unlikely I'll find anything to prove what Müller did.'

'Benjamin Blum could be a witness.'

'It seems that all evidence based on witnesses seeing their tormentors has failed,' said Richard, sadly. 'People change out of all recognition. You've only got to look at you own school photographs to realise that.'

He drove the car along the twisting back roads. The signs for Millingen appeared and Richard slowed down to enter the small town. A single, twisting, cobbled street lined by comfortable shops and pleasant brick buildings. There were a few people about and after a minute he found the Millingen Centre Hotel. Pulling up outside, he turned to Jane. 'What do you want to do? .... Check in, or go to Müller's house? It's ten minutes from here.'

She opened her handbag and took out a small mirror. 'If you'd asked me that twenty minutes ago, I would have said check-in. But now, I think I want to go straight there and get this meeting over with.' Staring intently into the mirror, as only women can do, she touched her eyebrows and felt her skin. Taking out a powder compact, she removed the pad and dabbed at her forehead and her nose.

Richard knew she was mentally preparing herself. 'Let's go and see this man' he said quickly. 'We can return to the hotel later.'

They crossed the German frontier and Richard drove slowly, giving himself time to gather his thoughts and check through what he wanted to say. There was a kind of numbness in his body, almost a feeling of inner calm. He felt he was ready for anything. The day was drawing to a close and long dark, shadows made driving that bit harder.

The house was exactly as he had remembered it.

'Some place,' said Jane, softly.

He drove down the drive and pulled up in front of the double wooden doors. Opening the car door, he walked round to help Jane from her seat. Together, they approached the imposing entrance. Richard held her hand and squeezed it. As he reached for the bell pull, one of the doors smoothly opened.

FORTY-EIGHT

The stiff following wind drove them across the black, choppy surface of Lake Havel. They made good time and reached the western shore just before dawn.

Hiding in the scrub near the shore line, they began to walk, all the time keeping to the paths and away from roads. After half an hour, Rolf paused for a moment.

Von Below saw him stop. 'What is it?'

'The silence,' Rolf whispered, facing back towards Berlin. 'For the first time for weeks, I can't hear bombs and explosions.'

'You're right,' he said. 'It could mean the *Führer* is dead and the Russians have taken Berlin. .... Come on, let's push on whilst we can.'

Skirting north of a small town, and travelling for two days, they kept away from all habitation. Eventually, they found a farm worker's hut and collapsed into a pile of straw.

'I don't know about you, Müller,' said Von Below, 'but I've had it. I couldn't walk another step.' Undoing his tunic, he reached down and pulled off his jackboots.

Rolf sat on a broken barrel. Glancing at Von Below's open tunic, he saw the strapping across his shirt.

'Yes, I'll answer your question,' he said, yawning. 'It's the *Führer's* Testament. How the hell I'm supposed to get it to Doenitz, I'll never know. We haven't seen anything on wheels for the last two days.' Reaching into his rucksack, he drew out some army rations. For a few minutes, they ate in silence. Von Below looked hard into Rolf's face. 'Tell me, what are you going to do now this war is over?'

'I had a woman back in Berlin,' replied Rolf. 'Although, she's probably dead by now.' He shrugged his shoulders. 'Hopefully, I'll practice medicine. What about you?'

Von Below took a deep breath. 'I'm an aristocrat and I've got a lot to lose. My estates are east of Berlin and I doubt whether the Bolsheviks will let me go back.' His eyes began to close. From under lowered lids, he said, 'You SS doctors who worked in the camps may have problems practising medicine. You do realise that, Müller, don't you?'

Rolf looked hard at this handsome man languishing on a pile of hay.

'Yes, I understand completely.' Here was a man he could use. 'What would you suggest I do instead of medicine?'

Von Below yawned. 'If you've any money at all, Müller, I'd buy land and farm it. This country will always need food and, when we've surrendered, there'll be plenty of cheap land. Buy it as quickly as possible.'

Rolf remembered the advice.

They slept alternately, each one keeping watch. Von Below woke up first and did all the talking. 'Look here, Müller,' he said with conviction. 'I've been thinking. By now Germany will have fallen and the *Führer* is probably dead. I think we should split up.'

'We have our orders,' interrupted Rolf.

Von Below's blue eyes blazed. 'Oh damn the orders! I'm not risking my life any more. I've got a family to go to and anyway there'll be nobody left to report to.' Rolf stayed silent. Von Below smoothly took over. He stood up and walked across to the window. 'I had a specific mission to perform but now I believe I can't succeed in that mission.' Undoing his tunic, he pulled the thin webbing straps that held the packet to this chest. Yanking the heavy envelope free, he glanced at the cover, and tore the document within it to pieces.

'*Herr Oberst*!' exclaimed Rolf striding across the bare room. He tried to grab the papers and Von Below pushed him to one side.

'Don't be stupid, Müller,' he said, angrily. 'It's all over. Forget it.' The two men faced each other. Von Below took Rolf's arm. 'Get out of uniform and go west.' For a moment, he thought Rolf was going to argue and then the two men relaxed.

'I'm an *SS* officer and sworn to be loyal to the *Führer*.' His face was deathly pale.

'There is no *Führer*,' said Von Below softly. 'He must be dead. Be realistic, man.'

Rolf's shoulders slumped, then, taking a deep breath, he snapped back, 'Right, we'll need a change of clothes. And a change of papers, ... identity cards.'

'Stop for a minute,' interrupted Von Below. 'Just hold on.'

Rolf stopped and waited, his face watching the man in front of him.

Undoing the flap of his rucksack, Von Below delved deep. Finding what he was seeking, he pulled it out. A package wrapped in oiled cloth. Tearing off the wrapping, he withdrew an envelope. 'Here, this is your new life.'

'What is this?' said Rolf, emptying the papers out onto the table.

'An identity card,' said Von Below, with a smile. 'Letters from your wife, photographs. Everything you'll need for a new life.'

Rolf picked up a photograph. He was quietly surprised; it was of Ulrika Hannsen. She wore a beautiful smile and it was a photograph he had never seen before. Keeping his thoughts to himself, he put it to one side and selected the grey army identity card. He could not suppress a frown. 'Who the hell decided this?' he said. 'I'm now a *Gefreiter* Jan Bildt of the *Wehrmacht*. At least you could have made me an officer.'

'Somebody made a wise choice,' said Von Below, grinning. 'All officers are usually taken for questioning. A mere *Gefreiter* would arouse no suspicion.'

'What about you?' said Rolf looking at Von Below.

'I'm an officer in the *Luftwaffe*,' said Von Below. 'Yes, they'll take me, if they can find me. I have no connections with the SS. My military knowledge is now of little use. Consider yourself lucky to have had these papers provided. You've obviously friends in high places. These were given to me by the *Reichsführer* and only to be used in an emergency, or if you were in danger of being captured. I think both of these reasons now apply.' Von Below scratched at his bearded chin and stared hard at the man in front of him. 'Müller, …just what the hell do you know?'

Then Rolf understood. Somebody was saving his skin. He had access to information and records concerning the very survival of Germany. He smiled grimly. 'Nothing in particular,' he said. 'Just some aspects of SS operations.' He went through the papers yet again. One address surprised him. 'Who decided that I live in Emmerich?'

Von Below shook his head. 'I don't know, Müller. I really don't know. Until you opened the package, I had no idea what was inside. Do you have family in Emmerich?'

'Just a good friend ,' replied Rolf, hardly able to conceal a smile.

The clothes that Von Below pulled out of his rucksack were old and had a sour body smell to them. At first, Rolf wanted to reject them but then he realised that it would be part of the disguise. A pair of ragged wool trousers caked in mud or something else too awful to think about. A collarless cotton shirt with holes in the elbows. The heavy boots had soles separating from the welts. Slipping off his uniform, Rolf began to pull on the trousers,

'A moment, Müller,' interrupted Von Below, eyebrow raised. 'I don't think a *Gefreiter* on the run would wear silk underwear and cotton socks. Do you?'

He stripped naked. The hairiness of the harsh wool on his skin made him shiver. Grabbing a belt, he baggily secured the trousers around his waist. The cap was missing its peak and it flopped over his forehead, forcing him to wear it sideways. Carefully, he folded his uniform and placed it on the floor. The leather belt and gun holster lay across the rank badges. For a moment, he stood back and looked at his past.

Von Below laughed, 'I'll bury them when you've gone and for God's sake, relax. You're not in the SS now. Look cowed, or at least hunch your shoulders.'

Rolf straightened his shoulders. 'I'll always be an SS officer and I'll never be cowed.' Von Below nodded. Carefully, Rolf patted the identity documents into his pockets and reached for his rucksack. He inclined his head to Von Below. '*Herr Oberst*, it's been an honour to know you. *Auf Wiedersehen*.' The two men shook hands.

He followed the map and made his way along a narrow track through the densest part of the forest. Rolf had another job to complete before he could arrive at the nearest village. Upending his rucksack, he emptied the contents onto the grass. Selecting only what a corporal would carry, he buried the rest. Only one item lay in his palm and then he remembered Ulrika's face when she had been faced with the same decision. Undoing the draw string, he tipped the diamonds into his other hand. The tin holding the cyanide capsule held the stones. He threw away the capsule and squeezed the diamonds into the container. Dropping his trousers, he crouched like a peasant shitting. Wetting his fingertips, he pushed the capsule up his anus, giving a grunt of pain as it slid in. Carefully straightening, he expected pain; there was none. 'Jan Bildt,' he said aloud, 'you amaze me.'

FORTY-NINE

The butler's face was expressionless. 'Do come in, sir, madam,' he said in English and then stood to one side.

The hall was just as Richard had remembered it. Precisely in the middle of the black and white-tiled floor stood a motionless Jan Bildt. Richard felt Jane at his side. Her hand slipped into his. There was absolute silence as the two men looked hard at each other.

'My dear, Richard,' said Bildt, across the echoing hall. 'It gives me so much pleasure to see you here again. Welcome to *"Grosse Bauernhof"'*

Richard saw a noticeable change in him. Gone was the erect stance. Replaced by slumped shoulders and a face with a yellowy drawn look about it. Richard hesitated and then took a single step forward. Bildt moved off the black tile rather like a pawn making its move.

'Mrs Cooper,' he said softly, 'ever since I first made contact with Richard, I've wanted to meet you.' He reached her side and extended his hand. Without thinking, Jane took it. Bildt, with a sweeping motion, lifted her hand to his face and brushed his lips across her knuckles. Their eyes met.

Richard watched the little act. Firmly, he said, '*Herr* Bildt, I'm here to sort things out properly and legally. The sooner we do this the better.' Richard looked about him. 'May we sit down somewhere?'

Bildt took a pace backwards. The bloodshot blue eyes looked Richard up and down. 'I quite understand your feelings, Richard. But, ... there's no reason why we shouldn't sort these matters out in a civilised way. .... Please follow me.' He walked as though one side of his body was not functioning, dragging his left foot behind the right. Richard said nothing and glanced at Jane. She frowned and still held his hand.

They went to the library. Three comfortable chairs were laid out in a circle around a low, antique table. On it stood a crystal decanter full of red wine. Three glasses were arranged on the tray in the same way as the chairs. Richard consciously pulled one chair closer to another and helped Jane to sit down. Bildt eased himself down into the other chair and pulled his left hand on to his lap. He wore a red bow tie, a black smoking jacket and matching evening-suit trousers.

'I have taken the liberty of opening a bottle of wine,' Bildt said with a gracious smile. 'Château-Lafite, 1946. A rather appropriate year, don't you think, Richard? The year you were born.' Richard remained silent. Bildt reached forward, grunting with some sort of discomfort, and poured out three glasses. He passed them out to his guests. 'May I offer a toast?' Without waiting for a reply, he raised his glass. 'I drink to the Cooper family and toast your long awaited arrival at my home.' They drank and then Jane spoke.

'*Herr* Bildt, my husband says that you claim to be his father. How do we know this to be true?'

Bildt looked at her coolly over the rim of his glass. 'Ah, yes, Mrs Cooper. The lawyer's opening gambit. I should have known.' Raising his glass to the half-lit chandelier, he peered through its crimson contents. 'This is my favourite vintage. I only have four bottles left.' Lowering the glass, he looked straight into Jane's eyes. 'What do you think of it, Mrs Cooper? Does it not taste absolutely divine?'

Jane knew the ploy; answer a question with a question. For some inexplicable reason, she found the man in front of her fascinating. It was not the house, nor the rich furnishings, nor the wine; it was the man that was interesting. He looked the urbane, civilised, older man. The iron-grey hair framed a sharp, firm face. Age enhanced his features and he knew it. A smile played round his thin lips. All that Simon Wiesenthal had said to her about a man called Rolf Müller was slowly fading away. She felt Bildt wanting to control her and she found it hard to resist.

'The wine is quite superb, *Herr* Bildt,' Jane replied. He had not replied to her original question.

Richard emptied his glass. '*Herr* Bildt,' he said. 'I don't think you've answered my wife's question.'

Bildt refilled his glass. 'Quite right, Richard.' He sat back in the chair, glass in hand. 'You will just have to believe that I'm your real father. .... Have you spoken to your mother?'

'Yes, I have.'

'What did she say?'

'She said, your real name was Rolf Müller. .... Not Jan Bildt.'

'And Ulrika, or should I say, Sabina, is quite right. That was my original name.'

'Why did you change it?'

'The needs of war, I'm afraid. Changing my name saved me a lot of unnecessary hassle.'

'You were an *SS* officer?' Richard watched every line on Bildt's face and there was not a flicker of movement.

'Now, why do you ask that particular question?'

'Answer it, please.'

'No, I was a mere *Gefreiter*. That's a corporal in your army.'

Jane placed her empty glass on the table. 'How can a man like you be just a corporal and yet live in these surroundings?'

Bildt relaxed and his eyes smiled at hers. 'Mrs Cooper. ... Adolf Hitler was once a corporal and, if I'm not mistaken, your Field Marshall Montgomery started off his brilliant career as a private.' He threw back his head and laughed through perfect white teeth. 'You British have this thing about the war and the *SS*. .... No, I was never in the *SS*.'

Richard waited like a hawk and then he struck. 'Simon Wiesenthal tells me otherwise. I have seen records that say you were a doctor at Auschwitz.'

The laugh disappeared from Bildt's face and his voice took on a harsher tone. 'Why did you have to contact Wiesenthal? The man has been proved wrong on so many occasions.' Then he regained control. 'My dear, Richard, you can go to any town in Germany and pick up a telephone directory and find a dozen Rolf Müllers. It's a common name.'

Turning his head, he called out, making Jane jump. 'Hans, ... another bottle of the Lafite.' Richard tried to protest but Bildt raised his hand. 'Let me return to Richard's original question. I admit my name is Rolf Müller.' He smiled at them both. The door opened and Hans delivered the open bottle and carefully decanted it. 'Richard, you've asked your mother whether she knew me and she has admitted to you that she did.' Folding his arms, Bildt reached for the decanter. 'As much as you may not like it, Richard, I am your father.' Hans gave a half bow and left the room.

Jane took the refilled glass. '*Herr* Bildt,' she said. 'Tell us a little more about Sabina, or Ulrika as you knew her.'

Bildt sipped quietly at the glass watching the two people in front of him. 'Tell me, did Sabina mention the *Lebensborn* Project?'

'Yes,' replied Richard.

'That's how I met her.'

Richard's eyes narrowed. 'I thought *Lebensborn* was only for the *SS*?'

'There you again, always suspecting me. *Lebensborn* was primarily for the *SS*. You're quite right. But other good German stock of the right blood and background was always acceptable. I was one of those people and our meeting was so wonderful.'

'I know,' interrupted Richard. 'Sabina told me all about it.'

'When you met her, you were already married,' said Jane.

Bildt smiled and wiped his good hand across his forehead. 'Yes, I was but it didn't work out. It happens during war.'

'Where is your wife now?' asked Jane, patiently.

'I don't know. The last time I saw her, fifty years ago, she was with another man. From that day, I have never seen her again.'

'And you've always lived here alone?' Jane watched his face.

Bildt placed his glass carefully back on the table and rose from his seat. It was not an easy task and Jane almost reached out to help him. He edged his way towards one of the book shelves. Reaching up to a shelf he took down a small silver picture frame. He glanced at it and the walked back to Jane's side. She could smell his old fashioned cologne. He placed the picture into her hand. 'This is a picture of Richard's mother, just after I met her. It's the only picture I have.'

Jane saw the head and shoulders of a pretty woman in her early twenties. Straight blonde hair swept back from a face with laughing eyes looking directly at the camera. Although taken fifty years ago there was no mistaking that it was Sabina Cohen. Jane passed it to Richard.

Staring at it for several minutes, he placed it on the table and then reached into his jacket pocket. Opening his wallet, he removed a colour photograph, glanced at it and then handed it to Bildt.

Bildt stared at the image and sighed. 'She is just as beautiful as when I knew her in Berlin.' His eyes moved from the photograph to Richard's face and back again. 'I can see the likeness and I can feel that I'm your father.' He brought the photograph closer. 'I presume the man at her side is Simon Cohen?'

'Yes,' said Richard.

'I never met him. I learnt about him from my brother.'

'You mean *SS-Hauptsturmführer* Edvard Müller,' asked Richard, staring at Müller's face.

Bildt stiffened and walked slowly back to his chair. Sitting down, he reached for the glass. 'So, you've found out about my brother as well?'

'Yes, I have,' said Richard softly. 'From a woman called Lottie Cohen, who is now the only survivor of the Dutch Cohen family. Edvard Müller had 42 Cohens transported from Holland to Auschwitz and there they were gassed by his brother Rolf Müller. These facts were corroborated by Simon Wiesenthal.'

Swirling the wine in the glass Bildt, said quietly, 'To use Mrs Cooper's words, "how do you know these facts to be true?" Have you any real evidence that my brother transported them and this man, with my name, at Auschwitz killed them?'

'There was a man at Auschwitz who was a Prisoner Doctor,' said Richard. 'His name's Benjamin Blum and two days ago I met him in Budapest.'

Bildt emptied the glass and placed it carefully back on the table. The cold blue eyes gave a single flicker, swept around the room and then settled back onto Richard's face. 'I've never heard of this man Blum. And, indeed, why should I have heard of him?' There was an edge of nervousness to Bildt's voice which Richard thought was a weakening of the man's defences.

Quickly, without any warning and with a cry, Bildt slumped forward, almost falling off his chair. Jane, jumping, to her feet, grabbed his shoulders and eased him back gently into his seat.

'What the matter with him?' said Jane, breathlessly, 'Look at his face. It's deathly pale.' She turned to Richard. 'He's not, ... he's not dead is he?'

Richard reached over and felt for the pulse in his neck. 'No, he's still alive. I can feel a pulse. Let's just undo the tie. .... That's better. .... Now straighten his legs.' Bildt moaned and muttered something.

'What did he say?' said Jane, bending closer to his face.

'I think he wants the butler.' Richard stepped back from the chair and called out, 'Hans, *hier, schnell.*'

The double doors flew open and Hans ran across the polished wooden floor. Reaching into his pocket, he took out a small bottle of pills, removed two and placed the bottle on the table. Carefully, almost reverently, he bent and opened Bildt's mouth. With infinite care, he slipped the pills under the tongue. The mouth closed wetly and the butler stood up and watched his master's face. The first indication of recovery was a change in the face colour, from yellowy white to blotchy red. Then the tongue licked the lips. Finally the eyelids flickered and then opened.

Within five minutes, Jan Bildt was acting as if nothing had happened. Smiling at Richard and Jane, he carefully explained in a voice that was barely a whisper. 'It's a heart problem I have. Normally, I can feel an attack coming on and I can take my pills. This time .... it caught me unawares.' He turned to his butler. 'Prepare the sofa in my study. I'll be there in a few minutes.' Hans nodded and, without a glance at Richard or Jane, left the room.

Bildt removing a white handkerchief from his pocket, carefully wiped beads of perspiration from his brow and cheeks. 'In the long room,' he said quietly. 'There's a buffet meal ready for you. Please help yourself. I must rest for twenty minutes.' Easing himself from the chair, he slowly stood up. Holding the chair arm, he shuffled carefully away from the table. Richard watched him but Jane took Bildt's arm and helped him across the floor. He turned to look at her.

Richard shrugged and went ahead of them to open the door. Hans, waiting outside, saw Jane and took Bildt's other arm. He nodded towards another door to his left. Slowly Bildt and his butler walked across the hall and into another room.

They stood alone. For a moment, they were unsure what to do. 'Richard,' said Jane. 'This is really the weirdest situation I have ever been in. It's like a film, ... it's totally unreal.' She looked about her. Together they walked out of the library.

A long room with curtained windows lining one side. Massive oil paintings hung on another wall. The smell of beeswax polish. Two fires, one at each end, burned brightly in big fireplaces. A superb Louis XIV table neatly laid with food.

Jane picked up a richly decorated plate and turned it over. 'Mmm,' she said, '.....Sévres porcelain. Nothing but the best for our host.' She paused for a moment. 'Richard, he's still a handsome man and that sun tan has to be seen to be believed.' Selecting several small sandwiches, she filled the plate.

'It's not a tan, Jane,' said Richard. 'It's not a healthy colour at all. I think he has jaundice. Probably something he caught at Auschwitz.'

Jane nibbled at a sandwich. 'Richard, ... do you believe him?'

'No, not a bloody word,' he replied, shaking his head. 'There's much more to this than we know. It's all too pat, ... too easy.' He bit into a chicken leg. 'I just know he's the Rolf Müller from Auschwitz. I don't why I know but I do.'

'Evidence Richard, evidence,' said Jane. 'Remember what Simon Wiesenthal said about proving it absolutely. Sabina's photograph looks nothing like her, it could be anybody.'

Richard stared at her. 'Are you beginning to doubt what Müller really is?'

Jane walked across and reached up to his face. She touched his cheek. 'Darling, I know you don't want to believe anything about this man. He could be exactly what he says he is. An ex-corporal from the wartime German army. Simon was just the same thing. Why don't you just take him at face value and let him believe he's your father. What harm can it do?'

Richard shook his head and his face was sad. 'I still keep seeing Auschwitz and the damned gas chambers and I keep remembering Lottie's words.' He slammed the plate back on the table. 'I can't eat a thing. I'll just have a cup of coffee and wait for Bildt, or Müller, or whatever his name is, to come back in.'

'He's a sick man, Richard,' said Jane, looking for the coffee. 'Very sick. When he collapsed in there, I thought he'd died.'

'Unless it was all a big show to earn our sympathy and,' he said firmly, 'for us to believe his story.'

'Richard, you've just lost one father. I think you're going to loose another.'

He shook his head. 'A man with two fathers. What a claim to fame.'

The door behind them opened and Richard was surprised to see another man walk into the room. He was dressed in a smart suit, white shirt and a red tie.

'Good evening, Mr and Mrs Cooper,' he said politely. 'My name is Willi Schmidt. Mr Cooper, how nice to meet you again.'

FIFTY

The first time the British caught and searched Rolf Müller took place on Wittenburg railway station.

There were few people about. Rolf watched the four soldiers approach from the corner of his eye and stiffened. He heard the sharp English words.

'You,' shouted the corporal. 'You over there, ... with the 'at on. Come 'ere.'

Rolf pretended not to notice.

They surrounded him and Rolf felt a rifle muzzle in his ribs.

'Papers!' shouted one of them into his ear. 'PAPERS!'

Reaching into his pocket, he pulled out his identity card and gave it to the corporal.

'What does it say, Corp?'

Their NCO scrutinised the piece of cardboard. 'He's a *Gefreiter*,' he said. 'A corporal.'

'Anythin' else?

'A photograph.' The corporal chuckled. 'Cor, she's nice. .... 'ere, 'ave a gander at that.' The men passed the picture round and stared at Ulrika. Rolf then noticed that even through their serious banter, the corporal's Sten remained pointedly fixed at his stomach.

'What's this bit of paper?' Rolf realised they were looking at Mengele's map. They waved it in front of his face. 'WHAT'S THIS BIT OF PAPER?' one of them shouted.

Rolf made sure he did not try to speak English. Dropping his head, he spoke as humbly as he could. '*Adresse, meine Frau, ... Meine adresse.*'

'It's where he lives. Give it him back,' said the corporal, 'and then arrest him.'

None of them were curious about why a man should have a map of where he lived.

'Right, Corp,' said one of the soldiers. 'What about the *SS* check?'

The corporal nodded. 'Under the left arm. Take his coat and shirt off.'

The men were rough and ripped his already tattered shirt in the process of removing it. Grabbing his left arm, they forced it upwards. 'Nothin' 'ere. Only a mole. Jesus, he stinks.'

Rolf inwardly smiled. At his *SS* training camp at Bad Tolz, the doctor had advised him not to have the SS tattoo under his left arm, because of the problems a mole might cause. Therefore, the number was under his right arm. In the distance, he heard the shriek of a train whistle.

'OK, he's not SS,' muttered the corporal, shoving the shirt back into Rolf's hands. Their search was thorough and he found it degrading. No man had ever touched him in those places before. 'Take him to the POW cage,' said the corporal loudly.

Two of the soldiers escorted him back into the town. People hardly gave him a second glance and, within twenty minutes, he arrived at a barbed wire enclosure.

Another surprise. At the gate, he was greeted by a German corporal in a grey *Wehrmacht* uniform. He checked Rolf's papers without raising an eyebrow and waved him into the pen. A thin, older man approached him.

'I've been watching you,' he said softly. 'You're no corporal.' Rolf tried to explain. The man pulled him to one side. In a corner of the enclosure, he told Rolf what would happen. 'The British don't have the men or the resources to handle us. Within three days, you'll be released to go back to your home. Do you have enough money?'

Rolf did not fall into the suspected trap. 'I have a little. Enough to get home.'

The man shook hands. '*Kamerad*, may I wish you good luck. HEIL Hitler.'

'HEIL Hitler,' whispered Rolf, wanting to get away.

The man was quite right. Three days later, the corporal who had arrested him, released him.

Some trains were operating. Tickets were unnecessary and there were few places. Rolf's train to Hamburg had eight carriages. The waiting cattle wagons made his stomach churn. Four of them, full of people young and old, children and some men of his age. The wagons were exactly the same as the ones at Auschwitz. Dark brown, oblong boxes, sitting on heavy, rusty wheels. The timber sides were covered in chalk marks and scraps of faded paper held in place by broken nails. The stencilled words "*Deutsche Reichsbahn*" could just be made out. One of the sliding doors was open and faces peered at him. He had no choice, taking a deep breath of fresh air, he pushed his way past an old man and fought for a place near an air-vent set high up the timber wall. It was the first time he had ever been inside one of the cattle wagons. The smell hit him full in the face and he only just managed to control his stomach. There were crying children, old people sitting with their eyes closed and others who pushed and shoved in every direction. The door slammed shut and the train jerked into motion. He lived every second of the journey with open eyes and a feeling of utter dread.

The journey lasted all day and, for Rolf, the train seemed to be shunted through every siding in Germany. He reached Hamburg at dawn and in the cold light of day, he managed to find some food which cost him dear. By travelling on smaller trains, he was able to make his way to Emmerich. He was stopped and searched every two hours and, as he stepped off the train, he had nothing left. No money, no watch; nothing personal.

Finding Willi Hossler was easy. In the officers' club at Auschwitz, Willi had told exactly where the farm was located. Emmerich was busy, occupied by the British since the end of March, the small town was trying to bring itself back to normality. Willi lived in the village of Hüthum to the west of the town. It took Rolf an hour to reach the village and he was exhausted by the time he reached the front of the small church. An old woman saw him standing alone.

'Are you looking for somebody?' she asked.

'The Hossler farm.'

'Oh yes,' she replied, with no expression on her face. 'Turn left by the church and it's the last building on the right.' Nodding, she went on her way.

The farm was stone-built in a neat, four square style. Rolf had never met Willi's wife but her recognised her from photographs. She stared at him as he went up the path to the front door.

'Good morning,' he said. 'Is Willi Hossler at home?'

She was a farmer's daughter. Beefy arms and a wide face. Her accent was pure country.

'Who's looking for him?' she asked, with doubt in her green eyes.

Rolf took a chance. 'My name's Rolf Müller.'

She nodded and a grin split her face. 'WILLI!' She bawled in a voice that could bring the cows home.

Rolf recognised Willi's familiar shape as he appeared from the back of the house. They stared at each other.

'Rolf Müller,' he roared. 'I knew you'd find your way here.' They bear hugged. Stepping back, he said quietly, 'Rolf, you look bloody awful. I thought you'd recovered from the jaundice. Come into the kitchen.'

As Rolf walked down the narrow hall, he glanced at the tall mirror. He did look awful. A drawn unshaven face with sunken eyes. What shocked him more than anything, were the grey streaks in his thick, brown hair. There had been no signs of grey when he had left Berlin eight days previously.

The kitchen was hot and the hanging herbs and a single pork ham gave off satisfying smells. Willi's wife beamed at him. 'I'm Lydia Hossler and I'm very pleased to meet you. I've heard so much about you.' She shook hands. 'Now, I'm going to make you the best meal you've ever had. You just sit down and wait.'

Rolf was about to drop into a comfortable wooden chair, when Willi beckoned him to the back door of the kitchen. 'Come on, Rolf, I'll show you the farm,' he said with a wink.

The concrete farmyard was spotlessly clean. One or two pigs grunted from their pens and a few chickens clucked about. Once out of Lydia's earshot, Rolf was the first to speak

'You obviously survived quite well, Willi. What was it like?'

'At first it was easy,' smiled a relaxed Willi. 'I wangled a pass and got home all right. Then I went into hiding.' He nodded to the pigs. 'Right under ten of those stinking bastards. Jesus, it was awful. Eventually, in March, the Allies came across the river.' Willi shook his head. 'That was a sight to behold. Thousands of vehicles, hundreds of planes. Nothing could have stopped them. They came to the farm and stripped it clean. These pigs and the chickens are all we have. They arrested me and locked me up for a few weeks. I had false identity papers saying I was a private in the *Wehrmacht*. I was beaten up pretty badly by the British. Without Lydia, I don't think I would have survived.' He laughed. 'Anyway, …. what about you, Rolf? What happened?'

As Rolf told his story, they walked across the fields to the fast flowing Rhine. He kept Mengele's message until the end. Then, carefully, he removed the folded map from inside his boot.

'And you say it's a map of the railway yards in Emmerich?' said Willi, turning the map one way and then the other.

'Yes,' replied Rolf.

'You could be right.' He pointed with a dirty finger. 'There's the main station. There's the road bridge over the Rhine and there's the railway line running under the main road.' Carefully folding the map, he handed it back to Rolf. 'Yes, it's about twenty minutes walk from here.' Willi chuckled and stood up, dusting mud of the seat of his worn corduroy trousers. 'I think you and I know a lot about railway yards.' They began to walk back. 'Why are these two wagons special?' he asked quietly.

Rolf took Willi's arm. There was now a slight breeze and a chill in the air. Rolf shivered. 'The two wagons have hidden compartments. They contain Mengele's medical records and mine. Also, certain "gifts".'

Willi gave a soft whistle. 'Christ, Rolf, that stuff's dynamite. If we find it, what the hell are we going to do with it?'

'I don't really know,' replied Rolf, hunching against the breeze. 'Let's find the wagons first and then see what we can do.'

Lydia shouted from the kitchen door and they walked towards her. 'Now, you two,' she said. 'The meal's nearly ready.' She waited until they came through the door. 'Rolf, there's some of Willi's spare clothes for you upstairs.' She frowned. 'I think you may need a bath.'

'Is it that noticeable?' said Rolf. She nodded. 'Excuse me,' he asked. 'May I use your lavatory?'

'At the end of the yard,' said Willi.

Rolf had no trouble excreting the container. It clattered down into the porcelain bowl. Fishing around, he found it. There was a cold water tap and a piece of soap. He managed to clean himself up and then placed the container in his jacket pocket.

They sat down together to Rolf's first decent meal for ten days. Simple food, potatoes, cabbage and slices of smoked ham. Rolf felt a new man. The clothes were a bit baggy but he looked the part of a typical farm worker. Lydia chatted about the farm, food and neighbours. It was as though a war had never happened.

'Rolf,' she said, ' Willi tells me you're a doctor. What're you going to do now the war is over?'

A simple question that Rolf had been thinking about for some time. 'As yet, I'm not so sure.'

Willi felt his hesitancy. 'Listen, my friend, stay with us. Soon I'll need some help getting the hay in. Then I can buy some more chickens and well, …. you know, …… the offer is there.'

Rolf made up his mind. Reaching into his pocket he took out the container. Splitting it open with his finger nail, he tipped the contents onto the wooden table-top. The diamonds rolled into a knot hole and sparkled back up at them.

'Are they real?' whispered Lydia, with wide-open eyes.

'Oh, yes,' said Rolf, gently moving them with his finger tip. Selecting two, he picked them up and placed them on Willi's clean plate. I want you both to have these. It's my way of saying thank you.'

Lydia said, 'Oh, we really couldn't …….. and anyway, where did they come from.'

Rolf saw Willi's startled glance. 'Don't worry, Lydia. They were part of a reward given to us after a battle in Russia.'

Lydia was a woman who knew a lie when she heard one and it increased her worries. 'We still can't take it,' she said firmly.

Willi took her arm. 'Oh yes we bloody well can. We're broke.' Rising from the table, he bent over, picked it up and placed it carefully in a waistcoat pocket. 'I know a man in Emmerich who's in the black market for diamonds.'

'Be careful,' said Rolf sharply, making Lydia glance at him. 'We don't want to arouse any suspicions.'

'That's right,' smiled Willi. Behind Lydia's back, he gave a broad wink. 'come on, Rolf, let's go for a walk. You said you wanted to look around.'

'A good idea,' replied Rolf, standing up. 'Lydia, thanks for the meal.' She glowed and began to clear the table. Willi left the kitchen and went upstairs.

'Rolf, I'm so glad you're staying,' said Lydia, frowning and looking up from the table. 'Willi, has been so lonely since he came back from the Russian front.'

'I understand,' said Rolf with a smile.

The walk to the railway sidings took thirty minutes. It was not a busy place. There were row after row of wagons of all types and sizes. Grass grew under some of the rusting wheels and a lot of the rolling stock was wrecked. Pushing their way past a pile of old sleepers, they came into another part of the sidings.

'Jesus,' whispered Willi, 'we've seen these before haven't we?'

'Yes,' said Rolf staring at the scene before him. Empty, they were different, as though the life had gone out of them. He wondered, whilst he was at Auschwitz, how many of these wagons he had seen.

Cattle wagons by the hundred. All arranged in neat trains of ten. Some looking brand new, others in a dilapidated condition. The rows seemed to stretch for ever. There was silence and the breeze gently moved the dust on the footpaths between the rails.

'Quick, Rolf,' called Willi, 'before somebody comes. .... Where's the map?' He ducked down under a wagon.

Rolf aligned the map so that the end of the tracks to his left were in the correct position. 'Follow me,' he said brusquely and marched off in the direction of the clearly marked arrows. Nearing the point that Mengele had drawn on the map, he slowed down and began to check every wagon. Most of the sliding doors were open. As he hurried past the never ending rows, he glanced into their dark, dank interiors and shivered. He remembered his own brief journey only too well.

It took them over an hour to find what they were looking for. Rolf was on the point of giving up, when he heard Willi call from two rows away. Crawling under the belly of a wagon, he straightened and saw Willi standing on the buffers of another.

'It's here,' he shouted, waving his arms. ' A red "M" just as you said.'

The wagon was no different to any of the others. The doors on each side were wide open and the usual scratches and damage were on the outside timbers. The felting on the curved roof had holes in it. Rolf walked down one side and looked up. Indeed there was a faded red "M", about as big as a hand. Willi jumped down. Together, they scrambled inside.

Rolf looked about him and shivered. He knew this particular wagon had been on the Ramp and the memories filled his soul. Even though the breeze blew through the open doors, he felt the world closing in on him and he began to fall. Willi silently caught his arm and leant him against the wooden walls. When he opened his eyes, he was centimetres away from the dark planks of timber. Blink focusing, he saw scratches running from top to bottom; nail scratches gauged into the wood. Initials, "G.C.", "D.J.C.". Names, one caught his eye, "*Rebecca Cohen*" He wondered who she was and if he had ever met her.

'Rolf, are you all right?' said Willi, anxiously.

Rolf shook his head. 'Just tiredness. Give me a minute or two.'

Willi began to pace round the walls banging and kicking at every plank. Twice he navigated the wagon and, nothing. 'I'm beginning to doubt Mengele,' he muttered. 'I never trusted the bastard anyway.'

Rolf sat on the wooden floor and looked about him. Mengele had clearly said the ends of the wagon. Hearing Willi lashing at the walls with his heavy boots gave no indication as to the truth of Mengele's instructions. Willi joined him on the floor. Rolf nodded and dangled his legs out of the door. The afternoon temperature dropped and he stared at the rows of wagons trying to put himself into Mengele's logical brain.

'Willi' he said and his friend jumped.

'What is it?'

'Go and kneel down inside the end of the wagon.'

'Kneel?' Scrambling to his feet, Willi walked down the wagon. 'You mean, …. like this?' He dropped to his hands and knees.

'Exactly,' said Rolf, standing up and facing the wall. 'I want to stand on your back for a few minutes.'

'What're you trying to do?' Willi was curious.

'The obvious is usually the answer. You've just checked this wall. You did it in a completely normal way. This wagon is higher than you can reach.'

'My God, you're right,' shouted Willi, staring upwards. 'Come on, climb up and have a look.'

Rolf gingerly stepped on Willi's broad back. With his fist, he started tapping. On the second blow there was a hollow response. 'That's it,' he shouted. 'Now we've got to find a way in.' Willi moaned as Rolf jumped off his back.

'Willi, we can't smash our way through these timbers. Mengele would have done it in a clever way. At Auschwitz he had the best cabinet makers to help him' Stepping away from the wall, he stared hard at every joint. Rolf craned upwards and put his finger into a large knot hole just below the roof line. Grunting with the effort, he pressed as hard as he could. 'Yes, ... it works,' he breathed. A soft click echoed round the wagon and part of the wall dropped downwards. Rolf caught it neatly and, together, they stared at what was revealed.

Files stacked hard against steel lined compartments. Layered to provide strength and solidity against casual searches. Rolf looked at the panel of wood in his hand. 'It's perfect,' he said to Willi. 'Every plank is grooved and precisely matched. And it's backed in aluminium to stop dampness.' He looked up at the files. 'Look at that.' He shook his head in amazement. 'Each one is placed on its own rack and catalogued.' Rolf reached up and took out a small notebook. 'This is the central card index. It's all in here, every detail of three years work. .... Amazing.'

'Rolf,' said Willi with a grin. 'Your mentioned other things. You know, "gifts".'

Rolf pushed files gently to one side and peered down into the cavity behind the remaining wall. 'Nothing in here. Let's try the next wagon.' Slotting the section of wall back into place, Rolf waited for the satisfying click as it locked. Together they jumped out of the wagon and searched for the second "M" mark.

'Got it,' said Rolf with a grin. 'It's the next one, just as Mengele said it would be.' In the next fifteen minutes, they found and removed the panels of the four ends of the wagons. Rolf laughed aloud when he saw his own neat writing and meticulous notes.

'Ah, ah,' he said.

'What is it?' said Willi, peering over Rolf's shoulder.

'I think I've found what we've been looking for.' Rolf replied with a smile.

Another panel moved smoothly out of place and there in neat boxes were carefully bound packages of all shapes and sizes. Rolf selected the biggest and laid it on the floor. Pulling the thick strings, he let the oiled wrappings fall lose.

He took a step backwards and drew in his breath. 'My God,' he exclaimed.

'It's a painting,' said Willi. 'Just a painting.'

'It's not just a painting,' said Rolf quietly. 'It's a Rembrandt.'

FIFTY-ONE

'Good evening,' said Richard staring straight into the man's eyes.

'I hear from Hans, that Jan is unwell again,' said Willi Schmidt. Richard glared at him.

'What exactly is wrong with Mr Bildt?' asked Jane, curiously.

'It's Hepatitis,' he replied. 'A disease he caught during the war in Russia. We had virtually no medicine in those days. Probably infection from some dirty needle in a syringe used by some foul Russian.'

'Is it serious?' said Jane.

Walking past her, he picked up a glass of wine from the table and turned to face them. 'It's fatal,' he replied. 'How he's lived this long, I do not know. Most people with Hepatitis die within a few years.' He sipped at the wine. 'He lives from day to day. In ten minutes,' he pointed with the glass, 'he'll walk though that door and look as well as when you first saw him this evening. Tomorrow, he could be dead.' He smiled. 'Now, Mrs Cooper, no doubt, you're wondering who the hell I am?'

Jane was defensive. 'I know you're a very close friend of Jan Bildt, or should we call him Rolf Müller?' The man shrugged. She looked him full in the face. 'My husband and I have reason to believe that he was an *SS* doctor who committed barbarous acts at the Auschwitz-Birkenau Concentration Camp.' She paused long enough for him to stare hard at her. 'What's more, we know your real name is *SS-Hauptsturmführer* Willi Hossler and you assisted *SS- Sturmbannführer* Rolf Müller in these criminal acts.'

He shook his head and swirled the wine round in the glass. His eyes were as cold as ice and his face held a mocking smile. 'Mrs Cooper, you make very grave accusations. Rolf and I were corporals in the *Wehrmacht*. Nothing more and nothing less. You're a lawyer and you know you can't prove anything without evidence.' Tipping his head back, he drained the glass. 'Where's your evidence?'

Jane did not answer.

Willi Schmidt sat down, crossing his long legs. 'I always thought the English were so well mannered. Jan invites you into his home to tell you, after fifty long years, that he's Richard's father and, all you can do, is accuse him of war crimes. Nowadays, with all this Nazi gold nonsense, it's quite fashionable to make such accusations.'

Richard watched Schmidt carefully. Then he went to the table and selected a thin slice of cheese. 'You talk of evidence,' he said. 'Where's the evidence that Müller is my father?'

Willi Schmidt was dressed in a beautifully cut, dark grey suit. Gucci loafers over silk socks. Broad shoulders and a balding head. He looked superbly fit. His English had all the correct inflections and the accent came from the very best language school.

An smile played over his face and the eyes softened. 'The evidence is with your mother, Mr Cooper. She has, I'm sure, told you exactly who your real father is. I'm sure Simon Cooper was a wonderful man, even though he was a Jew.' Richard felt his hackles rise. 'He left you some money when he died. What was it? £200,000, £250,000? Have you ever thought where a country town lawyer got such amounts from?' He raised his hand. 'Before you interrupt me, I want to tell you a story. ... At the end of the war, Germany was a ruin. Rolf and I had lost everything. Before the war, I had a small farm and when I returned to it, there was nothing. The British had taken all my livestock and the fields were overgrown. Rolf and I worked very, very hard and we built our farms up to what you see today.' He nodded. 'I suppose you could say we're one of the best examples of the German economic miracle.' He turned to look directly at Richard. 'You think you're reasonably well off. But as Jan's only heir, you'll be fabulously rich when he dies. .... You know he's named you as his heir?'

Richard's anger boiled out. 'I didn't know and I don't want his damned blood money. I'm more than happy with what my father left me. My wife and I wanted to come here to find out the truth from Müller. It seems that the truth is not to be found.'

Willi Schmidt uncrossing his legs, rose to his feet. 'Mr Cooper,' he said softly, 'no matter what you say or think, Rolf Müller is dying and you're his only son. At least have some modicum of consideration for a dying man.'

The door opened quietly and they all turned. Rolf Müller was just as Willi Schmidt said he would be. The smile was warm and the manner as gracious as ever. 'Ah, Willi, I see you've been entertaining our guests.' He walked unsteadily to a chair and lowered himself into it. 'I'm very sorry about my little upset. We old soldiers have war wounds to cope with. .... Now, where were we? .... Ah, yes, Mrs Cooper. We were talking about war crimes.' Jane shook her head. 'Germany will have this black shadow hanging over her forever. It is time to forget and forgive the past, because it's all a very long time ago and we must learn to go forward together. Great Britain and Germany are the masters of Europe. Together, we can lead Europe to become the most powerful economic force in the world.'

'I've heard that before,' said Richard quietly.

'Two wars between our countries haven't solved anything. Although, some races within Europe will never rise again. They deserve not to rise again because of their negative influences on our cultures.' He sighed. 'No, my dear Richard, war does not provide greatness; economic power does. The British and the Germans have the finest inventive geniuses in the world. For example, over the last fifty years, German medical research is second to none.' He paused to take a deep breath and hunched forward. 'I'm a rich man and, several years ago, I formed a new political association here in my home. Via my contacts, the idea is spreading across Germany. I am allied with Le Penn in France and several, shall we say, interested parties in Britain. The association is called, the Pan-European League and it's main purpose is to join the city-states of Europe into one super state with Germany and Great Britain as co-leaders.' He raised his voice slightly. 'Richard, you're my only son and you are German but brought up and educated in Britain. Surely the best of both worlds? You're my natural heir and I have approval from my supporters for me to name my successor. … I want you to be that person.' He dropped back into the chair, wiping his forehead with his hand.

'Rolf Müller,' said Richard very slowly. 'I can inform you here and now, that I'm not interested in your ideas and I completely reject your proposals.' Jane flashed a glance at him. Richard placed his wine glass back on the table, turned to Jane and said, 'Jane, I think it's time we left for our hotel. We've had a busy couple of days.'

Müller nodded and pushed a hand unsteadily through his hair. 'I understand your feelings completely. If I was you, I would've said exactly the same thing. I've worried about this day for fifty years. I've had you followed, checked on and photographed. I've engaged in subterfuges concerning your upbringing that I would never have dreamt of carrying out. I am an unhappy father that wants the love of his only son. Maybe that love will come when I'm gone and that time is not far away.'

Jane nodded. '*Herr* Müller and *Herr* Schmidt, Richard and I would like to thank you for your hospitality …. but we really must leave.'

Müller nodded and rose from his chair. 'All right. I hope this is not the last time we meet. Perhaps you could do me the honour of calling at my home in the morning to say farewell. I've tried my hardest to ask you both to regard my home as yours.' His head dropped and then lifted again. 'I've failed in my mission. Hans will see you to your car. Good night to you both.' He offered his hand to Jane and she shook it. Richard was a little slower and Müller's eyes looked straight into his. Then they shook hands. Richard felt a strange shiver go down his spine.

Richard and Jane checked-in to the Millingen Centrum Hotel. On the journey from *"Grosse Bauernhof"* they had said little to each other. Jane began to unpack.

'Richard, I'm more confused than I ever was.'

'I'm not,' replied Richard tersely. 'He's a lying bastard and I know it.'

'Evidence, evidence, evidence,' she said, hanging up a skirt. 'Has it ever occurred to you, that he could be telling the truth about the SS? After all, your mother's statements match his.'

Richard flopped onto the bed and sighed. 'I know, I know.' He tapped his chest. '….. In here, he's lying. Don't ask me how, …… I just know.'

'Müller …..,' she began.

Richard grunted. 'I see you now call him, Müller.'

'Yes,' replied Jane calmly, 'I'm sure that's his real name. Müller's a very sick man with not much time to live.' She placed her hand on Richard's shoulder. 'Surely, …. can't you just acknowledge that he's you father? It would help him to die in peace.'

Richard looked up at her. 'If there was no suggestion he was an SS war criminal, then I would happily do so. Because I can't prove what he is, I can't admit to being his son.'

Jane walked to the mirror and began brushing her hair. 'All right, I understand.' She sighed. 'I need a stiff drink. Let's go down to the bar.' Richard nodded.

The bar was small and busy. Collecting their drinks, they walked to an empty table near to the windows.

'I love the way the Dutch never close their curtains,' said Jane, looking through the glass into the narrow street. Richard did not answer her and she turned to find out why. A woman was standing at the side of their table.

'Good evening,' she said in English, to Richard. 'I'm sorry to interrupt you. Are you the man who called at my house a week ago to ask the way to Millingen?'

Richard rose from his chair. 'Yes, I am.' Then he smiled. 'I remember now. …. You're the person who gave me the directions. You live in that rather nice white house.' The woman hesitated, not knowing quite what to say. Richard turned to Jane and she raised a quizzical eyebrow. 'Why don't you join us?' he asked. 'You're very welcome.'

'Well, ….. yes please,' she replied. 'If that's all right. We don't get many English people in our small town. But, …. I'm with my daughter.'

'Please bring her as well,' said Richard, leaning forward to pull out two spare chairs. The woman returned. 'My name is Marijke Wulffraat and my daughter is called Manja.' Richard introduced himself and Jane and they all sat down. 'Did you find what you were looking for? Wasn't it some farm?' she asked politely.

'Actually,' replied Richard, 'I did find it. It's called *"Grosse Bauernhof"* near Bimmen.'

Her daughter nudged her. 'Mr Cooper,' said the woman, eyebrows raised, 'the place you mention is very well known around here.'

'Why is that?' said Richard, taking a mouthful of brandy.

'Pigs.' She grinned. 'They stink, we're always complaining but nothing ever happens.'

'Is it a big farm?'

'Big enough. The land extends for kilometres back off the main road. I've driven past it many times on my way for shopping in Kleve. There are rumours that the owner has armed guards patrolling the grounds.'

'Armed guards?' said Jane, speaking for the first time.

'So the rumours go. He's only been there ten years or so ......'

'Ten years!' interrupted Richard. 'Are you sure?'

'Oh, yes,' she replied quickly. 'Before then, it'd been very run down. Almost, what's the word? ....Yes, ... derelict.'

Richard wanted time to think, he glanced around the bar and saw happy people enjoying themselves. 'Where did the owner come from? Before taking over *"Grosse Bauernhof"*?'

'I'm not so sure,' she replied. 'My daughter knows, because the father of one her friends did some of the restoration work on the house.

The girl blushed. 'I'm sorry, my English is not very good,' she said, falteringly.

'Sounds fine to me,' said Jane, with an encouraging smile.

'The man was in medicine,' the girl added.

'A doctor?' said Richard, quickly.

'No, not a doctor. .... Eh, ... drugs, medicine drugs. You know, pills that kind of thing. He had factories and lorries. He has photographs in his house. That is how I know.'

'Thank you very much,' said Richard. 'Please can I buy you both a drink?'

The woman looked at her watch and shook her head. 'That's very kind of you, but no thank you. We have to return home because our dog needs his walk.'

Richard rose and shook hands with her. 'It's been nice to meet you.'

'Oh yes,' she said with a slight blush. 'If you get lost again, please call at my house. *Tot ziens.*' She and her daughter left the bar.

'Richard Cooper,' said Jane, shaking her head. 'Why is it women are so attracted to you?'

'It's my intelligence and natural charm,' he replied, slipping his hand into hers. 'Do have another drink.' They had another drink and then tiredness began to overtake them.

As Jane left the shower, she yawned. 'I may be tired but I want to finish off reading Simon's diary.' She busied herself, gently brushing her hair and carrying out those feminine bedtime routines that men like to watch.

"Would you like a cigarette?" I heard myself saying and I thought what a stupid question it was.

She smiled and replied, "No, thank you but I would certainly like something to eat."

"Of course," I said, realising she must be very hungry. "Please come with me. My barrack is not far from here."

Taking a step towards me, she tilted her head. "German nationals are not allowed into Allied barracks."

"You will be in this one." I took her hand. I didn't notice her smell and her clothes. She looked worn out.

We walked for a kilometre. The military police on the gate only let me in when I said that Ulrika had to be interrogated. The men in the cookhouse were more than helpful. At the back door, they gave Ulrika some bread.

Later, I took her to a place where I knew Germans were being looked after. It wasn't very nice but I was helpless to do anything else to help. I remember the smile on her face as she said good-bye.

I thought I'd lost her. For a week or so, I was involved in war crime investigations. I tried to find the records from Auschwitz but to no avail, the Russians had taken the lot. The search for Müller's brother was useless. I knew then I'd let Lottie Cohen down. Every day, I went back to where I'd last seen Ulrika; she was never there. On a last chance hope, I went to the guard on the gate, he recognised me.

"Yes sir. That Fraülein you were with last week," he said, stiffly to attention. "She's been back twice and I told her she wasn't allowed in here. Sorry sir, orders are orders. No German nationals."

"What time of the day was she here?"

He screwed up his face with concentration. "Oh, I'd say about ... 1400 hours, sir." A glance at the guard room clock told me I had an hour to wait.

I sat in my jeep and watched. The rain was sleeting down in buckets and I was sure she would never come. I reached for the starter and, as the engine turned over, I saw her. She was huddled under an old coat. I was out of the jeep in an instant and running across the road. She turned and saw me. In the pouring rain we looked at each other. She was much tidier than the last time we met and her face was more beautiful than I remembered.

"Simon," she said quietly, "is it really you?"

I just threw my arms around her and held her close. It was all I could do and all I wanted to do. I don't know how long we stood there for and then I heard somebody shouting. I turned, it was the corporal from the guardroom.

"Bring her in here, sir," he shouted to me. "You'll catch your death of cold." I laughed. The English have always amazed me.

I've never regarded the Military Police as friendly beings but these two could not have been nicer. Within a minute, they had a clean towel for Ulrika to dry her face and two big mugs of hot, sweet tea.

"Sir, we're going out on duty," smiled one of them and they left us alone.

There was a coal fire glowing in a stove set against the wall. We sat together, steaming in the heat of the fire, gripping the mugs of tea in our hands. She looked up and smiled.

"I'm so glad I found you again."

"I'm glad you found me." I nodded towards the rain-streaked window. "How are you coping with life out there?"

"It's hard. The Allies are bringing in supplies by train for us and local farmers are selling food on the black market."

I was curious. "Where's the food coming from?"

The smile faded from her face. "It's mainly preserved food from Holland. It was taken by our soldiers last winter and brought to Germany." I connected the comment with my experience and ignored it.

She had the finest hair I'd ever seen. Stretching out my hand, I touched it.

"My hair feels much better now I've washed it," she said, self-consciously. Then she sighed and smiled. "Now, please tell me about yourself?"

It was a simple request and my tea was cold before I'd finished telling her.

"You say your Jewish?"

"Yes. ... What about your background, Ulrika? Are you from Berlin"

Her story was shorter than mine. She told it clearly and precisely. Again I knew there were missing parts of her recent life. We both needed our privacy. "Look here," I said. "I'd like to see more of you. Would you like to come out with me tomorrow night. I know of a place where's there's music and dancing."

She gave a worried frown. "Simon," she said. "I'd love to come out with you but I've nothing to wear. Only what I stand up in."

I slipped my arm around her waist and felt her warm thinness. "All I've got to wear is my uniform and, please believe me, it doesn't matter what you come dressed in. You'll look beautiful in anything."

She blushed and leant over and kissed me gently on the cheek. Putting my mug on the floor, I reached across, held her and kissed her full on the mouth. We kissed a little more. I jumped when one of the soldiers came through the door.

"Excuse me, sir," he said politely. It was time for Ulrika and I to go.

I took her back to the hostel where she was staying. At least I knew she was safe. We kissed again and I felt that this woman was very special.

Later that night, I went for a drink in the mess. My friend was there. He walked across with the usual two double gins and grinned. "Hello, Simon how are you?"

"Fine thanks." I took the glass from him. "Cheers."

"Cheers." The smile vanished and his face became serious. "Listen, old boy." When he used those words, I knew it was something serious. "I hear on the grape-vine, you're seeing a Fraülein. *Is it true?"*

"Yes."

"I'm sorry to tell you this." He chewed quickly at his bushy moustache. "Officially fraternisation is forbidden. Monty has issued orders that members of the Allied forces must not mix with the Germans. Sorry but that's how it is."

It made me angry. "What absolute rubbish. I've seen soldiers walking down the Unter den Linden *hand in hand with German girls. The Americans have no such orders. Why the hell can't we be treated in the same way?"*

"Well, as I said, that's the official line." He swallowed a mouthful of the gin and smiled. "It must be love at first sight. Now, tell me, ... what's she's like?"

We chatted and the gin flowed. I went to bed at midnight and unashamedly dreamt about her. In the morning, I went about my duties of interviewing and interrogation with little real enthusiasm. The day could not go quickly enough.

The beir keller *was an old hotel that some crafty German had painted and changed into a kind of Berlin night club. It was a place used by allied officers. There were all sorts of girls waiting outside. I thought Ulrika hadn't turned up and then I saw her waiting some distance away.*

She looked really worried. "Are you sure I'm allowed in here?"

"Don't be silly," I said, taking her hand. "Let's go and enjoy ourselves."

In the bright lights inside the entrance, I looked at her. Her blonde hair was piled up onto her head showing the snowy white nape of her neck lined with the tiniest of curls. I found her very exciting. She wore a long blue dress that was too big for her but, somehow, she'd managed to tie it in a special way. There was not a speck of make-up on her face and the fact that she was so pale enhanced her simple beauty. We danced all night and drank quite a bit. I gave her cigarettes and chocolates and a pair of nylon stockings I'd swapped for a bottle of whisky. The real gift were the cigarettes. In Berlin they were better than gold and I knew she'd be able to live for several weeks on the black market. After midnight, I took her back to the hostel and we kissed like teenagers.

Life went on and I saw her nearly every day. I managed to find a tiny apartment near the Zoo and soon we were almost living together. Fraternisation was everywhere and nobody gave a damn. One night I was in the mess having a drink with my friend.

"I've got a question I want to ask," I said to him.

"It must be illegal," he replied with a grin.

"I want to marry Ulrika. Is it allowed?"

Preening his handlebar moustache with his fingers gave him time to think. "Interesting question, Simon. A very interesting question. Officially, no, you can't get married. Unofficially any German priest could marry you but you'd find it very difficult to get her out of Germany to England. Certainly as an officer, you'd find it impossible to obtain permission..

"Hang on," I said. "I'm Dutch, I'm a lawyer and I'm a Jew."

"Yes you are but you're still a serving officer in the Allied forces and bound by orders from Montgomery." He finished his gin. "I rest my case. Anyway, have you asked her yet? Because if you haven't, I think you'll find she won't marry you."

Just as I suspected, he was completely wrong. A month later a Catholic priest secretly married us in the ruins of a beautiful church near Lake Havel. We lived, quite unofficially, in the small apartment not far from my barracks. Everybody knew but nobody complained about me because I wasn't the only one.

One day, Ulrika wanted to give me something special. She presented me with a small steel box. When I opened it, I couldn't believe what I saw. It was a single diamond. The biggest one I'd ever seen. Ulrika told me it was from her uncle and she had managed to save it. Without any thought, I believed her. I remembered the diamonds Müller had found. Perhaps diamonds were the only currency that the Germans regarded as safe. I didn't hand this one over to the authorities. It was our nest-egg for my future law practise.

I became even more involved in the investigations leading up to the

Nuremberg War Trials. Edvard Müller had long since been taken back to Holland and I had to write out all sorts of statements about him and send them off to the Hague. I didn't shed any tears when I heard he'd been executed. In all my searches, I'd found no trace of his brother. Seyss-Inquart didn't last long, he was arrested by the British and imprisoned.

On another day in July, I heard the best personal news I could have ever received. Ulrika told me she was pregnant. We had a party in our apartment and our friends came. She was so happy and one of my doctor friends checked her out and said mother and baby were fine. I'm so glad we were married. I began to think of where the baby was going to be born and we both decided it would have a better chance in England. It's strange but I now regarded England as home. Holland seemed to be important but it just wasn't 'home'. The International War Trials were going to take place at Nuremberg and it meant I was away from Ulrika a great deal.

In October 1945, I spent two days interviewing Seyss-Inquart at an interrogation camp near Frankfurt. Not once did I hear him admit to any sort of crime. In fact, at one point, he pleaded mitigating circumstances because he had tried to save Holland from Hitler's scorched earth policy at the end of the war. In my opinion, he was guilty of all the charges that were laid against the Germans at the impending trials.

We had Christmas in Berlin and I was almost beginning to feel at home in the city. Orders concerning the marrying of German nationals were relaxed in early 1946 and we were able to travel to England. I returned to the north west and we lived in an RAF married quarters near Southport on the Irish Sea coast. Our son, Richard, was born on January 30, 1946. What a day! We had started our own family! Richard was beautiful and we sat for days watching him. I only had a week's leave.

I was ordered back to Germany again and continued assisting in the preparations at Nuremberg. I was beginning to lose interest in the whole thing. Many of the middle order Nazis had escaped or had just got away with murder. Still, I was involved with Seyss-Inquart and I had to send regular reports back to Holland. Europe was beginning to heal itself and all I wanted to do was to get demobbed and go back and set up my law practise. Richard was growing rapidly and Ulrika sent me letters every day with photographs; I was so proud. Then I was told that I was going to leave the army but only on condition that I would be recalled if, needed, during the trials. We set up home in Ormskirk, a small town in the County of Lancashire. We were so happy.

I was called back to Nuremberg just before the sentences were passed down to the 22 Nazi leaders. Only three were acquitted. He was found guilty and sentenced to death by hanging. Seyss-Inquart had often asked me if his son, who had served in the German armed forces, was still alive. I received a letter from the Russian delegation telling me that his son had been found alive in the USSR and I agreed to take the message to him. When I saw him, he was a changed man and said he regretted the 'fearful excesses of the Reich.' I gave him the message and he broke down and wept with joy.

On October 16, 1946, the executions were carried out under cover in the prison gymnasium of the Nuremberg court house where the trails had taken place. Seyss-Inquart's final words were selfless. Before he was hanged at 2-57pm, he said, 'I hope that this execution is the last act of the tragedy of the Second World War, and that a lesson will be learnt so that peace and understanding will be realised among the nations. I believe in Germany.' His body, when cut down from the gallows, was taken with the others, and, as rumour has it, burnt in the gas ovens at Dachau Concentration Camp and the ashes scattered to the four winds.

1st November 1946

<u>*Postscript*</u>   *22nd November*

Something strange happened today. I received a heavily franked envelope with German stamps. It contained a single sheet of paper with the words:

To Majoor Simon Cohen. Thank you for your kindness.

Artur Seyss-Inquart.   16 October 1946

I kept it as a souvenir.

FIFTY-TWO

'A Rembrandt,' said Willi. 'Even I know what a Rembrandt is. Are you sure?'

'Absolutely sure,' replied Rolf, picking it up from the wooden floor.

The portrait of an old man with a brown velvet hat hanging over his lined face, stared back at them. Dark, glowing browns, bright highlights of vivid yellows and flesh pinks that seemed alive. The swirl of the signature was unmistakable. Both men looked at it in silence. Rolf turned it over. On the back, In neat gothic print were the words, *Rijksmuseum-Amsterdam 2386.*

'How the hell did Mengele get hold of this?' breathed Willi.

'Favours for people in high places. Josef Mengele had fingers in many pies.' Rolf put his nose close to the rich surface and inhaled. 'That smell is unmistakable.'

'Yep,' quipped Willi, 'the smell of money.'

Rolf laughed and carefully re-wrapped the Rembrandt. 'Let's see what other little "gifts" the good doctor left for us.' The whole lower end of the false panel was stuffed full of priceless antiques. Gold plate, squashed flat. Massive silver ornaments and neat packets of different gems. Unmarked gold ingots and wads of currency.

'Jesus Christ' said Willi with a beaming face. 'With this lot we could buy the whole of Germany.'

Richard pushed it all back into the space. 'No, we can't do that,' he said, matter of factly.

'Why not?'

'If we walked into a German town with any of this loot, then the military police would be onto us very quickly.' Rolf thought for a moment. 'No, what we have to do, is move these two wagons to somewhere safe and store them away until things have quietened down.'

Willi scratched his head and laughed. 'I suppose you're right. But they're a bit big to push back to the farm.'

Black clouds scudded across the sky and rain threatened. Rolf looked again at the first wagon and he was surprised to find his own files. All neatly labelled in his own hand.

'What is it?' shouted Willi from outside. 'Any more gold?'

'No, just papers.'

'Burn the lot,' he called back. 'It's evidence.'

Rolf spent twenty minutes looking at his own work and that of Mengele's. He had not realised just how much they had achieved. Rolf shook his head, when he saw his signature everywhere. On the 1944 Ramp lists, certificates of death and jottings about individuals. For a moment, Rolf thought about burning the whole lot and then he stopped. The research and the records were, as Mengele had said, of tremendous value. Fitting everything back into place, he jumped out of the wagon onto the track.

Willi, leaning against a stack of old sleepers, smiled. 'Quite a day, Rolf.'

'Yes, indeed,' he replied. 'Now we've got to try and work out how we can move them to a secure place.'

'Look here,' said Willi. 'Let's go home. After all, they've been here for months a few days won't matter.'

They walked between the rows of wagons, pulling up the collars of their old coats against the wind. Rolf was lost in thought and Willi sensed it. As they cut across a rusty length of track, they saw a fire burning and thick black smoke billowing into the sky. Willi, ducked behind a small worker's hut. Rolf was curious.

'Willi,' he called out, 'let's find out what's happening.'

There were four men, older than Rolf and Willi. The fire was burning fiercely as they threw on railway sleepers and timber from the wagons. One of them saw Rolf and they all turned to stare. Rolf nodded. 'Hello. Do you mind if we have a warm at your fire?'

The oldest one shrugged his shoulders. That's all right.' He kicked listlessly at the embers. 'Where're you from?'

Rolf made up some story about working on a farm, which was not too far from the truth.

'Are you ex-*Wehrmacht*?' asked one of the others. He wore a dirty grey *Wehrmacht* greatcoat.

'Yep, that's right,' replied Rolf, picking up a splinter of timber and throwing it on the fire.

'You don't look like *Wehrmacht*,' he muttered.

Rolf stared hard at the man's face and he quickly looked away. 'Listen,' Rolf said, they turned to face him. 'What's going to happen to all these wagons?'

The oldest one spoke again. 'They're no good. Most of 'em are rotted or just sitting here. The connection to the main line is gone, the British blew it up. We sell them for firewood and scrap iron. There's a few more men in the workshops over there.' He pointed back towards the town. His face screwed up with curiosity. 'Why do you ask?'

Rolf put his hand in his pocket and produced a solid silver antique spoon. It gleamed in the flickering light of the fire. 'My friend and I need two wagons urgently,' said Rolf. 'I would like to buy them and have them moved. Can you do that?'

With smiles all round, the man licked his lips. 'Dead easy, my friend. We unbolt the wagons off the bogeys and transport them wherever you want us to. Mind you, it'll cost you more than what you've got in your hand.' Rolf nodded and took out another spoon. 'It's a deal,' said the man, reaching for the spoons.

'Oh, no,' said Rolf, sharply. 'You'll get the other spoon, when we've finished.'

The rain poured down and they walked back to the farm. Lydia had a meal waiting for them. Willi showed Rolf to his bedroom and left him alone to change. When he came downstairs, Willi and Lydia were waiting for him.

'Willi tells me you've found a few things that will help us for the future?' said Lydia, ladling out a bowlful of soup.

'Yes,' replied Rolf, blowing on a spoonful of hot soup. 'It's something I had sent from Berlin before I left.'

She smiled and looked hard at their faces. 'You two are up to something and I'm with you all the way. What exactly is it?'

Rolf swallowed the soup and carefully laid his spoon on the table. 'Lydia, Willi, we are going to be very rich. I can't do anything for a long time, it could be years. Whilst I'm waiting, I want to stay here and help you and Willi on the farm. There'll be times when I have to leave on business.'

'That's not a problem,' she said, refilling his bowl.

'Lydia,' said Willi, taking a deep breath, 'I want to tell you, that as SS officers, the Allies are looking for us. We both have very good false identities and, so far, we've managed to avoid anybody finding us.'

She shrugged her shoulders and grinned. 'That's not a surprise. Anyway, I'd managed to work it out.'

Rolf turned to look at Willi. 'If anybody comes to look for me. Then both of you must deny all knowledge of me. Do you understand?'

'Absolutely.'

'A woman may come looking for me.'

'You mean the woman you knew in Berlin?' Willi flashed a wink.

'Yes.' Rolf, tapped his finger on the table. 'Not a single word of what we were, or what we did, or what we've found, must ever leave this house.' His gaze turned to Lydia. 'It's a matter of life and death to all of us.'

'I understand,' she replied, with shining eyes.

Rolf rose from the table and picked up his glass of watery beer. Standing rigidly to attention, he said softly, 'Willi, Lydia, I give you a toast.' They rose to their feet. 'To Germany and the Fatherland.'

FIFTY-THREE

The day was overcast and it rained intermittently. Richard and Jane sat at breakfast with the few other guests. He had not slept well. Dreams about faces and people constantly woke him.

'I still think we ought to go,' said Jane, finishing her coffee. 'Whatever we've found out, can't do any harm now.' She looked up at his face. 'Can it?'

'I suppose not. Last night I dreamt about Simon. It was as though, having finished reading his notes, he was still here with me.' Richard, resting his head in his hands for a few moments, looked up. 'Come on then. Let's get it over with so we can go home. I'm missing the children and I'm missing home.' Taking her hand, they left the dining-room and went to reception. Checking-out took ten minutes.

The rain had stopped but everywhere was still wet. Richard helped Jane on with her raincoat and she opened the door of the car and stepped inside. Richard drove back over the German border and hardly spoke a word. As they turned into the gravel drive of "*Grosse Bauernhof*", he stopped the car and turned to face her. 'Jane, I don't want to stay long.'

She smiled. 'I understand, darling. I just want you to do one thing.'

Richard frowned. 'What's that?'

'Please be courteous?'

Leaning sideways in his seat, Richard kissed her gently on the cheek. 'Don't worry, in my mind the whole thing is over and done with.'

She held his face with both hands. 'Thank you for saying that. But I know it'll never be over.'

Smiling back at her, he slipped the Volvo into gear and drove up the drive. As he stepped out of the car, he paused and looked at the house. There was no movement from anywhere and even the birds were silent. It reminded him of something he had read about Auschwitz; it was a place where the birds don't sing. When he had first seen "*Grosse Bauernhof*", he had thought it beautiful. But now it was a dark dismal place with no life about it.

Jane took his arm. 'Come on.' They walked together to the front door.

Before they reached for the bell pull, the doors opened. Willi Schmidt stood in front of them. 'Good morning,' he said, quietly. 'Do come in, I'm glad you came.' Richard sensed something was wrong. Schmidt's face was pale and his voice dropped to a whisper. 'I have to tell you that Rolf is seriously ill.' He shook his head. 'In fact, I'm surprised that he's lasted the night. Mr Cooper, he's asked to see you as soon as you arrive. Would you follow me please?' Without waiting for a reply, he turned his back and walked across the hall to the stairs. Jane took Richard's arm and they followed him. Down a long gloomy corridor lined with old paintings and thick carpets. Willi Schmidt stopped outside a door at the end. Hans stood guard outside his master's bedroom. Without a change of expression, or a spoken word, he opened the door and stepped to one side.

The bedroom was huge and exceptionally ornate. Dark, wood-panelled walls gave out a sombre atmosphere. Heavy curtains cut out the daylight from tall windows, making all eyes concentrate on the one light at the side of the bed. Against the wall farthest from the door, stood an old four-poster, with the drapes closed on three sides,

As Richard walked across the room, his nose wrinkled. It was a cloying smell he remembered from Simon's final hours; the smell of impending death. Rolf Müller lay propped up on a pile of pillows. He wore a white, old-fashioned night-shirt drawn tight round his neck by silken cords. The suntan of the day before had gone, to be replaced by a deathly yellow pallor. Lank grey hair lay on the pillow. Richard stood at the side of the bed. Müller heard the footsteps and his eyes opened.

His voice was a feeble whisper. 'Is that you, Richard?'

'Yes.'

There was a long exhalation of breath. 'I'm so glad you came.' He muttered something in German and his eyes closed. Richard leant over the bed and strained to hear the words. Müller's mouth lay half-open but nothing came out. A string of yellow spittle dribbled from between his lips. Richard stepped back, holding his nose.

'May I suggest,' said Willi Schmidt, respectfully, 'that you and Mrs Cooper might like to wait downstairs? Rolf keeps lapsing in and out of consciousness. I'll call you back when he's fully awake.' Hans opened the door and waited. As Richard walked back towards the door, he suddenly stopped and stared at the small picture hanging on the wall directly opposite Müller's bed. For a full half-minute, he stared at it and then he turned away, taking Jane's hand.

They waited alone in the long dining-room. For a moment, neither of them spoke, then Richard turned to face her. 'The picture on the wall was a Rembrandt.'

Jane's mouth dropped open. 'A Rembrandt? Are you sure?'

'Absolutely sure. It looked like a self-portrait to me.' He folded his arms. 'How the hell does he have a Rembrandt hanging in his bedroom?'

'He is a very rich man, Richard. It's quite possible he bought it at some time in the past.'

'This man is a doctor and was a major in the SS. How does he get enough money to buy a Rembrandt?' He paused and a slow smile spread across his face. 'Unless, of course, it was Nazi loot from the Jews.'

Jane shook her head. 'You just can't let go, can you. Fifty years ago, Rembrandts were probably cheap enough to buy on the open market.'

'Rembrandts have never been cheap and few private people can afford to buy one.' Richard shook his head and ground a balled fist into his palm. 'This could be the answer. If we can prove the Rembrandt is stolen and we can find the name of the last owner, then we can prove who Müller really is.'

'Richard, Richard, stop it,' Jane said, loudly. 'Previous proof of ownership will prove nothing at all. Unless it used to belong to a national museum.' She reached out and took his hand. 'Look here, Müller is dying: let it be.'

Richard let go of her hand and walked across the carpet to the long windows. 'It's stopped raining,' he said. 'The atmosphere in this place is getting on top of me. Come on, let's go for a walk.' Turning the heavy iron handle, he stepped out onto a stone terrace.

Outside the wind had dropped to a gentle breeze and the heavy rain clouds had moved away. There was an earthy smell in the air and the ground underfoot was wet. Richard and Jane walked arm in arm off the patio and away from the looming rear of the house.

After twenty minutes, Jane stopped. 'Don't you think we'd better be getting back?' At the precise moment she spoke, the first heavy rain drop fell on her head. Then another and another until Richard grabbed her arm.

'Quick. ….. We must find a shelter or else we'll get soaked.' He stared about him. 'Over there! … Look over there.' He pointed to a low wooden structure half hidden by heavy foliage and thick ivy. They ran hand in hand with the rain just beginning to pour. Breathless, they managed to run through the half-open door.

Richard stopped dead and turned to look for Jane. She was at his side. An awful sense of foreboding came over him. He looked around. A wooden hut higher than head height with a curving roof and dark timber sides. Old wooden boxes piled in the corners. On the wall opposite the door, through which they had entered, was another door. This one closed and overgrown with ivy tentacles. Richard's clenched his fists. He looked hard into the gloom. On both sides of the hut, just below the roof, were two small windows. Each one barred and blocked with foliage. A heavy cloud outside stopped most of the daylight from entering and the rain beat down on the roof like a drum. Richard moved and felt the heavy air holding him back.

'Richard, what is it?' said Jane, worriedly.

'Shush.'

Walking back to the door, he pushed it, nothing happened. Placing his back against the frame he reached out with one leg, placed a foot against the door and pushed; with a groan, the door slid back.

'Holy mother of God,' he said softly.

He tried to calm himself and walked slowly across the broken floor. The other door moved much more easily. Richard ran back across to the other door. He was muttering something Jane could not hear. Stepping half out of the hut, he began to pull the ivy creeper away from the outer wooden walls.

'Oh, no!' he shouted, turning pale. 'Oh, my God, no!'

'Richard,' said Jane with panic on her face. 'What is it?'

With drooping shoulders and rain streaming down his face, he shook his head from side to side. 'Look,' he said angrily. 'Look there. On that piece of timber, underneath the branch.'

Jane looked hard and then, as one heavy cloud moved away from the sunlight, she saw the faintly painted words.

"Deutsche Reichsbahn"

Pulling again at the creeper, Richard tore strings of it away and then he stared at the timber walls. Many curling pieces of paper held on by rusting nails. Pulling one away, he showed it to Jane.

'Read it,' he shouted, with the two words grinding out from behind clenched teeth.

'I can't see what it says,' she said, trying to hold the crumbling paper flat in her palm.

'Read the letters.'

'I can make out an "A", as "S", and "H" and then "W", yes I think it's a "T" and a "Z".' Then it dawned on her. 'Oh, Richard! Oh, no! It says, "AUSCHWITZ"'

Richard snatched the shreds of paper. 'What we're standing in, is a cattle wagon that took Jews to Auschwitz. Can you feel it? … Can you feel what must've happened in here? … The horror! … The terror! … The misery!' Walking to the corner of the wagon, he dropped to the floor. 'This is an evil place,' he said, shaking his head. 'I can't believe it.' Jane sat down with him.

'Oh my darling, what can I say?' Jane held him and pushed his head against her shoulder. 'What the hell is this monstrosity doing here?' she said. 'Come on, let's get out of here and go home.'

He pushed himself away from her and crawled away to another part of his prison. The rain still beat down on the roof and there was the distant roll of thunder. As great black clouds rolled by, occasional flashes of pale sunlight threw themselves into the wagon.

Jane watched her husband cry. He put his head in his hands and she saw him rocking backwards and forwards. She felt trapped in this awful place and yet, she could not leave him. Another moment of brightness illuminated a patch of woodwork near her shoulder. Moving her eyes to the light she saw long, deep scratches in the dark wood. Jane tried not to admit to herself what they were. Her brain told her that some poor wretch, in the misery of certain oncoming death, had gouged his or her fingernails into the very grain of the innocent wood. She reached out and carefully, fitted her ten nails into the narrow deep grooves. She knew instantly that these gouges fitted a woman's hands. With an awful shiver of pure horror, she pulled her hands away and then her eyes caught two words scratched into the wood. Lifting herself off the floor, she peered more closely.

'NO!' she shouted from the very depths of her being. 'NO!'

Richard lifted his head. 'Jane, …. Jane. …. What is it?'

'Look,' she said, tears streaming down her face.

There were two words scratched onto the dark timber.

"Rebecca Cohen"

Richard groaned. Scrambling to his feet, a low moan came from his throat. Walking away from his wife, he kicked the timber walls. Again and again and again. With his fists he hit the surrounding planks of solid wood. Every metre, every inch, he hit, either with foot or fist.

Jane watched him and was helpless to do anything. She wanted to run out of this awful place but, like Richard, was compelled to stay.

Richard suddenly froze. The flowing tears stopped and, with a quick jerking motion of his hands, he wiped his cheeks. 'Listen,' he said urgently, '….. Jane, …. listen.'

She found her voice, 'What, my darling. What is it?'

'The walls are hollow,' he said, with sweat streaming off his face. 'The walls are hollow. The end walls of this wagon of death are hollow. ….

Something is hidden.' Strangely humming, he began to tap and touch the dark wood. Every plank, he examined minutely. With a grunt, he pulled a box towards him, jumped on to it and found the key he was looking for. His fingers jabbed into the knot hole. 'Look out.' he shouted, as a huge panel dropped away from the wall.

Richard stepped down off the box. Slipping his arm around Jane's shoulders, he held her close. A calm smile spread over his face. In a very quiet voice, he said, 'Jane, this is it. .... I know it is. .... This is your evidence.'

Before him stood a steel rack with row upon row of neatly stacked files. Outside the rain stopped and there was only the drip of water off the roof to break the absolute silence. Bright sunshine slanted in through the open doors. Fresh air blew across their faces. Richard pulled one of the files down and looked at it. At first the German confused him and then he reached for another and another and another. The yellowing paper blew out of the door into the pouring rain and dropped sodden onto the muddy grey soil. Throwing great heaps of them down onto the floor, he knew what he was searching for. Then he found it.

Taking a deep breath he turned to Jane and said, with enormous sadness, 'I've found it.' He waved the file in the air. 'Thank the good Lord, I've found it.' Opening the file, he translated. 'Transport 4,386. Westerbork (Netherlands) to Auschwitz-Birkenau. Via Hannover, Dresden, Breslau. Arrived Birkenau 0800hrs. September 13, 1944.'

Richard paused. 'There's a list,' he said, throwing the yellowing sheets to the floor. 'It's here! It's here!' he exclaimed. 'The whole Cohen family from Leeuwarden. Every name is listed and there's Rebecca's name,' jabbing his finger at the correct line, 'just there.'

Jane looked hard at the gothic writing; precise, neat and thoroughly correct. Without thinking, she extended her hand and touched Rebecca's scratched name on the wall. Turning to look at Richard, she saw he was still reading.

Without a word, he passed across another list and pointed at the script. 'Read it,' he said simply.

Jane took the flimsy piece of paper to the open door. With a low moan of expectation, she read it aloud. 'Transport number 4,386. All disposed of and cremated. Signed *SS-Hauptsturmführer* Rolf Müller. September 13, 1944.'

Whilst she was trying to take it in, Richard, with a cry of pain, ran past her into the clear morning air. 'Richard,' she said, running after him and throwing her arms around his neck. 'Oh, my poor darling I'm so sorry.' She held him close.

'In that awful place,' he whispered into her ear, 'are Mengele's medical records. They're too unbelievable to look at.' Easing the paper from her hand, Richard put it together with his then he said, 'There's something I have to do.' Gently pushing her away, he stepped to the threshold of the cattle wagon.

Richard stood still and bowed his head in silence. Then, with a deep breath of decision, he pulled out a book of matches. Jane saw the logo and the name *"Millingen Centrum Hotel"* across the cover. He pulled out a single match and struck it. Shielding the flickering flames with his cupped hand, he stepped into the wagon and threw it into the pile of rustling documents. The brittle-dry paper burst into life and the yellow flames licked upwards. The heat was intense and soon, with a whooshing roar, the timbers of the wagon began to burn.

Richard was so close that his face turned red. 'Burn, ...burn! May all this be cleansed from the face of God's earth,' he whispered softly.

They returned back across the wet, tranquil gardens and, behind them, roared the flaming inferno of the cattle wagon with its evil contents belching black smoke into the air. Richard's mind was at rest. He had one more task to carry out and then it was over.

Before he reached the open windows, Jane stopped him and said simply, 'Tell your mother.'

It was a thought that had passed through his mind. 'I'll tell her about what happened today,' Pausing, he shook his head and wiped away his tears of anger. 'I have sympathy for her. To have known what she must have known for over fifty years was a massive burden. I don't think I could have talked about it.' They walked on.

Willi Hossler stood at the door, waiting for them. There was anger on his face, gone were the smooth manners. 'What the fuck have you done?' Richard pushed his way past him and strode across the carpet of the dining-room. 'You swine, Cooper,' he shouted. 'You've destroyed vital records.'

Richard whirled round on him. His voice quivering with anger. 'Those are not records. They're disgusting and vile pieces of criminality. Now, thank the Lord, they're gone. In the same way as the people whose names are written on them.' He brandished the two documents in his hand. 'And I have what I need to expose the likes of you and Müller.' Hossler lunged towards Richard with a swinging fist. Behind him, with a smash of breaking porcelain, Jane broke a huge Chinese vase over Hossler's head and he dropped, pole-axed to the floor.

'Nice one, my darling,' said Richard.

'A pleasure,' she replied, taking his arm and stepping over Hossler's inert body.

Running across the tiled hall, they climbed the stairs two at a time. Hans was at the bed room door. 'Get out of my way!' shouted Richard, poised to hit him if necessary. With a glare, the man stepped to one side.

Rolf Müller looked barely conscious. His head was sunk into the big pillows and his mouth was drawn with the rictus of death. A foul odour rose from his body. Richard stared down at him, covering his nose with his hand. He then leant over and shook Müller's arm. The eyes opened and looked at Richard.

In barely a whisper, he said, 'My .... son. ... My son.'

Richard held up the list of Cohen names and said so quietly, 'Read this you bloody murdering and lying swine.' Müller's eyes flickered across the letters and he tried to sit up. Richard was absolutely calm and his voice was cold. Then he showed Müller the signature on the certificate of death. '.... And this, Müller and this.'

The body on the bed moaned and spasmodically jerked. A talon-like hand grasped Richard's wrist and, with a flow of new strength, pulled him closer. Words came from the mouth but Richard could not hear them. Putting his ear next to Müller's lips, he heard the hoarse whisper.

'Say it again, Müller,' said Richard. 'Say it again for the whole world to hear.'

Müller's eyes closed and then flickered open. The exhalation of fetid smelling breath from his mouth was long and drawn out and then with, a final rattle, it stopped. The eyes stared wide-open but, there was no life in them.

'He's dead,' said Richard without emotion and picked up the two pieces of paper. Slowly and deliberately he tore them into pieces and threw them across Müller's face. Turning to face Jane, he tried to speak. No words came out. His face was pale and he walked away from the bed.

Shaking himself, he said, 'Now, my love, let's go home.' Jane took his hand.

FINALE

(Notes made by Richard Cooper)

I was not looking forward to my journey to Auschwitz. I knew it was something I had to do for my family, past and present. It was Rebecca who had persuaded me to travel there via Budapest. I suppose it would have been logical to go from Westerbork but the railway line had long since been removed. It was the continuing contact with Benjamin Blum that had really persuaded me.

One Sunday, we'd sat down as a family and worked out exactly how to make the journey. My children, as usual, had surprised me. Jane made contact with Lottie and Marieke and they would meet us in Amsterdam. Benjamin would wait at Budapest. Before the meeting, everybody agreed that Sabina should come and, when I asked her, she cried and said she would. I was concerned about Lottie's reaction and, when I phoned her, she said quite simply that fifty years was a long time and she wanted to meet Sabina. And so everything was arranged and we made ourselves ready.

We had agreed that English roses would be laid at the entrance to the crematorium where the Cohen family had been murdered. Rebecca felt that it was something she wanted to do. When she returned from a visit to Lottie, she brought with her a history of the teenage Rebecca Cohen. A faded black and white photograph of her stood on Jane's dressing table. Simon would have been proud of his granddaughter.

There was no doubt that since Simon's death and the revelations about her past, Sabina had changed. She had aged ten years and the doctor at her nursing home had told me that she was just worn out. One morning, a couple of weeks ago, Sabina told me that she had always wanted to go to Auschwitz. When I asked her why, she said it was to apologise for Rolf Müller's sins. I respected her for saying that.

I left the kitchen and walked down the hall. I had one thing to do before I left the house. Closing the study behind me, I paused and looked at Simon's photograph on the wall. It was taken whilst he was still in war time uniform. I had found it amongst his papers and had it framed.

David's voice made me jump. "Come on, Dad, time to go." I left the study and helped with the bags.

We were all together in the hall and I thought it was a good time to say something. Casting my eyes around, I saw a slight smile on Jane's face and she imperceptibly, nodded.

"Right, everybody," I said softly. "We may be going on a journey of remembrance

but we've no need to be sad or miserable. Let's enjoy being together." I looked at each of their faces. "Agreed?"

"Agreed," they chorused and, together, we left the house.

We were all quiet. I think the enormity of what we were doing was finally sinking in. Thoughts ran through my mind about everything, apart from where we going. Jane had persuaded me to retire early and now I knew she had been correct. Life for me had a new meaning but I still missed teaching. Rebecca wanted me to write about what had happened to us all. I really was not quite ready for that.

When, after Simon's death, I visited Holland, I went as half-Dutch and half-German. The next time was when I found out I was all German. Now, I most determinedly came as an Englishman.

We had decided to travel in March as the cold winter in Central Europe would have lost its grip, much more comfortable for the older members of our group.

At Schiphol, Amsterdam, we had to meet Marieke who was not travelling with us. I was unsure where to meet her and then, suddenly, standing near an information desk, there she was. Jane waved and laughed. We needed two baggage trolleys and David and I pushed them, whilst Jane and Rebecca strode ahead. Sabina threw a concerned look at me and I realised what she was thinking. I slowed down.

"Don't worry, mother," I said, reassuringly. "Everything'll be all right."

She took my arm and I felt her trembling. "Thank you, Richard." She looked up at me with her watery blue eyes. "You, know, I've always dreaded this moment. I'm now going to meet the last surviving member of a family that my lover murdered. Then later today, I'm going to meet a man that watched Rolf Müller gas thousands." Her grip on my arm tightened. "I hope I can cope with it. "She looked straight ahead.

I stopped my trolley, turned to face her and said, "It's been a long time and now you're with your family. We'll help you."

I introduced my mother to Marieke.

"Mrs Cooper," she said with a smile, "it's a real pleasure to meet you. Welcome to Holland." The kisses were absolutely genuine.

We stood in the main concourse and rather self-consciously looked around for Lottie. Marieke knew what we were thinking. "Well now," she said, "Lottie's in the bar. She thought you would all like a strong drink. I've checked in her baggage and I think I'd better be going."

Marieke said her good-byes and then turned to me. She grasped my hand. "Richard," she said, "I know how much this journey means to you. God bless you." With a nod and tears in her eyes, she left us.

My family kept together and Sabina remained firmly at my side with Rebecca holding her hand. David deftly pushed the trolley in and out of the hurrying crowds. I could feel my mother's tension and I felt for her. I stole sideways glances at her and she stared stonily ahead with an expression that I knew was pure worry. As soon as we turned a corner, I realised where Lottie was. The bar was small and full of people. Somehow, she had kept two tables reserved.

Lottie rose to meet us. Warmly dressed in a woollen two-piece suit and brown boots, a short fur coat lay draped over her baggage trolley. For an eighty-six year old, she looked great. There was a moments pause and then Sabina brushed past me and walked straight up to her. The two women looked at each other and we watched in silence. The hustle and bustle of terminal life ebbed and flowed around them.

Sabina was the first to speak. "Hello, Lottie. I'm so pleased to meet you." The confidence in her voice surprised me. She leant forward and gave Lottie a single kiss on the cheek.

Lottie froze and I tried to guess what was going through her mind. "Sabina," she said, quietly, "ever since I found out about Rolf Müller, I've dreaded this moment." There was a faint smile on her face. "I still find it difficult." And then she seemed to relax. With a sigh, she held Sabina's hand. "Let's just see how we get on with each other, shall we?" Sabina nodded.

The idea of us all going to Auschwitz seemed, at the time, the right thing to do. But now I was beginning to wonder whether it was all going to work.

"Richard," said Lottie, "Sabina tells me that Simon left a very detailed diary. Some time, I'd really like to read it."

I took a long gulp from my glass. "I'll send a copy to you. He writes about how beautiful you were when you were younger and, I must say, you haven't changed."

Lottie, for the first time, since we had all met, laughed. "You're just as charming as your father was." The word 'father' made Sabina's head turn but she covered up her thoughts.

Our flight left dead on time. After the meal most of us dozed. My mother and Lottie had chosen to sit next to each other and occasionally they broke into quiet conversation. The aircraft began its descent to Budapest. The flight crew were really kind, they let us leave first and helped Sabina and Lottie down the steps to the concrete parking area. The coach took us the short distance to the terminal.

Jane saw Benjamin Blum first and she waved to him. I made the introductions. He was absolutely charming and carefully shook hands with all of us. He wore what was obviously a new, dark-blue, double-breasted suit. Benjamin presented a small bunch of flowers to each of the ladies.

"Richard," he said, "I've ordered a driver and a mini-bus and they're waiting outside." He frowned to concentrate his English. "Is there anything else I can do?"

"No thanks," I replied, "and it's good to see you."

For the first time, he smiled. "I must say, I'm very nervous about this journey."

David surprised me, he put his hand on Benjamin's shoulder and said quietly, "Don't worry, Doctor Blum. I'm nervous as well. We'll look after each other."

The old man nodded. "That's very kind of you, David."

Outside the air was cold and refreshing. A bright blue cloudless sky made everything stand out pin-sharp and crystal-clear. The young driver chattered away in a confusing mixture of English and Hungarian. David listened in awe.

I was sitting near the front of the bus and I felt the apprehension. "Look here," I said carefully. "We're all making this journey for very individual and personal reasons. Tomorrow is special to us all but there's no reason for us not to be happy together."

"I absolutely agree," said Lottie. "And I, for one, am looking forward to us being together." Reaching across the narrow gangway, she grasped Benjamin's bony hand and gently squeezed it. His face lit up and he grinned.

I settled back into my seat and glanced through the window. Traffic on the narrow dual carriageway was beginning to thicken. The mini-bus slowed and, now and then, jerked to a stop. Jane nudged me. She nodded over to my left and I saw what she was looking at. Sprayed in black on a concrete wall was a Nazi swastika and written in large words, **GO HOME ENGLISH JEWISH BASTARDS!!** Everybody saw it and everybody remained silent.

Lottie said softly, "It never stops does it."

"I'm sorry," said Benjamin. "The neo-Nazis are active here. The Government is trying hard to stop it."

"Don't let them beat you, Doctor Blum," said Rebecca, with tears in her eyes. "You've got to keep fighting them, ... all the time." I was proud of her.

Keletyi station teemed with life. Benjamin knew exactly where we going and led the way. Lottie and Sabina helped each other. I heard Benjamin grunt something in Hungarian and then he waved us towards a train. There were only four carriages. I expected the same luxury as we had on our last train to Budapest, what stood on the tracks was different. Painted in a faded red colour, the carriages were dirty and looked years old. They seemed massive and I looked for a way to climb up the steps leading to the open doors. We all hesitated and Jane looked at Benjamin.

"Are you sure," she asked hesitatingly, "this is our train?"

He nodded and said, "Yes, it is. Sometimes they use older trains and, it seems, they have done that tonight. I'm sorry."

Lottie laughed and cheered us up. "Look here all of you. A train is a train, let's get on board and make the best of it." She glanced at me. "Some people had no choice." I knew what she was thinking.

The first class carriage had a foul smell of unwashed bodies, old urine and dirt. It consisted of a narrow corridor and compartments. Each one held two people on narrow bunks. Once the baggage was sorted out, we all somehow met in the corridor.

Sabina looked worried. "I'm really rather tired. I'll just go and lie down for a while. Please wake me if anything happens."

After another brief chatter, we went to our compartments. Jane made up her bunk bed and lay back, resting her head on her hands. "Richard, it's a long journey, longer than I thought. Do you think everybody will be all right?"

I stood near the window and watched the outer suburbs of Budapest grind past. "Oh yes," I replied. "Remember, for all of us, this is a pilgrimage of remembrance rather than a simple journey. It's that fact that'll keep us all going."

"I suppose you're right," she replied, with a yawn.

The clackety-clack of the wheels on the rails had made everybody relax. I walked back to the corridor, the open countryside took over from the city and I watched it going by. My mind was a mix of emotions. The journey was something I had to do. Auschwitz was part of my life, part of my history. I had to go to this place for the memory of every human being that Müller had murdered. What I would do, and what I would feel when I got there, I had no idea.

Rebecca stood at my side and slipped her arm through mine. "What are you thinking about, Dad?" I told her. "Is Auschwitz a real place?" Biting her lip, she sought the right words. "I mean, is it still there? Or is it just a big cemetery?"

I loved my daughter very much and, as I looked into her eyes, I just wanted to hold her close and protect her from what she was going to see. "Auschwitz is real," I said quietly. "It's just as the Nazis left it."

"What do we do when we get there?"

I pushed a strand of hair away from her eyes. "Just walk about and remember people. It's a time for trying to understand what happened."

"Can we ever understand?" she asked, staring through the window.

"Probably not."

She sighed. "Dad, I'm tired. I think I'll go to bed. Do you mind?"

"Of course not, Rebecca. Sleep well." She kissed me on the cheek and gave me a hug.

I watched dusk fall over the flat Hungarian landscape. I stood there for another ten minutes or so and then walked along the corridor to see who was awake. Only Benjamin's door was open. He was reading a book and looked up when I walked past. "Hello Richard," he said quietly. "Would you like to join me?"

"Yes, ... thank you," I replied and sat at his side on the bottom bunk. "Well," I said with a smile, "who would have thought after our meeting in the Hotel Géllert last year that we'd be sitting on a train together travelling to Auschwitz?"

He smelt slightly of alcohol and then I found out why. Reaching under his pillow he produced a nearly full clear glass bottle. He nodded and said, "Can I offer you a drop of Hungarian Palinka?"

"Thanks, Benjamin."

Frowning with embarrassment, he wiped the top of the opened bottle with his sleeve and passed it across to me.

Taking the bottle from his hand, I upended it and took a mouthful. It burnt its way from my lips to my stomach and then kicked me hard. "What the hell?" I spluttered. "That's strong stuff." I wiped the neck of the bottle and passed it back to him.

"Oh yes, Richard ...." He smiled. "Very strong. I like it almost as much as Scottish whisky." Raising it to his lips, he drank another good measure. We both sat back against the compartment wall.

The palinka had the right effect. For the first time since leaving England, I was completely relaxed. The bottle found its way into my hand and I drank again.

"It's my second time," said Benjamin quietly, taking the bottle from my hand.

"What's that?" I asked.

"It's the second time I've travelled to Auschwitz by train."

I understood what he was saying. He just wanted to talk.

"It took over three days and nights. I was lucky, half the people in my wagon died and so we had more room. No food, no water, no fresh air. It was like hell on earth. The temperature was below freezing for the whole journey." He took another swig, this time without wiping the bottle. "The stench, the screams, and the inhumanity of it all." He stopped talking and his eyes closed. "I dream about it. I relive every terrible minute every night. It never goes away. That's why I drink this stuff." He passed the bottle to me and I drank from it.

"Benjamin, how do you live with this thing?"

He shook his head and I saw the tears in his eyes. "I've just accepted it. It's a fact of life. It's as simple as that." His head dropped onto his chest. "I wanted to help you to clear the demons from your soul. .... I've learnt to live with it. .... You'll have to learn to go through that whole process." He squeezed my arm. "You have a family and friends. I have one or two friends. Since Auschwitz, I've not found it easy to make friends." Benjamin paused. "I regard you as a friend."

"Thank you," I replied, with a lump in my throat.

Suddenly, he pushed himself into a sitting position. "One thing I remember very clearly. Somebody said that if you relive your worst experiences, then they'll disappear. I never wanted to do this journey by myself, it would have been impossible. But, travelling with you and your family seems to me, just right. I travel, feeling helped and cared for. I hope that my demons, like yours, are exorcised."

I felt for this old man. He trusted me and I wanted to help him as much as I could. We sat very still, feeling the motion of the train.

"Your father saved my life." Benjamin said it with such aplomb that my alcoholic blur almost cleared.

"What did you say?"

"I had to tell you," he said. "Mengele was carrying out an experiment with transfusing blood into twins. The donor was in terrible pain and I knew that afterwards Mengele would have him killed. I injected a bubble of air into his artery and I killed him." He stopped talking and took a deep breath. "Müller saw me and told a lie to Mengele. I'm still here. There were other times when he turned his head."

"Why didn't you tell me this before?"

Shrugging his shoulders, Benjamin looked down and fiddled with the cuff of his dressing-gown. "Richard," he said softly, "the saving of my life is nothing but a grain of sand in the total suffering that took place at Auschwitz. I believe that Müller's act towards me was an attempt to save himself. He knew I'd been watching him. As I told you the last time we met, he was different. He took no pleasure in what he did." Benjamin looked up. "He carried out his duties like a robot. Most of the others seemed to enjoy it. Müller believed that his medical experiments were for the benefit of mankind. The fact we were Jewish, or Gypsy or anything, did not occur to him."

The train rumbled on into the night. The wheels sometimes humming along the steel rails or rhythmically clattering over the joints. I was really very tired but I wanted to hear more.

"How did you actually feel at Auschwitz, Benjamin? What were your deepest emotions?"

His eyes closed and I could see the lines and folds of age etched into his face. He thought for a moment. "At first there's a feeling of total disbelief that one man can do this to another. That feeling does not last long because there was no respite in what happened. Then you wish you could die. Death was always an easy way out. You wanted it to be easy and painless. But, there were no easy ways to die. You could risk attacking an officer but they always let you die slowly if you tried that. Joining the queue to the gas chamber was another way. But, inevitably, the Nazis had you sorted and selected." Benjamin shook his head. "It was strange, if they didn't want you to die, then you didn't. As a doctor, they wanted my services and, therefore, I was allowed to live. Later, when you knew how the awful system worked, there was a burning desire to live. I killed hundreds of my own people. I remember each face as though they are photographs. I remember how they died and when." He tapped his forehead with a bony finger. "Its all in here, every second, every minute." For a minute Benjamin was silent and I waited for him to start again. His eyes opened. "Richard, you asked me what my deepest emotion was. I had no emotions. No feelings, no hopes, no desires and no future. I lived for each second and no more." His head lolled and I realised he was suddenly asleep.

Rising from his bed, I gently swung his legs horizontally onto the bed. By lifting him, I was able to slide a pillow under his head. He didn't utter a sound. I reached up for the bed cover and then covered him gently. I looked at him for a moment and smiled. This was a very brave old man. Switching off his light, I picked up my shoes, closed the door and made my way back down the swaying corridor.

Jane lay in her bunk and, by standing on tip-toe, I could see her eyes were closed. My bed light was on and I began to slip off my pullover.

"Is everybody all right?" she whispered.

"Yes. ... I've been talking to Benjamin."

"I thought so." She moved under the covers.

Then the train braked hard, throwing me off balance. I grabbed the curtain and peered into the darkness. Suddenly bright lights and the train ground to a juddering, squealing stop.

"What is it, Richard? What's happening?" Now she was wide-awake.

"I'm not sure."

Barking dogs and raucous voices echoed outside the train. Then a hammering on the door. I tried to reach for the lock but it was thrown open and there stood a man with a snarling Alsatian dog.

He was big and dressed in some kind of uniform. Anyway, there was a peaked cap and a gun in a holster. "What the hell!" I said. He shouted something at me. The whole thing was really quite scaring. He had a bright torch and its beam shone straight into my eyes. I tried to remain calm. Still the man shouted and the dog barked.

Then I heard a calmer voice; it was Benjamin's, illuminated by the swinging beam of the torch. The contrast was amazing. A thin, wizened old man with baggy pyjamas facing a uniformed giant. After a few words Benjamin turned to me. There was silence in the corridor.

"It's Hungarian customs and passport control," he said. "Do you have your passports?"

I found them and then I thought of the others. I opened my mouth but Benjamin interrupted me.

"Don't worry," he said with an understanding smile. "I've looked after the others."

The man grunted something and I heard the thump of a passport stamping machine. As quickly as he'd arrived, the man was gone.

"What the hell was all that about?

"I should've told you. We have to leave Hungary, go through Slovakia and then enter Poland. This will happen two more times before we arrive at Krakow."

"I found it very scaring. They were a bit like ...."

"SS guards?" said Benjamin, eyebrow raised. As he spoke, the train jerked forwards, almost throwing him to the floor. "Richard, you have to realise that communism has only just left eastern Europe. The Nazis came first and the Russians came next. Some people say there was no difference."

After passing into Slovakia, the lights disappeared and the inky blackness fell over the train. It was as though we were driving through one everlasting tunnel. I felt Benjamin's arm on my shoulder.

"That was one thing that didn't bother me the last time I travelled this way," he said.

"What was that?" I asked.

"There no passport controls on the transports to Auschwitz."

Sleep came easily for Jane and, above me, I could hear her steady breathing. A plethora of thoughts went through my head. Every time I closed my eyes, I could see people. Faces, bodies, babies, young, old. They were all going somewhere, I didn't know where. There were no faces I could recognise, no voices I knew. Behind them were flames and smoke. The only sound was the clackety-clack of the wheels on railway lines. Even then I wasn't sure whether it was reality or a dream.

Through the slightly open curtain I could see a tinge of dawn in the sky and I leant out of my bunk.

"Good morning," said Jane and I saw her looking down at me.

"Morning," I called back. "Quite a night."

"What time is it?"

"Six-thirty."

My mouth felt gritty and my eyes were sore and yet I felt a tingle and a sense of awareness that I had not felt for many years. Pulling the curtain to one side showed a flattish landscape punctuated by small fields and clumps of trees. The train rolled slowly on.

Jane filled the tiny washbasin with tepid water. I left her to it and went to look for the others. The children's door was already open and David looked up from a book.

"Morning, Dad. Had a good nights sleep?"

A fully dressed Rebecca swung down from the top bunk and smiled. "How long will it be now?"

We chatted for a few minutes as the final hour of the journey ticked by. Within twenty minutes, we all met in the corridor and watched the approaching outer suburbs of Krakow. I was pleased to see Sabina and Lottie becoming good friends.

They all stopped talking when Rebecca said, "Doctor Blum, is this the same railway line that you came along to Auschwitz?"

We all leant against the rail in the corridor and waited for him to speak. He looked kindly at Rebecca. "Yes my dear. This is exactly the way I came. I travelled courtesy of the Deutsche Reichsbahn and I had to buy a one-way ticket. My carriage was not first-class like this one. It was an old wooden wagon normally used for cattle or for horses. There were sixty of us crammed in closer than sardines in a space that was no bigger than a small room in your house. The toilet was a single bucket in the middle. When it was full, we did it where we stood. Water was a joke. There was another bucket for water and, after several hours both buckets were full of our excreta. Fresh air was impossible. Above head height was a small air grill. If you were lucky enough to be near it, you lived. If you were away from it, you died. After the first day of the journey, eight people out of the fifty people in my cattle wagon died of suffocation. The Germans stopped the train every twelve hours and threw in mouldy bread and another bucket of water. The water never reached our mouths and there was never enough bread." He stopped talking and stared through the window. The train clattered over junctions and passed slowly through miserably dark stations. "The journey was the beginning of the worst nightmare imaginable," continued Benjamin. "In the wagon, I remember the stink, the noise of screams, the dying, clawing and fighting for air. Trying to think about escaping when there was no escape. The night was better because you couldn't see the nightmare, only touch it. I still don't know how I survived." He turned to Rebecca and touched her cheek softly with the back of his fingers. It was a moment of pure tenderness. "Does that answer your question, my dear."

I could see the words sticking in her throat. "Yes," she replied. "It answers one question for me but raises many others."

Jane was packed and ready. "What now?" she asked me.

"Breakfast at the station and then on to a coach for Auschwitz," I replied.

"As simple as that?" said Jane with a hard look in her eyes.

"As simple as that," I replied.

The train slowed to a crawl through the drab suburbs of Krakow. Eventually, it juddered to a halt and we gathered near the open door.

The station was full of people. Two porters appeared and, took our baggage away and directed us to the cafeteria. We had agreed to stay in Krakow after Auschwitz. We ate breakfast making small talk and none of us daring to mention what we were really thinking. Eventually, everything was eaten and I decided we should leave. Nobody disagreed.

I was surprised when I saw at the bus station, signs, again in English, saying "Auschwitz Concentration Camp - Tour Buses. Please wait here."

Benjamin saw my curious stare. "Oh, yes," he said, "Auschwitz is a World Heritage Centre."

David heard the comment. "Who would want to go there. I mean, I can understand why we are going. But why other people?"

"Most people go for the same reasons as us. Others go for different reasons." He smiled at David. "Not everybody is like us."

The final part of the journey took over an hour. Benjamin fell asleep but everybody else listened. The coach pulled into the visitor centre at Auschwitz.

"Richard and Lottie," said Benjamin, as they stepped down the steps into the bright spring sunshine. "I have arranged something a little special for you. Perhaps you could follow me."

There were crowds of people around and it struck me that they could be visiting an English stately home. Book stalls, ice cream sellers, tour groups, all intermingling in the worst of all the Nazi death camps. Lottie and Sabina were silent and I found it easy to imagine what they were thinking about. David and Rebecca, rather strangely, held hands and stared stonily ahead.

At the reception desk, Benjamin took a card out of his pocket and presented it to the stern faced woman. After glancing at the card, her whole demeanour changed. She became all smiles and pleasantries. I didn't understand a word but I knew respect when I saw it. Smiling, she waved us to comfortable seats in a quiet area near the desk. She picked up the phone and animatedly spoke to somebody. We waited. I turned to Benjamin.

He placed his hand on my arm. "Patience, my friend. Patience."

We all said little to each other and then a door opened and a man approached us. Smiling at me, he said something to Benjamin and beckoned us back to the door.

A largish room with all the walls completely hidden by racks of books and periodicals. There was the same smell as Simon's diary.

"Good morning, Mr Cooper," the man said in English. "Please will you all sit down and then I can explain." We did as we were told. "I'm an archivist here at Auschwitz. My work is to search out and catalogue all the people who passed through here during the time Auschwitz was in operation. Doctor Blum contacted me some weeks ago to prepare some documents for you." He smiled with satisfaction. I was totally unaware of what was about to happen. "I believe," he continued, pulling a file from an open drawer, "both you and Mrs Cohen lost members of your family here at Auschwitz?" He did not wait for an answer. "I believe the date your family arrived here was September 13, 1944. Am I correct?"

"Yes," replied Lottie, quietly.

Opening the file, he carefully pulled out two sheets of very brittle paper, yellowed with age. I knew exactly what they were and my heart nearly stopped. "These are original copies of the lists from Transport 4,386," he said, sliding them across towards me. "As you can see, there are the names of members of your family." His finger pointed out the words.

"You're now going to tell me," I said, "that the other document is the certificate of death signed by the SS officer in charge?"

He was surprised. "Mr Cooper, how did you know what it was?"

"I just knew, that's all."

He nodded. "Doctor Blum here, says that you would like copies for family research and I have these ready for you with my compliments." With a polite smile, he gave to Lottie and I, two large, brown envelopes. Rising from his chair, he said, "Is there anything else I can help you with?"

I stood up. "No, ... thank you."

Birkenau was just as I imagined it to be. The dominant feature was the brick entrance tower under which the transports used to arrive. We all stood on the single track and looked under the arch and then back towards Auschwitz station. The track was overgrown with weeds and rubbish. I suppose that's how it should be. As a group, we said little. Benjamin occasionally gave a brief description of what was around us and we listened. The Ramp was quiet and there were few people around. We stood in a line on the compacted dusty soil and just stared and thought. My eyes caught something in the soil near the rails and I bent down to pick it up. A shoe buckle, rusted but perfectly preserved. I looked again at the soil, there were tiny circles of brass.

Shoelace eyelet's, the only remaining parts of leather shoes and boots long rotted away. I moved the soil gently with my fingers and other artefacts of the Ramp's history of suffering emerged. The arm off a pair of spectacles; another shoe buckle; pieces of green and brown glass; metal buttons; twisted pieces of steel. Eventually, I neatly covered them with the soil. I wanted to leave them there because that's where they belonged. Benjamin's quiet voice made me stand and turn.

"It was here," he said, pointing at a bare patch of soil. "Just here, where SS Hauptsturmführer Rolf Müller sent me to the right and life." There was no emotion on his face and his eyes were fixed at some point on the horizon. Turning away, we followed him. Lottie and Sabina linked arms and said nothing, although I could see they were crying.

The focal point for people who visit Auschwitz-Birkenau is the International Monument to the Victims of Fascism located precisely between the remains of Crematoria II and III. Rebecca, without a word, left us and approached the Monument. In her hand, she carried our bunch of English roses. So carefully, she bent down and placed them in a stone crevice. Straightening, she paused, bowed her head and then slowly turned to face us.

"It's done," she said quietly and came and stood at my side.

Lottie took a pace forward. Undoing her handbag, she took out a small scrap of yellow cloth. Holding it flat in the palm of her hand, she showed it to us. It was her Jewish star. The one that she had to wear in Holland during the war.

"Sabina," she whispered, "Take my arm," Lottie looked at me. "Richard, take the other." We walked with her and then she stepped away from us. Obviously in some discomfort, she bent and placed the yellow star carefully on top of Rebecca's roses. She did not bow but looked up at the Monument.

"It's done," she said. Then she let us take her arms and we walked back together to where the rest of our little group waited. We stood for a long time.

Auschwitz is a terrible, Godless place. Totally unreal and chilling to the depths of the human soul. I was sick of it and I wanted to leave. Quietly, I took Jane's hand and we walked away back down the side of the Ramp towards the towered entrance. Sabina joined us. Thoughts went through my mind.

"Mother."

"Yes," she replied softly.

"Ever since all this happened to us, I've always been curious about my actual time of conception. My birth certificate says January 30, 1946. Which means that I was conceived about the end of April, 1945." She glanced sideways at me.

I stopped and looked around me. The Ramp was empty of people and there were only the two of us. "But, Mother, if I was born prematurely, then I was conceived at the end of May 1945."

"What are getting at?" she asked, with her eyes full of tears.

"It's occurred to me that if I was conceived at the end of April, then I'm Müller's son. Conceived at the end of May, then I'm Simon's son. Who was my father?" My eyes focused on the arch at the end of the Ramp

Sabina shook her head and took me in her arms. Releasing me for a moment, she stepped back, looked me straight in the eye and said quite firmly, "Richard, only God knows the answer to your question."

Photograph by John Cross, Standish Photographic

ALAN CLEGG
AUTHOR

Writing is Alan Clegg's third career. His first was in the Royal Air Force and the second as headmaster of a secondary school in his home town of Wigan. He has an abiding interest in the Second World War and particularly how it affected the Netherlands. Probably because he is married to Aukje Clegg-Kingma, a Dutch citizen. Educated in the grammar school system as a boy, he then later in life graduated from the University of Southampton in 1973. Alan has travelled widely all over the world and has lectured on educational matters in Russia and Sweden.

"Windmills" was his first sell-out major novel. **"Where birds don't sing"** is the much demanded second story in his Dutch Holocaust trilogy. The third and final part is being written. He has an enthusiasm for detail and characterisation, skills clearly shown in his novels. Writing successfully has been a long held dream.

Published by the same author.
"WINDMILLS" the first in the Dutch Holocaust trilogy. (Also published in Braille by the National Library for the blind.)